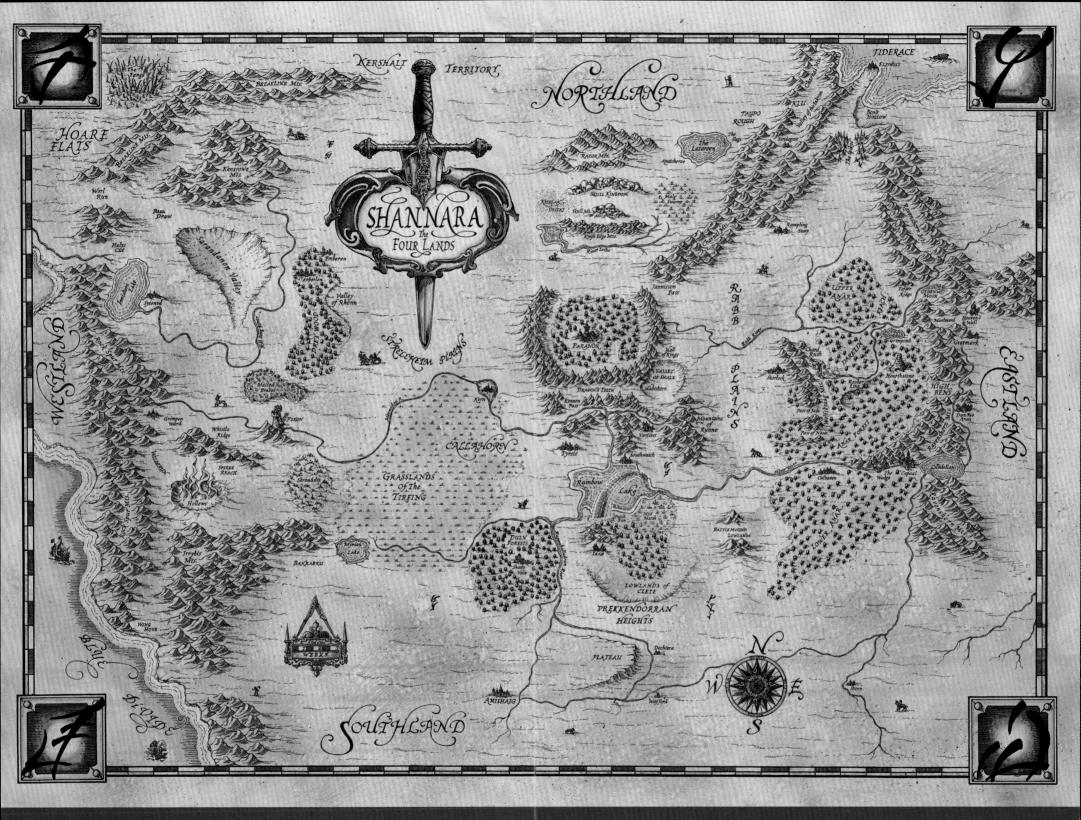

SHANNARA ■ THE FOUR LANDS

ARTWORK BY RUSS CHARPENTIER

GOBLIN DEMONS SWARM APHENGLOW AND CYMRIAN

ARTWORK BY TODD LOCKWOOD

By Terry Brooks

BLOODFIRE QUEST

BLOODFIRE
QUEST

THE DARK LEGACY OF SHANNARA

TERRY
BROOKS

BALLANTINE BOOKS NEW YORK

Copyright © 2013 by Terry Brooks
Insert map copyright © 2013 by Russ Charpentier
Insert illustration copyright © 2013 by Todd Lockwood
Excerpt from *Witch Wraith* by Terry Brooks copyright © 2013 by Terry Brooks

Published in the United States of America by Del Rey, an imprint of the Random House Publishing Group, a division of Random House, Inc., New York.

DEL REY and the Del Rey colophon are registered trademarks of Random House, Inc.

This book contains an excerpt from the forthcoming book *Witch Wraith* by Terry Brooks. This excerpt has been set for this edition only and may not reflect the final content of the forthcoming edition.

Library of Congress Cataloging-in-Publication Data
Brooks, Terry.
Bloodfire Quest : The Dark Legacy of Shannara / Terry Brooks.
pages cm
ISBN 978-0-345-52350-1 (hardcover : alk. paper) — ISBN (invalid)
978-0-345-52352-5 (ebook)
1. Shannara (Imaginary place)—Fiction. 2. Quests (Expeditions)—Fiction. I. Title.
PS3552.R6596B56 2013
813'.54—dc23   2012041705

Printed in the United States of America on acid-free paper.

www.delreybooks.com

2   4   6   8   9   7   5   3   1

First Edition

Book design by Liz Cosgrove

For Jim, Carol, and Mark, and Katie and Karla
inspirations all

BLOODFIRE QUEST

I

---◆---

ARLINGFANT ELESSEDIL SAT FROZEN BENEATH THE BROAD canopy of the Ellcrys, the words a whisper echoing in her mind.

Child, I have need of you.

Had she actually heard that, or only imagined it? Whose voice was she hearing? Her eyes were still closed, and her presence in the Gardens of Life carried little more impact than the space she occupied and the soft sound of her breathing. Sunrise approached, bringing the new day to life. The world was mostly asleep, and the Elves of Arborlon were just beginning to stir. Dreams still held sway.

She felt again the soft touch and opened her eyes to find its source. A slender silver branch adorned with scarlet leaves rested gently upon her shoulder. It moved slightly, a feather's touch she could feel through her clothing, strange and reassuring.

–Child, do you hear me–

Heart hammering, a flush of fear and expectation rushing through her, Arling rose to her knees to face the ancient tree, rocking back on her heels and looking up. She was aware of the branch that lay across her shoulder moving with her, maintaining contact as she shifted her position.

"I am here, Mistress," she whispered.

All around her, the light was changing, darkness giving way to daybreak, blackness turning silvery with the brightening of the eastern sky. And in that strange, in-between time the world seemed to hold still around her.

–Long years have I kept the faith of my calling, strong against the elements and the whimsies and vicissitudes of nature and Man. Long years have I been true to all expectations and challenges, never once regretting what I gave up to be so. But time wears down all living things, and so it is with me–

It was not her imagination, Arling thought. The tree was speaking to her. The voice she was hearing belonged to the Ellcrys. She could feel a connection between the voice and the branch resting on her shoulder. She could feel the link between them.

Could feel the link to herself.

Arling tried to parse this out, to understand what was happening, but now the tree was speaking again.

–It happens slowly, but there is no mistaking its direction. There remains time to do what is needed, but for that to happen I need you first to understand. You are a Chosen in service to me. Many others have been so. Others besides yourself are so now. But you are special to me, child. You bear the blood markings that tell me no other will serve my purpose so well or so long–

Arling blinked rapidly, aware that the Ellcrys was praising her for something the tree found in her that she had not found in others. But Arling had no idea what that something was. Blood markings?

"I don't understand, Mistress," she blurted.

She felt a wash of shame when she admitted this. She wanted to be helpful, was anxious to serve in whatever way she could. But the Ellcrys was telling her she was failing, that time was taking its toll, and Arling did not know what it was she was expected to do.

–I am dying–

There it was. The truth of things, the words clear and unmistakable. The Ellcrys was coming to the end of her life. Arlingfant felt tears spring to her eyes and found it suddenly hard to breathe. How could this be happening? The Ellcrys was showing no signs of deterioration—no wilt, no shedding, no loss of color or form. All looked to be as it should, yet the tree was telling her otherwise. Telling her! Arlingfant didn't want to be the one made responsible by knowing. She had done everything she had been asked to do and more in the course of her time as a Chosen. She did not deserve this!

–Child, you are precious to me–

"Don't tell me that!" Arling cried out. "I have failed you! I did everything I could, but it wasn't enough. Could you be mistaken? Could you be given medicines and special care to keep you from . . . ?"

She couldn't finish, her words dying away into a series of hiccuping gasps. She was crying uncontrollably, and she couldn't seem to make herself stop.

Then the branch shifted against her body, and she felt a strange peace settle through her, bringing an end to the tears. She went still, the sounds of her lamentation ceasing. All around her the air turned soft with the scents of flowers and grasses and leaves, smoothing away the hurt and fear.

–There is much you can do to help me, Arlingfant. My service has been long and successful, and that service must continue. All of the Chosen must care for me in my final days, and you must tell them so. All must band together to keep me safe and comfortable during the time of my passing, but pass I must. Back to where we all one day will go. Back to our birthroots, to our pre-life, to where we await our next appointing. Try to understand–

Arling did not understand. Asking her to bring word of this to the others was unbearable. Why choose her as opposed to another? Why ask this of her when so much else was happening?

But this was selfish thinking, and she would not speak it aloud to her mistress. She was a Chosen, and the Chosen did not complain—ever—of what was asked of them during the time of their service.

"I will tell the others," she agreed. Then she hesitated. "And we will do much more than you ask. We will find a way to stave this off, to cure you of what afflicts you and make you well and strong again!"

There was a long pause.

–Oh, child, no. You ignore the truth at your peril. Hear me once again. I have need of you. I have need of your strength and your dedication. I have need of what you are and what you will be when I am gone. Do you not see–

Arling shook her head in despair. "I see only that you need help and I don't know how to give it."

–You will give it in the same way that I once did, a long time ago—when I was a girl no older than you are now. When I was one of the Chosen. You will carry my seed to the Bloodfire and immerse it and then return to me, and through you I will be renewed and the Forbidding will hold–

"I will . . . carry . . ."

That was as much as she could manage to repeat before the enormity of what the Ellcrys was saying tightened her throat in such an iron grip of fear that she choked on the rest. She saw it now. She saw what she was being asked to do.

–You are my Chosen one. You are . . . –

Instantly Arlingfant was up and running, her dark hair flying out behind her in a tangle. She had broken away from the touch of the Ellcrys, from the voice in her head, from the realization of what was being asked of her and how her life would be altered forever. She felt cold and hot all at once.

She knew the story. All of the Chosen had known since the time of Amberle Elessedil, who was the last to be called. The tree was said to live forever, and some believed it was so. But the truth was a different matter. The tree had a finite life—centuries long, yes, but finite. When its time was up, the tree always selected one among the Chosen to take from it a seedling, to carry that seedling to the Bloodfire, to immerse it in the flames, and then return to become . . .

No, I cannot do this! It is too much to ask! I will lose everything. I will have to give up my life!

. . . to become the next Ellcrys, reborn into the world at the death of the old, and linked forever in an endless line of talismans that would keep the Forbidding intact and the demons imprisoned.

I cannot do this! I am only a girl and nothing special. I was not meant to bear this burden!

She exploded past Freershan and a couple of the other Chosen coming into the gardens, not even slowing to acknowledge them but racing for the concealment of the trees and the waning darkness, anxious to hide and not emerge again for weeks or months or however long it took for this impossibility to vanish. She ran for her cottage and the comfort of home, trying to regain something that was already lost. She refused to acknowledge it, but she knew it anyway in her heart.

Then, abruptly, she remembered Aphenglow. She needed her sister—the one person who had always been able to make things right.

But Aphenglow was leaving for the deep Westland, off on her expedition with Cymrian to find the other Druids and to tell them what had become of abandoned Paranor, following the Federation attack, and of poor Bombax.

Had she already departed?

Changing directions in midstride, Arling turned toward the airfield, fighting down the panic surging through her, her face streaked with tears, her breathing ragged. *Don't let this be! Don't make it so!* She darted through the trees—a slight, almost ephemeral figure in the growing light of dawn—taking paths and byways that shaved seconds off the time required to reach her sister.

Aphen! Please be there, please!

Then she burst onto the grassy flats where the airships were anchored, their dark hulls glistening with early-morning dew—great tethered birds hovering in the windless morning light, their sleek curved shadows cast earthward. She gasped in relief as she caught sight of *Wend-A-Way,* her mooring lines still fastened in place.

"Aphen!" she screamed, closing the distance as swiftly as she could, desperation providing her with fresh strength.

Then her sister was running to meet her, flying across the open fields beneath the canopy of airship hulls, tall and strong and safe. Arling threw herself against Aphen, crying out her name, her face buried in Aphen's shoulder.

"She's dying, Aphen, she's dying, and she wants me to take her place and I can't do it, Aphen, I can't!"

Arling sank to the grass, pulling Aphen down with her. Aphen held her sister close, soothing her. Hushing her, saying it was all right, that she was safe.

Arling drew back, her face stricken. "She touched me on the

shoulder with her branches and spoke to me. She said she had need of me. She said . . ."

It all poured out of her, a jumble of words riven with emotions that she could barely control, all of it released in a torrent of need and despair.

"Arling, stop now," her sister said at last, taking her firmly by the shoulders and turning her so that they faced each other again. "I understand. But we don't know enough yet to be certain of anything. There are Chosen records of the history of the Ellcrys and those who have served her. We should look at those, read what has been written of their history."

Arling shook her head in denial. "What difference will that make? I know what she expects of me. I heard her speak the words."

"And then you fled, right in the middle of her explanation." Aphenglow pulled her close, hugging her anew. "You need to go back to her. You need to hear the rest. But before you do that, we'll read the records of the Chosen. We may find something of value that will turn things around. Stop crying. I am here with you. I won't leave you to face this alone."

Cymrian appeared, rushing up. "What's happened? I didn't even realize Arling was here." He knelt beside them, his eyes finding Arling's. "What's wrong? Tell me what it is."

But it was Aphen who repeated the story, keeping alive the possibility of more than one interpretation of the Ellcrys's words. Cymrian listened without interrupting, his eyes never leaving Arling.

Then he reached out and took her from Aphen and held her against him. "Do not fear, Arling," he whispered. "I will be your protector now. I will stand with you as I have with Aphen, and I will give up my life before I let anything hurt you."

Arling shook her head. "But you were leaving to find the Ard Rhys. Both of you. You can't stay because of me. Finding the Druids and telling them of Paranor's fate—"

"—can wait," Aphen finished. "What matters now is discovering what is needed to help you, and what can be done about the Ellcrys. If she is truly dying, then we face a far more important task than seeking the missing Elfstones."

Cymrian nodded, his features somber. "If the Ellcrys fails, it doesn't matter whether or not we find them."

Arling looked from one to the other. She had ceased crying, and her wilder emotions had quieted. She felt better having reached her sister and Cymrian. Maybe Aphen was right and things would turn out differently than she had feared when she fled the Ellcrys. She experienced a momentary shame for having acted so foolishly, for responding in such a childish way.

"Thank you both," she said to them.

"We will face this together," Aphen assured her. "Starting right now."

2

---◆---

APHENGLOW ELESSEDIL WAS ACHING.

She kept it hidden inside, not allowing even the smallest hint of what she was feeling to escape, but that didn't make it go away. She was going to lose her sister to a twist of fate she could not in all likelihood change. For reasons she could only pretend to understand, the dying Ellcrys had chosen Arling—out of more than a dozen who served her—to take her place.

She hadn't stopped to question that this might not be true. She didn't take time to go into the details to be certain of their accuracy. All she knew was that Arling felt as if her heart had been ripped to pieces and would never heal. She could see the terror and despair reflected in her sister's eyes; she could hear it in her voice as she gasped out her story.

Casting every other consideration aside, almost without thinking about it, she responded in an old and familiar fashion, bringing order to the chaos of the moment. Making clear that there was always a way to work things out. Suggesting a plan to start things moving. Staying calm and steady, containing the screams of rage and frustration she wanted to give vent to. She comforted her sister and told her what she needed to hear.

That she was there for her and would not leave.

That she would help her find a way through this darkness.

That she would comfort and protect her against any harm.

It was what Arlingfant needed to know, what she could depend upon Aphen to provide. Reason and discussion and hard decisions could wait until another time. For now all that mattered was helping Arling regain her balance so that she would not be mired in a fear so paralyzing, she could do nothing.

Together they departed the airfield, heading toward the cottage that housed the records and, from time to time, a handful of the Chosen themselves who had moved to Arborlon for the duration of their service. Aphen kept her arm around her sister as they walked, telling her that everything would be all right, that once they had explored the Chosen history and had examined accounts of the actual rebirth, they would better understand what needed doing. She spoke softly and with as much reassurance as she could muster—all the while feeling herself dying inside.

She had already lost Bombax. She had watched the rest of her order fly off in search of a myth and not return. Her mother had abandoned her years ago. All she had left was Arling, and now she might lose her sister, as well.

She could not bear it. And yet she knew she must.

Cymrian walked closely behind them. "We must tell no one of this," he said quietly, his eyes scanning the woods as though word might already have leaked out.

Aphen glanced back. "What do you mean?"

"I mean you are already being hunted by someone who doesn't like what you are doing. Three times now they have attacked you. I think it would be wise to assume they might move against Arling if they got even a whiff of what she was told by the Ellcrys."

Aphen gave him a look.

"It's about perception, not reality. We need to keep this to ourselves until we know more." He shrugged. "And if we need to tell someone then, we'll think carefully about who it might be."

They passed down pathways that skirted the city proper, avoiding the main roadways, the palace, the Gardens of Life, everything that might bring them into contact with anyone who would want to stop them and talk. They used the dawn as a shield, keeping to the shadowy, less traveled byways until they had reached the cottage at the edge of the gardens where the Chosen records were housed.

There was no one inside when they entered. The Chosen were performing the ritual dawn greeting, a welcoming of the Ellcrys to the new day. They would be missing Arling, but several had already seen her fleeing, and they would not come looking for her until their duties as Chosen were fulfilled. The sisters and Cymrian had at least several hours to complete their search.

Aphen had never examined the Chosen records. These were unofficial writings that belonged solely to the order and consisted of everything from personal diaries to catalogs and lists of those who had served. Even Arling, who had never had reason to consult them, wasn't certain what they contained. But she knew where they were kept and how to open their keyless locks, and she went to them immediately upon entering the cottage and brought them out for her sister and Cymrian to examine with her.

Together they sat down at the communal dining table and began to read through the papers, beginning by searching for references to Amberle Elessedil, the last Chosen to become an Ellcrys. Most of the serious record keeping had begun with her transformation, hundreds of years ago. If there was anything to be found, it would most likely be found there.

As she perused the records, Aphenglow was consumed by a fresh wave of despair. Having come to terms with losing both Bombax and Paranor—and needing to seek out the rest of the Druids to let them know of it—she was now sidetracked by the possibility of another, even more terrible loss. She felt pulled two ways at once, and the combination generated an overwhelming feeling of inadequacy. Dealing with one only made her more certain she should be dealing with the other, and she felt as if the fabric of the world had been pulled apart beneath her and she had been left hanging in midair, unable to move and waiting to fall.

She forced herself to read the diaries—still more diaries!—in their entirety, hating every minute she was giving up to do this. She was searching, but what was she searching for? What was it she expected to discover that would change anything? Something more about Aleia Omarosian, whom she had once intended to seek out in these pages? How would that help? It all seemed so futile.

"Here," Cymrian said suddenly. "Read this."

She had no idea how much time had passed. But when he handed her the logbook he had been reading, she took it and began to read aloud.

After resuming her role as a Chosen in service to the Ellcrys and there-after accepting her mission to carry the seed of the tree to the Bloodfire, Amberle Elessedil left Arborlon in the company of the Valeman Wil Ohms-ford and a contingent of Elven Hunters under the command of Captain of the Home Guard Crispin Islanbor. Traveling south toward the Wilderun, they were tracked and set upon by a demon that had broken free of the Forbidding, and all were killed but the Chosen and the Valeman.

Within the Wilderun, the Chosen immersed the seed of the Ellcrys in the Bloodfire as she had been commanded to do by the Ellcrys, and thereby quickened the process of transformation. The demon found them engaged in the process, but was killed by the Valeman. On returning to Arborlon, the Chosen found the city besieged by demon hordes, but completed the transformation and restored the wall of the Forbidding in time to save the city and its Elves.

Written and recorded in the days immediately following the death of the Elven King Eventine Elessedil. Peace and long life be ours now and forever.

There was no signature and no indication of who had made the entry.

"That's all?" she asked, glancing at Cymrian. "Isn't there anything more of this business?"

"Only records compiled from various sources of what happened during some of the preceding centuries. I didn't read them all. That was the last entry, the only one dealing with Amberle Elessedil. There's more. About her childhood, her family, her choosing, her . . ."

He gestured at the logbook. "Why don't you study it for yourself? I only wanted you to read the last part first because there doesn't ap-pear to be any mention of where the Bloodfire can be found."

While the other two went back to searching the remainder of the records, Aphenglow did as Cymrian had suggested. What she found was either disturbing or heartening, depending on your point of view. Amberle had begun communicating with the Ellcrys early on in her service, very much like Arling. As a consequence of what she had begun to understand from the tree, she had rejected her choosing and had fled Arborlon for the wilds of the Eastland, where she had remained until the Druid Allanon had found and persuaded her to return to her Elven homeland. But the implication of what this must have meant to the young girl—though not expressly stated—was heart wrenching. She had given up everything, lost everything, in order to fulfill her service as a Chosen. It was impossible not to wonder whether Amberle had ever been able to come to terms with her fate in a way that provided her peace of mind.

Aphen looked up, gazing at Arlingfant, barely able to stop the tears from coming as she envisioned this fate for her sister. She closed the book and set it aside. There would be plenty of time later for Arling to read it.

She picked up a fresh logbook, one compiled more recently that had exhumed bits and pieces of records from the times before the destruction of the Old World. It was the third of three volumes, and she dug around until she found the first and second, as well, and began reading the former. It was a mess. There were various references to the Chosen and their service, but they were haphazard and there was a noticeable lack of continuity. Obviously, much had been omitted or lost from the chronology, leaving gaps of dozens of years. She read through it all dutifully, one volume after another. But there was nothing personal, no stories that would help explain why one Chosen was selected and another was not.

Nor were there any stories of those who had become transformed into an Ellcrys in the years before Amberle Elessedil.

Aphenglow set the books aside with a sigh. Neither Arling nor Cymrian had said a word in some time, so she knew they had failed to unearth anything useful, either. Perhaps this had been a bad idea. What they had discovered of Amberle Elessedil was of no help at all in deciding what to do about Arling. It was one thing to promise her sister that she would help her find a way through this. It was another to actually make that happen.

She was shoveling the stack of books, diaries, and loose-leaf notes closest to her back into a pile when she caught sight of a slim, leather booklet bound in copper that had oxidized to a dark greenish color. She pulled it free and read the letters carved into the leather front of the casing.

LIVES OF THE SPECIAL CHOSEN

Holding her breath, she opened the cover and skimmed the pages quickly. It was a recitation of all the Chosen who had become the Ellcrys since back in the time of Faerie when the sacred tree was first created, with names, dates of birth and death and rebirth, family and history, the ways in which they were selected, and how they came to accept their choosing.

She went quickly to the last entry. There was Amberle Elessedil's name, along with everything about her life.

She skipped back to the front and caught her breath in shock and disbelief.

The first name entered was printed in bold, black letters:

ALEIA OMAROSIAN

Aphen stared at the name, and suddenly the pieces of the puzzle that was Aleia began to fall into place. Aleia wasn't just another Chosen serving in the order or even one of the few who had sacrificed themselves to become an Ellcrys; she was the very first Chosen ever. She was the original Elf to become the Ellcrys, the one whom all the others had followed.

Aphen read the tiny print just below Aleia's name, print that was smaller even than the dates of her life and her heritage:

Forgiven; embraced; remembered.

Aleia's final entry in the diary had referred to a chance for redemption that she knew she must take. It suggested she had found a way to make up for her foolish assignation with the Darkling boy—one that would restore her good standing in the eyes of her parents and the Elven people. Her reckless infatuation had cost her people possession of the powerful magic of the Elfstones and placed them in further danger from the dark creatures of Faerie. But what if there was a way to imprison those creatures so they could do no harm to the Elves ever again—even if they somehow found a way to use the Elfstones? Offered a choice to transform herself into the Ellcrys, create the Forbidding, and thereby save her people and all of Faerie, wouldn't she have jumped at the chance, even if it meant sacrificing herself?

Aphen checked the dates recorded in the book next to Aleia's name, then pulled out Aleia's diary, which Bombax had reminded her to take just before they had departed Paranor. Then she rifled through the pockets of her backpack until she found the notes she had made on the rule of Pathke and Meresch Omarosian.

All the dates matched.

By now both Arling and Cymrian had stopped what they were doing and were looking over at her. She started to say something and stopped. Neither one could appreciate what she had just discovered. They did not know of Aleia Omarosian or her diary, or how it had launched a search for the missing Elfstones. They knew nothing of what the Druids sought and why it was so important—not only to the Druids, but to the whole of the Four Lands. She had kept that secret from them, following the dictates of the Ard Rhys and her own conscience.

To explain it now would require that she reveal the truth of everything that was happening, and that would violate the trust bestowed on her by Khyber Elessedil.

Yet hadn't these two, who had stuck by her through everything, saving her life, healing her body, and providing reassurance and strength, earned the right to know? If they were to continue to support one another in their efforts, surely it was necessary that she stop keeping the secret of the diary and Aleia and the missing Elfstones and make them both privy to what was at stake.

It all came down to Aleia Omarosian—the first of the Chosen, the original Ellcrys, but also the one responsible for the theft of the missing Elfstones.

Forgiven; embraced; remembered.

She put her questions and doubts aside and forced a smile. "I have something to tell you," she began.

3

◆

After she finished telling Arlingfant and Cymrian of her discovery of Aleia Omarosian's diary and how it had triggered the search for the missing Elfstones and all the attendant consequences—including the attack on Paranor—Aphenglow apologized.

"I should have told you sooner. But I was following the dictates of the Ard Rhys, who made me promise to keep everything a secret, even from you. There wasn't really a reason to reveal it before. But now there is."

She gave them the slender logbook that chronicled the names of the Chosen who had transformed into the Ellcrys. Arling went white at the sight of those names, clearly envisioning her own being added to the list, but somehow she managed to tamp down her fear.

"What does all this mean?" she asked.

"There is more to the connection between yourself and Aleia than the fact that both of you served as Chosen. More than that she transformed into the Ellcrys centuries ago and now you are being asked to do the same. It has to do with the fact that she was the first to become the tree, the one who established the Forbidding and locked away the demonkind of Faerie."

"And what is it?"

Aphen took a deep breath. "After finding the diary, I made it a point to search out the details of the Omarosian family tree. I found a direct connection to the Elessedils. The surnames of the various generations of the two families clearly link them intimately. And those surnames appear again and again in the list of Chosen that appear in the logbook you are holding."

"Wait a minute!" Cymrian jumped in. His bewilderment was obvious. "Are you saying that this girl and Arling are related?"

"I'm saying more than that. I'm saying that by becoming the first of the Chosen, the original flesh-and-blood Elf transformed by magic to become the tree, Aleia apparently set in place the pathway for all those who followed in her footsteps. Without checking the lineages thoroughly, I can't be certain, but what little I've seen suggests I am right. I think every new generation of Chosen contained at least one who bore the blood of the Omarosian line—which includes the Elessedils—so that the tree could be assured of a successor should the need arise."

"The Special Chosen are all a part of the same bloodline?" Arling demanded. "My choosing as a bearer of the seed was preordained?"

"In a sense, yes."

There was a stunned silence as Arling and Cymrian exchanged a quick, uncertain look.

"But what does this have to do with the missing Elfstones?" Arling pressed. "Aleia and I might both be Chosen, but even if I must . . ." She paused, the words too bitter to speak. "Even if it turns out I must take her path, what does this have to do with the Stones?"

"Does it go beyond the fact that she sacrificed herself to make up for losing the Elfstones to that boy?" Cymrian pressed. "That she became the Ellcrys so her people would be protected?"

"I don't know," Aphen admitted. "I'm not sure the two have any connection beyond the fact that Aleia Omarosian was responsible for both."

In truth, she hadn't been able to give enough thought to any of this to understand all the ramifications. What she needed to do was to get word to the Ard Rhys and the other Druids so that they could puzzle it through. By now, perhaps, they had found the missing Elfstones and would have answers to these questions. But before going after them, she had to help her sister absorb the immediate impact of what the Ellcrys was demanding of her. What was happening with

Arling and the tree that maintained the Forbidding took precedence over everything else.

"Have we searched everywhere we can think of to learn about the transformation of those Chosen who became the Ellcrys?" Cymrian asked.

That was when Aphen remembered Woostra.

"Maybe not," she answered. She got to her feet quickly. "I want you to finish up here. Keep the Chosen logbook; take it with you. Wait for me back at the cottage."

Leaving Arling and Cymrian to put away the Chosen records, she raced off to speak with the keeper of the Druid Histories. Perhaps he had encountered something in his years of study of the Druid writings that would help them. Or at least he might know where else they might look.

She found Woostra at the inn where they had agreed he would await her return from her now-aborted search for the Ard Rhys. She knew that if she were too obvious in asking the necessary questions about the Ellcrys and the transformation, she would risk involving Arling, so she decided to approach the matter from another angle, leaving Arling out of this discussion altogether.

"Aren't you supposed to be flying west by now?" he asked, setting aside a book as she approached.

She sat next to him, smiling. "Something's happened, and I've decided to delay for a day or two. I had Arling gain access to the records of the Chosen, and I discovered that Aleia Omarosian was not just one of them, but the very first. She was the one who originally agreed to sacrifice herself to create the Ellcrys. She would have done so to help make up for losing the Elfstones and shaming her parents. So I need to know more about the history of the Chosen. I have searched the whole of the Elven records, but there is little on the actual transformation process. Do you think there might be something more on this in the Druid Histories?"

He stared at her. "Are you telling me you want to return to Paranor? After having just barely escaped with your life?"

"I'm telling you I will do whatever is necessary to find a way to help the Ard Rhys."

He admitted that there were places in the Histories where the purpose of the Ellcrys was documented. Including, he believed, a description of how to reach the Bloodfire, the magic of which would quicken an Ellcrys seedling and allow the transformation to take place.

"So I'll have to go there to find out," she finished.

He snorted. "You mean *we'll* have to go. It would take you days to find what you needed without me."

She returned to Arling and Cymrian to tell them what she intended to do. Both would go with her, the latter because an additional pair of hands were needed to fly *Wend-A-Way*, the former because Aphen wanted to keep her close.

"I don't know what we'll find," she hastened to add. "I don't know if we'll find anything. But I think we have to try. As things stand, we know almost nothing about what's needed if we're to save the Ellcrys."

"We know it wants Arling to be her successor," Cymrian pointed out bluntly. "And we know Arling's not happy about it. How are we going to resolve that?"

"We'll find a way," Aphen snapped back, and immediately regretted the sharpness in her tone. "I don't know," she added.

They departed the next morning for Paranor, a company of four. Admittedly, there were real concerns about taking Arling away from her Chosen duties. She was conflicted about it herself and had already told them so. But in the end it was agreed she was better off coming with them than being left alone in Arborlon. She would stay aboard ship during the incursions into Paranor and whisked away quickly if threatened.

Aphenglow didn't attempt to minimize the danger of what she was doing. Getting back into the Druid's Keep meant circumventing whatever forces the Federation had left behind to guard it and then, once that was accomplished, eluding or banishing altogether the dark magic she had released from the Keep's lower reaches. It was a formidable challenge under the best of circumstances, but she couldn't convince herself that delaying the attempt until she had found the Ard Rhys and the others and brought them back into the Midlands was a good idea, either. There were too many variables that might prevent this, and just knowing the location of the Bloodfire was crucial. It might not be Arling who ended up making the journey, but whoever went would need to know where to go.

Standing at the railing several hours into their flight, watching the Dragon's Teeth draw steadily closer, she allowed herself a moment to accept how small their chances of changing Arling's fate were. There was no record of any Chosen selected to serve as the Ellcrys's successor having failed to do so. What she might do—what any of them might do—to release Arling from her obligation was impossible to imagine. It was only her love for her sister and her dislike of destinies dictated by factors beyond her control that made her determined to press ahead. She knew this visit to Paranor was ill advised, but Arling was precious to her and terrified of what she was being asked to accept, and Aphenglow would do whatever she could to find another way.

Even risk her life, as she was doing now.

Even give up her life, if it came to it.

She would do anything for Arling.

They brought *Wend-A-Way* in from the north, after sunset, using the deep gloom of the Northland skies to shield their approach. Aphen knew of a clearing within a mile of the Keep, well back from where they might be spotted in the darkness, and they set the airship down there, within the shelter of the ancient trees of the Forbidden Forest.

The plan was to get back into the Keep by means of the secret tunnels that linked the fortress to the outside. Any direct approach to the walls or gates would almost certainly risk detection. But entering through the underground passageways—while it would risk an encounter with the dark magic Aphenglow had released when they departed—was at least marginally safer. She did not believe the Federation had been able to find a way to penetrate the walls and survive what was now waiting there for them, but that didn't mean Drust Chazhul and his minions would have stopped looking.

In any case, she was prepared to deal with the magic. After all, she had released it; there was at least a chance it would recognize her and let her pass safely. Whatever the case, only she and Woostra could risk trying to enter the Keep. Theirs was an established presence, and the magic was less likely to attack them. Arling and Cymrian would be viewed as intruders and dispatched without a second thought. Even Woostra was at some risk, she had to admit, given that he was not a Druid. But he insisted on coming, and Aphen knew that without him there to help her, she would be left at a severe disadvantage. She would do her best to keep him safe. She would ward him with magic of her own.

His response was a dismissive snort and a curt insistence that he didn't need any warding in his own home.

Leaving Arling and Cymrian with the airship, the Druid and the keeper of the records crept through the trees to where the nearest entrance to the tunnels was concealed. By then, they were within a hundred yards of the fortress walls but still had not encountered anyone at all. Woostra, leading the way, had no trouble finding the trapdoor, but it took him awhile to release the hidden locks. Whether due to rust or weather or the tightness of the seals, they refused to budge at first. But eventually his efforts prevailed and the locks released.

Pulling back on the hatch cover, he led the way inside.

They stood next to each other, searching the gloom. A rack of torches was fastened to the bedrock of the wall, and Aphen and Woostra each removed a pitch-coated brand and ignited it. From there, they wound their way ahead, descending several sets of stairs until they were deep underground and far enough forward of where they had entered that Aphenglow was certain they were beneath the Keep proper.

Woostra stopped. "Do you hear anything?"

She shook her head.

"Good. But keep listening, anyway."

"I sense something, though."

He looked at her. "What is it?"

"I don't know."

They stayed where they were awhile longer as Aphen struggled to decide what her instincts were telling her.

"We'd better keep going," she said finally.

Not long after, they reached an ancient iron door set into the rock with pins and metal plates, its surface overgrown with mold and crawling with insects, its metal dull and rusted. She brushed off the handle, seized it with both hands, and twisted hard.

Nothing.

She looked at Woostra. "What's wrong?"

"There are locks in the plates above and below the handles," he told her, peering closely at the door. "A combination of touches to the pins releases them. Here, let me try."

Moving ahead of her, he worked the pins in a particular sequence, then seized the handle and twisted. The locks released at once, and the door opened.

He gave her a look, cocking one eyebrow. "It's all in the wrists."

They entered a corridor formed of stone blocks and plank floor- ing that led to a second door, this one less formidable. Aphen led the way through, and they found themselves inside the stone well of the furnace chamber. Its circular walls rose into the body of the Keep, where heating ducts carried warmth to the various rooms of the for- tress, and dropped away into the pit where the earth's fires provided that warmth. Once, tenders had been used to mind those fires and control their output. But during the time of Grianne Ohmsford, the Druids had devised a system that tended the fires automatically. With the Keep deserted, the heat was diminished and the fires reduced to a dull red glow.

A long, circular metal stairway, its interlocking sections con- nected by catwalks and platforms that formed ramps and thresholds to dozens of closed doors, wound in serpentine fashion about the stone walls.

"We need to go up," Woostra advised.

They began to climb, ascending the steps at a cautious, steady pace, listening for sounds and watching for movement that would signal danger. But as the minutes drifted past, nothing happened save for the echo of their footfalls on the stairs. The pit was silent, and the Keep empty of everything but ghosts.

When they reached a door that opened onto the ground floor of the fortress, Aphen took the lead, her magic summoned and poised at her fingertips. They stepped out of the furnace room into a long corridor where dozens of bodies lay piled atop one another, twisted into positions that clearly indicated they had suffered an agonizing death. Federation soldiers, all of them, clumped against the walls for as far as the eye could see. From the marks on the stone and the damage to their hands, it could be deduced they had died trying to claw their way out. Some of them had worn their fingers down to the first and second knuckles. Some of them had torn out their own throats.

Aphen bent close to her companion. "Can we find a way to go other than through this?"

He nodded wordlessly and led her into a short corridor that branched off to the right and from there through a doorway to a narrow set of stone steps leading upward. Again, they began to climb. There were still no sounds, no signs of life anywhere. But Aphen sensed something once again—the warning stronger this time. A presence, unseen but lurking close. She hunted for it as they ascended, but couldn't track it. The magic, she thought. It was there, and it was aware of them.

They reached the floor on which the Druid Histories were housed and made their way down the empty, cavernous hall, pressing through the weight of the silence.

Aphen.

The voice whispered in her head.

A voice she knew well.

I am here.

She kept moving, saying nothing to Woostra, who might have heard it as well but wasn't acknowledging it.

Aphen. She caught her breath. *I see you.*

This time Woostra glanced over his shoulder, and there was no mistaking the look he gave her.

Reaching the door to the archive room, the old man released the locks and let them inside. Then he carefully closed the door and re-locked it. He led the way through his office and a series of reading rooms into the storage vault—a box with bare walls and a massive wooden table set at its center. Once upon a time, only Druids had been granted access to this chamber and possessed the magic that would reveal the hiding place of the books. But Grianne Ohmsford had changed that, too, when she had become Ard Rhys. Now there were keepers of the records who were not Druids themselves but in service to the order. Woostra was the most recent of these, and like his predecessors he knew the secret of the books and the magic that would reveal them.

He used that knowledge now in Aphen's presence, touching the wall here and there in a complex sequence that dissolved the concealment and revealed hundreds of tomes shelved in the stone, the whole of the Druid Histories emerging into the circle of light cast by their smokeless torches.

Woostra went straight to the book he wanted, pulled it out, set it on the table, and began to page through it. It took him several minutes before he found what he wanted. "Here," he said, indicating where he wanted Aphenglow to read.

She bent close to do so.

The Forbidding endures only so long as the Ellcrys. The tree lives a long time, through many generations, but not forever. When it begins to fail, it selects one among the current order of service to carry its seed to where the Bloodfire burns, there to be immersed and quickened so that Chosen and seed can merge and become one. The old Ellcrys passes away and the new takes root, keeping the Forbidding intact or, in the case of a diminishment, restoring its former strength.

The Bloodfire can be found in only one known place in the Four Lands. It burns deep underground within the Safehold, warded by the mountain of Spire's Reach in the country of the Wilderun within the middle regions of the Westland.

Written in the aftermath of Amberle Elessedil's choosing and transformation.

I am Allanon.

"A transformation many witnessed," Woostra said, "but which few now believe actually happened."

She looked at him. "Are there any other entries that you have found?"

He shrugged. "A few, but nothing more revealing. I think Allanon determined the exact location from Wil Ohmsford, who made the journey with Amberle, thinking that a more complete record of where the Bloodfire could be found might help when it was needed again. Fortunately, that hasn't happened." He paused, studying her. "Yet."

Aphen said nothing. She could tell he suspected. She read a few more entries from farther back in time, ones that Woostra pointed out to her, but he was not mistaken in his assessment of their worth. All were cursory, almost negligible references to things that were already common knowledge about the value of the tree.

"Since you already searched for any mention of Aleia Omarosian and her parents," she said, "I assume you found nothing regarding her connection to the Chosen?" She wanted him to continue to think that this was the object of her search.

He shook his head. "Nothing."

She closed the books and helped him reshelve them. She had memorized the passage detailing the location of the Bloodfire and could help Arling make the journey if it came to that. But she had discovered nothing that would prevent it from being necessary, nothing that would provide her sister any way out of this mess.

Woostra resealed the books within the walls of the room, and everything disappeared once more.

He turned to her. "The magic is waiting for you. It knows you are here. I believe it has something to say to you."

"I know. I sense it, too."

He sighed. "Are you ready?"

She nodded. "I want to go to the south wall to see if the Federation still watches the Keep. I've sensed no human presence anywhere since we left *Wend-A-Way*. I'm not even sure anyone from the Federation is out there now. But I need to know if they are. It might change my mind about what we need to do."

He led her from the room, relocking first the vault and then the door leading into the chambers of his office. They walked down the hallway in the opposite direction, south toward the parapets of the Inner Wall. Suddenly tinges of a misty greenish light began to appear, pulsing softly against the surface of the walls, emanating from deep within the stone.

Aphen noticed Woostra hesitating as he caught sight of the eerie glow. "Keep moving," she said.

Once outside the Keep, they rushed across the courtyards to the Outer Wall. Bodies lay everywhere, scattered like windblown stalks of corn in an abandoned field. No birds pecked at them, and no four-legged scavengers fed. Nothing had disturbed them since they had died. They were twisted and broken, but their remains had been left alone.

"Nothing living wants any part of these poor dead creatures," Woostra muttered as they hurried past.

Aphenglow was looking around, searching the shadows and listening for the voice, but everything was silent and blanketed in soft, white light. The night was clear and empty of everything but a quarter moon and stars. Shadows cast by the towers, the walls, the parapets, and the trees of the forest themselves draped the stones of the Druid's Keep.

Climbing to the battlements where they could peer over the side of the Outer Wall, they crouched in silence while Aphenglow used both her senses and her Druid skills to layer a skein of magic over the surrounding forest. She found no evidence of a human presence. She found scant evidence of any life at all.

She looked at Woostra when she was finished and shook her head. Nothing. Nodding, he motioned for her to follow him down again. Together they descended the battlement steps.

They were halfway across the courtyards and heading back toward the Inner Wall when tendrils of greenish mist began seeping out of the stone ahead of them. The mist advanced toward them, reaching the clusters of dead, penetrating the lifeless bodies and turning them to dust. Aphen and Woostra began to run, skirting the mist until they had passed once more into the Keep. Winding through a series of secondary corridors, they found their way back to the furnace tower and its metal catwalk.

That was when they both heard the voice.

Aphen.

They stopped as one, looking at each other.

None can leave.

Aphen felt her heart catch in her throat. *We are not like the others.*

All the living are the same. All must become the dead.

She saw Woostra close his eyes in mute acceptance of his fate. He knew this was the risk they had taken. As did she, but she refused to embrace it.

Your task is finished here. The Keep is intact. The Druids are safe. Let us be.

Then release me!

Its scream shook her to the soles of her feet, reverberating through her body like a shock wave. She could feel pain and rage emanating from the words. But what was it asking of her? She had released it already.

You are released already.

No!

She hesitated, having no idea what her response should be. What was it seeking from her? She could feel its presence now, pushing closer, drawing near. She glanced down into the pit and saw the greenish mist rising from the depths. Instinctively, she backed away, flattening herself against the stone of the chamber wall. Woostra was beside her, his face drawn and gray.

The voice screamed again. *Release me now!*

It was coming for them, and there was little doubt of what it intended once it reached them. She started to summon the magic she could use against their attacker. Release it? Release it how?

Then abruptly, she saw what it was asking of her. She rushed to the railing, looking down at the approach of her own death.

"I release you back into your resting place! Listen to me. The Druids are returned!" She screamed the words, the sound echoing off the walls of the Keep. "I release you from your task and send you back!"

There was a long, deep, endless sigh, and the greenish mist began to recede back into the gloom, withdrawing into the depths, a roiling haze slowly losing color and presence until it was gone.

Aphenglow felt the tension and fear recede within her, and she exhaled slowly in response.

"Hurry," she told Woostra.

She was thinking of the future now, of what it meant to leave

Paranor. The Druid's Keep would be abandoned, with no Druids in residence and no immediate prospect of any returning. With the magic that warded the Keep sent back into seclusion, all of Paranor was again at risk. But there was nothing to be done about it. Not when so much else was at stake, as well.

Unspeaking, they made their way down the circular stairway to the entrance of the underground tunnel, passed through, and went back out into the world.

4

◆

ABOARD *WEND-A-WAY*, ARLING ELESSEDIL WAITED ALL night for the return of her sister and Woostra. She did not sleep much, but sat with Cymrian on the forward deck of the airship, staring out into the darkness and worrying about Aphen. She was dismayed she was the cause of everything that was happening, but at the same time grateful Aphen had come to her aid.

She was not meant to be a Chosen; she had decided that some time ago. She was meant to go to Paranor and become a Druid like her sister. The heart-stopping news that she had been chosen to replace the tree—a fate she could not have imagined in her wildest dreams—simply reinforced her conviction. If Aphenglow could find a way to help her walk away from this, everything could be as it was meant to be. It wasn't that she felt no obligation toward the Chosen order or her service. It was just that there was a limit to what could be expected of a person no matter what you had agreed to do or how much you wanted to do it. She had found hers yesterday at sunrise.

There would be others among the Chosen who would better serve the needs of the Ellcrys in this business. If she was truly dying—a conclusion that Arling was not yet ready to accept—another descended from the Omarosian bloodline could carry her seed to the Bloodfire and undergo the transformation to replace her. Another who was more devoted and spiritual than Arling and better prepared to do what was needed.

She cringed at her own thoughts, but at the same time could not shake the certainty that she was not ready for this. She was still a young girl with her whole life ahead of her. She had entered into the Chosen order with the expectation of serving a single year. It was a much-sought-after honor, and she had embraced it readily enough. But never with the expectation that more would be required of her than was required of anyone else.

"Are you all right?" Cymrian asked her at one point. "It's cold out here. Would you like a blanket?"

She was wrapped in her travel cloak, but even so she was shivering. "I would," she admitted.

He left her side to retrieve one and was quickly back again, placing it about her shoulders, then sitting close with his arm around her to help keep her warm. She leaned into him, grateful for his reassuring presence. She wished Aphen would return. She felt so much better when her sister was close.

"You must not think much of me right now," she said.

"Because you don't want to be a martyr for our people? Because you don't want to transform into the Ellcrys?" He shook his head. "I don't know anyone who would want that. I certainly wouldn't."

"But I have been asked, and there is so much at stake. What if there is no one else who can do this? Or no one who will?"

"We don't know enough yet to be certain of anything. Give Aphen a chance to see what she can discover."

She lowered her face against his shoulder. "I'm just so scared."

The hours slipped away, and for a time she dozed. She felt Cymrian holding her, never moving. Each time she drifted awake he was there, keeping her warm and safe, protecting her as he had promised he would. One day, she thought drowsily, she would find someone like Cymrian to love.

It was still dark when she heard voices whispering and sensed movement on the deck of the *Wend-A-Way*. She opened her eyes to find Aphen smiling down at her with Woostra looking on.

"Time to go," Aphen told her.

They sat together while Cymrian went off to release the mooring lines and take the airship back to Arborlon. Woostra retired to the aft deck to give them some privacy.

"The Federation has left Paranor," Aphen told her. "Not one sol-dier remains. I don't understand it. They wanted it so badly. Hun-dreds died to take it. But now only the dead remain. Something unexpected has happened, I think."

"The magic frightened them away?" Arling was fully awake now, anxious to hear what her sister had learned.

Aphen shook her head. "But they would have left guards, wouldn't they? Even if they remained outside and didn't try to go back in, they would have wanted to keep watch to see what happened."

"I don't know, Aphen."

Her sister smiled. "Did you get some rest while I was away?"

"Not much. What did you find out?" Arling could keep still about it no longer. "Was there anything about the Ellcrys in the Druid His-tories?"

"A little. Most of it had to do with where the Bloodfire could be found. There wasn't much on the transformation or how the choosing is made." She leaned forward quickly and put her hand on Arling's shoulder. "But we're not finished. This matter isn't settled yet."

Arling shook her head, discouraged. "Where else is there to look? What else can anyone do?"

Aphen hesitated. "I don't know. I only know that we are not giving up." She took her hand away and rocked back. "I need to find Khyber Elessedil and the others and ask them. I need to bring them back to Arborlon—both because of this and because of what's happened at Paranor. They need to give up this search for the Elfstones and re-claim the Druid's Keep. And they have to help you. I will insist on it."

She tightened her lips and exhaled sharply. "While I'm gone, I want you to go back to the Ellcrys and speak to her again. I want you to tell her how you feel. She needs to know you are not ready for this. You have to tell her you want to seek a place in the Druid order. It may help if she understands how strongly you feel about this."

"I fled from her," Arling answered. "She already knows."

"She knows you are frightened, but she doesn't necessarily know the rest of it. Besides, you don't want to leave things like this. You have been a good and faithful servant to her; she will expect you to come back and explain yourself. You owe her that much, Arling. You owe yourself. Go speak with her again."

Arling didn't want to do any such thing. She was afraid of going back to the Ellcrys. It was a nameless, pervasive fear that originated in her mix of shame and disgust at having fled. But she knew it was the right thing to do, and she would not disappoint her sister. Aphen expected her to be strong enough to confront the Ellcrys and try to convince her to choose another. If she did not, Arling would live out the rest of her life knowing she was a coward.

"I will," she said to Aphen.

Then she hugged her sister and tried not to think of what a second encounter might mean.

A day later, Arling joined Woostra on the Elven airfield to bid farewell to her sister and Cymrian. *Wend-A-Way* had been resupplied, and the journey to find the Ard Rhys and the Druids was about to begin. The sisters hugged and kissed, facing each other with smiles and tears in the early-morning light.

"Look after yourself, Arling," her sister told her. "Do what you need to do. Be strong."

Arling nodded. "I can be strong as long as I know you are there for me."

Aphenglow looked stricken. "Oh, Arling. I will always be there for you. You know you can depend on that. We will be there for each other." She paused and wiped away her tears. "Will you speak to the tree today?"

Arling hesitated, wanting more time and space to consider. But she knew that she was only putting off the inevitable, and there was nothing to be gained by doing so.

"Tonight. When the other Chosen are asleep," she promised. "I will try then."

"It won't be so bad. She's an old friend to you, a companion. She's asking for your help. If you can't give it, she will understand."

"I know," Arling said, but she did not know anything of the sort. "Please come back soon."

Aphen's strong features tightened. "As quickly as I can. But you need to remember something while I am gone. Someone in the Elven community is hunting me and now, perhaps, you. I want you to be especially careful. Cymrian thinks you are safe enough for the moment, but I am not so sure. I thought I was safe, too. So stay alert. Do your work as a Chosen and keep to yourself. If you have a problem, go to Uncle Ellich or Grandfather and ask for help. Do not take chances. Promise me."

Arling nodded, beginning to cry anew. She embraced her sister and held her close for a long time before releasing her. "Good-bye, Aphen. Please be safe."

She stood then with Woostra and watched as her sister and Cymrian boarded *Wend-A-Way,* released the mooring lines, and lifted off into the brightening morning. *Wend-A-Way* swung about until she was facing west and slowly picked up speed.

Arling stood watching until she was out of sight and the sky was empty once more.

Woostra cleared his throat. "If there is something I can do to help you while she's gone, you have only to ask me."

Arling nodded, not looking at him. "Thank you."

"She didn't say what is happening, but it is clearly important to her. I don't need to know what that something is. I'm not asking you to confide in me. But Aphen is dear to me, and I will do what she expects of me in her absence."

It was a strangely formal proclamation, and Arling almost smiled in spite of herself. "I will see to it when she returns that she knows you offered. And I will come to you if it is needed. I appreciate your offer, Woostra."

He shrugged. "I'm just doing what I know Aphen would want." He hesitated. "I saw how you were when the Keep was attacked and we were struggling to hold the Federation back. You were as brave as anyone. I respect you for that. You are much the same person as your sister."

Maybe not, Arling thought. Not so brave, not so certain about herself, not so confident in who she was. Not like Aphen. She had never compared herself favorably to her sister, always aware that Aphen was older and had accomplished so much more in her life, even in the face of criticism and disapproval. Even though she was alienated from their mother and much of the Elven community. Arling could never have done that. She wasn't strong enough.

She gave Woostra a quick smile. "I have to go now."

She was aware of the old man's gaze as she walked away, though she did not look back.

The remainder of the day was spent working in service to the Ellcrys. She returned to the Gardens of Life and was warmly greeted by the other Chosen. Before flying off to Paranor, she had explained her absence by leaving word with Freershan that she had been taken with a fever and stomach sickness that would put her in bed for a few days. When one of them asked why she didn't answer her door when they had come to check on her, she covered by saying she had gone to stay with her mother. No one questioned her further. She was given hugs and kind words and welcomed back. It made her feel like a liar and a cheat; it made her feel ashamed of herself. But she got past it as quickly as she could and spent the remainder of the day absorbed in her tasks, keeping her head down and her thoughts to herself.

When her work was finished, she went to see her mother. It was not something she particularly wanted to do, but she craved the reassurance that being in her mother's house—the house she grew up in with Aphen—would provide. But on this day Afrengill was dark-tempered and distant, moving like a ghost through the cottage while Arling sat watching, saying almost nothing to her daughter, so far gone inside herself that she almost wasn't there. Arling tried speaking with her, hoping for just a few words in response that would make her feel as if she belonged here. But her mother couldn't give her those words, and after a short while she left feeling none the better for having come.

She ate dinner alone, listening to the silence of the cottage and thinking of her sister. She glanced out the window repeatedly, watching as the light dimmed and the darkness settled in, knowing what was coming, what she must do. She tried more than once to rationalize her way out of going to the Ellcrys. What harm could it do to wait another day? Or even two? But she knew better than to give in to such arguments. Waiting would only make it harder and confirm that she was as much a coward as she feared. She could not afford to feel any less secure and capable than she already did. As frightened as she was of doing this, she was even more frightened at the prospect of what it would mean if she gave in to her fears. She might not want to do this, but doing nothing would be even worse.

So when it was suitably dark and most of the city's inhabitants were in bed or on their way there, she wrapped herself in her travel cloak to ward off the chill and headed toward the gardens. She walked quickly, afraid that any delay or diversion would be enough to tip the scales and send her back to the refuge of her home. It took only minutes before she found herself standing on a slight rise at the eastern edge of the gardens, looking down to where the Ellcrys glimmered crimson and silver in the pale moonlight. She hesitated then, trying to think what she would say, to gather her thoughts so she could make the best argument for asking that another be sent in her place. Even the thought of trying to do so made her queasy, her stomach churning at the idea of seeking to be relieved of a responsibility she already knew was hers.

Though it wasn't one she had asked for.

Taking a deep breath, she crept into the gardens and up to the tree. She stood beneath its canopy and stared, momentarily entranced by its perfect beauty. She waited for the tree to respond, blinking against the brilliant wash of starlight that spilled out of the night sky and streamed through the silver and crimson limbs.

Finally, she knelt, bowing her head in open acknowledgment of her position as a servant to the order of the Chosen. She closed her eyes and waited patiently, hardly daring to breathe, listening to the beating of her heart.

Then a slender branch brushed her shoulder, and the familiar voice whispered inside her head.

–You are returned to me, child–

Arling shuddered. "I am returned."

–You are so frightened–

"Terrified."

–Your fear caused you to flee from me–

"I am ashamed of this."

–You need not be. Your fear is real and justified. I was once as you are. Frightened and confused. I, too, fled–

Arling opened her eyes and looked at the tree. "You fled when you were told what was expected of you?"

–Even before I understood. I was a young girl, like you. I barely remember it now. The tree spoke to me. She touched me. I grew frightened of what that meant, and I fled–

"But you came back?"

–Why are you so frightened, child? There is no pain in what I ask of you. There is so much good that you can do–

The voice was calm and measured. It filled Arling with a sense of peace that she found oddly reassuring. She shivered at the feelings it roused in her.

"I am not meant to do this. I am meant to be a Druid, like my sister. It was what I planned all along to do when my time as a Chosen was finished."

–You would be a Druid so you could help others. Like your sister–

"I would. I would do that instead."

–Even though you would be helping so many more by doing what I have asked? Even though you would be saving a world–

Arling hesitated, not knowing what to say. "Someone else would be a better choice."

–You say this to me, knowing I am the one who makes all the choices? Knowing I chose you because there was reason for doing so–

Arling squeezed her eyes closed. "Was I made a Chosen because you knew you were dying and needed another of the Elessedil line to replace you? Is that why I was chosen?"

A long silence followed.

–I choose all of my children instinctively, with no prior knowledge of who or what you are. I know nothing of your histories. Not then and not now. In the beginning, I do not even know your names. When you, child, passed beneath me in the time of your choosing, you felt right to me and so I took you–

"I shouldn't have agreed."

–But you did agree. You accepted your choosing. Would you abandon it now–

"I must. I cannot do this."

–Because you think it will be too hard–

"Because it isn't something I thought I would ever have to do."

–You would do only those things for which you were already prepared? You would accept only hardships you already understand? Will it be like that for you if you become a Druid–

Arling burst into tears, burying her face in her hands, momentarily unable to continue.

"I don't know what else to say."

The Ellcrys went silent again, and Arling fought to stop crying, wiping away the tears, telling herself to be strong, to stand her ground. She couldn't be forced to do this. She couldn't be made to take the Ellcrys seed and carry it to the Bloodfire. She didn't have to do anything she didn't want to.

–What if there is no other to take your place–

The words broke the silence like the shattering of glass, and Arling flinched in response.

–What if you are the only one who can do this–

Arling exhaled sharply. Her oval face lifted and she tightened her lips in defiance. "But I'm not the only one. There are others. Lots of others. You choose us for this. You know which of us will be able to serve you in the ways you have need of being served. You can always find another to do what is needed."

–You sound so certain of this. I was like you once. I believed this, too. There would be others to do what I was being asked and did not want to do. How difficult would it be to find one–

Arling brightened. "Then you understand what I am saying. I think another Chosen would be more ready than I am to take the seed to the Bloodfire. To become the next Ellcrys. More ready and capable than I am to do it."

–More ready and capable? A sweeping conclusion, child. Think a moment. Whoever does what I ask must be strong enough to survive a journey to a distant place, one filled with dangers. This Chosen may be hunted, just as I was hunted. This Chosen must have family and friends willing to die for her. This Chosen must be able to withstand both physical and emotional hardships and be willing to sacrifice herself for the good of her people–

Arling felt her momentary elation fade.

–This Chosen will need courage and resilience and strength of will that exceed those of others. The journey to find the Bloodfire and immerse my seed is a terrible trial. The journey back and its inevitable ending will be no less so. When an Ellcrys chooses a successor, all this must be taken into account. All these qualities must be considered when searching for the one who will become what I became–

"But I am not . . ."

–Hush, child, hush. Let me finish what I would say to you–

Arling flushed at the rebuke and went silent.

–My decision to choose you as the bearer of my seed was not arrived at in days or months or even years. It took a long time to find you. Generations of Chosen came and went. Death comes gradually if not hastened by chance or misfortune, and so it has been to me. I have seen its approach for a long time and only of late have felt its touch. The Forbidding I ward has been eroding incrementally. At first, it did not matter; the erosion was slight. But with the passage of time, the danger has grown more immediate. My search, therefore, needs resolving–

–So when I ask you what I should do if I cannot find another, it is not because another does not exist. It is because I lack the time I need to find that other. My predecessor faced this same dilemma when she chose me. The erosion of the Forbidding accelerates. The risk of the imprisoned breaking free from their world and invading this one is upon us–

The Ellcrys fell silent again, but Arling could not find the words to respond. She felt trapped and overmatched by this ancient creature, and she lacked the means to do anything about it. She slumped back on her heels and kept her head lowered against the fear that would undo her completely.

Finally, the tree whispered once more in a soft, soothing voice.

–Enough talk for tonight, child. I have sat where you are sitting and argued as you have argued and struggled to decide as you are struggling. I know how difficult this is for you. Go to your home and sleep. Come again tomorrow night, and we will speak further–

Arling shook her head. "I don't know if I can make myself come back."

The leaves of the tree shivered in a soft gust of wind, rustling like tiny creatures.

–You will do what you know is right. You will come to me. If you fail to appear, I will know I was wrong to choose you–

Then the Ellcrys went silent, and although Arling sat where she was for a very long time, the tree did not speak to her again.

5

In the hostile and blasted country of the Forbidding, the survivors of the search party for the missing Elfstones stared at the Ard Rhys in disbelief.

"What did you say?" Carrick was the first to break the silence, his stance aggressive. He glared at the Ard Rhys. "Tell me I misheard you."

Khyber faced him squarely. She was not in the least intimidated, Redden thought as he stood off to one side, watching the confrontation unfold.

"We are inside the Forbidding," she answered. "Just as Grianne Ohmsford was a hundred years ago. Trapped."

Carrick shook his head. "That isn't possible."

"I'm afraid it is. The shimmer of light we passed through was a breach in the wall that had been deliberately altered to suggest it was something other than what it really is. Even my magic failed to detect it. As did your own, Carrick."

"But you can't be sure of this! How do you know?"

"The look of the land. The creatures that attacked us on our way in—things not of our world but very much of this one. Giant insects, Goblins. The dragon that attacked us and then took away Oriantha and Crace Coram—when there aren't any Drachas left in the Four Lands. The way the opening was there one minute and gone the next.

There's no mistaking what we saw. Anyone who knows the history of the Four Lands and its Races would know the truth of it. We are inside the Forbidding."

There was a stunned silence.

Then Pleysia, still on her knees, began to laugh hysterically. "How much worse can this get? We've lost half our number. A dragon has carried away my daughter and the Dwarf. We found our way in and can't find our way out." Her laughter died away into sobs. "All of us are caught out on the wrong side of a door we can't even find, let alone open! Caught among creatures that will tear us to bits once they discover we're here. It's madness!"

Carrick whipped around to say something, and then stopped short. "Your daughter? That odd girl is your daughter? Why didn't you tell us?"

Pleysia hauled herself to her feet, her eyes dark as they fixed on him. "Would it have made any difference to you? What do you care about me and mine, anyway?"

The Trolls were pressing forward as well, talking among themselves, lapsing into their own guttural language as they gestured at the bodies of Garroneck and the other dead. Redden took a step back in spite of himself, even though he wasn't the one being threatened. If anything, he was being ignored. It was Khyber Elessedil who was bearing the brunt of everyone's rage and fear.

"Stay calm," she ordered, raising her voice only a little.

"Stay calm?" Carrick looked wild and dangerous. "We have to get out of here, Mistress. Right now!"

"I'm not leaving my daughter!" Pleysia screamed at him. "We don't go anywhere until we find her!"

Redden looked around uneasily. They were standing out in the open, and the sound of their voices would carry a long way. If there was anything else out there hunting, anything as dangerous as that dragon, it would find them with no trouble.

"Come close," the Ard Rhys ordered them, indicating both Druids and Trolls. She did not look at Redden, but he stepped toward her anyway. "Now listen to me," she said, looking from face to face. "We can't go back the way we came. The way we came is gone. Or if not gone, lost to us. But before we give up completely on finding it, we should use our magic to see if it can be revealed. Carrick? Pleysia? We should at least try."

So they did, each one of them separately, conjuring Druid magic and sending it abroad, sweeping the countryside for a hint of where the door might be concealed. But even though they kept at it for long minutes, it showed them nothing.

I could try using the wishsong, Redden thought. But then something else occurred to him.

"Maybe we shouldn't be doing this," he said suddenly. All heads turned. "Doesn't the use of magic attract other magic? Especially here, where there is so much of it?"

"He is right," Khyber Elessedil said.

"But we can't stand here and do nothing!" Carrick insisted. "What does it matter if we use our magic or not? The things that hunt us in this monstrous land will find us sooner or later anyway. Our only chance to escape them is to discover a way out and take it!"

The Ard Rhys shook her head. "Maybe nothing is hunting us. Except for the dragon, the creatures that inhabit the Forbidding might not even know we are here. Not yet, anyway. Remember how we got here. The blue Elfstones showed Aphenglow that this was the way to the missing Stones. Her vision was clear enough to get us this far, and everything we have done has followed that vision exactly. Even the shimmer of light was a part of what she was shown. We were not lured here. We came of our own free will at the direction of the seeking-Stones. Whoever created this trap didn't know that we would be the ones to fall into it."

"What difference does that make?" Carrick demanded. "We don't have the blue Elfstones now. We can't use them to find a way out."

"No one is suggesting we can. But we shouldn't make the mistake of thinking we're trapped by something that hunts us. We may yet find a way out. We mustn't panic. We must stay calm and remain together. If we are judicious about it, we can still use our magic to find another doorway. If the Forbidding has eroded in one place, it has probably eroded in another."

Redden wondered about that, but since he knew nothing specific about the way in which the Forbidding worked, he kept still about his doubts.

"Redden," the Ard Rhys called to him, and he glanced over quickly. "Just to be certain that we overlook no possibility, will you try using the wishsong?"

He nodded and summoned the magic to seek out the shimmer of light through which they had passed, picturing it in his mind. Quickly enough the blue light flashed to a place perhaps a hundred feet away from where they stood, flaring out in a broad swath. But open countryside was all they saw. Nothing else was revealed.

Nevertheless, acting on the wishsong's response, the three Druids went at once to the place where the magic had spun out, searching for anything that would suggest a doorway back through the Forbidding. But their efforts were in vain. No opening appeared, no sign of a way through the invisible wall that imprisoned them.

"I've had enough of this!" Pleysia snapped. "I'm going after my daughter. Those who want to come with me can. Otherwise, I'll go alone."

She stalked away from them, suddenly looking much stronger and more determined. Redden and the others watched her for long minutes before Carrick muttered, "We shouldn't let her go off without us. Besides, there's nothing for us here."

Khyber Elessedil nodded. "Let's stay with her, then. We can keep searching for a way out as we go."

Which meant she had no better idea to offer and perhaps recognized that their situation was much more hopeless than she wanted to admit aloud.

They set off—the three Druids, the four Trolls, and Redden—heading in the direction that the dragon had flown. It felt futile to Redden, who would have preferred staying where they were. Maybe Seersha, who had been left behind with Railing and the others, would come looking for them and be able to guide them back again. Maybe the opening would reappear after a while.

But the decision wasn't his to make, and he could feel the despondency and loss of hope that appeared to infect the others working its way through him, as well. He wished he had never agreed to come with the Ard Rhys but instead had remained behind with Railing. He wondered how Railing was. At least his brother wasn't inside the Forbidding like he was, but matters might not be going so well on the other side of the wall, either. After all, those Goblins would still be hunting them, and possibly other things by now. They were still deep in the interior of the Fangs, and if Seersha didn't get word to Mirai to come rescue them, it would be a long and dangerous trek back out again.

And Railing couldn't walk with his broken leg. He would have to be carried. Helpless.

Redden walked in silence for a long time, watching Pleysia lead them—almost as if she knew where she was going. He tried to imagine Oriantha as the Elf Druid's daughter and failed. They seemed nothing alike. Yet there was a clear connection between them, one that went beyond friendship. He shifted his gaze to Carrick and watched the tall Druid for a time, his aspect somber and detached. Then he glanced over at the Trolls, muttering among themselves as they lumbered along.

Finally he moved up alongside the Ard Rhys.

"Do you think one of the others might come looking for us?" he asked her quietly. "Maybe Seersha or Skint?"

"Maybe. If they do, the tag I left on the opening will alert me. If it's Seersha, she will recognize it and know it for a warning to stay back until I return for her." She glanced over. "Is that what you were wondering? If I made a mistake in deciding to leave and come along with Pleysia?"

He flushed. "It had crossed my mind."

She smiled, the wrinkles in her face smoothing in a way that made her seem decidedly younger. "I thought so. I considered staying where we were. But we would have had to come looking for Oriantha and Crace Coram eventually. We couldn't leave either of them behind." She paused. "You have your wits about you, Redden Ohmsford. You'll be fine."

He nodded, not so sure about that. "So you think the Elfstones are really in here somewhere? Like Aphenglow was shown by the vision?"

She nodded. "It would explain why they couldn't be found for so long. Aleia Omarosian's Darkling boy must have had the missing Elfstones in his possession when the Forbidding went up. The magic took all the dark creatures and whatever possessions they had on them and locked them away. Others trying to find the Stones after that wouldn't have been looking in the right place—not even in the right world. And the seeking-Stones wouldn't have been able to penetrate the wall of the Forbidding until now, when it's begun to fail. The blue Stones found a chink in the armor. Too bad we didn't recognize it for what it was."

"But at least now we know where they are, and we have a chance of finding them."

"Maybe we know. Maybe we have a chance. But finding the missing Elfstones isn't necessarily what we need to do at this point. Even if we found them, we couldn't be sure they would help us get out of this mess. With the Forbidding crumbling, our priorities have changed. If the wall goes down, everyone in the Four Lands is at risk. We need to escape and give warning of the danger. We need to find out why this is happening."

She shook her head, as if to emphasize the dilemma. "I would like nothing better than to complete our search. But to find the Stones now, we would need time to search them out—and that's time we don't have. Even then, I wonder if it would be worth it. I wonder if any of this has been worth it."

There was more than a hint of discouragement and frustration in her voice. He walked on with her for a few minutes more and then dropped away, leaving her to her own thoughts, thinking how hard it must be for her to know she had been seduced and deceived by the vision. Lives had been lost because of it, and more still might be lost before this was over.

His own among them.

The trek continued through the remainder of the day, but there was no sign of the dragon or their missing companions. They came down from the mountains to the plains of the south, moving in the general direction the dragon had taken. The terrain was barren and empty, a mixture of rutted earth dotted with scrub and rock, and forests in which leaves and grasses had turned gray and the trees had a skeletal look. There was no sign of water. There was no movement on the ground or in the air. The land looked dead and broken.

Every so often, the Ard Rhys or one of the other Druids would use magic to search the countryside ahead, but each time the effort failed. Once, they caught sight of something huge in the distance, a massive creature lumbering across the plains toward the mountains beyond. The Ard Rhys had them stop and hold their positions until it was safely past before allowing them to continue on. More than once, they came across piles of bones, sometimes acres of them. It was hard even to guess at their identity from what remained, and they skirted these killing grounds warily.

By nightfall, they were confronted by an impassable wilderness of swamp and saw grasses, and they were forced to turn west to seek a way around. After walking awhile longer, the Druids agreed they should make camp before it got too dark to see. The Ard Rhys chose a patch of desiccated spruce that offered cover and at least marginal protection from the things that might be hunting them. No one felt comfortable spending the night in such an exposed position, but there was nothing better anywhere close at hand. The Ard Rhys strung a warding chain around their sleeping ground that would sound an audible alert should anything try to attack. The company agreed to set a watch that would work through the night in two-hour shifts.

They arranged themselves in a circle so that the ravaged spruce trees provided a wall around them. The trees were almost completely stripped of needles, and their twisted limbs cast crosshatched shadows over the little party like a cage. Redden was so uncomfortable and on edge that he offered to sit the first watch, hoping that by the time it ended he might be tired enough to sleep.

They ate their meal cold, aware that their supplies were meager and would not last more than another day or so. They might be able to replenish their food, but water would become a problem quickly. How could they know what was safe to drink in this world? Sitting together and speaking quietly, aware of the darkness deepening as night closed in about them, they tried not to talk about it.

We don't belong here, Redden kept repeating.

He was dirty and hot, and his skin itched. He found a pool of stagnant water while it was still light and took a quick look at his reflection. Same red hair, blue eyes, and sunburned face that he remembered, but all three looked leached of color and the rest of him resembled a scarecrow set free of its pole. He brushed at himself for a moment and then gave up. Nothing he did would make any difference.

When the others went to sleep, Redden kept the first watch in the company of one of the Trolls, sitting back to back with him at the edge of the circle of sleepers. Time dragged like an anchor, and to ease its weight he summoned his best memories of Railing and himself flying Sprints through the tangle of the Shredder and out over the flat blue surface of Rainbow Lake. It was as good a way as any to distract himself, replaying the twists and turns of the courses they had flown, remembering the rough spots and the wild dips and leaps, and even letting himself recall what he had felt on seeing Railing crash on their last flight before leaving for Bakrabru and the start of this journey.

Eyes sifting through the layered shadows in the darkness, ears sorting out sounds that he recognized from those that were new, he kept himself alert and wide awake. But when his watch was finished and he rolled himself into his blanket and closed his eyes, he was asleep in moments.

And then awake again faster still.

Something was wrong.

He forced himself to remain perfectly still while he scanned the darkness, trying to determine what had woken him. It took him only a moment.

Carrick and another of the Trolls had taken the second watch. Redden saw the body of the latter sprawled on the ground close to where he had been sitting when the boy fell asleep. It was clear from the twisted position of his limbs and the way his head was thrown back that he was dead and had died hard.

There was no sign of Carrick.

Redden sat up slowly, looking around in all directions, finding nothing but the still forms of the other sleepers and the dead Troll.

Then he looked up.

Carrick was hanging head-down about twenty feet above him, firmly grasped in the jaws of something that resembled a giant insect. His eyes were open and rolling wildly, but he hung limp and unmoving as he was hauled upward through the skeletal branches. His eyes found Redden's and his mouth worked in silent anguish.

Then a second of the insect creatures appeared from out of the trees to seize the body of the Troll and begin to lift it away.

In the shadows, just visible as bits of movement in the gloom, more of the creatures were advancing.

Redden threw off his blanket, scrambled to his feet, and summoned the wishsong. He reacted instinctively—not out of bravery or daring, but out of fear. The magic surfaced in an explosion of brightness that lit up the whole sleeping area, brought all of the sleepers awake instantly, and caused the insects to hesitate. Fighting to keep it under control, Redden concentrated the magic in the cradle of his hands and turned it on the creature that had hold of Carrick. The wishsong flared upward in a burst of power that exploded into the monster with such force that it was cut in half. Down came the beast and Carrick both, the severed pieces of the former thrashing as if still alive, the latter a limp rag doll unable to do anything to help himself.

Redden threw himself aside as the head of the insect slammed into the ground only feet from where he was standing, mandibles snapping wildly.

By now Khyber Elessedil and Pleysia were striking out at the other insect creatures, using their Druid magic to drive their attackers away from the camp. The Trolls were clustered next to them, weapons extended in a circle of sharp steel. But the insects kept attacking, trying to find a way past the fire and sharp blades. One or two would hang back while the others tried to distract the defenders and then rush in suddenly, hoping to catch someone unprepared.

But Redden had regained control of the wishsong and quickly joined the battle, sending a wall of sound from his magic into the largest cluster of the giant insects, throwing them back, slamming them into trees and rocks. Overmatched, the advantage of surprise lost, the insects wheeled about and skittered back into the darkness and were gone.

Redden was suddenly drained. He slumped to one knee and was surprised to find Pleysia next to him, holding him. "Are you all right, boy?" she asked, leaning close. He nodded. "Good. I don't think we can afford to lose you. That was quick thinking."

A few feet away, the Ard Rhys had gone to Carrick, carefully turned him over, and laid him on the ground with his head cradled in her lap. The Druid's eyes had stopped rolling and his gaze had steadied, but he was bleeding from his nose and ears, and his face was as white as chalk. Khyber was murmuring quietly, her hands making small gestures as she fought to hold back the death that was already claiming him.

"They came right over the top of my wards," she muttered to herself.

"They knew they were there!" Pleysia snapped. "The wards drew them!"

"Steady, Carrick," Khyber soothed. She leaned close so that he could see her. "Don't give up."

His eyes shifted to find her. "So quick . . . no chance . . . to do . . ."

He shuddered and went still, dead in her arms.

Pleysia released her hold on Redden and stood next to him. "We're all going that way before this is done," she whispered. "All of us."

Then she turned her back on them and walked off.

6

---◆---

THEY WAITED UNTIL IT WAS LIGHT AGAIN BEFORE THEY in-
terred the bodies of Carrick and the Troll. The ground was so hard
they couldn't have penetrated it even if they had possessed digging
tools, which they didn't. Nor did the Ard Rhys think it wise to try
burning the bodies, since that would almost certainly attract the attention of the very things they were trying to avoid.

So they lay the dead in shallow depressions and covered them
over with heavy rocks hauled and set in place by the surviving Trolls,
hoping that this would be enough to discourage scavengers. When
the cairns were complete and the Ard Rhys had used magic to help
seal them, the others gathered around and she said a few words about
the commitment and sacrifice both had given to the Druid order. She
took a moment at the end to thank Redden for his alert response to
an attack that might very well have meant the end of all of them if he
hadn't realized what was happening. Redden felt sheepish and embarrassed; he still didn't know why he had come awake like that. Presumably, it was the wishsong's magic that had alerted him—something
it had never done before. But then he had never been in a situation
like this one, either. In any case, the recognition bestowed a new responsibility on him; now everyone expected him to be able to give
warning if danger threatened. They didn't say as much, but he could
see it in the way they looked at him. He wouldn't have minded so

much if he could have been certain the wishsong would respond in the same way again when the need arose. But he didn't know if the magic was something he could depend upon to ward even himself, let alone his companions.

He was new to this. He was riddled with doubt. The wishsong had always been something of a toy. His mother had discouraged the boys from using it at all, and both brothers had experimented sparingly. They knew they could use it to enhance the power of their Sprints and to provide protection against the mishaps they were forever encountering in their wildness. But Redden wasn't at all sure he could use it to defend himself successfully against the things that lived within the Forbidding.

Leaving the bodies of both their companions and the giant insects behind, they set out walking again, moving once more in a southern direction, still tracking the Dracha that had carried off Crace Coram and Oriantha. There were only six of them left—less than half their original number. Carrick, Garroneck, and five other trolls were dead. Crace Coram and Oriantha were missing. That left the Ard Rhys, Pleysia, three of the Trolls from the Druid Guard, and Redden himself. With so few remaining, he thought they should turn back. They should return to the place where they had found their way in and wait for someone to come for them or the passage back to the Four Lands to reappear. But Khyber Elessedil seemed convinced that continuing on was the best choice. With Pleysia equally committed to that course of action—still adamant that she would not leave her daughter behind—there was no chance that either the Trolls or he could change the course of things.

But his thoughts were as dark and empty of hope as the land through which they passed, shifting between agonizing over Railing's fate and despairing of his own. He was just a boy, and he had come a long way to die for nothing. He was scared and he was lonely. Nothing had gone the way he had imagined it. He was trapped in another world, with no real expectation that he would ever get out again. His original purpose in coming—the search for the missing Elfstones—seemed distant and unimportant. Given their present circumstances, it even felt pointless. Staying alive was all that mattered now, and he was having difficulty imagining that.

He said nothing of his fears to the others; there was no need to do so, because they would almost certainly be struggling with the same feelings. He told himself not to be distracted, but to remember that while there was life there was hope. He was not helpless; he was not without intelligence and common sense. The magic of the wishsong was a formidable weapon. He just needed to stay alert and keep moving. Sooner or later, something would happen that would help them all get free again.

He told himself all of this, and believed almost none of it.

Time stretched out in singularly bleak fashion as they made their way through country that never changed in any appreciable way. Already Redden was beginning to wonder what they were going to do for water when their own ran out. They had encountered only stagnant swamp water, none of it drinkable. Eventually the food would run out, too. He was wondering how long Khyber Elessedil would let them go on without finding anything before she turned them back. He could not imagine it would be for much longer.

In fact, he told himself when they were hours into their march and the first suggestion of real twilight crept over the land, she would announce it that night.

And then they saw the dragon.

It was flying out of the south, coming toward them in an unmistakable looping, undulating fashion, great wings spread wide, legs tucked up close to its body.

"Mistress!" Pleysia hissed, bringing them all to a halt.

They crouched down at once, doing the best they could to blend into the terrain as the dragon approached at an oblique angle that would carry it just west of them. Redden knew it at once for the dragon that had carried off Oriantha and Crace Coram—unless this was an exact double—thanks to the strange striping along the trailing edges of its wings.

When it flew past them, heading north and west, they could see clearly that it carried no passengers.

Pleysia climbed to her feet slowly in the wake of its passing, her face twisted and grim. "It's left them somewhere," she declared at once.

"If it's the same beast," the Ard Rhys answered.

Pleysia wheeled on her. "No two Drachas share the same mark-ings! You know that as well as I. All the histories say so. Drachas are unique. You, boy!" She turned the bright glare of her eyes on Redden. "Was it the same beast or not? You saw it clearly when it flew off. Were the markings on its wings a match?"

Redden nodded reluctantly. "They were."

"There! Even the boy agrees. It is the same beast. Oriantha and the Dwarf have escaped it. We must go on!"

The Ard Rhys gave her a brief smile. "No one ever said we wouldn't, Pleysia. Please take the lead."

The other woman did so, striding out with grim determination. Within seconds she was twenty yards ahead of the rest of them.

Redden moved up alongside the Ard Rhys and whispered, "I'm sorry. I didn't think I should lie."

"Don't apologize for telling the truth. I wouldn't expect anything less from you. I know it's the same dragon."

"But you think they're dead, don't you? Crace Coram and Orian-tha. What's going to happen when she finds out?"

"I'm not so sure either of them is dead, Redden. But knowing is necessary before she will agree to give up the search." She gave him a long look. "I know you want to go back. I know you worry for your brother. I worry for him and for the others, too. But until we know there is nothing more we can do for our missing friends, we can't quit looking. We owe them that."

They marched on through the twilight until Khyber Elessedil brought them to a halt on a broad, open rise that gave them a clear view of everything approaching from all directions.

"We'll spend the night here. Three on watch, three asleep in four-hour shifts. We won't be caught by surprise again. Pleysia, I can see by your face that you want to continue on. But it is too dangerous to go farther this day. We don't know enough about what's hunting out there. We'll wait until morning."

"Waiting is a mistake," Pleysia snapped. "Morning may come too late for us to be of any use to my daughter or the Dwarf."

"We won't be of much use if we are dead or crippled, either."

Pleysia stared out at the sweep of the land south. "I could go on alone. You could catch up to me in the morning."

The Ard Rhys shook her head. "We agreed to stay together. Tomorrow will be soon enough."

They sat down on the rise and ate their meager dinner, their eyes scanning the horizon, watchful of shadows, uneasy with the growing dark. In the lengthy silences, they tightened their resolve and prepared themselves for how they would confront the hours ahead. No one had put the events of the previous night entirely in the past, and no one expected to sleep well.

When the meal was finished and the darkness was complete—the sky so overcast with haze you could barely see in front of your nose—Pleysia and two of the Trolls rolled into their blankets while the Ard Rhys, Redden, and the other Troll took the first watch.

In the distance, something cried out—a long and mournful wail—and the echo seemed to linger through the hours that followed. Time drifted. Redden's eyes adjusted to the dark, and he found he could see better than he had imagined as he sat with his knees pulled up to his chest and his blanket wrapped about him to ward off the chill. Once, a small creature approached, getting close enough to him that he could just make out its features. It looked like a lizard—maybe a foot long, covered with spikes. Its body was supple and lean, its eyes gleaming as it studied him. It was there and then gone again, vanished as if it were a ghost. He stared at the space it had occupied for a long time afterward, waiting for it to reappear. He had a faint memory of having seen it—or one just like it—the night before. He had caught a glimpse of it just after the attack by the giant insects, and then it had skittered away, a flash of movement in the darkness. He remembered it now and was certain his memory was not playing games with him.

When his watch ended and he lay down to sleep, he knew the effort was a waste of time. He was too awake, too nervous. He could not possibly sleep this night.

But then he did, and when he woke it was morning and something was prodding his leg. He glanced down and found the lizard nudging him with its horn-encrusted head. It would move close, poke at him once or twice, and then withdraw, waiting a moment before repeating the action. When it saw it had succeeded in getting his attention, it backed off just a little farther than he could reach and crouched down, watching him.

That was when he saw the second creature. This one was bigger and had the look of a Spider Gnome, although it was clearly something else. It was sitting cross-legged about a dozen yards away, its elongated arms folded in like wings, its body hunched forward with its head cocked. Patches of coarse black hair sprouted from leathery skin, and its face was crisscrossed with wrinkles. It wore plain clothing decorated with colored thread; clusters of feathers and knots of what appeared to be bones were sewn to the fabric. Even sitting, it seemed disproportionate, as if its arms and legs were too long for its body and its head too small.

Redden raised himself up on his elbow and looked around. The others were all asleep—even those who were supposed to be on watch.

Except for Pleysia. She wasn't even there.

The Spider Gnome look-alike made a short hissing sound and the lizard prodding Redden bolted away—a blur of motion until it reappeared at the watcher's side. The creature reached down with bony fingers to pet the lizard, then looked up at the boy and smiled, revealing a mouthful of sharp white teeth.

Redden sat all the way up, eyes locked on the creature and its pet lizard. The creature didn't appear threatening, and a quick look around revealed that it was alone. Redden didn't miss the curved, serrated blades it carried—two shoved in a leather belt at its waist and a third, much longer knife slung over one shoulder on a strap—but it showed no interest in using either.

"Mistress," Redden called softly to the Ard Rhys.

She came awake at once, pulling off her blanket and sitting up, her eyes looking where he was pointing. She took a moment to count heads, obviously noting the absence of Pleysia, and then she moved over to sit next to him.

The creature said something to them, but it was in a language the boy didn't recognize. She shook her head at it, and the creature's smile broadened.

"You are not Jarka Ruus?" it asked her in broken Elfish. "You are not of the free peoples, the *ca'rel orren pu'u*?"

Jarka Ruus. The name given to those imprisoned by the Forbidding. She shook her head. "No."

"Then you don't belong here. Why are you come?"

"We came by mistake. Through the wall of the Forbidding. What are you?"

The creature shrugged. "An Ulk Bog. What do you think I am?" The sharp eyes brightened. "Do you know of us?"

Khyber Elessedil nodded slowly. "I knew of another Ulk Bog. One from a long time ago. His name was Weka Dart."

"Ha!" The creature clapped its hands in glee. "At last! You are the one I have been waiting for."

"No, I don't . . ."

"For very long. For years. I wait for so long!" The Ulk Bog talked right over her. "All through years after my uncle passes to other side, long since. I have wait and wait. Now you return, finally! You! I know of you! Your story, your name, your history, I know all!" It released a deep, explosive breath. "You are *Straken Queen!*"

For long seconds, there was a shocked silence. Then Khyber Elessedil held up her hands in a gesture of denial. "Wait. Your uncle was Weka Dart?"

The Ulk Bog danced to its feet, quick and lively. "Yes, yes! Do you remember him?"

"Only from the stories I was told. I am not the one who came here before. I am not the one your uncle knew. That was a different woman, one who served as Ard Rhys before me. Not a *Straken* or a *Straken Queen,* but an *Ard Rhys.* We are not witches. We are Druids. This other woman, the one your uncle knew. Her name was Grianne Ohmsford?"

"That was her name!" The Ulk Bog darted closer, crouched, and cocked its head. "Why do you say it isn't you?"

The Trolls were awake now, standing behind Khyber and Redden and staring at this strange creature. Since they didn't speak much Elfish, they had no idea what was going on.

"Grianne Ohmsford is gone. I am her successor. I have never been inside the Forbidding before now. I have never met Weka Dart."

The Ulk Bog looked unconvinced. "You are described to me. It must be you! You have Straken magic. You know of Weka Dart. Of the Jarka Ruus. Why do you lie?"

"No, she isn't Grianne Ohmsford," Redden interjected impulsively. "I would know. Grianne Ohmsford was my great-grandfather's sister. We are family. This isn't her."

As soon as the words left his mouth, Redden Ohmsford knew he had made a mistake. The look that flashed across the Ulk Bog's face was of anger as black as demon's blood. It appeared and was instantly gone again. The boy saw it—or maybe he just *thought* he saw it because he *felt* it so strongly—reflected in the creature's eyes and in a twisting of its features.

"Who are you?" the Ulk Bog asked, the words a soft hiss. "What is your name?"

"Redden Ohmsford."

"Ohmsford. Of the family of the Straken Queen?"

"Of the . . ." He stopped himself, angered he was suddenly feeling so intimidated. "Who are you?"

The creature smiled, revealing all its teeth. "Tesla Dart is my name." The smile vanished. "What are you doing in the land of Jarka Ruus?"

"Trying to get out!" Redden snapped.

"Trying to find two of our friends," the Ard Rhys corrected, putting a warning hand on the boy's shoulder. "We are here by accident. I told you before. We came through a breach in the wall we didn't know was there, and it closed behind us. Now we are trapped."

The Ulk Bog scooted back a few feet, his eyes darting left and right. "I think you lie. There are no others. Only the woman who left during the night."

Pleysia. "Did you see which way she went?" the Ard Rhys asked.

Tesla Dart pointed south. Of course, Redden thought. Still searching for Oriantha. Going it alone.

"How long have you been tracking us?" the Ard Rhys pressed.

The Ulk Bog looked angry. He yanked on a patch of black hair in irritation. "Why do you ask stupid questions? I don't track you. I don't have to. My Chzyks do so for me. This one"—he gestured to the lizard—"is called Lada. He tracks you. He was there last night when you fought the Mantis Styx." He gestured at Redden. "This one saw him."

The boy glanced at the Ard Rhys. "He's right. I did see him. Right after we were attacked. I forgot about it until I woke just now and found him poking at me."

Tesla Dart nodded. "He watches you fight. Sees you and comes to tell me of it. Brings me here so we can talk." He scrunched up his face. "But you are not who I thought? You are sure?"

"You've never seen Grianne Ohmsford, have you?"

"No. But I hear the stories. From Weka Dart. He tells me. You have magic like hers. You can do what she could. You are a Straken. Perhaps a Straken Queen, even if you say you are not. Lada knows this. So he tells me."

"Wait," Redden said, jumping in. "You can speak with Lada? But how did Lada find us? How did he even know we were here?"

Tesla Dart looked confused. "The Chzyks are a community. The community shares. One knows, all know."

"And communicate with you," the Ard Rhys surmised. "How many Chzyks are there?"

"Many. Everywhere. One saw you come through the wall and told me. Lada went to find you and told me. I am looking for you a long time, but now you are not the right one."

"You were looking for Grianne Ohmsford? How long were you looking?"

Tesla Dart's wizened face turned away in disgust. "Forever."

"Why would you do that?"

The Ulk Bog jumped to his feet and danced away. "I can help you, if you want. Like Weka, I track. Nothing escapes once I begin to search. You want to find your friends? Missing friends? Ask me!"

His dark face was bright and animated; he appeared eager to demonstrate his worth. He hissed at Lada, and the Chzyk raced over, leapt onto his arm, and scurried up to his shoulder. Together Ulk Bog and Chzyk waited for a response.

Khyber Elessedil hesitated. "You can find them for us?"

"Ha!" the Ulk Bog shrilled, dropping once more into a crouch. "Tesla Dart can find anything! Lada!"

He made a series of hissing sounds to the lizard creature, and Lada responded in kind. Then the Chzyk flashed away, tearing out across the flats south and disappearing from view.

"You see? Lada goes to find them. When he does, he will return to tell me. We can start walking now."

He turned and began to follow the Chzyk, not bothering to look back at them. Redden and the Ard Rhys exchanged a look, and then Khyber called after the Ulk Bog to wait long enough to let them gather up their things. She spoke to her Druid Guard, who hastened to do as she asked. It took the members of the little company only minutes before they were ready.

But then Tesla Dart returned to them, leached of animation and excitement, suddenly serious. "What we do is very dangerous," he said quietly. "In the land of the Jarka Ruus, you are trespassers and not welcome. You understand, do you?"

Khyber nodded. "This country is treacherous . . ."

"No! No! Not this country!" The Ulk Bog was suddenly angry. "Not to an Ulk Bog. Not to a tracker of my skill." He took a step closer. "Tael Riverine!"

The Straken Lord. Khyber Elessedil had heard the stories from Grianne Ohmsford. Redden had heard them from his grandfather Pen when he was only five or six. The land of the Jarka Ruus was ruled by Tael Riverine, and all of its creatures, great and small, were his subjects. He had captured and imprisoned Grianne Ohmsford more than a century ago when she was trapped in the Forbidding, and he had very nearly killed her before she managed to escape.

"If he finds out you are here . . ." Tesla Dart trailed off, making a curious twisting motion with one finger pressed up against his neck. It was hard to mistake what he meant by it.

"Then we must be careful," the Ard Rhys finished.

"You must be quick!" the Ulk Bog hissed. *"Ar kallen rus'ta!"*

"We still have to find a way out again. We have to get back to where we came from. Can you help us?"

The Ulk Bog shrugged. "A way out is no problem. Not to me. I know many ways out."

Redden stared. Was this so? Was the Forbidding eroded so badly they could cross through it anywhere? He glanced at the Ard Rhys and could tell she was wondering the same thing. For the Forbidding to fail, the magic that sustained it must be completely compromised.

But that happened only when the Ellcrys was dying and in need of rebirth. It had been hundreds of years since the last time, and there had been no word of a diminishment in the Elven magic, no word of the Ellcrys showing signs of sickness. Wouldn't the Druids have heard about this before setting out? Yet the Ard Rhys seemed as surprised and confused as he was. Something was wrong with all of this.

"Stand around long enough," Tesla Dart snapped, "and the Straken Lord will have no trouble finding you. Everything that lives in the land of the Jarka Ruus will want to tell him. Will you help them?"

The Ard Rhys shook her head. "Take us to our friends, Tesla Dart."

The Ulk Bog smiled, and all those sharp teeth reappeared.

7

◆

WITH TESLA DART LEADING THE WAY, THE LITTLE COMPANY
set off south in search of Crace Coram and Oriantha. They kept an
eye out for the missing Pleysia, as well, thinking they might at least
cross her trail. But they lacked a true Tracker to read whatever sign
had been left, and while they searched diligently they found no trace
of her passing. The country remained barren and wasted, a combination of hardpan and scrub interspersed with groves of withered trees
and patches of swamp. At times, they skirted fissures in the ground
that disappeared into darkness and stretches of broken rock that
looked to have been pushed up through the earth in cataclysmic upheavals. There were no signs of life save for things distant and indistinct that the Ulk Bog mostly ignored.

That changed when, several hours into their march, he brought
them to a hurried halt and ordered them all to crouch down and remain perfectly still. Redden peered out from the cover of the broken
rise behind which they all hid and watched a swarm of creatures with
cat faces and sleek, supple bodies lope across the plains west, dozens
moving together in an undulating mass. Separately, they seemed
small and vulnerable. But as a pack they had a dangerous look to
them.

When the boy asked Tesla Dart afterward what they were, he
smiled his toothy smile and said, "Furies."

They spied many other creatures after that: ogres, Goblins, Wights,

Harpies, and things that Redden had never even heard mentioned before. Everything seemed to be hunting, and none of them seemed too particular about what they found. Some scoured the land alone and some did so in packs. Now and then, the company came upon hunters absorbed in eating prey they had caught. Twice, they watched killings take place. Much of their traveling time was spent hiding in plain sight, crouching down and not moving until the danger was past. All of it was vaguely surreal, backdropped by a setting in which everything already seemed half dead and flattened by a sky that was hazy and dark and pressed down upon the earth like an anvil. The stench of death was everywhere, animal and vegetable alike—the world a giant cairn in which everything born into it was already on its way to dying.

As he walked through this grim wilderness, Redden found himself repeating the same words over and over.

I just want to get out of here. I just want to go home.

"They are called the Jarka Ruus, but the meaning for them is not the same as it is for us," Khyber offered at one point while they were walking together. Tesla Dart had scurried on ahead and was out of hearing. "Jarka Ruus for them means 'the free peoples.' For us, as recorded in the Druid Histories, it means 'the banished peoples.' They have never accepted that they are anything but creatures tragically wronged by us, put here in this prison of magic for no reason other than being different. Grianne told me of this when she returned. She said no one would ever be able to persuade them otherwise."

"How did she manage to survive this place?" he asked her.

She shook her head. "She wouldn't talk of it."

"I wouldn't either, I guess."

"She was aided by Weka Dart after she was taken prisoner by the Straken Lord. He helped her get free and find a way back to where she had come into the Forbidding. He probably saved her life by doing so. I seem to remember that he wanted her to do something for him in return, but I don't know what it was. In the end, she left him behind and returned with your grandfather, then took Paranor back from Shadea a'Ru and the rebel Druids who had aided her in seizing control."

"And then she disappeared," he finished.

"She entrusted the Druid order to me and those who had survived the war with me. She abdicated her position as Ard Rhys and went away with Penderrin, and no one ever saw her again." Khyber Elessedil glanced over. "Did your grandfather ever tell you what became of her?"

Redden shook his head. "Only that she went somewhere far away to live out the rest of her life. Too many still saw her as the Ilse Witch, and she could never escape what that meant. She'd had enough of Druids—and magic, as well. She didn't want to be part of that anymore. My father told me this when I was little. Railing and me. But he never said anything about where she had gone or what she had done afterward."

He paused. "I remember asking my grandmother once. I always thought she knew something that she didn't want to talk about. But I asked her anyway. I was young, persistent, and didn't know anything about boundaries when it came to asking personal questions. I pushed her for an answer. She broke down in tears and wouldn't talk to me afterward for almost two weeks." He smiled sadly. "I never asked about it again."

"It was a long time ago," the Ard Rhys said. "A lifetime ago. It doesn't matter anymore."

Redden nodded. "I still think about it. I still wonder where she went. I wonder if she was happy then."

"She was solitary and aloof when she was alive, always conscious of how she was seen by others. I don't know that she was ever happy."

She moved away from him, leaving him with his thoughts.

Midday passed; the air thickened and the heat grew intense. Water was running dangerously low, and food was being rationed. They had never had much of either to begin with, carrying only enough for personal use when they'd passed through the waterfall. Soon, they would have to begin foraging. Tesla Dart seemed uninterested in the problem, leaving them to their midday meal as he danced off into the distance, looking this way and that, always active and eager, always moving. Redden watched him in fascination. How could anyone have so much energy?

When they set out again after eating, the Ulk Bog beckoned for

Redden to walk ahead with him, making a series of quick, demanding gestures that the boy felt compelled to obey. Reluctantly, he moved up to where the other was waiting.

"You are family to the Ard Rhys, Grianne?" Tesla Dart asked as they walked together.

"She was my great-grandfather's sister. But I never knew her."

"She died?"

He hesitated. "She went away before I was born. I guess she must have died."

The sharp eyes watched him. "She is friends with my uncle, Weka Dart. He helps her."

"The Ard Rhys." Redden indicated Khyber Elessedil. "She told me this. She said he helped save Grianne when she was trapped here."

"A prisoner of Tael Riverine. Very bad. The Straken Lord wanted her to mate with him. He wanted her child for his own. But she escapes with Weka."

Redden looked over at him. "I didn't know that. About her child and the Straken Lord. I only knew she was trapped here and your uncle helped her get out again."

Tesla Dart laughed. "Think of it! A child with the Straken Lord! Who would want that? I would not want that. My child will be Ulk Bog–sired."

The boy stared for a moment, realizing suddenly he had made a big mistake about Tesla Dart. She was a woman. Or maybe just a girl. But female, not male.

"You would like a child someday?" he asked, trying to be certain of what he was thinking.

"I will have many children. My family will be large. Ulk Bogs, like me and Weka. But I will need a mate, and he is not yet come to me."

"Um," Redden mumbled, not sure what to say.

"We can be friends, you and me. Families are the same. Weka helped Straken Queen, and now I will help you! It is for us as it was for them. Friends!"

"Friends," he repeated.

Then, from out of nowhere, came that dark look she had given him earlier, the one he couldn't understand. "But better friends than

Weka and the Straken Queen. Real friends, who don't fail to help when needed. Keep promises we make, stand by our word. Is this right, that we can promise this?"

She seemed so desperate for him to say yes that he did so, nodding for emphasis. There was no reason not to. There were no promises to be kept, were there?

"We can promise," he said.

"This is good!" Tesla Dart announced with a yelp.

Then she darted away, quick and wild, skittering ahead on all fours like an animal, laughing as she went, leaving Redden still trying to come to terms with the idea that such an odd, wild creature was female. He trudged along in her wake, wishing he had her stamina, thinking he could feel his strength ebbing even now. How much farther would they have to go, he wondered, before they found some sign of their missing companions?

It was late in the afternoon when they reached a stretch of deep ravines and high, broken ridges worming their way across miles of stark, empty terrain. A flock of huge scavenger birds circled the skies perhaps two miles farther on.

Khyber Elessedil called a halt and stood staring at what lay ahead. "Tesla Dart!" she shouted to draw the other back from where she was scampering about.

The Ulk Bog girl rushed back. "Yes, Straken Queen?"

"Don't call me that." She gestured forward. "You intend for us to go in there?"

Tesla Dart looked at her questioningly. "You wish to find your missing friends? The ones the Dracha took?"

"I do. But why would they be in there?"

"Why? Because that is where the Dracha has its nest. It would go there without thinking about it. It would want to shed parasites it carries. So it would go there."

"You know of this particular Dracha?"

The Ulk Bog shrugged. "This one, yes. Do you want to go on or not?"

The Ard Rhys considered. "How far ahead is this nest?"

"Not far. Maybe two miles."

Right where the birds were circling, Redden thought. And then he wondered suddenly how Tesla Dart knew which dragon it was that had taken Oriantha and Crace Coram. Her Chzyks had been watching the company when it entered the Forbidding, not her. Had she learned which dragon it was from speaking to them?

"What has become of Lada?" Khyber asked suddenly, as if reading Redden's thoughts. "Shouldn't he have returned by now?"

"If he finds something, he returns. Come! We waste time. Let us hurry before the night arrives."

But Khyber Elessedil shook her head. "I don't think so. We aren't going in there without knowing if our friends are alive. Why don't you go in for us, Tesla? Find the nest, see if our friends are there, then come back and tell us."

"That is a bad idea. To leave you is bad."

"I think it is necessary. You must go."

The Ulk Bog stamped her foot petulantly. "I will not go! You cannot tell me what to do. I am free to do what I want. I will leave you!"

"But I thought you wanted to help us, like your uncle Weka helped Grianne Ohmsford. Don't you? Are you afraid?"

Suddenly Tesla Dart was incensed. She screamed something unintelligible at the Ard Rhys and stomped away a short distance, then whirled around and screamed some more. Then she sat down and refused to look at them.

The Ard Rhys glanced at Redden and motioned for him to come away. With the three Trolls trailing after them, they moved to an open stretch of ground and sat down together, taking out food and blankets and making camp. The minutes slipped away. Tesla Dart stayed where she was, staring off into the weather-riven wilderness. Those with the Ard Rhys let the Ulk Bog be.

"We are not following her any farther until we know something more," Khyber whispered to Redden at one point.

The boy didn't care if they ever took another step. He was ready to turn back, to retrace his path to where he had found his way in and hope he could find his way out again. He was sorry about Oriantha and Crace Coram, but he had lost all hope of finding them alive. It had been too long. There were too many bad things that could have happened. He didn't feel much hope for Pleysia, either. There should have been some sign of her by now. They should have caught up to her, or she should have come back to them.

It made him feel cowardly to think this way, but he was beyond caring. He was sick at heart and filled with despair, and he wanted to put all this behind him and get back to his brother.

He was picking at the scant pieces of his meal when Tesla Dart gave out a fresh scream, leapt to her feet, and began jumping up and down. At first Redden thought she had been attacked, but then he realized she was holding Lada, who had reappeared out of the twilight.

Redden and Khyber climbed to their feet as the Ulk Bog charged over, Lada now riding on her shoulder. Tesla Dart was singing and chanting as if it were a day of celebration.

"I will go now!" she exclaimed. "I will do what you asked me! Lada comes back, so all is well. Your friends are not far. I will go to them and bring them here!"

Khyber Elessedil rose. "We can come with you."

"No, no, you can't! It isn't safe. Night is too close. Too many hunters, all bigger and stronger than you. Dangerous to use magic, too. The Straken Lord senses this if you do. Better you stay. Wait here for me."

Without waiting for a further response, she took off running into the darkness, Lada atop her shoulder, holding on with his claws to her leather vest, hunched down so close that they seemed a part of each other.

Redden and his companions stared after her until she was gone and all they could hear was the sound of her voice, singing in the darkness.

Tesla Dart did not return that night. When morning came, she was still missing. Khyber Elessedil stood looking off into the wilderness where the Ulk Bog girl had disappeared, waiting. Redden sat watching her, growing increasingly anxious. She had been up all night, staring into the darkness. Redden had seen her every time he had come awake, which was often. She was clearly trying to make up her mind about what to do, and he was afraid she was going to come up with the wrong answer. Not for her, necessarily, or maybe even those she sought to rescue. Just for him. But he knew he couldn't interfere, even though the urge to do so was so strong he could barely contain himself. She was the leader of this expedition, and she was experienced and capable in ways he was not. He would only cause trouble by trying to guide her actions.

So he kept silent and willed the time to pass and the answer to come.

When it did, it was a surprise.

"We're not waiting any longer," the Ard Rhys announced suddenly, wheeling back to where Redden sat with the Trolls. "We're going back. If Oriantha and Crace Coram could be found, Pleysia would have found them. Or will, if she is still looking. I've used magic to search for signs of the Ulk Bog, but found nothing. Enough is enough. I won't risk any more lives. We're wasting our time sitting about. We need to find a way out of the Forbidding and back to the Four Lands."

Everyone climbed hurriedly to their feet, gathered their gear, and in minutes were walking north again, retracing their footsteps. This day was a mirror image of all the others, the sky iron gray and hard, the air thick with dust and the smell of decay, the land empty and barren everywhere.

"If we find a way out, we will think about coming back to see if the others managed to survive," Khyber said to the boy. "But we need better preparations and a stronger company to attempt it."

Redden nodded in agreement. Going on was too dangerous. They had already lost half their number, and there was nothing to say they wouldn't lose the other half before any of them got free of this place. Only five left, he thought in disbelief. All of the Druids save the Ard Rhys, all of the experts they had recruited to aid them, and most of the Trolls—dead or missing. All in less than four days' time.

He felt a tightening in his chest just thinking of it.

Nothing could be worse than this.

The trek went on through the rest of the morning, and neither Pleysia nor Tesla Dart reappeared. They moved cautiously, but steadily, keeping a sharp eye out. Khyber used a small scrim of magic to sweep the land just ahead of them, searching out predators and hidden dangers. When she found them—less than half a dozen times altogether—she steered the company clear. When at one point they crossed paths unexpectedly with a huge four-legged beast that was armored and horned, she had them stand still and wait for it to pass. It did so without more than a disinterested glance, lumbering off into the distance.

When they stopped for a brief rest, Redden caught sight of a brilliant green flash that appeared suddenly and was gone again. It reappeared later, after they had set out again, and this time Khyber Elessedil saw it as well. It stood out in sharp relief against the gray of the landscape, and every time it appeared after that—which was often—it caught their attention. But they were never able to get too close, and it didn't seem to have any particular source.

"What do you think it is?" Redden asked the Ard Rhys after they had seen it appear and disappear repeatedly.

But she only shook her head and kept walking.

Finally, they came to a stretch of heavy woods, the trees barren and skeletal, the grasses gray and dusty and dead. When they began to skirt the woods, the green flash reappeared and settled on a tree branch not fifty yards away, just inside the barren grove. Redden turned and walked toward it, hypnotized by its brightness and mystery, wanting to have a closer look. He heard the Ard Rhys tell him to come back, then heard her coming after him. But he kept going anyway, just wanting to see it a little more clearly, thinking it might be a sort of bird.

He was within twenty feet of his goal when the ground opened up and his feet were yanked from under him as a heavy rope net closed about him. He had just enough time to thrash in response and to witness the Ard Rhys releasing Druid magic in all directions before attackers bore her to the ground and thick, suffocating fumes filled his nostrils.

He woke again to the creaking of leather traces and the rumble of wooden wheels rolling across uneven terrain. He could smell the heated bodies of two huge beasts pulling the wooden cart in which he rode before he could see them, so thick was the dust. He was imprisoned in a cage constructed of iron bars embedded in huge beams, his arms and legs chained to rings set into the floor of the cart. He was sitting upright, his body and limbs pinned in place so that he could barely move.

The Ard Rhys was chained across from him, her head sunk against her breast. She was still unconscious. A blur of memory recalled itself, and he saw her fighting back against the things that had come out of the earth, fire bursting from her fingertips, engulfing those closest. He saw the Trolls rush to her aid, falling one by one to a barrage of arrows and spears.

He closed his eyes again, fighting back against the stabs of pain that lanced through his head. He still felt disoriented and weak, and it was all he could do to keep from passing out again. He forced his eyes open, made himself look outside the cage to find the heaving, straining bodies of the massive horned creatures pulling it. He caught sight of movement next to where he rode and found a wolfish creature pacing the cage, its huge, lean body covered in thick gray fur. When it saw him looking, it opened its jaws wide and revealed rows of blackened teeth.

Redden slumped against the bars of his cage and tried to calm himself. They'd been lured into a trap, snared and rendered unconscious, then imprisoned. He had no idea who was responsible, but his first thought was of Tesla Dart.

He tried to reason it through, but everything fell apart when he looked through the bars at the back of the cage and saw Pleysia's head impaled on the butt of a spear embedded in the cart's wooden bed.

8

---◆---

STILL TRAPPED ON THE PLATEAU WITH THE OTHERS WAITING for Khyber Elessedil, Railing Ohmsford levered himself up on one arm and tried to get to his feet. Seersha had announced that they had to get out of there before nightfall to avoid an impending attack, and he wasn't about to waste time doing so. Broken leg or not, he wasn't going to let those sharp-clawed creatures in the deep woods below get to him again.

"Here, here!" The Druid was bearing him back down again, her grip surprisingly strong. Her rough face pressed close, her good eye fixing on him. "I said we had to move to safer ground. I didn't say you had to *walk* there."

He started to make a retort, but then thought better of it and simply nodded. "Don't forget," she added, "you have the use of magic. You can protect yourself better than most. Stay calm. I will likely need *your* help when they come for us."

She turned away, all business now. He felt better knowing she depended on him, that she expected him to do more than lie there helplessly. For a moment, he had panicked. Redden wouldn't have allowed that to happen. His brother would have pulled himself together and prepared for a fight. So Railing would do the same.

Nevertheless, he couldn't try to pretend their situation wasn't desperate. They were trapped on this ledge somewhere in the middle of the Fangs, too far away from their airship to make a run for it, the surrounding countryside awash with creatures waiting for a chance to tear them apart. There were few enough of them left as it was— Seersha, Skint, Farshaun Req, the Speakman, a pair of Trolls, and himself. Everyone was still recovering from the last attack, and there was every reason to think another would be mounted soon enough— likely right after it got dark. The Ard Rhys and those who had gone with her had left only hours ago, but it seemed like days.

Railing tried not to think about how vulnerable his broken leg would render him when the next attack came.

"Skint!" Seersha called. The Gnome Tracker, who had returned by now, came over at once. "Go back up into those rocks and look around until you find a place where we can make a stand. Make sure those creatures can't get to us once we're in place. Don't rush. There's plenty of time. They'll wait until dark to attack."

Skint left without a word, heading into the woods behind them, back toward the cliffs where Redden and the others had gone earlier. How long had it been now? Railing tracked the sun—what little of it he could distinguish—across the gray, hazy sky, a whitish blur sliding westward. When night fell they would be left in complete blackness unless the moon broke through. Farshaun Req came over and knelt beside him. "How is the leg doing, boy? Is it giving you much trouble?"

Railing snorted. "Only if I try to walk on it. Which I'd better learn to do fast if I want to get out of this. I can't just lie around hoping someone can carry me everywhere."

The old Rover clapped his hand on the boy's shoulder. "Well said. Wait here. Don't go away."

He disappeared into the trees, leaving Railing to peer after him in confusion. The boy glanced over to the edge of the plateau to find the two remaining Trolls from the Druid Guard in heated conversation with Seersha. They were still keeping watch where she had left them, making sure no fresh attack caught the little group unprepared, but they seemed decidedly unhappy about something. Railing found himself wishing that Khyber and those with her, especially Redden, would return from wherever they had gone so the brothers could be together again. He was being selfish, but he didn't care. He hated having been left behind. Farshaun had explained why the Ard Rhys had insisted Redden must go with her, but that didn't make Railing feel any better.

There was a clear sense of urgency now, even though Seersha had told Skint otherwise. She moved away from the Trolls toward the Speakman, who huddled with his legs drawn up to his chest in a clear attempt to make himself less noticeable. She knelt next to him, and while Railing couldn't hear what she was saying, he could tell that her words were having a calming effect. The long scarecrow body gradually dropped its defensive posture, and the Speakman eventually got to his feet and went to join the Trolls.

Farshaun reappeared from the trees bearing a heavy staff cut from a tree limb. He had fashioned one end to form a cradle, its wooden surface wrapped in cloth.

"Take this," the Rover said, handing it to Railing. "You can use it as a crutch to help you walk. In a pinch, it will make a good weapon. In my opinion, a cudgel is worth a dozen swords."

Railing took the cudgel, glanced over to see if Seersha was looking, saw she had disappeared into the trees, and held out his hand to Farshaun. Using the Rover's firm grip and the solidity of the staff, he raised himself to a standing position. His leg pulsed with sudden pain and he grimaced in response but kept his feet. He wished he had taken the time when he had it to learn how to use the wishsong to heal injuries of this sort.

"Chew on this," Farshaun said, handing him some leaves he had extracted from a pouch.

"Deadens the pain?" Railing asked.

The old man shrugged. "Something like it."

He turned away, moving over to join the Speakman. The two stood at the edge of the precipice with the Trolls, all four of them peering down into the woods below, watching the lengthening shadows cast by the cliffs. Railing stayed where he was, conserving his strength for the trek to the cliff and the likely climb that waited. He was thinking how badly things had gone on this expedition, and how little success its members had found. A handful of them were already dead or injured, and for all he knew the group that had gone with the

Ard Rhys might have suffered losses, as well. But he didn't want to think that Redden was at risk, so he brushed the matter aside.

Seersha returned, scanning the group swiftly before coming over to Railing.

"I see you took my advice about staying off your feet," she deadpanned.

Railing shrugged. "I don't like feeling helpless. I don't want anyone to have to worry about me."

"Well, it's your choice. Just don't hold us up by being too proud to ask for help. You stumble, you call out. Understand?"

"Don't worry, I can do this."

"You'll get your chance to prove it." She began rummaging through her pockets. "Shades and shadows, where did I put it? Ah, here it is."

She pulled out a thin metal coin stamped with the image of Paranor and held it up so he could see. "We're not waiting any longer on the Ard Rhys. We're getting you and the seer and your Rover friend out of here. One of these was given to me; Mirai Leah has the other. Once I break it, Mirai's will shatter, as well, and she'll know to come to us." She studied the coin. "I don't know how long Khyber expected me to hold off, but I'm out of patience."

Without waiting for his reply, she snapped the coin in two and shoved the pieces in her pocket. "The coin will lead Mirai here. Now we have to hope that she comes soon."

It happened too quickly for Railing to object, which he might otherwise have done. He didn't want Mirai to come into the Fangs, even if it was to save him. Or maybe *especially* if it was to save him. It was bad enough that she had come on this expedition in the first place. But he had taken some comfort in the fact that the Ard Rhys had chosen to leave her behind with the *Walker Boh,* where she would be comparatively safe.

Now, thanks to him, even that small reassurance was gone.

"Seersha!"

Skint reappeared from the woods, trotting toward her. "I've found what we need, but it's not easily reached. We should go there now, at once, while it's still light enough to see the trail clearly."

She nodded her agreement and walked over to the precipice, motioning for the Trolls to remain where they were. Then she rejoined the others.

"Show us," she said to Skint.

The Gnome took them back into the trees, winding through heavy grasses and scrub for several hundred yards and then farther on through a series of rocky outcroppings and ravines. It was a slow, difficult slog, and it took everything Railing had—even with help from Farshaun now and again—to make the journey. By the time they reached the base of the cliffs, the boy was sweating heavily and his leg was aching badly enough that he had to sit down.

"Where do we go from here?" Seersha asked.

Skint pointed upward. "A short distance away, there's a series of cuts in the rock where you can find footholds to climb. About a hundred feet up, there's a wide ledge and an overhang farther back that offers shelter. The ledge can't be reached any other way than by climbing unless you can fly. There's no way in from the sides or down from the top. At least, none that I could see. I think we can hold off just about any attack from up there."

"All right. Well done." She glanced at Railing and his companions. "Take these three up with you. If the boy can't make the climb with his leg, use a rope to haul him. I'll go back for the Trolls. We'll wait until twilight and then we'll slip away to join you. With luck, those little monsters hiding out below won't know we're gone until it's too late to stop us." She held up a warning finger. "Wait. How far is it from here to where the Ard Rhys went through the cleft in the cliff wall?"

The Gnome glanced ahead. "It's close to where we'll be. You want me to have a look?"

"As soon as these three are safely up, see if you can find a sign of the others. Any sign. But don't get caught down here after dark."

She gave them all a sharp glance and hurried away.

Skint spent the better part of the next hour getting first the Speakman and Farshaun and then Railing Ohmsford up the cliff face to the ledge he had discovered. Railing required the most help. He could not put any significant weight on his injured leg and had to make the climb by planting the foot of his good leg in one foothold and then pulling himself upward using his hands and arms to the next. It was slow going, and his strength was quickly depleted. Skint, who was much stronger than he looked and patient with his efforts, pushed from below and kept Railing steady on the rock face. He made the boy pause often to rest and insisted he drink water when he did. Several times Railing began to slip or sway out from the wall, and each time Skint was there to help him.

When he finally reached the ledge, the Gnome patted his arm, told him he'd made a good job of it, and went back down in search of the mysterious waterfall.

Farshaun sat down next to him and shook his head. "We'll be well out of this business when Mirai comes to get us. This was never a good idea."

"Do you think she can find us?" Railing asked, gesturing toward the low ceiling of mist and haze.

Farshaun shrugged. "She'll find us. She's resourceful, that one. But she won't get here until morning. She won't bring the *Walker Boh* into this mess under darkness. We'll have to hold out until it's light."

Railing looked over the edge of the precipice to the rocks below and the dark smudge of the trees beyond. "Maybe we can do that," he said doubtfully.

They sat without saying much, looking out over the bleak countryside from their elevated vantage point, waiting for either Skint or Seersha and the Trolls to appear. Every so often, Farshaun would leave the boy's side to talk with the Speakman. He didn't say anything about his reasons for doing so, but the boy could tell that the Speakman was in need of constant reassurance. It made him wonder how the man had survived out here alone for so many years. But he supposed that if you hid in a cave and pretty much kept yourself out of sight, you could survive anywhere. Or maybe it was just that you could survive in surroundings you knew well enough to avoid the things that would do you harm, and that being taken out of those surroundings made you vulnerable.

He spent most of his time thinking of home. He would not have joined the expedition if he had known what it was going to be like. He wouldn't have come if he had thought he would be separated from

Redden. He wasn't all that different from the Speakman. He was removed from familiar surroundings, and his own fears and insecurities were being exposed as a result. What he wished now was that he and Redden and Mirai were back home, flying Sprints or scavenging pieces of downed aircraft or doing anything but what he was doing here. What he wished was that things could be put back the way they had been.

It was almost dark when a scrabbling sound on the cliff face announced the arrival of Seersha and the Trolls. They hauled themselves up the cliff face and onto the ledge, where the Druid set the guards at immediate watch and ordered the Speakman and Farshaun into the shelter of the overhang. She kept Railing out in the open, positioning him about six yards in front of the other two.

She looked ragged and spent, and her face was smudged with dirt. "From here, you can see most of what happens when we're attacked. I want you to do two things. I want you to watch our backs. If anything gets behind us, anything we don't see but you do, your job will be to send it back over the edge. Second, I want you to protect Farshaun and the seer. And yourself. Can you do all that?"

Railing nodded. "I can do it."

"It's a lot to ask."

"I know. I won't let you down."

Seersha gave him a flash of her crooked grin and clapped him on his shoulder with her strong hand. "I don't expect you will."

Afterward, when she had gone back to the edge of the precipice and was repositioning the Trolls to her left and right and putting herself in the middle, he found himself wondering if he was being overconfident. He had use of the wishsong's magic, but was that enough? He had used it only once in a fight, when the company was attacked coming into the Fangs. The attack had happened without warning, and he had reacted instinctively. But this time he knew what was coming, and he wasn't sure if knowing and reacting were the same and would produce an identical response. Sometimes thinking too much about something or even anticipating it for too long caused you to freeze at the crucial moment.

Hesitation in this case would likely be the end of him. So he must remain clearheaded and focused when the time came. He must not fail his companions.

He sat there in the darkening of the light and told this to himself over and over, all the while trying very hard not to panic. At one point, he stopped fretting long enough to wonder what had become of Skint. He had been gone an awfully long time now—far too long for Railing to feel comfortable about it. The boy didn't like just sitting while someone who had done so much to help keep him alive might be trapped out there in the dark. Seersha, crouched at the lip of the ledge, had shown no apparent interest in the other's failure to return. Railing thought to ask her what she intended to do, then realized there was no point. The Druid would not risk the safety of the others by leaving them to look for the Gnome. Either Skint would return on his own or he wouldn't return at all.

He had just about convinced himself it would be the latter when he sensed a stirring from those who kept watch at the edge of the cliff, and suddenly the Gnome Tracker hove into view atop the ledge, scrambling up hurriedly and flattening himself against the rock. He immediately motioned for the others to crouch down, gesturing them away from the edge. Seersha bent close, speaking quickly to him, listening to his rushed reply. She turned to where Railing was sitting, motioning for him to stay put, pointing out into the darkness to indicate something was coming.

Seconds later they were attacked.

Their assailants had returned for another try, scaling the walls of the cliff face like ants. They swarmed over the edge of the precipice, clearly not in need of the footholds that Railing and the others had required, bodies hunched over and skittering across the ledge, claws and teeth flashing. They were all over the two Trolls in seconds, flinging themselves on their armored bodies, tearing at them. Seersha held firm at the center, using Druid Fire to fling their attackers away, keeping most from getting past her.

But from either end of the ledge, where there were no defenders, the crookbacked little monsters gained the precipice unchallenged and came at Railing in droves.

Skint had dropped back to stand with him, knives held in both hands, and he was even quicker than his attackers. Blades cutting and slicing, sharpened metal edges flashing, he tore into them. In seconds, bodies lay heaped all around him.

But he couldn't be everywhere, and the rest charged the boy out of the dark, squealing and hissing like cats.

By now, Railing was on his feet, leaning on his crutch and summoning the magic of the wishsong. He reacted smoothly and calmly even though his stomach was roiling, standing his ground more because he had no choice than because he was brave. The attack came from three sides, but he stopped it cold, sweeping the magic in a broad swath that tumbled his attackers backward. He advanced a step at a time, taking the attack to them. Fire ripped across the ledge first one way and then the other, catching up the snapping, screeching creatures and flinging them away. One or two got around him by keeping to the darkness of the cliff face, but Farshaun was waiting with his heavy staff and put them down with swift, solid blows.

The members of the little company fought hard until the attack was broken up and their assailants driven off.

In the aftermath, the defenders stood panting for breath, ready for a fresh assault, waiting for it to come, and knowing it would. Skint moved over to Railing and put a hand on his shoulder, saying nothing. At the edge of the precipice, Seersha spoke quietly with the Trolls and glanced back to where Railing and Skint were standing together, giving them a satisfied nod.

Railing took deep breaths, his heart racing. He didn't feel good about any of this.

"Above you!" the Speakman shrieked.

Down from the cliff face behind them dropped several dozen fresh attackers, springing off the rocks like cats. Railing had only seconds to realize what had happened—they had used the screen of the previous attack to come up from behind—before they were all over him. He caught a glimpse of Farshaun going down, felled by a blow to the head. Beside him, Skint whirled away, quicker than he was, knives flashing. Then Railing's crutch was knocked out from under him, and coarse, hairy bodies swarmed over him and bore him to the ground.

But the wishsong saved him once more, reacting to the danger faster than he could think to command it, surfacing on its own to explode out of him and throw his attackers away. It happened so swiftly that it took him a moment to realize he was free again. Ignoring the pain in his broken leg, he scrambled up, using the crutch for leverage, and lashed out at the crouched forms. Out of the corner of his eye, he watched Seersha's magic ignite her attackers in bright blue flashes, setting them afire and sending them screaming into the night. A crush of the gnarled creatures had overwhelmed one of the Trolls. It fought to get free, veering dangerously close to the edge of the drop, then lost its balance and tumbled over the side, carrying its attackers with it.

The creatures were climbing up onto the ledge again, attacking from the front as well as dropping from the cliff face behind. The defenders were surrounded. Railing saw Seersha sweeping Druid Fire all along the edges of the cliff, trying to turn back these new attackers, to purge the entire front ranks. Skint and the last of the Trolls were standing shoulder-to-hip on his right, blocking the few who slipped past the Druid.

He swung back toward the overhang and found Farshaun on his feet again, struggling to break free from a pair of the attackers that had come down off the cliff face. They had his arms and were trying to wrench the staff from his hands. The boy dispatched both with quick bursts of the wishsong, his voice a hoarse shriek by now, his throat parched and raw. Quickly, he limped through the tangled bodies to stand next to the old Rover, reaching him just as a fresh wave of attackers scrambled over the cliff edge to his right and came at them.

"Stand fast," he heard Farshaun say.

Tightening his resolve, he did so, summoning the magic of the wishsong one more time. But he was weakened from the struggle and the effort drained him of the last of his strength. There were too many of them. Then he saw Seersha mount a counterattack, flinging herself into the heart of this fresh assault, and he responded with a wild cry and a counterattack of his own. Magic flaring, he tossed aside the crutch and began advancing toward the spidery attackers in a steady shuffle. The pain in his leg was intense, but it caused him to focus on what he was doing, generating a raw strength of will that would not let him quit. Fire burned across the ledge from both directions as the Druid and the boy struggled against this fresh surge, hammering into it, slowing it, stopping it, and finally throwing it back.

The attackers broke and scattered the way they had come, leaving the ledge smoking and ash-clouded and littered with the dead.

Railing staggered awkwardly, barely able to stand. He scanned the precipice for signs of movement, then for signs of life, and found neither.

Seersha reached him a moment later and braced him, waiting for Farshaun to place his crutch back in his hands. "Better hold on to this," she whispered. "We need you strong enough to stand and fight, Railing Ohmsford." She exhaled sharply. "Without you, I think we're lost."

Farshaun helped steer him to where he could sit down, one arm around his shoulders. The old man was bleeding heavily from a head wound, and his clothing was ripped and bloodied. "Wicked little monsters, aren't they?" he muttered.

"Have we beaten them?" Railing asked, leaning on his crutch as the old man helped support him.

Farshaun shook his head. "I don't know, boy." His eyes were vacant as he stared out at the darkness. "Have we?"

Time slipped away, and no further attacks came. The smells of death and dust cleared, and the night's wildness faded into silence. The bodies of their attackers littered the broad surface of the ledge, but the defenders were too exhausted to clear them away. Their strength drained, they sat hunched over in small groups—Seersha and the Rock Troll at the edge of the precipice, Farshaun and the Speakman at the back of the outcropping, and Skint and Railing midway between—conversing in quiet tones and waiting for the inevitable.

"You did well," Skint said to the boy. "You showed real courage."

Railing shook his head. "I was too scared even to think about being brave. I was just trying to stay alive."

"Which is the point." The Gnome's wrinkled face tightened in what might have been a grimace. "Maybe it's always the point."

They were silent for a moment. Railing was thinking, *That's right. That's the point exactly. That's all we're doing now. Trying to stay alive. All that stuff about searching for the missing Elfstones is gone. No one cares about that anymore.*

"Did you find any sign of the Ard Rhys or my brother?" he asked Skint impulsively, remembering he had never heard the other's report.

The Gnome gave him a look. "I didn't even find the opening they went through. That's why I was gone so long. I was searching for it. Everywhere. I knew where it had been, but when I couldn't find it there, I started searching the cliff walls, thinking I was mistaken." He shook his head in disgust. "I never found anything. It was as if the opening just disappeared, and everyone who went in disappeared with it."

Railing stared at him. "You couldn't find anything? How can that be possible?"

"Couldn't say. Seersha thinks there's magic at work. Someone else's magic. But there's nothing we can do about it. Not until we're out of this mess." Skint looked away. "I'm sorry about your brother."

Railing was stunned. "Well, I can tell you one thing," he managed. "I'm not leaving Redden."

Skint nodded. "No one said anything about leaving anyone. Calm down. Maybe you should try to sleep a bit."

He got up and moved away, leaving Railing alone. The boy stayed awake, trying to come to terms with what he had been told, unable to believe his brother could just be gone and no one know anything. It didn't make any sense.

The night faded into morning, and still their attackers did not return. They sat together and watched the sunrise, faint gray light filtering down through the haze and mist, the stark world of the Fangs slowly revealing itself. They ate a little food and drank some ale, and then they cleared the ledge of bodies, throwing them over into the precipice and onto the rocks below, where they lay in crumpled heaps.

No one came for the bodies.

No one came for them. Not Mirai or the *Walker Boh* or the Ard

Rhys or any who had gone with her or the fierce little creatures that had attacked them during the night.

No one.

Finally, darkness approached with a thief's silent cunning, the shadows lengthened in a cool hush, and the stillness that comes with day's end deepened with night's soundless fall.

Reluctantly, the little company prepared for a fresh onslaught.

9

ABOARD THE *WALKER BOH*, MIRAI LEAH WAS ENGAGED IN A
knife-throwing contest with members of the Rover crew when she
felt the coin shatter inside her tunic pocket.

A day had passed since the second time the Ard Rhys had taken
the bulk of the members of the expedition off the ship and into the
Fangs in search of the missing Elfstones, leaving Mirai once again
behind with the Rover crew and a handful of Trolls from the Druid
Guard. Not the kind to sit around and wait on a resolution of events
that might not happen for days or even weeks, she had, on both occasions, immediately begun spending time with the Rovers—a couple of whom she already knew from her previous trips to Bakrabru
on family business. She had a natural affinity for friendship and was
possessed of a sociable personality. Because she was a flier like they
were, it was not strange that she should feel a connection with the
airship riders who had accompanied Farshaun on this expedition,
and within the first twenty-four hours it felt as if they had been
friends for years.

But even as friends, they were competitive with one another and
with her, as well. Of varying ages and backgrounds, they were wild
and adventurous and eager—even in some instances compelled—to
prove they could measure up to whatever challenges they might encounter. Everything was a competition. It was the way they lived; it

was a big part of how they defined themselves. Having Mirai with them simply added fuel to the fire. Some were content to tease her, suggesting that no one who wasn't a Rover could ever compete with them. Some carried it much further and offered direct challenges. Mirai was a tall, strong girl, athletic and talented, and she was a match for any of them. But mostly she met their bantering with smiles and shakes of her head. Once or twice, she agreed to test her known skills against theirs, and once or twice more she agreed to be taught a skill she didn't possess. Knife throwing was one of the former, and scaling the mainmast without using the rigging one of the latter. To her credit, she declined Austrum's offer to wrestle, knowing full well his intentions in suggesting such a thing.

A heady mix of emotions fueled the verbal bantering and posturing of the Rover men, but in every case it was grounded to some degree in sexual attraction. Mirai was beautiful and charming, and while she kept them at bay during their time together, she did not discourage their attentions. Some of the men were partnered and some were not, some had families and some did not, but all were far from home and used to a life in which relationships were not measured in traditional ways. Many Rovers had more than one wife or partner. Others would never be able to settle even for that. Opportunity was always knocking, and Rovers were usually the first to respond.

Mirai knew all this, but she was not the sort to denigrate openly what she did not herself embrace. She was here on the *Walker Boh* with men she liked and admired, and there was no reason for her to spend what time they had together being rude or aloof. It wasn't in her nature to hold herself apart even as it wasn't in theirs to let her. She might be only a girl—not even a woman yet—but she was wise and experienced beyond her years and knew how to handle both them and herself.

Mostly.

Austrum was the only one who wouldn't let up. No matter how many times she rebuffed him, he kept coming back. He pushed at her constantly, taunting and challenging, always with a faint undercurrent of sexual innuendo that left her irritated and unsettled.

That was how the knife-throwing contest had come about.

He had started that morning by suggesting it, making comments about how men were physically superior to women and therefore better able to compete in contests of strength, but that maybe, just maybe, a woman might be able to win a knife-throwing contest—although probably not against him or any of the other Rovers. He didn't press the matter at first, just talked it up for a time—first while the crew ate breakfast and then afterward while they washed the decks and railings and replaced sections of the rigging. Mirai was not persuaded—not even interested, actually—but Austrum slowly began to gather support from the rest of the Rover crew.

By midday, they were clamoring for a contest and insisting that Mirai participate.

In the end, she relented, even though she thought Austrum was being boorish. There was really no way of avoiding it. They already knew she was proficient with knives. She had made the mistake of mentioning that Farshaun Req himself—one of the most accurate throwers in Bakrabru—had taught her. She was trapped by her own words and by a growing sense of resentment toward Austrum. If she could best him in a contest he felt so confident he would win, it might shut him up for a while. It might even persuade him to stop challenging her to contests where he could demonstrate his supposed superiority—although she knew better than to hope for too much.

They began the contest at midafternoon, standing twenty feet back from the mainmast. A black circle six inches wide was drawn on the mast, and the main hatch was removed and lashed in place to serve as backing against errant throws. Each participant was given three throws. The best of each set would be counted, and one participant would be eliminated in each round.

There was much anticipation and excitement, and soon even the Trolls had wandered over to watch the competition. All eight of the Rover crewmen and Mirai participated. Aleskins were passed around and large quantities of their contents consumed amid laughter and teasing. Only Mirai abstained from drinking, and that was only through the first four rounds, in which Arben, Chance Boy, Drendonan, and Pursett were eliminated.

Then she took several long swallows because she was parched and hot and feeling confident that a drink of ale would not cost her the victory. She was already throwing better than anyone but Austrum, and she could see the worry in his eyes. He was as good as if not better than she was, but she could tell he wasn't dealing with the pressure of the contest as well. Even so, he was good enough that she could easily lose. So she took nothing for granted, especially when all of the others were eliminated and only the two of them were left.

Austrum was throwing first. Tall and lean, he was a few years older than Mirai, a ruggedly handsome man/boy with dark, exotic features and a rakish smile. He usually wore his black hair loose and wild, but he had tied it back for the contest. She would have found him attractive if not for his taunts and teasing and the fact she was convinced no one would ever find him half as interesting as he found himself. Given a choice, she would have preferred the older, more stable Edras for a partner.

If she had been in the market for one, which she wasn't.

She took several more swallows from the aleskin and handed it to Austrum, who declined. "Still not too late to call it a draw," he offered.

It was odd, but he said it in a way that suggested the offer was not intended as a taunt. It almost felt like a compliment. She gave him a cool look. "Worried?"

He shook his head. "Not really. But you've proved your point. We don't need to take it farther."

She nodded, suddenly feeling stubborn. They were thirty feet back from the target now, a long distance for an accurate throw. "But I want to. Go ahead. Make your throw. Let's finish it."

He shrugged. Without pausing, he whirled and threw his knife, the blade flashing in the gray afternoon light as it buried itself in the center of the black circle. He did it so smoothly and quickly that Mirai caught her breath in spite of herself.

He finished his follow-through, straightened, and turned to face her. He looked uncomfortable. "Give me a minute and I'll remove my knife to give you a clear field."

"Don't bother," she snapped, fighting hard to ignore the sinking feeling in the pit of her stomach.

"But it's obstructing the target."

"You heard me. Leave it where it is."

She stared at his knife protruding from the center of the black circle and felt an unreasonable rage sweep through her. He hadn't even looked before throwing! How was she supposed to match that? But she was determined to try. She would not give in. Not to him.

She took a long, steadying breath, braced herself, and whipped the throwing knife underhand at the target. The blade shattered the handle of Austrum's weapon and fell to the decking.

She waited for his response, unable to look at him. "Doesn't count, my lady of skills and beauty," he said at last. "You have to stick it for it to count."

"It was dead on top of your own throw." She now held his gaze, refusing to look away. "It would have stuck if your own knife hadn't obstructed it. It counts."

He shook his head. "Not according to the rules. You should be penalized, if anything. You damaged my knife. Even if I can salvage the blade, I'll have to replace the handle."

She was livid. She knew she had been lucky with her throw, but now he was trying to steal the victory from her! She looked around at the other Rovers, aware that the boisterous crowd had gone mostly silent. She couldn't tell whether it was a result of discomfort over her confrontation with Austrum or astonishment over the accuracy of their throws.

"Who agrees with Austrum?" she snapped. "What do the rules say about this?"

Edras, older and even more whipcord-thin than Austrum, gave her a wry smile. "There isn't any rule. I don't think anyone's ever even seen this happen." He hesitated. "I say we call it a tie."

There were nods and murmurs of agreement from the others. *Declare it a tie and leave it at that. No need to choose between the two of you.*

But Mirai didn't want it to end in a tie. She hadn't even wanted to be a part of this competition, but now all she could think about was winning it. Calling it a tie was condescending and demeaning, and she would not stand for it.

"We'll throw again," she insisted, wheeling back on Austrum.

He flushed a deep red. "You still owe me a new knife."

She laughed at his petulance, unable to stop herself even though she knew it was the wrong thing to do. He was immediately furious, but stood his ground, insistent. "You find this funny, do you, little Highland girl?"

That was when she felt the coin break in her pocket.

She bit back the retort on the tip of her tongue, reached into her pocket, and extracted the pieces of the coin to make certain she was not mistaken. "We have to stop this," she said at once.

Austrum, mistaking the reason for her demand, threw up his hands. "You just said you wanted to continue! You really don't know your own mind, do you, *chilchun*?"

In Rover slang, that name was the worst insult possible. So bad, in fact, that she almost hit him. Edras was upset enough that he grabbed Austrum by the shoulders and pulled him around threateningly.

"No, stop," Mirai said quickly, not wanting this to go any further. "Let it be. He misunderstands, that's all." She faced Austrum. "The coin given me by the Ard Rhys has broken in two. Just now, in my pocket. That means she needs us to come to her. She's in trouble."

Austrum stared at her, caught off balance. He started to say something and stopped. Then he shook his head in disgust and walked off.

The Rovers already knew about the coin and the signal it would send if the Ard Rhys needed the *Walker Boh* to come to her aid. Mirai had discussed it with them after the others had departed for the first time, seeing no reason for them not to know and every reason for them to understand the urgency should the coin break. They were the lifeline for those on the ground who had gone into the Fangs, and it was their responsibility to come to the rescue of their companions if the need should arise.

Even so, they knew better than to respond recklessly and without consideration for the dangers involved. Foremost among these was the darkness that was fast closing around them. As much as Mirai wanted to leave at once in response to the coin's signal, she would have to wait until morning. Any attempt to penetrate the heavy mists of the Fangs would involve avoiding the clusters of stone pillars that could tear apart the underside of the *Walker Boh*'s hull, and that would require as much daylight as possible. Going in at night was suicide.

Reluctantly, the group agreed to postpone any rescue until dawn, spending the interval between then and now making the ship and themselves ready for the following day. They put away their throwing knives and went to work coiling up lines and tightening down stays and fastenings, clearing off the decks, and talking over how they would attempt an entry, bringing the Trolls into the discussion so that they could prepare themselves, as well.

No one thought for a minute that this would be easy. It was one thing to sail an airship high enough to avoid the treacherous forest of stone spears clustered below; it was another to make a descent into their midst. But that was what would be required if they were to be of any use to the Ard Rhys and her little company.

They ate their dinner late and after glasses of ale rolled into their blankets, anticipating an early rising. The night was deep and clouded over, and there was little light from moon or stars. The air was windless and infused with a metallic smell, and no sounds penetrated the stillness save for the snores of the men sleeping.

Awake and unable to sleep, Mirai Leah rose and walked back to the aft railing to sit and think. She was worried about Redden and Railing, wondering if they were managing to keep their wits together, if they were all right. Because if the Ard Rhys was in danger, so were they. She felt protective of them even in the best of times and distraught in times like these when she wasn't there to help them. The twins were too wild and reckless for their own good, and while she was the same age as they were she was far more mature than both of them put together.

She thought a bit about their relationship, wondering if the brothers would ever see it in the same way she did, deciding almost immediately they would not. She could pretend otherwise, but that was the truth of things. Each wanted her to belong to him; each believed she favored him. Both were in love with her and visualized her as an important part of their future. She understood why they felt this way.

The three of them had been close for a long time. They had spent hours together flying and exploring and sharing adventures. She had encouraged their attentions, a young girl anxious to know that boys found her attractive and desirable.

But she hadn't needed or sought that sort of validation of late, sufficiently grown up to be comfortable in her own skin and satisfied with who she was. She had worked hard ever since not to give either one the wrong impression about how she felt, while at the same time making sure they all stayed friends.

Even so, things hadn't worked out quite as she wished. While they accepted her friendship they continued to believe strongly that eventually there would be something more. They were so eager and awkward and funny about it. Each tried to outdo the other. Each made a special effort to lift his profile above the other's so that he would be seen differently in her eyes.

She gave a mental shake of her head. Hopeless. One day soon, she would have to do something about it.

A shadow moved in the darkness to one side and Austrum appeared, moving over to her. She was surprised and immediately irritated, but she resisted the urge to get up and leave. He sat down and for a moment said nothing.

"Why is it you dislike me so?" he asked finally.

She rolled her eyes. "I don't dislike you."

"You work hard enough at making it seem like you do."

She sighed wearily and faced him. "I just don't like it that you taunt me all the time. I don't need you trying to prove you're better than I am at everything. And if you're so worried about me not liking you, then don't call me terrible names."

He nodded, looking at her sideways for just a second. "I was wrong to call you that. I lost my temper. I thought you were trying to make me look foolish about the contest when you demanded we continue and then said we couldn't. I reacted without thinking. I didn't mean it. Any of it."

"But it hurt."

He shifted slightly in the dark. It was difficult to see his face. "I won't do it again. I promise. I'll tell everyone I was wrong to do it this time. Will that help?"

"Just don't do it again."

"I said I wouldn't."

"Maybe you should just stay away from me for a while."

The silence was longer this time. He seemed to be mulling over the idea, giving it weight. Finally, he locked his hands and pulled his knees up to his chest like a little boy caught out.

"I like you. I think you're beautiful. You're funny and smart. I feel good just being around you. I wanted you to notice me. So I teased you and did stupid things so that you would. I'm not very good at this courting business. I don't really have any practice." He finished abruptly and kept his eyes averted.

"You're courting me?" she asked in amazement.

He nodded wordlessly.

She was stunned. "Why would you court me? You don't even like me! Look how you behave around me!"

"I said I wasn't very good at it."

She stared at him. Big, strong, and handsome, he was someone she might be attracted to under different circumstances—although she couldn't think what those circumstances would be. Maybe if she didn't think him so hopelessly idiotic and dense. Maybe if they were in a different setting and not wandering the wilderness of the deep Westland. She was almost willing to concede that she had been wrong about his self-absorption, given the self-effacing way he had tried to explain his behavior, but she couldn't think of any reason why telling him this or otherwise encouraging him would be a good idea.

"I'm not interested in being courted by you or anyone else, Austrum," she said. "I just want you to leave me alone. I appreciate the apology. Now do what you said and don't keep after me all the time."

He looked confused. "What about those twins? You seem to want them to court you."

"Redden and Railing are friends from way back. That's all."

He shook his head. "They don't look at you like they're just friends."

She'd had enough. She put a finger into his chest. "I want you to go sit somewhere else. Right now."

He hesitated, looked down at her finger, then looked up again and smiled. He got to his feet without a word and walked off.

That had been entirely too easy, she thought, looking after him, and wondered why it bothered her.

Daybreak brought an unexpected change in the weather. Mirai woke to the feeling of cool wind and dampness on her face and rose to find dark clouds moving in from the west. Huge, tumbling black thunderheads filled the sky from horizon to horizon, and it was immediately clear that rain was on the way. Most of the others were already awake and sliding into cloaks and rain slicks, and she was quick to join them.

Austrum walked by, grim-faced and aloof, and did not bother even to look at her. Edras was in the pilot box, unlocking the gears and levers and readying the airship controls. She joined Chance Boy and Rideout, who were trimming the rigging in expectation of the blow, reducing light sheaths to a bare minimum. The rest were lashing down everything that might shift in flight. This was not the sort of day she had envisioned after so many dry and windless ones. Today would be something altogether different, and she did not like to think of what that would mean to their efforts to find the Ard Rhys.

They took time to eat in shifts, their meals quickly prepared and eaten. There was a decided sense of urgency. If they could get moving quickly enough, they might be able to reach their unknown destination before the storm hit. What it had taken the Ard Rhys and company days to reach on foot they could expect to reach in a couple of hours. No one thought this would happen, given the speed and look of the approaching storm, but at least they could make significant progress before they had to anchor and wait it out.

The wind was blowing harder but the rain was still holding off as they hauled in the anchor and lifted away from their mooring site. Mirai stood with Edras in the pilot box, the pieces of the broken coin clutched in one hand, reading the brightening and dimming of their glow to determine the direction the *Walker Boh* should take. She had not known before what she would have to do in order to find the way. But as soon as the airship had begun to fly, the coins had responded, and it had immediately become clear what was needed. Still, knowing and acting on that knowledge were two different things. The high winds buffeted the *Walker Boh* like a toy, and she was continually knocked off course. Edras fought the wheel until he was exhausted and suddenly Austrum was there to take his place, seizing the wheel and holding it steady. Mirai glanced at him, but he refused to look back.

When the rains came, they had still not reached their destination. With sheets of rain whipping over them, the light sheaths reduced to tatters, and the ship caught in the grip of a north wind shaking her like a cat would a rat, there was every reason to believe they might go down.

"We have to get out of this!" Mirai yelled at Austrum.

The Rover shouted something back that was lost in the wind's piercing scream. But his hands flew over the airship's controls, and the airship began to descend toward the layers of mist and the stone spears they concealed.

Forward, Chance Boy on the starboard railing and Pursett on the port shouted back and gestured for them to not go any lower. It was clear they had caught at least a glimpse of the wicked tips of the Fangs right under them.

Austrum reached over and pulled Mirai close. "We have to get down farther if we don't want to be shaken to pieces," he shouted in her ear.

"Watch for my signals!" she responded. And without waiting for his response, she rushed forward.

Positioning herself next to Chance Boy, who was barely out of his teens, she peered into the shifting haze of the mist and rain, searching for an opening. She pulled the pieces of the coin from her pocket and took a quick peek through her fingers. The glow was sharp and clear; the Ard Rhys was not far away. Putting the pieces away again, she braced herself against the railing and peered over the side. She could just make out the dark spear points of the Fangs below. She held up her hands where Austrum could see them through the darkness and downpour, motioning him left and then right, guiding him toward a place where a landing might be possible. All they needed to do was to descend far enough to secure mooring lines and ride out the rest of the storm.

Worried that she might be thrown overboard by the turbulence, Chance Boy had secured a safety line about her waist—something she had failed to do herself. She was balanced against the railing, her boots hooked into the struts to help hold her in place. She was being knocked about, but she was holding on and the safety line assured she would not fall even if she was dislodged.

But then she missed seeing a cluster of the spikes materialize right underneath the hull as she signaled Austrum to maneuver toward a hole in the mist. The jagged stone ripped through the planking, knocking the *Walker Boh* askew and tearing out the hull far enough up on the bow that it took out the railing to which she was tethered.

With a startled gasp, she went over the side and tumbled away.

10

---◆---

Pain.

It ratcheted through Mirai's body as she woke and tried to move. It flooded her senses and made her go instantly still.

Something is wrong.

She was hanging upside down, she realized, suspended by the safety line fastened about her waist, swinging slowly back and forth through a shroud of haze and grayness and damp. Rain was lashing her face, blown by storm winds that had not abated in their fury.

How long have I been unconscious?

She tried moving again, and this time realized that she was wrapped up in the safety line in a way that pinned her left arm to her side and tangled her legs. The pain seemed to be generated as much by this as by any injury, although on looking up to where the broken piece of the ship's rail anchored her to the branches she had tumbled through, she wasn't so sure.

But at least she was alive.

All was rain and howling wind, so she knew she was still in the thick of the storm and not much time could have elapsed. Maybe hardly any at all. Her head ached fiercely, and she supposed she had struck it hard enough falling through the tree branches to black out.

Then she looked down.

She was hanging over a line of jagged rocks forming part of the lip of a broad ravine. The ravine itself was little more than a black gash in the mix of rain and mist, and she couldn't tell how deep it went. Huge trees ringed everything, some of them shredded of all foliage, all of them old and gnarled, their limbs twisted together in knots. The ravine zigzagged its way right through their center, in some places exposing huge roots that hung into the deep split like the arms of dead men in an open grave.

She looked away quickly. If her safety line had not caught in the trees, she would have fallen into the ravine.

And she would probably never have been found.

Her thick blond hair had come loose from its bandanna and was plastered against her face, obscuring her vision and causing her further discomfort. Using her free hand, she brushed it away, being careful to move slowly. She couldn't tell how securely she was fastened to the trees, and she didn't want to do anything that would cause her to shake loose. Bound up as she was by the safety line, she wouldn't stand a chance of saving herself.

Peering upward for a long moment, she searched the grayness for some sign of the *Walker Boh,* but there was no hint of her. In a storm like this one, the airship had probably been blown away from where she had fallen overboard, and the Rovers had no idea how to get back to her. Especially not while the storm was still raging.

She was going to have to get out of this by herself.

The wind caught her in a sharp gust, and she found herself swinging in wide arcs over the chasm—out into the void and back over the rocks—a pendulum out of control. She gritted her teeth and tried to will herself to stop, to make her body be still.

Then the rope that suspended her gave way, and she dropped several feet before it caught again.

She closed her eyes against the wave of fear that coursed through her.

What can I do to save myself?

She looked down again, searching for something that might offer a way out. But there was nothing within reach she might grab on to and nowhere to attempt to swing herself and land safely.

Even if she managed somehow to free herself from the safety line.

Then she remembered her throwing knife. She had tucked it into her belt when the coin had broken and the throwing competition had ended. It should still be there.

She reached back, fumbling for the handle, grasping at hope.

But the knife was gone.

She felt all the air go out of her. No surprise, she told herself. She must have lost it in the fall. And she had no other blade. No other weapon at all.

She heard something beneath her, a kind of hissing sound. She glanced down and saw a lizard looking up. Or something like a lizard, only much more unpleasant. It was big, fully eight feet long. Its mouth opened as it lifted its head toward her, perhaps thinking she might fall into it like a piece of fruit. Except she didn't think this creature ate fruit. Not with so many sharp teeth and such strong jaws for snapping bones and chewing flesh. No, this was a meat eater, and it was hoping to make a meal out of her.

Her eyes shifted.

A second lizard had appeared off to one side, even bigger than the first.

Mirai took a moment to catch her breath. She had imagined this expedition would be dangerous, and she had prepared herself for what she might encounter. But she had not prepared for this, and suddenly all she could think about was how foolish she had been to come. How foolish *all of them* had been. She should have refused to accompany Redden and Railing, and then perhaps they wouldn't be here, either. Now all of them were caught up in a world of monsters and bleakness and rapidly vanishing possibilities.

Or that was how she saw it as she dangled helplessly over a chasm with a pair of hungry lizards waiting for her to drop.

But Mirai Leah was not the kind to give way to either despair or fear, so she gathered up the shreds of her courage and resolve and tried anew to find a way to save herself.

Then a shriek sounded off in the darkness to one side, piercing even the sounds of the wind and rain. The lizards turned at once, hesitated only a moment, then skittered off into the brush, leaving the clearing empty.

Mirai waited, searching the gloom. A stout figure wrapped in the black robes of the Druids stepped into view, moving toward her.

"Mirai?"

She exhaled sharply. "Seersha!"

"Are you all right?"

"As all right as I can be, trussed up like this. Can you help me?"

The Dwarf moved over to the edge of the chasm, glanced down, and stepped back again. "Close your eyes and keep them closed. Hold tight to yourself. Don't move, no matter what you feel. Not until I tell you to. Ready?"

Mirai closed her eyes, hugged herself as best she could, and grunted affirmatively. Almost instantly she felt herself being lifted away, and then she was floating weightlessly. The wind and rain still buffeted her, but she was no longer swinging in midair. Mirai wanted desperately to see what was happening, but she had been told not to try and she wouldn't have been told that if there wasn't a good reason.

She felt herself moving, and then the rain-soaked earth was pressing up from beneath her, and she was lying on the ground.

Seersha was next to her at once, cutting away the remnants of the tangled safety line, tossing the pieces aside. "Must be a good story behind all this," she said.

Mirai finally opened her eyes. "Not if you're me." She stretched her arms and legs as the rope fell away. "How did you find me?"

The bluff face wrinkled with her smile. "The pieces of the coin. It works both ways. When they started to glow brightly enough, I knew you were close."

"We got caught in the storm, and the *Walker Boh* struck a cluster of stone spikes. I was tied to the railing, but it tore away and took me with it."

"Not a good time to be looking for anyone," Seersha observed as she helped the Highland girl to her feet. "For either of us. We have to get out of here. This whole place is crawling with things that want to kill us."

Although Mirai could stand, she could barely walk, her legs numb from being trussed up. Seersha had to support her, an arm wrapped around her waist as she helped her move away.

"Is the ship still flying? Or did it go down, too?"

"Still flying, so far as I know." Mirai hobbled along as swiftly as she could, casting anxious glances over her shoulder in the direction the lizards had taken. "What's happened?"

"Good question. I only know a little of it. Let's save that for when we're safe. Was it the coin breaking that brought you?"

Mirai nodded.

"Not very quickly, though."

"The Rovers and I decided not to risk it at night. Too dangerous to try to maneuver a big airship. So we waited until this morning to set out."

Seersha snorted. "Which didn't turn out to be of much help, did it?"

"No. The storm just made things worse. I'm sorry."

The Dwarf tightened her arm about Mirai's waist in a brief hug. "Don't be. I'm just glad you came at all."

The hissing sound was back, suddenly right behind them. Without releasing her grip on Mirai, Seersha wheeled about, stretched out her free arm, fingers extended, and sent an explosion of blue fire into the creature that was reaching for them with open jaws. The lizard flew backward into the dark and disappeared.

"And that's not even the worst of what's here," the Druid said, exhaling sharply.

They moved ahead as swiftly as they could, and slowly Mirai regained the feeling in her legs and her strength began to return. Twice more the lizards came at them, and each time Seersha used quick bursts of her Druid Fire to fling them away.

"Trouble is," she said, panting for breath as they slogged through the mud and rain, "the more I use the magic, the more of them I attract."

"How many are there?"

Seersha gave her a look that said it all.

Mirai was moving on her own now, stumbling a bit but able to support herself. Together they pushed on, making their way through a tangle of woods and heavy grasses and then clusters of boulders and empty flats. The lizards had been replaced by something that resembled Gnomes with lots of teeth. These new creatures were smaller, but attacked in packs. There seemed to be more of them gathering with every step.

"We have to climb that cliff just ahead," Seersha said suddenly, pointing. "The others are up there."

Somehow they made it to the base of the cliff and found the trail. Together they started up, clawing their way from handhold to foothold, the pursuers snapping at their heels and trying to pull them down again. The rain made their grip on the rock uncertain, and the gloom hid their attackers until they were almost on top of them. Mirai kicked out behind her as she climbed, trying to keep the creatures at bay, but they seemed able to scale even the sheerest of surfaces and came at her from both sides, grasping her arms in an effort to dislodge her.

Then brilliant light flooded the darkness from above, illuminating the climbers and their attackers. A surge of white fire swept across the face of the cliff, peeling the creatures off like bits of lichen and sending them tumbling away. Seersha and Mirai scrambled the rest of the way up and tumbled over the edge to safety.

Mirai lay on her back, gasping for breath. Dark figures clustered around, and one leaned close, a familiar smile on a familiar face.

"Took you long enough," Railing Ohmsford said.

They sat huddled together at the back of the precipice, the little company that had been defending this ground for the better part of two days and Mirai Leah. The overhang gave them some shelter from the storm, and the wind kept their attackers from trying to mount a sustained assault. One had been attempted at the storm's onset, Railing informed Mirai, but it had been hampered by the damp and the wind and been thrown back easily. Since then, the Spider Gnome lookalikes had been mostly quiet.

"But they'll come again once the storm stops and things begin to dry out. Especially when night comes." Railing was huddled close to her, his broken leg stretched out, and his cloak bundled about both of them. "Unless the ship finds us," he added.

"It will," she said quickly, wanting to reassure him that there was hope, even though she was not at all sure there was. With both sets of coins on the ground, the mist obscuring their position, and the *Walker Boh* already damaged from one attempt at landing, there wasn't much reason to think an attempt would even be made without something to guide the Rovers besides guesswork.

Seersha had already told her what had happened to the company since they had come into the Fangs. She had heard about the division of the company, the loss of contact between the two commands, and the ongoing attacks by the creatures she had just barely escaped. She understood how desperate their situation was and how much more desperate things might be for those who had disappeared into the defile.

"What have you decided to do about the Ard Rhys's party once the airship finds us?" she asked Seersha, who was huddled within her black cloak, nose and mouth tucked down inside its heavy folds.

The Dwarf's eyes shifted to find her. "Wait here with Skint until they come back. Or until they contact us. We'll have to ask you to come back for us once you've gotten Railing and the others safely out."

"But you have no idea where they are, do you?"

Seersha shook her head. "Skint looked, but he couldn't find a trace of them. Couldn't find the crevice they went into. Couldn't find the waterfall that isn't a waterfall."

"Redden will find a way back," Railing said, his voice muted by a burst of wind. "He has the wishsong to help him. He'll use it to find a way if things get too ugly."

No one said anything to that. Mirai knew what they were thinking. What if there wasn't a way back from wherever Redden and the others had gone? What if the company was trapped? It seemed clear enough that magic had lured them in, but maybe even magic wasn't enough to get them out.

"Here, eat some of this," she offered, pulling out packets of white paper in which bits of something hard had been carefully wrapped.

Seersha opened hers and ate it. "Honey candy. Where did you get honey candy, Mirai Leah?"

"I made it." She grinned at the Druid, who was passing pieces down the line to the others in the company. "I carry it with me for occasions just like this one."

"What a liar!" Railing exclaimed.

Seersha laughed. "Guess you were thinking further ahead than the rest of us."

"I think further ahead than some." She glanced over at Railing, who crunched his piece of candy noisily.

They waited out the storm, which lasted most of the rest of the day, and then Skint disappeared up into the rocks, searching for a better defensive position. The precipice on which they were settled was adequate, but it was too broad for six—now seven—defenders to continue to hold against the hordes of attackers they had been fighting off. Sooner or later, they would be overwhelmed. Mirai hadn't said anything to Seersha of their chances of being found, but she guessed the Druid had already surmised the problem and decided to act on what she perceived to be the unfavorable odds.

With the approach of sunset, Mirai helped Railing to his feet and walked him to the cliff edge, where they stood looking out over the rumpled blanket of trees and rocks amid the jagged stone towers of the Fangs. Everything was sodden and wrapped in trailers of mist and looked to be better suited for the dead than the living.

"How bad is your leg?" she asked. "Does it hurt much?"

Railing shook his head, staring off distractedly. "I should have gone with him. We should have stayed together."

She nodded. "We should have stayed home. All three of us."

"He left while I was unconscious. I wouldn't have let him go otherwise. I don't know why he did it."

"He did what he thought he had to do." She put her arm around him. "He did what he thought was the right thing. He's like that. You're both like that."

Railing looked unconvinced. "If anything happens to him—"

"Nothing will happen," she interrupted quickly. "Redden is tough and smart. He'll find a way. And if he doesn't, we'll find a way for him. You and me. We won't abandon him."

He looked over at her. His face was suddenly stricken. "I'm sorry we ever asked you to come with us. I wish you weren't here, Mirai."

She gave him a look. "Maybe we should stop talking about this. It's all said and done, anyway. I'm here. You and Redden are here. We can't do anything about it. Regretting it now doesn't do much to make things better." She leaned over and kissed him on the cheek. "We just have to help each other get through this."

He nodded. "Just get home again, right? Just get back."

She left her arm draped around his shoulder and looked out over the wilderness, trying not to think about what that meant. "Just get back," she repeated quietly.

Skint returned just before sunset, weary and discouraged. There wasn't anywhere else they could make a stand that was any better than where they were. They would have to stay put for another night. Seersha nodded grimly and gathered the others together, explaining how they would position themselves when night fell. She asked Railing to take one side of the precipice while she took the other, dividing their use of magic equally. Mirai and Farshaun would stand with Railing. Skint and the last of the Trolls would stand with her. They would put their backs to the wall of the overhang, their defensive line reduced to less than a dozen yards. There was no longer any point in trying to defend the precipice. Their attackers could not be kept off the heights—the past two nights had shown them that much.

She did not mention the Speakman. There was no need to. Everyone already knew how useless he would be. He had lapsed into a state approaching catatonia, barely able to converse with Farshaun and seemingly unaware of any of the others. It had been a mistake to bring him, Mirai knew. He wasn't up to this. He crouched in the lea of the overhang, hunkered down with his face averted, muttering and hugging himself.

"He's never going to be the same after this," Railing muttered to her at one point.

She stood close to Railing as the darkness deepened and the twilight hush began to fill with night sounds. Seersha had provided her with a pair of short swords, weapons with which she was familiar and skilled. Oddly, although Railing was the better equipped of them to defend against what was coming, she couldn't escape the feeling that he was the one who needed protecting. The loss of his brother had unnerved him; she could see it in his eyes and hear it in his voice. Their separation, so unfamiliar to both, was wearing on him. Railing was strong, but the thought of anything happening to Redden was breaking him down.

There was little time to consider it further. Their attackers swarmed over the precipice shortly after the darkness had drained away the last of the light. Seersha had ringed the defenders inside a thin line of liquid she had conjured with magic and now lit with Druid Fire, giving them a protective barrier. When the Gnome creatures tried to come through it, they caught fire instantly, turning into balls of flame that skittered this way and that, howling in anguish as they died. But the fire lasted only as long as the magic, and when it finally went out their attackers were on them.

Mirai fought side by side with Railing, each protecting the other and both trying to protect Farshaun. But the old Rover was soon too weak to continue and dropped to the ground senseless. Railing's use of the wishsong threw back most of their assailants, and Mirai's quick hands and sure use of her blades cut down the rest. Whatever manner of beings these creatures were, they seemed to possess no threshold point where they would break and run. No matter what the defenders did to drive them off, they refused to quit. It was disheartening and eventually terrifying, and after a while Mirai began to sense that there was no way this battle could be won.

Then Skint went down, felled by a blow from a club, and suddenly they were four. A moment later the last of the Trolls went down, and then they were three. A handful of their attackers got behind them and seized the Speakman. He shrieked and howled as they dragged him out into the open and then gave a strangled gasp and went silent as they cut his throat.

Railing, Mirai, and Seersha were backed up against one another, surrounded on all sides. It was over for them, Mirai knew. Their strength was depleted and their numbers reduced to where they were too few to hold off their attackers. One by one, they would be cut down. Even their formidable magic was not going to be enough. Already it was showing signs of failing both the Druid and the boy, leaving them ashen-faced and gasping for breath.

"Get behind me," Railing told Mirai as the creatures massed for another rush.

He was covered in ash and grime, and his face was hard in the darkness. He looked a dozen years older, and she was stricken at the thought of losing him.

"I'm right here," she said, tears flooding her eyes.

Right to the end.

But suddenly light flooded the darkness overhead, spearing down to the precipice and illuminating the hordes of attackers. A familiar whine broke through the sounds of battle, and a flit shot out of the darkness and plunged into the fray. Rail slings released their deadly missiles, sweeping aside scores of attackers, and a fire launcher's deadly beam incinerated dozens more. Instantly the tide of battle shifted. Even for creatures as determined and blood-crazed as these, this was too much. They broke and ran, disappearing over the edge of the precipice and into the night.

Mirai wanted to shout aloud what she was feeling, but she settled for hugging Railing instead. Somehow, against all odds, the Rovers had found them!

Still holding on to Railing, who was swallowing hard and murmuring, "It's all right, it's all right," over and over, she watched the flit swing around and settle onto the bluff. The pilot, wrapped in leathers and a protective mask, stepped out of the cockpit and looked around cautiously before coming over.

Mirai felt a twinge of surprise. She knew at once who it was.

Austrum reached her, pulled off the mask, took her out of Railing's arms, and kissed her hard on the mouth.

"Are you hurt?" he asked her.

She shook her head no, too shocked to speak.

"Courting you is very hard work," he said, looking her in the eyes and holding her gaze. "But worth it."

Then he kissed her again.

I I

---◆---

In that same hour, far to the east in Arishaig, the assassin Stoon approached the sprawling compound that housed the offices and residences of the Federation Coalition Council. It was raining—a torrential downpour, thunderclouds massed overhead and the skies filled with flashes of lightning and long peals of rolling thunder. Cloaked and hooded, a wraith abroad on a gloomy night, the assassin passed through a door used by servants and laborers—a door that was locked, but to which he possessed a key.

Keeping to the shadows, he made his way along the courtyard walls and then through a little-used rear door to the building that housed the Prime Minister's residence. He slipped inside a darkened entryway, pausing to make certain he was alone. But there were no guards at this level or any servants about at this time of night. He shed his cloak and moved swiftly down the hall to the secret passage, triggering the release to the hidden door and passing through to an even deeper darkness.

It was musty and cobwebbed within, and he could hear rats scurrying in the walls. He found the candle he required to light his way, lit it, and started up the stairs to the next floor, moving on cat's feet, his senses straining to catch any unusual or unexpected noises. But there were only the rats and the sound of his breathing.

Just like old times.

He thought momentarily of Drust Chazhul, dead now for over a week, lying in the ground to which he had been hastily consigned by a handful of the soldiers who had followed him to Paranor—a handful lucky enough to survive the doom that had overtaken their fellows and with no love for the late Prime Minister and no reason not to want him dead and buried. They would keep their mouths shut; they did not wish to be connected to the deed and had been made to understand that silence was what would keep them alive. It was an easy bargain to make. Drust Chazhul was nothing to them. He was just another in a long line of politicians who had found countless ways to make their personal lives difficult and their lot as soldiers more trying.

Stoon thought of Drust without sadness or regret. He had killed Drust because the Prime Minister had become an obstacle to his own ambitions. In his trade, you looked out for yourself first and foremost. He might serve a master or mistress from time to time, but it was never for long and never with any thought of permanent attachment. That he had stayed with Drust for as long as he had was something of an oddity. He doubted it would ever happen again.

Even with her.

He reached the next floor and turned down the hidden passageway leading to the Prime Minister's chambers. How many times had he made this journey? How often over the years had he followed this very route through the bowels of the compound to meet in secret and plan great things? It would have been impossible to say, and in any case unnecessary to speculate. The past had no meaning in these matters. It was always about the future and what great promises the future might hold.

Farther down the corridor, several twists and turns later, he reached another set of stairs and climbed to the third floor. As he did so, he flashed back to the killing and recalled Drust's face as the knife slid home and his life thread was severed. An image of it hung suspended in the air before him, fully remembered from the moment the killing had occurred. Shock and dismay, confusion, and a clear sense that something was terribly wrong—all had shown in the man's dying features. Stoon savored the memory. It gave him an undeniable satisfaction. There were many others like it, but none that provided such a clear sense of fulfillment. Drust Chazhul had been a monster, bereft of any sense of moral obligation or purpose in life. He had only wanted to achieve power and then hang on to it. Such men were plentiful and always replaceable. Such men needed purging, and when the chance came to remove one, it was an opportunity to be exploited.

Or so Stoon believed, and at the end of the day what else mattered but his own beliefs?

At the head of the stairs he found a landing and a locked door. He looked to see that the signal candle was lit and then knocked softly, waiting for her voice before he used the second key. He entered the bedchamber, closing the door behind him. The light was better here, thanks to a series of lit candles arrayed about the room and the pale reflection of the torchlight that illuminated the courtyards, its rain-washed glow streaming through the windows.

"You have news for me?" she asked softly, her voice low and seductive. She was sitting in her bed, wrapped in a silken robe, propped up by pillows and holding a tablet on which she had been writing.

"Yes, Mistress," he answered. "I do."

He extinguished the candle he was carrying and moved over to the chair he favored on these visits, wondering how the rest of the night would go.

"Have you missed me?"

He shrugged. "Always."

"Life with me is so much better than it was with Drust, isn't it? So much more interesting?"

"I'd be a fool to say otherwise."

"And you are not a fool, are you, Stoon? Not where I am concerned. Are you?"

He watched Edinja Orle set down the tablet and rise from her bed. She walked over to where he sat, bent down, and kissed him on the lips. Her dusky skin smelled of sandalwood, and her long silver hair spilled over his face. "I didn't hear your answer."

"I didn't give it. I don't need to. You own me body and soul, Mistress. You already know that."

She smiled, the teeth behind her lips as sharp as those of her cat.

"I know men aren't to be trusted," she said quietly, moving away.

Drust would have appreciated knowing who had orchestrated his death. He would have liked the symmetry of it, had he been able to look at it objectively. He had been so anxious to rid himself of Edinja that he had overlooked the obvious when he found himself the recipient of those threatening notes. When the possible doesn't fit, one must take a closer look at the impossible. Certain that Edinja was dead, it had not occurred to him to wonder why no one had been able to verify her death. He had even accepted Stoon's story about the disappearance of the body—that it quite likely had been spirited away by family members, a common practice among magic users. Seeing her poisoned right in front of him had been sufficient proof, and he had never even considered the possibility that she had arranged all this for his benefit, in order to catch him off guard and finish him.

Stoon had made certain it all went as planned. He and Edinja had become lovers and accomplices several months before, not long after Stoon had decided that things were not working out with Drust as he had expected. The "permanent position" he had accepted was leading nowhere. Drust was ambitious and clever, but he was not well positioned in the hierarchy of Federation families and there was a limit to how far one could rise when personal circumstances were unfavorable. Stoon had seen the need for a different alliance if he were to improve his situation—something he was always looking to do. He had been looking around already when he met Edinja.

The meeting had been carefully planned, though not by him. It was she who had approached him as he was coming back to his quarters late one night; she stepped out from the shadows, cloaked and hooded, to confront him. How she had found him in the first place was a mystery, but the reason she had done so was never in doubt. She asked him if she could come in, she told him what she had in mind for him as they sat drinking cups of ale, and then she asked him to take her to his bed. He let it happen; she was eager and he was curious. It occurred to him that she might be lying, that she might have another purpose in doing this, but he saw no harm in taking the time to find out what it was.

He began seeing her regularly after that, but always on her terms and always making certain they would not be discovered. He realized she was a good match for him, and soon enough curiosity turned to attraction and attraction to infatuation. She wanted him to become her assassin; she wanted him to leave Drust Chazhul. She made it clear that he would never improve himself with Drust, no matter the promises made or the heights the other might strive to achieve. None of it would last; in the end, Drust would go the way of other over-reaching, ambitious amateurs. She intended to see that this happened. It would be wise of him to join her in this effort. Didn't he find the idea attractive?

Eventually, he agreed to join her. The decision to be rid of Drust Chazhul was made the moment he did. Stoon might not have agreed to the arrangement had he not been so certain that Drust had over-stepped himself and that his demise, however it came about, was imminent in any event. Allying himself with Edinja Orle made perfect sense. She was a member of a powerful family of magic wielders and politicians. She, herself, was an extremely talented sorceress. She was beautiful and smart, and she wanted him. The benefits were obvious. In the beginning, there had been no specific timetable for eliminating either Drust or Federation Commander Lehan Arodian. Once Edinja had faked her own death, Stoon had simply waited for the right opportunity to dispatch the other two. Arodian's killing had been simple; Drust was looking to eliminate the commander and had been more than willing to help achieve that end. Killing Drust after the debacle at Paranor had been inspired by Stoon's realization that there would never be a better time. The Prime Minister had led his soldiers into a disastrous engagement, and the fury and hatred he had called down upon himself as a result assured that no one would question too closely what had happened when he didn't return.

Of course, Stoon understood the danger inherent in the game he was playing. Edinja had been quick to resurface and lay claim to the position of Prime Minister once Drust was out of the way, explaining how she had gone into hiding to save her life and convincing by various means the members of the Coalition Council that she was the logical choice. Many, it might be pointed out, knew of the tower in which she lived and the rumors of what happened to those who disappeared within because they had incurred her disfavor. The salient point, so far as Drust was concerned, was that once she was named to the office, he became dispensable. At any point thereafter, Edinja might decide she would be better off rid of him. But Stoon was drawn to the riskiness of the relationship, and he trusted his instincts to warn him when it was time to quit playing the game. His instincts exceeded those of most and had saved him before on repeated occasions. He had no reason to think they wouldn't save him again.

"What have you come to tell me?" Edinja asked, bringing him out of his reverie. She was standing across the room, looking out the window.

He caught sight of Cinla now, stretched out beneath the sill, eyes bright lanterns of green in the shadows. The moor cat was staring at him, gaze fixed and steady.

He forced himself to look away. "Aphenglow Elessedil has left Arborlon and is flying west toward the Breakline, possibly in search of the Ard Rhys, but perhaps for another reason."

"Another reason?"

"Before she left this last time, she flew back to Paranor and apparently went into the Keep. The birds you set on watch after we withdrew brought word only hours ago; she was seen on the south wall, inside the Keep." He paused. "Those birds. How do you get them to report to me like that?"

Somehow, in a way that was a mystery to him, she had trained ravens not only to keep watch for her but also to report what they had seen by a form of communication that projected images into the mind. It was magic, of course, but magic of a sort he had never before encountered. Edinja was the possessor of many such skills, and it only served to strengthen his belief that abandoning Drust Chazhul had been the correct choice.

She shook her head dismissively. "I just do. Now finish what you were saying."

He backed off at once. "On returning, she resupplied her vessel, bid good-bye to her sister, and flew off with her bodyguard. Just the two of them. So perhaps she searches for the Ard Rhys, but perhaps she found something at Paranor that sent her west. We can't know."

Edinja smiled. "Not right away, we can't. But perhaps soon. Our source in Arborlon has nothing more to add?"

"I received a message about the Elessedil girl's return and subsequent departure. Nothing more. She seems to have spoken to no one about why she either went back to Paranor or later flew west."

"Her sister will know," Edinja said softly.

Stoon hesitated. "Do you wish me to find out?"

"What interests me is the reason behind the Ard Rhys's departure and the nature of her destination. There is something important happening."

She walked over to stand beside him. She was small, but it always seemed she was the larger and stronger of the two when he was in her presence. He had never felt that way with Drust Chazhul.

"I want to know the moment any of the Druids return or are sighted in any part of the Four Lands. I want to find them and I want to track them. Send more of my birds to search them out. Send word to my creature in Arborlon. I want to know what is going on. All of it."

"I will see that it is done, Mistress." He paused. "Do you wish to have Paranor occupied now? Perhaps the protective wards have been removed."

She reached out and stroked his cheek gently. Then she sat down across from him. "Do you know why I wanted Drust Chazhul dead? Not because he was Prime Minister when I should have been. Nor because he was any real threat to my ambitions—certainly no more than Arodian was. I could have killed them anytime and gotten what I wanted. No, it was because Drust was so determined to put an end to the use of magic in the Four Lands."

She got up again, crossed the room, poured wine into goblets, and returned, handing one to him. She smiled as he hesitated in accepting. "It is only wine, Stoon."

He took it from her, and she sat. "Drust believed that magic had run its course and that once again science had become a viable alternative. He ignored history and common sense, believing that the advent of the Great Wars and the destruction of the Old World were things of the past and that the future should not be shaped by what had happened several thousand years ago. The discovery of diapson crystals and the inventions that were generated as a result led him to embrace this theory. Magic seemed dangerous to him. He perceived it as a threat—not only to himself because he had no use for it, but to the larger world as well, because its power rested in the hands of a few, and that could never change. Magic wasn't an object that anyone could master and command. It was genetic and therefore elitist. It could be studied and learned or it could be acquired by chance and sometimes diligence, but never possessed by more than a few."

"He hated magic's unpredictability, as well," Stoon added. He sipped at his wine and found it satisfactory. "He didn't trust it."

"He didn't understand it. He preferred science because it could be contained and manipulated by everyone who had access to it. He could see its source; he could hold it in his hands. This isn't so with magic, which is ephemeral and intuitive—even when you hold a talisman. In any case, he was determined to stamp it out, in spite of what he suggested to me in our final meeting. He thought to placate me and later would have betrayed me. Had he been allowed, he would have advanced science to the position it occupied in the world before the advent of the Great Wars. He would have relegated magic to the pages of ancient history."

She shook her head. "Magic is the foundation of the Orle family and the source of what keeps the Four Lands in balance, whatever anyone else might say or think. Men and women like Drust Chazhul would manipulate and deceive their way to power that is beyond them. They would gain their positions and then squander their opportunities. When Drust became Prime Minister, all he could think to do was to strengthen his hold on his office. He gave no thought to how he might use the chance he had been given productively. He simply decided magic was bad and science was good, and that he would seize control of the one and stamp out the other."

Stoon finished his wine and set the goblet on a small table at his elbow. "He was obsessed with making certain no one would challenge his grip on the Prime Minister's office."

She sniffed. "It was a grip he would never have been able to hold, even had he lived. But here is my point. I align more closely with the Druids of Paranor than with the politicians of Arishaig and the Federation. I am kindred to the Druid order in my history and in my worldview. They would not accept this, but it is so. We seek the same ends. What separates us is their unwillingness to use their magic to take control of the Four Lands. It isn't that I am suggesting they need to do this to gain further power; I am suggesting they need to do more to make the Four Lands safe from predators. Once a central government is established, there are better uses to which magic could be put than in fighting the constant civil wars that have raged since the time of the First Druid Order."

"And you would be the one to make this happen?" he asked.

"Of course. Who better? I am well positioned for it. I command the strongest government in the Four Lands. I have the means and influence to bring the others into line. As Prime Minister, acting on behalf of the whole of the Southland people, I can make anything I wish come to pass."

"So you have a plan?"

"I have a plan. But it does not involve seizing Paranor and tearing down its walls. It does not involve engaging in a war with the Druids and eventually with the Elves, who at some point will ally themselves. It means taking a different approach."

She did not offer to explain what that approach was, and Stoon knew better than to ask. He simply nodded in casual agreement. "So I am not to go back into Paranor?"

She rose from where she was sitting, reached out and pulled him to his feet, and then pressed herself against him. "The wards might be down, but the Druids would never leave anything valuable lying around unprotected. Try to take anything out of Paranor and you will pay a price for your arrogance. Besides, going back into Paranor at this point will undermine everything I hope to accomplish. The order will associate all that has happened so far with Drust Chazhul. I hope to leave it that way. His time has come and gone, and I will do my best to make it clear that his actions were not mine. I wish to disassociate myself—and the Federation, as well, if it is at all possible—from everything he did. Am I clear about this, Stoon?"

He felt her fingers working at the buttons of his tunic. "You could not be more clear, Mistress."

She slid her hands inside his clothing and ran them up and down his chest. "You can stop calling me Mistress now," she said. "Think of something a little less formal, will you?"

Then she took him to her bed.

When the assassin departed her chambers some hours later, the first rays of sunrise were just beginning to show on the eastern horizon, the light silvery and muted. Stoon returned the same way he had come, alone and unseen, his mind on fire with memories of his time with her. Edinja was like no one he had ever been with, and he did not want their relationship to end. Even knowing that one day it would—that she would have it no other way and he would not be able to prevent it—he did not want it to happen. So he would make the most of it while it lasted, and he would not give himself cause to look back on this time with even the smallest of regrets.

For now, he had other business to attend to. He must send word to their spy in Arborlon. He must dispatch Edinja's birds to seek out the Druid and her Elven protector. It would be their assignment to find the pair and then to track them to wherever they might be going, all the while sending messages back to him.

Messages he could carry to Edinja.

Messages of sufficient import that she would allow him to come to her and be with her as he had this night.

Stoon was a practical man with few vices and dependable instincts. But he was not perfect; he was not without weaknesses. He knew that she was one. But he also knew that for all her talk about serving a higher purpose and seeking a peaceful unification of the Four Lands, she was every bit as bloodthirsty as her former rivals. Why else had she allied herself with him? Why else had she been so keen to dispatch both Arodian and Drust Chazhul?

He slowed outside the walls of the compound, checking to make certain he had not been seen. Then he began navigating a complex network of alleyways that would take him to his quarters nearby. It was best, she had told him early on, if they were never seen together, not even by chance. It would increase his effectiveness and diminish the chances of them being connected even in the smallest of ways.

It would make their clandestine meetings just that much sweeter, she had insisted. Didn't he agree?

Oh, yes, he agreed.

His thoughts drifted. He had come a long way since his days as the son of a blacksmith. His father had been a big, strong man with a mean temper and a penchant for taking out his anger on his son. Stoon had been badly beaten on more occasions than he cared to remember, frequently for no reason other than his father's mood. The beatings had continued right up until the moment he took a hammer to his father's head while he lay passed out after a bout of drinking. Then he dragged the body to the river in the dead of night and sank it with weights. A street boy after that, he had allied himself with an assassins' guild and learned the trade well enough that eventually he was smarter and more skillful than any of them and had set out on his own.

Years of practicing his chosen trade had provided him with distance from his childhood and safety from any who might try to mistreat him ever again. It had provided him with everything that had led to his meeting with Drust Chazhul and now Edinja Orle.

His future seemed assured.

But there was a nagging concern, one that had been with him since the ill-fated assault on Paranor. Aphenglow Elessedil. He had almost caught up to her in the courtyard between the Outer and Inner walls of the Keep, but had he done so he would be as dead as Drust Chazhul. He knew that as surely as he knew he must face her again. There was a certainty to it he could not shake. She should have been his; she should have gone the way of all the others he had dispatched. Yet she had turned on him, and it was only by the slimmest of margins that he had managed to escape her. A step here, a turn there, a bit of smoke and ash, a momentary distraction—almost any of these could have changed the outcome of their meeting.

Now he would have her tracked along with the other Druids, and while he did not fear the Druids as an order or even their formidable magic, he did fear her. He could not help himself. The fear had attached itself to him and would not release its grip.

. . .

Deep within the Fangs, the new day crept like a predator from out of the eastern horizon. On the precipice where they had made their stand the previous night, Railing Ohmsford was sitting with Mirai Leah, looking out over the clusters of dead attackers to the dark and silent sweep of the forest wilderness. Nothing moved in the shadows of the jungle of rocks and trees below. No sounds broke the silence. The last attack had ended more than six hours earlier with the arrival of the Rover Austrum aboard his armored flit. The dead lay where they had fallen, and what was left of the defenders huddled together in hollow-eyed anticipation of what might happen next.

"They'll come again," Mirai said, as if reading his mind. She was ragged and covered in blood and dust and might have been a stranger for all that he recognized of her.

"Why did you let him kiss you like that?" he asked.

He had kept the question to himself all night, even though he could barely contain it. It ate at him in a way that was unbearable. Now it was out there, released just like that.

She gave him a look. "I didn't have a chance to stop him. I was as surprised as you were."

"But you didn't even try. You let him kiss you twice."

She started to say something and stopped. Then she looked away. "It isn't your concern, Railing."

"I'm your friend."

"That doesn't mean you have the right to question me like this. I am the one who needs to deal with Austrum, not you. Let it go."

He did not want to let it go. He wanted to see dismay and regret from her, not acceptance. She had been forcibly violated and did not seem much concerned about it. It was maddening.

He glanced over to where the Rover was sleeping next to Skint and Seersha. The Speakman was dead; there hadn't been time to save him once their attackers dragged him out from under the overhang. The last of the Trolls had died during the night. Farshaun, however, had recovered. He was sitting off to the other side of the sleepers, just far enough away that he couldn't hear what they were saying.

"They won't come again before nightfall," Railing said, trying to regain his footing. He did not want her to be angry with him. "Whatever they are."

She shook her head. "I wouldn't want to bet on that. We need to get out of here before then."

"Maybe Austrum's right. Maybe the *Walker Boh* will find us before then." He glanced up at the thick blanket of mist and was immediately discouraged. Nothing could find its way through that. "Or maybe he has a way to signal her. He said the flashes of magic caught his eye and guided him down to us."

But mostly down to her, he knew. He had come for her, and it made him crazy to know that she understood it as well as he did and was doing nothing about it.

"It's a big place," she responded absently. "The storm blew the airship off course. Austrum took a big risk when he left to come look for us. A foolish risk. I don't know what the others will choose to do."

"Maybe we should send him back up there to look for them," he suggested.

"Maybe you should stop talking about him."

Seersha was awake now, on her feet and stretching. Her black cloak was ripped and dirty, her face a mask of harsh lines and rough determination that made her look dangerous. She walked through the dead creatures to the edge of the precipice and looked over. Mirai rose and went to join her. Railing, hampered by his leg and exhausted from the struggle, stayed where he was. It was his turn to sleep after having kept guard all night. But it was Mirai's time, too, and he stubbornly refused to lie down until she was beside him.

He closed his eyes against his weariness and dismay, feeling suddenly alone and abandoned. Redden was gone and Mirai felt removed and distant and he was sick at heart because of it. He hated that he had come on this expedition and hated even more that he had been the one who had pushed for all of them to come. He had thought it would be such a big adventure. Now he just wanted things back the way they had been before, with the three of them returned to Patch Run and the Highlands of Leah. He wanted Mirai's attentions focused on him, and he wanted Austrum gone. He wanted them all safe, and he was beginning to think that might never happen.

Then he realized how he sounded and was instantly ashamed. This wasn't like him. The brothers had never been the sort to feel sorry for themselves or whine about their situations. They had never despaired of being able to work things out.

What is happening to me?

Farshaun ambled over and sat next to him. He had a nasty wound on his head and bruises on his face. "You need to sleep, Railing. You look terrible."

The boy nodded. "I know that."

"You did well last night. You saved us all. You and Seersha."

"Not the Speakman, we didn't."

The old man nodded. "No, not him. But I don't think he expected to be saved. He came here to die. Maybe he believed his own prophecy enough to want it to come to pass. We did what we could to prevent it from happening, but sometimes there just isn't any way. And maybe he was right and none of us is coming back from this."

The boy stayed silent, watching Mirai return across the precipice. When she reached them, she knelt down and embraced him and kissed him on the cheek. "Let's be friends again, Railing. Let's not argue about things that don't matter."

He couldn't help himself. He nodded and smiled gratefully. "I want that, too. I'm sorry about before."

She leaned in again and this time kissed him on the mouth. "It's forgotten. You told me how you felt. I understand. I worry about you, too."

He wasn't sure she did understand, but he didn't want to say so. It was enough that they were talking again and not angry at each other. He knew he was being foolish; all this nonsense about Austrum would pass. Once they were out of this place and on their way home, things would go back to the way they had been.

Seersha had turned and was heading toward them when she abruptly stopped and looked back. A soft white glow was emanating from somewhere below the precipice. Seersha moved back over to the edge and then quickly beckoned to the others. Railing, in spite of his exhaustion and the damage to his leg, levered himself to his feet with Mirai's help and hobbled over to where the Druid knelt. When he peered over he saw a bright splash of light spilling out of a cleft in the rocks.

"Shades!" Mirai Leah hissed.

A moment later Crace Coram passed through the light and stood looking up at them.

12

WITH THE NEW DAY BRIGHTENING IN A HAZE OF GRAY MIST and dull light and the remnants of the Druid expedition gathered about him, Crace Coram told his story. He had climbed up to the ledge to join the little company, the light through which he had passed having disappeared the moment he emerged from it. Now they were arrayed in a tight circle—Railing, Mirai, Seersha, Skint, and Farshaun Req—listening intently to the Dwarf Chieftain.

Oriantha was still inside the place in which they had all been trapped, he began, but he would get to that in a minute.

When the dragon lifted off in the midst of its battle with the members of the expedition, the Dwarf Chieftain, still riding its back and trying to bring it down, was caught by surprise. He tried to jump clear, but his clothing was tangled in the dragon's spikes, and by the time he had torn himself free the dragon was already too high up. All he could do at that point was to hang on and try not to fall off.

It helped that he was immensely strong, but even so it took every-thing he had to keep his balance as the dragon's wings rose and fell and its long body undulated like a snake's. The wind whipped at the Dwarf, threatening to tear him loose, and he flattened himself against the scaly body to reduce its force.

At some point during his flight, he became aware of someone else clinging to the dragon, a flash of movement or color drawing his attention. When he glanced back down the dragon's body, he found a creature he didn't recognize plastered against its hindquarters, a thing that looked half human, half wolf. Its face lifted to find his, and for just an instant he saw the girl Oriantha looking back at him. Then the green eyes narrowed and the creature's jaws drew back in a snarl, and what he might have thought was human disappeared.

But the creature did not try to advance on him, and so the Dwarf let it be and used his energy to fight back against the wearing demands of keeping his seat. He did his best to try to get a fix on his position during his flight, sighting various landmarks that he thought he might be able to use to find his way back once he got down off the dragon—something he never doubted would happen eventually. There were distinctive mountain peaks and a huge lake and a large stretch of rugged wilderness, and he could determine where he needed to go by noting where these lay.

But heavy clouds stretched from horizon to horizon, hiding the sun and making it impossible to determine the direction in which he was moving. When the dragon underwent an unexpected shift in its flight pattern, his landmarks disappeared into a range of mountains that eventually obscured everything he had memorized and left him totally turned about and unable to determine how he had gotten to where he was.

The dragon flew on until finally it reached a forested lake and made an abrupt downward plunge. Crace Coram barely had time to register what was happening before the dragon was diving into the lake waters and he was forced to fling himself clear. He landed with an enormous splash, struggled back to the surface gasping for air, and immediately began swimming toward a spit of land several hundred yards away. Burdened by his mace, which was shoved into his belt, and by his heavy clothing, he nevertheless completed the journey in record time, looking back only once when he heard the dragon surface with a thrashing that sounded like a thousand waterbirds taking flight.

But the creature began moving in another direction, and once the Dwarf Chieftain was certain it was not coming back, he continued his swim until his feet were again on solid ground. He collapsed momentarily but quickly hauled himself upright and off the exposed shoreline until he was hidden in the trees. Out on the lake, the dragon had reached a small island and was disappearing into a rocky stretch at its center—a place in which the Dwarf assumed it might have its nest.

He lay back, his heart pounding, exhausted by what had happened, safe for the moment but wondering how he was going to find his way back to the others.

Then a shadow fell over him, and he jerked upright to find Oriantha standing next to him, her young face bruised and her clothing ripped almost to shreds. She looked pale and disoriented, and without saying anything she dropped down next to him and looked back out across the waters of the lake to the island where the dragon had gone.

"Why did you do it?" he asked her after a minute.

She looked at him with her strange eyes. "What?"

"Grab hold of the dragon and let it carry you off as it did me. That was foolish."

"I didn't think about it. I just did it."

"So that *was* you I saw back there hanging on to its hindquarters, wasn't it?"

She nodded. "My other self. I had to stay that way in order to keep my grip. I am much stronger that way." She paused. "You know what I am, don't you?"

"A shape-shifter. I've seen one or two. But you're no full-blood. You're a Halfling."

"Elven mother, shape-shifter father. Hard to tell the difference between them, though, sometimes."

"But Pleysia must have known the truth when she brought you along. Why did she keep it secret from the rest of us? Why did you?"

Oriantha hesitated. "I don't suppose it will hurt to tell you at this point, since the Ard Rhys already knows. Pleysia is my mother—a full-blown witch who mated with a creature of magic and produced me. All this before she came to live with the Druids. But she never told anyone. She wanted me to follow in her footsteps. She wanted to bring me to Paranor when I was older and offer my skills to the order in exchange for being admitted as a member. Then she found out she was dying. She suffers from a rare disorder that is eating her body from the inside. There is no cure. So she brought me along on this expedition, thinking that if I distinguished myself I might gain admittance after she was gone. That the Ard Rhys would have to take me in."

The Dwarf nodded. "She didn't think she was coming back from this, did she?"

"She was certain she wasn't. But she made me promise to say nothing until we were far enough out that the Ard Rhys couldn't make me return. I think a few of the others saw what I was during the attacks in the Fangs, though. Those boys saw me, I know."

Coram nodded. "The Ohmsfords, Redden and Railing. Those two don't miss much, even if they're still a bit on the new side of knowing. But they didn't say anything to the Ard Rhys?"

She shook her head. "I don't think so."

He looked down at his boot tops and scuffed his feet along the earth absently. "How are your tracking skills? We have to find our way back, but I don't think I know where we are."

"I don't think I do, either," she said, "but I might be able to get us back anyway."

He shifted his stocky body to a different position. "How?"

She shrugged. "Look at me. I am half animal, maybe more. I can find direction as my animal self much better than any human could. I can sense how and where to go. But you will have to bear me looking the way you saw me on the dragon."

"I've borne much worse in my time." He paused. "Tell me. Which is the way you really are?"

She laughed softly. "There is no one way with me. I am both ways and others, too. I have no real self. I shift back and forth as need dictates. But each form gives me something that helps me. So I just accept that I am not one thing or the other, but many."

He gave a quick snort. "You can be any one or all at once if it helps us find our way to the others." He fumbled his pack off his shoulders and began fishing through it. "I have some food. We ought to eat something before we start out."

They sat together in silence, the burly Dwarf and the young girl, sharing a little of the food stash that had survived the dragon ride and lake plunge, keeping an eye on the distant island and an ear pricked for other predators. When they were finished, they rose and faced each other. Oriantha smiled at the Dwarf almost apologetically and then abruptly changed into her other self, wolfish and dangerous. The young girl was gone completely, and the predator returned from hiding once more.

The Dwarf only barely managed to hold his ground until the shape-shifter wheeled away with a snarl.

Their journey took them through the remainder of the day. Oriantha's animal self took the lead, loping ahead of the slower-moving Dwarf, seeming to sense which direction they needed to go even without knowing either their destination or the distance they must cover. Now and again, she circled back to him, her wolfish face staring up at his, looking savage and hungry enough to give him pause. But each time she wheeled away quickly and was off again.

They encountered no visible threats that day, perhaps because they were in the dragon's territory and nothing it might want to eat chose to live so close by. They did not see the dragon, either. Perhaps its struggle with the company had been enough for one day; perhaps it had flown off again in another direction. Whatever the case, they made good progress and avoided any confrontations.

That night they took turns keeping watch, finding shelter within a rocky overhang that enclosed them on three sides and required only that they defend themselves from the front should something come after them. But nothing did, and when morning returned they were well rested.

"Where do you think we are?" she asked him as they ate a little dried beef and fruit from the stores he still had in his pack. She had changed back again to the girl, and there was a winsome quality to her that made her seem little more than a child. "What part of the Westland is this?"

Crace Coram had been wondering that, too. "I've never seen or heard of country like this. Nor of dragons. Not for a long time. They were all sent into the Forbidding, weren't they? Back in the time of Faerie?"

"It is said. But they must have missed this one."

"Those creatures that attacked us in the Fangs—the four-legged ones with all the teeth?" He shook his head. "I've never seen them before, either. Where did they come from that no one has ever run across them before now? You would think the Elves might have encountered one or two at some point, no matter how deep inside the Westland they live."

His face clouded. "If we find our way back, I'm not going on. This is madness. If the Ard Rhys wants her Elfstones so badly, she can go get them herself. I'll tell Seersha I've had enough."

She looked at him doubtfully. "Will you?"

He started to say something and stopped. "Maybe. I don't know." He paused. "But that's what I should do. What we all should do."

They set out again shortly afterward, heading toward a line of mountains that provided the only landmark they recognized, traveling through bleak country marked by stretches of dead and dying trees and rocky flats empty even of that. They found no other water on their way, not even a stream, and the mountains seemed as distant today as they had the day before. Crace Coram could not be certain, but it seemed to him they were weeks away from where they needed to go.

On this day, they encountered a huge horned beast that resembled a bull crossed with a lizard. They saw it coming from a long way off, lumbering across the flat land, slow and ponderous, and had plenty of time to avoid it. They did not have quite so much warning of the cat creatures they caught sight of several hours later from atop a rise overgrown with dead grasses, which was probably what saved them. The cat things found something else to occupy them—a creature that neither the Dwarf nor the girl ever had a chance to identify—converging on their victim and tearing it to bits in short minutes.

Afterward, safely off to one side as the cat things moved on, the Dwarf said, "Those aren't anything I've ever heard of or seen, either. Not anywhere in the Four Lands."

She was silent a moment. "I don't think that's where we are," she answered quietly.

This took him aback. "What do you mean? Where else would we be?"

Her face began to change again, the wolfish side emerging. "Somewhere no one has ever been, maybe. Somewhere bad."

He thought about it for a moment. They hadn't crossed any large bodies of water, so they had to be still on the mainland. She was saying they were in a place within the Four Lands—or maybe just outside the known boundaries—that no one had been before. But even that didn't feel right.

"Wherever we are," he finished, climbing to his feet again, "we shouldn't be here."

They walked for the rest of that day and for two full days afterward and still didn't reach the mountains. Time and again, they encountered new dangers, ones that neither had come across before. A huge lizard attacked Crace Coram, and it took all of Oriantha's animal skills and strength to drive it away. A strange plant threw spikes at the shape-shifter, and the poison on the tips of the three that penetrated her animal hide would have killed her if the Dwarf hadn't cut into her skin with his hunting knife and sucked it out. Twice more they encountered the cat things, and once they saw the dragon fly overhead, scouring the ground below for food.

It was becoming increasingly apparent that the chances were shrinking of finding their missing companions—if they were even still alive, which Crace Coram was beginning to doubt. Sooner or later, something bad was going to get one of them—or, more likely, both at once—and that would be the end. He kept his thoughts to himself, but they burned like live coals in the back of his mind.

Then, midway into the fifth day, Tesla Dart appeared.

They saw the small lizard first, a swift, momentary glimpse of it as it raced toward them and then away again. Because it was not threatening, they paid little attention. Even when it reappeared several hours later for a second look and a second quick disappearance, they barely gave it a thought. They were trudging along as before, trying to keep themselves alert enough to watch for predators, trying to stay focused in spite of the fact that their food had run out and their water was down to a single skin they had filled two days ago at a tiny stream where they saw other creatures drinking. They had ceased talking to each other except when it couldn't be avoided, conserving their strength, knowing it was seeping away with each hour's passing.

Oriantha was in the lead, as usual, having reverted to her lupine shape, her attention riveted on the landscape and the things that lived there. They had gone all morning without a threatening encounter, and there was reason to think they might reach nightfall without having to endure one. This day was darker than those that had preceded it, and a misty rain had been falling since first light.

They had just crested a low rise, climbing through jagged rocks and loose stones, when they first saw Tesla. Neither knew who or even what this new creature was, and they stopped where they were. Tesla was sitting just ahead of them, back resting against a stump, watching them. Crace Coram had the distinct impression that Tesla had been waiting for them, but he could not imagine how that could be. Even so, his hand tightened on his iron mace as he made a quick survey of his surroundings.

The creature rose and waved. "Greetings, friends of Straken Queen! Come speak with me."

"Straken Queen?" the Dwarf muttered.

Oriantha had come loping back to him and was changing to her human self, her feral features fading as she stood upright once more. "Nothing hides here," she said. "The girl is alone."

"Girl?" He snorted. "How can you tell *what* that is?"

Oriantha gave him a look. "Who are you?" she called out to the creature. "Give us your name!"

"I am Tesla Dart! I am Ulk Bog. Like my uncle, Weka Dart? You know of him? Come here! I have searched for you for two days! What are you doing out here?"

The girl and the Dwarf walked over to her, and she rose to greet them—a mass of bristling black hair that seemed to grow in clumps, a gnarled body that was wiry and misshapen, and some very sharp teeth that revealed themselves when she attempted what appeared to be a smile.

"You are in dangerous country," Tesla Dart advised, looking from one to the other. "You need to come with me."

"Why were you searching for us?" Oriantha asked her. "How do you know of us at all?"

"The Straken Queen tells me you were lost. We looked for you, she and I and the others. For several days. But then I left them and went ahead to see if you were in a dragon's lair. But you were not. So I know it is a different dragon that takes you away, even though I think it was this one. You can never be sure about dragons."

"The Straken Queen?" Oriantha was suddenly animated. "You mean the Ard Rhys? Khyber Elessedil?"

Tesla Dart frowned. "She is the Straken Queen. She says not, but she is. These others, I don't know of these names. But nothing matters now. They are all gone."

Crace Coram exchanged a quick glance with Oriantha. "What do you mean?" he asked. "Gone where?"

The Ulk Bog wrung her hands in a peculiarly helpless fashion. "I tell them to wait for me. I tell them not to go anywhere until I come back. But the creatures that serve the Straken Lord come. His Catcher sees something that tells him they are close and is waiting for them. I wish to warn them, but I must hide until it is safe. But they do not wait as I say, and then they turn back. Tarwick is waiting. A trap."

She clapped her hands together to demonstrate the trap closing, the emphasis clear.

"Are they dead?" Oriantha asked.

Tesla Dart nodded. "Dead. All but the Straken Queen and the boy. They are Tael Riverine's prisoners now, taken by Tarwick to Kraal Reach. Lost to us."

"All of the others dead?" the girl pressed. "All of the rest? You are certain of this?"

"Certain."

Oriantha exhaled sharply. "Mother," she whispered.

The Dwarf could not believe what he was hearing. The entire Druid expedition was gone? All those who had come with them through the cleft in the rock and the shimmer of light were dead save Khyber Elessedil and Redden Ohmsford? He felt his throat tighten and his stomach clench, and he saw again, clearly and unequivocally, how wrong it had been for any of them to come on this journey.

"Wait!" Oriantha said sharply. "You said it was Tael Riverine? The Straken Lord?" She had a frantic look in her eyes as she wheeled abruptly this way and that. "Where are we? What is this place?"

The Ulk Bog was taken aback. "Why do you ask such a stupid question? This is here! The land of the Jarka Ruus! We are the free peoples. *Ca'rel orren pu'u!*"

Crace Coram watched the shape-shifter's young face undergo a terrible transformation. "Oriantha!" he snapped at her. "What's happening here? I don't understand any of this! Where are we?"

Austrum, who had been asleep for most of the discussion—exhausted from his efforts to find them—now woke up and wandered over. "What's this all about?" he asked, looking from face to face. "Has something happened?"

The others hushed him, their collective attention on Crace Coram.

"You were inside the Forbidding!" Seersha exclaimed.

The Dwarf Chieftain nodded, the weariness returning to his face. "Oriantha said so. She learned the name from her mother. Jarka Ruus. The free peoples." He shook his head. "There was no mistake."

"Is my brother still in there?" Railing demanded.

"We couldn't get to him. Tesla Dart said he had been taken with the Ard Rhys to the Straken Lord's fortress at Kraal Reach. She said no one could get in there, not even with the use of magic. She told us we had to get ourselves out, that it would be hard enough just to do that."

"And the rest are dead?" Skint pressed, his narrow features twisted in disbelief. "All of them?"

"Killed at one point or another along the way. Apparently Redden told this to the Ulk Bog." He looked at Seersha. "It was suicide going in there. It was a mistake we should never have made."

"Coming into the Fangs at all was a mistake," she agreed. "But we're here, and there's nothing we can do about it." She paused. "I want to get the rest of you safely away, but I have to go back for the Ard Rhys."

"What are you talking about?" Skint demanded angrily. "Don't you realize what's happening? If the Forbidding is opened, it means the demons locked inside are breaking free! The Elves have to be told of this and then do something to stop it! And the other Races have to come together to defend the whole of the Four Lands in case doing something isn't possible!"

A rush of objections and protestations followed, but Crace Coram quickly silenced them. "You had better hear the rest of my tale first. Then you might want to rethink everything."

Tesla Dart led them on through the remainder of the day, still pointing toward the mountains, and found shelter for them for the night, kept watch while they slept, and at daybreak marched them ahead once more. She talked incessantly, mostly about Ulk Bogs and herself, but sometimes about the other peoples and the Straken Lord. She responded to questions, but her answers were frequently vague and meandering.

On one point, however, she was very clear.

"The Straken Lord seeks Grianne Ohmsford and will not rest until she is his. If the woman he has now is not her, he is *ut disonqjer*—very displeased. He searches again, not just in the land of the Jarka Ruus. The wall of our prison comes down; everyone knows. Tael Riverine will lead his armies out and find the Straken Queen, wherever she is."

"That might be difficult," the Dwarf observed.

But before he could say more, Oriantha motioned for him to be silent. "She is the Straken Queen no longer. She lives in a faraway place now."

Tesla Dart shrugged, her twisted features tightening. "Doesn't matter. He finds her. He does not give up. He brings her back. His mind is set on this. She bears his children as his Queen. Tael Riverine is the Straken Lord. He has whatever he wants, and he wants her."

The girl and the Dwarf exchanged a quick look, but said nothing. It would not help things if the Straken Lord were to learn that Grianne Ohmsford was dead.

Or was she dead? She had disappeared, but who knew what had become of her? Pen Ohmsford had gone with her on that last flight, but whom had he told of her fate? Did Khyber Elessedil know?

"I will lead you out," Tesla Dart told them. "When you are free again, you find the Straken Queen Grianne and bring her. Let her face him. He will free the others, if you do."

She paused, grinning broadly enough that all her teeth showed. "Then she can kill him and take his place!"

She scampered ahead at every opportunity, all energy and excite-

ment, constantly moving, never still. Oriantha and Crace Coram
followed dutifully, but with mixed emotions. Getting out of the Forbidding was a desperate need for both, but leaving Khyber Elessedil
and Redden Ohmsford behind felt like a betrayal. Oriantha was
grieving for her mother, and the Dwarf could tell she was tremen-
dously shocked and distressed by the loss. He saw her cry only once,
late at night, when she must have thought he was sleeping, and did
not otherwise give herself away. But her grief was mirrored in her
eyes and present in her voice, and though she might appear stoic
otherwise she could not hide the truth from him.

Later that day Tesla Dart told them to wait and disappeared
toward a cluster of hovels and outbuildings. Within minutes, she was
back driving a wagon drawn by a pair of four-legged creatures that
might have been horses but for their burly bodies, shaggy coats, and
tusks. She urged them to climb aboard quickly, glancing back at the
buildings from which she had driven away before whipping the creatures hard enough to send them galloping away into the haze.

A day later, after long hours of travel, they reached the place from
which the Druid expedition had emerged from the shimmering light
a week earlier. The mountains were still hazy and distant, and the
gloom from clouds and shadows uniform across the landscape from
horizon to horizon. Stiff and sore, Crace Coram and Oriantha
climbed down from the wagon and faced Tesla Dart.

"Go quickly," she said. "When you return, come here. The way will
be open again. But for now, once you pass through, it will close behind you. It is the Straken Lord's magic that makes this protection.
Entry allowed, but no exit until later. Do you see?"

She brushed at the scrub of hair bristling from the top of her head,
eyes shifting from one to the other. "Find the Straken Queen. Quickly.
If you do not, Tael Riverine brings his armies into your land and
finds her himself. He plans this already. His armies assemble already.
Time is very short for you."

"Why are you helping us?" Oriantha asked her.

The Ulk Bog looked confused. "Weka Dart is my uncle."

Oriantha shook her head. "I don't understand. What does he have
to do with you helping us?"

"Weka was Straken Queen Grianne's friend. He helped her escape. She said she would come back for him."

"But what if she can't come back for him?" Crace Coram interjected. "What if we can't find her?"

Tesla Dart cocked her head, her strange face taking on an entirely new look. "Weka is dead. When the Straken Queen leaves him, he goes to hide in Huka Flats. But Tael Riverine hunts him down and kills him. Weka dies for helping her. Now she must come back and revenge him. This is a debt she owes."

She pointed toward the shimmer of light. "Tell her my words. Tell her she must pay it."

"So now we must find a dead woman in order to keep the Straken Lord from invading the Four Lands?" Skint summarized. "Is that what you're saying?"

"The Ard Rhys is not necessarily dead," Seersha said quickly.

"She's not?" Railing asked in surprise. He had always thought she was. Both he and Redden had thought so.

Seersha made a dismissive gesture and shifted her gaze to Crace Coram. "What happened to Oriantha? Why isn't she with you?"

The Dwarf shook his head. "She wouldn't come. Right at the last, she said she was staying."

"Why would she do that?"

"She said she was going back for the Ard Rhys and your brother." He looked over at Railing and shrugged. "If you spent as much time with her as I have, you might understand the why of it."

"She wants revenge for her mother," Skint declared. "She's going back to find Tael Riverine and kill him."

Crace Coram nodded slowly. "That's what Tesla Dart said. That's why the Ulk Bog agreed to go with her." He looked back at Seersha. "Madness." He took a deep breath and exhaled wearily. "Do you have anything to eat?"

13

---------------------------◆---------------------------

STILL MANY MILES TO THE EAST, APHENGLOW AND CYMRIAN
flew the airship *Wend-A-Way* in search of the missing expedition.
Using the vision revealed weeks earlier by the blue Elfstones, they
had tracked their way across the Westland from Arborlon to the wilderness of the Breakline. Without any real idea of where the Ard
Rhys and her party had flown, the pair were forced to rely entirely on
Aphen's memory. At least the landmarks shown by the vision had
materialized as she remembered them, and they were now approaching a huge stretch of stone pillars that she recalled having glimpsed as
the vision had moved her swiftly onward toward the shimmering waterfall. Her memory of this mist-shrouded marshland gave her no
real idea of what she was to do once she reached this point, but it was
enough to reassure her that, three days into their journey, they were
still on course.

"I think we have to land *Wend-A-Way* somewhere in there," she
said to Cymrian, pointing ahead into the mix of pillars and mist. "If
they were following the vision they will have done the same thing,
and that's where we will find them."

He stood next to her in the pilot box, looking doubtful. The air
was heavy and damp, and strands of his white-blond hair were plastered against his face. "Unless," he answered carefully, "they have already moved on somewhere else."

She shook her head. "No, the waterfall was in here. They had to pass through it on their way to finding the Elfstones, so they had to land and leave the ship. The *Walker Boh* is too large to have passed through the opening the vision showed me."

"Big place," he said, taking in the sweep of the marsh below. "Can't see much of anything down there. This isn't going to be easy. It will be dangerous to try to land the ship with all those stone spears waiting to tear her hull apart."

He was right, of course, but she didn't see that they had a choice. If the *Walker Boh*—a much larger vessel than *Wend-A-Way*—had done it, so could they.

She eased back on the thrusters and slowed the airship to a crawl. "Maybe it will clear as we get closer," she said hopefully.

He glanced over, smiling. "Maybe. In case it doesn't, I'm going forward where I can get a better look at what's down there. Keep it slow. Watch for my hand signals."

He left her, moving to the bow. She watched him go, thinking how hard this would have been without him. Once, in the beginning, she had tried to discourage his insistence on acting as her protector. Once she would have welcomed his decision to leave her. Now she had no idea how she would have managed without him. He was always there for her, ready to help when needed. He didn't have to be asked; he anticipated what was required and provided it. He never seemed to want or even expected anything in return, not even a word of thanks. She couldn't imagine why he was putting himself out this way when there was no reason for him even to be here, but she was grateful nevertheless.

Her thoughts drifted to Arlingfant, still back in Arborlon struggling with the terrible charge the Ellcrys had given her. She knew she must help her sister find a way to refuse it, but so far her efforts had failed. Nothing she had found in the Druid Histories offered a solution. Nothing she had found in the Elven archives or Chosen records had helped. She had come up with no answers on her own. Even talking about it with Cymrian—something she would never have done before now—had provided no useful answers. She was stymied at every turn and beginning to feel desperate.

But she had put all that aside for now, consigned to a compartment in the back of her mind where she could find it again after her present efforts were successful and the Druid expedition found. Perhaps the Ard Rhys would have something useful to suggest. Perhaps in discussion with the Elven High Council and the King, a solution might be found.

Although she could not help thinking that perhaps things had already gone beyond that, and that the loss of Paranor and the failing of the Ellcrys were symptomatic of much larger and more complex problems.

As the mist-shrouded stone pillars drew closer, she turned her full attention back to sailing *Wend-A-Way*. From the pilot box, she could see gaps in the hazy cover through which the floor of the wilderness was visible. All they needed, she thought, was just a glimpse of the *Walker Boh*. Then they could find a way to reach her.

At the bow, Cymrian motioned for her to slow down even more. Breathless, filled with expectation that their search might be ending, she did so.

But for a long time, nothing happened. They eased their way across the vast expanse of brume, blinking away the rain as they searched for something recognizable and found nothing. The hours drifted past, and the landscape took on a senses-deadening sameness that suggested anything that had dared to come into it had been long since swallowed and forever lost and they were wasting their time looking. They spelled each other regularly, moving between the pilot box and the bow, hoping fresh eyes and fresh hands would aid them in their search.

But the landscape remained endless and empty.

Then Cymrian, forward again at the bow, held up his hand, signaling for her to stop. She did so, swinging the airship about in a slow circle, a virtual hover as she waited for something more. Her companion seemed to be sniffing or perhaps even tasting the air, casting about this way and that.

After a moment, he hurried back to her. "I can smell tar and burning timbers somewhere close. Circle the area slowly. I'll try to pick out where the smell is coming from."

He hurried back to the bow, and she began the process of widening the search in a slow spiral to cover a larger area. She watched Cymrian as he braced himself against the forward railing, leaning over to seek the source of the burning scent. She was thinking already about what it meant if he was right—especially about the burning timbers. But she told herself it might not be the *Walker Boh*. It might be something else entirely. This was strange country to them. Burning wood could have any number of sources.

She continued to sail *Wend-A-Way* across the roof of the mist, the rain still falling in a steady wash to mix with the ever-present haze.

Then Cymrian abruptly held up his hand once more, a hard push this time.

He had found something.

He turned and signaled that she should keep watching him, and then motioned for her to take *Wend-A-Way* down. She signaled back that she understood, dropping the airship just a little. Using his hands to dictate direction and speed, he guided her toward the floor of the marshy jungle. It was harrowing to respond without being able to see what was down there, especially when the stone spires began to appear to either side of her, rising up like monolithic creatures from a frothy sea.

Their descent was slow and treacherous. Twice Cymrian stopped it entirely and had her take the airship back up again, apparently having seen something that had been hidden from higher up, and then reposition before starting down once more. She worked hard to keep their maneuvering steady and her hands responsive to his signals. As they dropped lower, the mist began to close in around them, and soon they were swallowed up in it.

Once, *Wend-A-Way* scraped against one of the pillars, and the sound of wood cracking caused her to catch her breath as she made a quick adjustment to ease the airship away.

But finally they were down far enough that Cymrian signaled her to stop entirely and came loping back to the pilot box. "We need to anchor and go on foot from here," he said.

They secured the ship fore and aft using ropes and grappling hooks they swung over the side and maneuvered until they were caught in the limbs of a pair of skeletal trees, then dropped the rope ladder and went over the side. They descended cautiously, a distance of about twenty feet, eyes scanning the gray haze. Both wore dark-mottled forest clothing to blend in with their surroundings, loose-fitting to allow for easy movement. Aphenglow carried no weapon other than a hunting knife, but Cymrian carried a small arsenal of blades and throwing stars.

At the foot of the ladder, they paused. "Over there," Cymrian whispered, pointing into the haze.

Aphen nodded, listening and assessing. It was hard to see any-thing in the swirl of brume and shadows, but she could detect the pungent odor of charred wood and ash. She wished suddenly they had brought a few other Elves along with them. She did not feel com-fortable leaving the airship unprotected.

Cymrian led the way, moving into the gloom with Aphenglow close on his heels. The stone pillars loomed all about like frozen gi-ants, sections of them visible through the shifting mist, huge and rugged sentries. The floor of the jungle was damp and soft, and their boots sank into it as they crept forward. Aphen listened carefully for sounds that would warn her of the presence of enemies; she scanned the gloom for movement. Nothing. But even so she wasn't convinced.

Ahead, minutes later, they caught a strong whiff of burning, and moments after that a glimpse of embers.

Cymrian pointed to one side. A body lay sprawled on the earth, torn apart and partially eaten. They moved over for a quick look. It was a Troll, one of the Druid Guards.

They eased their way ahead once more, this time quickly finding other bodies—all of them either Trolls or Rovers, and all of them sav-aged and partially eaten. She searched for the Druids, dreading what she would find, but there was no sign of them.

A fresh stench, raw and overpowering, brought them to a halt. The *Walker Boh*, a huge gash in her port bow, her planking ripped apart and sections of the railing torn away, lay broken and ruined. Radian draws had been severed, parse tubes smashed, and the main-mast broken off midway up. All of the light sheaths were ripped apart and pulled down. A quick examination revealed that the airship had suffered a wound that had impacted her controls. The initial damage had crippled her, but most of the rest of what they were seeing was from the crash.

There were more bodies aboard the vessel, a handful of Rovers and Trolls crammed together around the pilot box. The attackers had swarmed aboard, and these few had made a final stand here. They were armed with weapons of all sorts, but whatever they had faced had been too much for them.

"They're all dead," Cymrian murmured after checking each. He seemed anxious to move away.

Aphen took a final look around at their surroundings from her vantage point atop the wreck. "All Rovers," she said. "Where are the members of the order? Where are the Ohmsfords and Mirai Leah?"

There was still no sign of black robes, nor any hints of them. Had the others escaped? If so, where had they gone? But there was nothing to find here that would answer those questions and no reason to stay any longer. She signaled Cymrian, and together they climbed down and started back toward *Wend-A-Way*.

They had gotten no more than a dozen yards before the creatures appeared. With gnarled bodies and wizened faces, they were vaguely similar to Spider Gnomes. They came out of the shadows like ghosts, creeping toward the Elves on all fours, eyes bright with anticipation. Mouths yawned wide to reveal rows of teeth. Aphenglow could guess at what had drawn them. Not sated by those they had already dispatched, they had returned for something more to eat.

She stood with Cymrian and watched the creatures close in on every side. Their ship was too far away to make a run for it, even assuming they could get past the ring of bodies that was tightening steadily around them.

"What do you want to do?" Cymrian had blades in both hands, but even in the face of such terrible danger, he sounded calm and unhurried.

"Stand behind me," she said suddenly. The creatures were very close now, easing forward soundlessly, eyes watchful. "Quickly!"

He did as she ordered, still holding the blades ready. "What are you doing?"

"Stand closer," she said. "Put your arms around me. Do it."

She felt his arms tighten about her body while leaving her arms free. His blades glinted right next to her face. She took a deep breath. "Whatever happens, don't let go of me and don't panic. Trust me."

She felt his head press to her own, nodding. "Always."

Then she summoned her magic and lit them both on fire.

She heard Cymrian inhale sharply as they were enveloped in a column of flames that soared forty feet into the air, crackling and burning with such ferocity that the encircling creatures immediately fell back, cringing and ducking away, their interest in pursuing the attack vanished. It was an illusion, of course. But to all outward appearances, Aphenglow and Cymrian appeared to be burning up.

She moved ahead instantly, almost dragging Cymrian with her. To his credit, he kept his feet and stayed close in spite of his shock and the awkwardness of the advance. They appeared to be trying to flee the flames, rushing ahead in a swirl of fire, stumbling now and then as they fought to keep their feet while their bodies were slowly consumed.

By the time their attackers had determined that nothing was actually happening, Aphen and Cymrian had already forged ahead through the disintegrating lines and were in the clear.

"Run!" she screamed as she caught sight of *Wend-A-Way* resting at anchor amid the stone pillars and damaged trees, and she extinguished the magic and the fire with it.

The creatures were after them instantly, a massed pursuit that fell back only when she turned long enough to sweep their front ranks with real fire and create a momentary barrier between them. Then she was running again, racing to catch up to Cymrian. A pair of the creatures appeared out of the trees before them, but the Elven Hunter cut them down without slowing, his blades quick and deadly. Aphen could hear their attackers coming up behind them, closing the distance rapidly, and she was forced to turn and create a fresh wall of fire before fleeing once more.

The pursuit was gathering momentum now, skirting the ends of the wall of flames and running parallel to them, closing in from both sides. There were many attackers, and they were quick. Aphen stretched her arms wide and sent explosions of Druid Fire into the midst of the tightening pincers; the ground erupted in clots of earth and sparks, and again the attack was momentarily scattered.

Then they were at the rope ladder and she was scrambling up as he held the ropes steady for her, following her a moment later, kicking back at the creatures that leapt at him, snatching at his legs. She could do nothing to help from where she hung, not without risking that the fire would burn him, as well. All she could do was keep climbing as fast as she could, hearing him behind her as she did so—hearing, too, the grunts and snarls of their attackers, feeling their combined weight shake the ladder as they scrambled to catch up.

Hearing the sounds of their breathing.

Breathing the stink of their bodies.

At the top of the ladder, she flung herself through the opening and clawed her way forward. She felt Cymrian land atop her as he launched himself over the lip of the decking, and then he was rolling back to his feet to meet the first wave of climbers. He stood his ground against them, shielding her, his blades whipping in silvery blurs. But it took a final explosion of her Druid magic to clear the decks entirely.

Then Cymrian was cutting the anchor lines while she stood at the top of the rope ladder and burned away the last of those trying to climb up.

Seconds later *Wend-A-Way* was lifting past massive stone spikes toward the ceiling of thick clouds that hung over it and from there into the safety of the open sky.

Blood-spattered and exhausted, Aphenglow and Cymrian cleaned themselves off with a bucket of water as *Wend-A-Way* hovered just above the canopy of the mist.

"What were those things?" Cymrian asked, mopping off his face and wiping his hands.

Aphen shook her head. "No idea."

"Something like Spider Gnomes, but much more dangerous."

"Those men on the *Walker Boh* never had a chance." She was breathing hard, and her heart was still pounding. "But there were no

Druids. No sign of Crace Coram or Skint or Oriantha. Not all the Troll Guards were there, either. A lot of those who were on that ship are still missing."

"Without the *Walker Boh,* they're all trapped down there. We'd better find them right away, Aphen."

She nodded. "Well, they can't have gotten far on foot."

He grunted noncommittally. Then without a warning, he tore off his tunic. He was lean and sinewy, and his muscles were sharply defined. There were scars all over his body. "I can't wear this. I need something else." He glanced at her. "I'll bring you fresh clothes, too."

She started to object, and then gave up. She knew she didn't look any better. "Just a tunic."

Her black robe was still lying on the decking where she had left it. She had taken it off because she didn't want to be encumbered when they went into the wilderness below. She leaned back against the pilot box and closed her eyes. They had almost not made it back, she thought suddenly. It had been very close.

"That was quick thinking," he said, reappearing from the hold. He handed her a fresh tunic. "Using your magic like that. I almost thought we *were* on fire. How did you learn to do that?"

She brushed back her hair and finished wiping off her forehead and hairline. "Experimenting. An accident, really. I would have told you what was going to happen, but there wasn't time."

He pulled on the tunic he had brought for himself. "Doesn't matter. I trust you." He shrugged. "Besides, I had hold of you." He gave her a small smile. "Whatever happened to me was going to happen to you, too."

She remembered his arms around her. The memory gave her a funny feeling. "You did well."

"You did better. We wouldn't have made it out except for you."

She looked away, suddenly embarrassed. "Turn around so I can change."

He did so, and she slipped off her ruined tunic, wiped herself down, and then slipped on the fresh one. "That feels much better," she said, signaling that he could turn back.

They talked over what they should do next. Dropping low enough to try to catch sight of the others was not only risky but also unlikely to produce results. Cymrian suggested he should take a flit and go in search, but Aphen didn't like that idea, either. There were too many things that could go wrong and leave them separated, and then they would both be on their own.

"Wait, I have an idea," she said finally. "Druids have a way of letting each other know where they are if they are close enough—a quick spurt of Druid Fire launched skyward at regular intervals. If you steer while I go forward, I can give that signal, but I'll angle it downward into the mist. One of the other Druids might see and signal me back."

He nodded at once. "Let me take the helm, but use a safety line and give me time to begin circling outward from where we are now. Call back to me if you see anything."

She hurried to the forward railing, lashed herself to an iron ring embedded in the decking, and set herself in place. As the ship began to ease forward, she sent the first burst of magic into the gloom and shadows below.

They continued their efforts throughout the remainder of the day, hour after hour, easing their airship over the Fangs and sending out signals. Now and again, they heard screams of rage or distress from within the haze or saw sudden bursts of frightened movement, but no return signal appeared. The hours slipped away and with them Aphenglow's fading hopes that there was anyone left to find. It was entirely possible, she knew, that the remainder of the expedition had met with the same fate as those they had found at the crash site. She didn't like thinking that way, but she couldn't ignore the possibility.

She pondered the creatures that had attacked them, bothered by the fact that even though she had never seen them before, they reminded her of something. Not Spider Gnomes, but something else. She ruminated on it, left it alone, came back to it again, mulled it over some more, and finally realized.

They were Goblins!

She had seen pictures of them in the Elven histories. They had accompanied descriptions written down in the time of Faerie of the creatures that had been imprisoned within the Forbidding. Even knowing it was impossible, she was certain those were Goblins she had seen.

Except, of course, it wasn't impossible at all. In fact, it made perfect sense. If the Ellcrys was failing, then the Forbidding was breaking down. That meant any number of imprisoned creatures might be starting to escape, Goblins among them.

And almost certainly there would be others.

A chill ran through her. What else was down there? What else might the missing members of the company have encountered after the crash of the *Walker Boh*? Had worse things than Goblins escaped? Were they already beginning to spread throughout the Four Lands, freed of their imprisonment and anxious to take revenge on those who had put them there?

An instant later a reddish streak of fire exploded out of the mist—one she recognized at once as having been given in response to her own. Startled by both the suddenness and the unexpectedness of it, she nevertheless leapt to her feet and raced back to tell Cymrian.

In seconds *Wend-A-Way* was descending into the haze, and Aphenglow Elessedil was about to have all of her questions answered.

14

WHEN SHE WOKE THE FIRST MORNING FOLLOWING HER RE-
turn to Arborlon, Aphen lay in bed for a long time before rising. In
part, it was because there was no rush to do anything else—no immediate crisis to be faced and resolved, no desperate need to be met.
In part, it was because it felt so comforting just to lie there and let the
last vestiges of sleep drift away. But mostly, it was because she felt
the weight of her life bearing down on her and needed to collect her
thoughts and marshal her resolve.

Everything had changed.

She still could not believe that the Druid order was decimated.
Bombax, Pleysia, and Carrick—all dead. Perhaps the Ard Rhys was
dead, too. Of the rest, there was no better news. Almost all of them
were dead, as well. It still seemed impossible, three days after finding
the handful of survivors and hearing their stories. She could not find
a way to make it seem real; she could not come to terms with the
enormity of its truth.

But even that paled when her thoughts shifted to what lay ahead.
The future she faced was darker and harsher still. The Forbidding was
coming down; the demons were breaking out. The Straken Lord—
a creature whom history had consigned to the past—was alive and
well and seeking revenge not only against the Four Lands and its
people, but against a woman who was a hundred years gone. The

demon was determined to find Grianne Ohmsford and bring her to its bed, to make her its wife and the mother of its child—an image that even now caused Aphen to shudder.

Then, too, there was the matter of finding the Bloodfire, of carrying the seed of the dying Ellcrys to its source, immersing the seed, and then returning it so that the tree could be reborn and the magic that protected them all could be restored. Arling's fate, her sister's destiny, bequeathed to her by the magical creature she served as a Chosen, was to become the tree's successor by accepting responsibility for all of this and seeing that it came to pass.

Arling, who was so young and so afraid and so unwilling to be the One.

Arling, who now depended on Aphen to find a way to save her.

She glanced over at her sister's bed and found it empty. Arling had already gone to begin her day of service to the tree. It was after sunrise, so she would be down in the Gardens of Life with the other Chosen, having welcomed the Ellcrys to the new day and begun her work as its caretaker and provider.

Aphen rolled over and faced the wall. Mirai Leah and Seersha were likely still asleep in the other bedroom. Skint, Crace Coram, and Railing Ohmsford shared guest quarters elsewhere with Woostra in a house Arling had found for them. Cymrian could be anywhere, probably outside her cottage, keeping watch. Did he ever sleep?

The Ard Rhys and Redden Ohmsford were still inside the Forbidding. Oriantha was still there, as well, hunting for them.

Farshaun Req and the Rover Austrum had returned to Bakrabru.

All the others were dead and gone.

She kept coming back to it. How many had there been? How many were lost? She tried counting the Trolls of the Druid Guard and could not seem to remember how many had gone with the Ard Rhys. She had never been told the number of Rovers. Then there was the Speakman, three Druids—four, counting Bombax—along with those Trolls who had died at Paranor . . .

She trailed off abruptly, awash in anger and dismay. Where was this getting her? Thinking of the dead did nothing to help the living. Thinking of the dead was pointless.

She rose, threw on her robe, then slipped from the bedroom. Once downstairs, she disdained tea for a glass of ale and carried it outside onto the porch where she sat with it and looked out on the new day. It was early still, and the cottages nearest hers were quiet. One or two Elves passed by on the roadway, but none of them turned to look or tried to speak to her. She was a ghost, she thought. She was a wraith come out of the night, and perhaps they thought she should go back into it again. Perhaps they wished her gone forever. Or perhaps they no longer even knew who she was.

Perhaps she didn't know, either.

She finished the glass of ale and sat there, thinking through what she must do next. It was clear enough. She would go with Arling to see their grandfather and Uncle Ellich and tell them what was happening to the Forbidding. She would warn them, and together they would try to find a way to prevent the inevitable from coming to pass. She would have done so immediately on her return, but Arling had insisted that she sleep first, that she rest and then clean herself up before going to the King. How she presented herself would count for something with the old man. Going as she was might give him a heart attack.

So she had reluctantly agreed, seeing the wisdom in her sister's suggestion, noting as she did that there was something changed about Arling, something fundamental and compelling.

Arling seemed calmer, more assured than when she had left.

She seemed more grown up.

Seersha appeared suddenly, hair wild and tousled, her face a scarred and bruised mask surrounding the black patch that covered her right eye. Her crooked smile was grim and somehow reassuring.

"I slept well," she offered quietly, sitting next to Aphen. She was carrying her own glass of ale and a fresh one for her friend. "You?"

"Well enough. But now I'm awake and thinking about everything."

"Welcome to the new day." Seersha handed her the second glass of ale and toasted her. "At least we have a chance to make something useful of it, which is good."

Aphenglow brushed back her hair, which had grown long enough by now that it was as flyaway as Seersha's. "There's that. I wish I had a better plan for it."

The Dwarf shrugged. "At least we know what needs doing. That's a reasonable start."

Aphenglow wasn't sure that either statement was true, but she nodded agreeably. "It's the number of things that need doing that troubles me. There are so many of them and so few of us. How do we make up for that?"

They were quiet for a time, thinking again of their dead friends and pondering the fate of Khyber Elessedil. The entire Fourth Druid Order, save the two of them, was gone. Destroyed. Paranor might still be theirs, but it had become an empty shell.

"Good morning."

Mirai Leah came through the door and sat down beside them. She looked as beat up as they did, but her smile was bright and welcoming. She was washed and dressed and looked ready for the day. She carried tea rather than ale and sipped at it gingerly.

"You look rested," Seersha observed. "Falling off airships must agree with you."

"Escaping impossibly dangerous situations agrees with me," the Highland girl replied. "But I am already thinking about going back to look for Redden and the others, so maybe the fall damaged me after all."

The Dwarf nodded. "I'm thinking about it, too. Perhaps we suffer from the same affliction."

Aphenglow said nothing, sipping at the cold ale. She wasn't considering going into the Forbidding because that wasn't where she needed to go. Not if she was to help Arling, and by now she had pretty much resigned herself to focusing entirely on that goal. Not just because it was Arling, although that was reason enough, but also because if the Forbidding were to be sealed and the Four Lands made safe, then helping her sister resolve the dilemma of how to renew the Ellcrys had assumed paramount importance.

"I might try some of that tea," she said.

She rose and went back inside, found the kettle of brewed tea, and poured herself a cup. She inhaled the hot fumes, the steam filling her breathing passages and clearing her head. Better than the ale, she thought.

When she went back outside, she found Arlingfant waiting.

Her sister looked pleased. "I went to Uncle Ellich and asked him to arrange for us to speak privately with Grandfather. An audience has been set for midday. Uncle Ellich will meet us outside the palace when it is time."

Aphen was caught off guard. Arling had already done what she had intended to do. When had Arling last shown initiative of that sort?

Arling seemed to sense that she might have overstepped herself. "I just thought it would help. You needed to rest, and I didn't want Grandfather to think we were ignoring him."

"No, you were right to speak with Ellich," Aphen said quickly. "We will all be ready to go when it's time." She laughed. "Mirai is ready now."

Arling looked embarrassed. "The audience is only for you and me, Aphen. Grandfather wants to see us alone."

"Probably better that way," Seersha said at once. "You can say what needs saying without Mirai and I tagging along. If there's more to tell, we can have our time later."

Aphenglow was not entirely happy with this. She had not experienced events in the way that Seersha had, and Mirai, to a lesser extent. But she knew she should not go against her grandfather's wishes.

"Sorry, but I have to go back to the gardens and finish my work," Arling said, interrupting her thoughts. She turned and started off. "I'll be back before midday."

Aphen watched her go, then she said to the other two, "We had better talk everything through one more time. I don't want to leave anything out when I go to see Grandfather."

So, in painstaking detail, Seersha and Mirai went through it all again.

The morning passed quickly, even taking into account the slog entailed in retelling the fate of the doomed Druid expedition, and by midday Aphenglow was dressed and ready to meet with the King.

She hugged Seersha and Mirai both, as much for her own reassurance as for theirs, and set out for the palace with Arling beside her.

"I should have let you be the one to talk to Uncle Ellich," Arling said to her after a few minutes of silence.

Aphen moved over and put her arm around her sister. "I should have *asked* you to do it in the first place. You're just as able as I am."

"Maybe now, but not so much before." She leaned into Aphen. "I feel . . . more capable, somehow. I think it's because I have finally stopped denying what the Ellcrys wants me to do."

"You seem stronger."

"I'm doing the best I can."

Aphen could barely make herself ask. "Have you come to terms with what's being asked of you, Arling?"

Her sister didn't look at her, clearly uncomfortable with the question. "I've accepted what it means. I've found that I can face the idea of it. I don't know that I can do it, though. Maybe I can. Maybe I can find a way through it." She shook her head. "I don't know."

They walked on a bit farther without speaking. Then Arling said, "After you left, I went back to the Ellcrys and spoke to her again, as I said I would. I spoke with her a long time. Then I went back again the next night. I went every night. Each time, we spoke a little longer, a little more openly. It became easier, even though I was still terrified. She was kind to me. She made me understand what it was like for her. She was a girl like me once, and she remembers how she felt when she was chosen. She ran far away, trying to escape what she had been asked to do. In the end, she came back. She felt strongly enough that she had to. Even so, her delay cost lives. Many lives, I think. She still lives with that memory. She can't forget, and she wants to save me from the same fate. It's a powerful argument, Aphen."

Aphenglow felt a chill in her heart. "Are you saying she has persuaded you? Have you decided to do what she wants?"

Arling shook her head. "I am saying that at least I begin to understand her. I am not saying I *am* her. I am not saying her path should be mine. But maybe if it is required of me, I might find a way to accept it."

Aphen nodded and said nothing. She did not want to lose her

sister, not for any reason. She didn't know how she could prevent it, but she was as determined now as she had ever been to find a way.

They walked the remainder of the way in silence and found Ellich Elessedil waiting for them at the edge of the palace grounds. He was out of sight when they first appeared, but stepped into view at once and motioned them down a side path that was heavily sheltered by a grove of conifers. When they had gone a short distance, he turned and embraced Aphenglow warmly.

"I'm so glad you are back safely, Aphen. It must have been terrible for you. Arling told me some of it."

She nodded. "It's inconceivable. Almost the whole order is gone. Seersha and I might be all that's left. And Paranor is abandoned. Drust Chazhul has shown he will do anything he can to destroy the Druids. It says a great deal about his disregard for magic and its uses that he attacked us with so little hesitation."

"Your grandfather is anxious to hear everything." Ellich paused. "Is it as bad as I think?"

"Worse," she told him. "But you will hear for yourself."

"A word with you about your grandfather, first." His strong features tightened, and he kept his voice low. "My brother is not well. In fact, he is as bad as he has ever been. It will be a shock to you when you see him, but try not to show it. The stress of his position and its demands have worn him down. That, and dealing with Phaedon. The Prince no longer makes any attempt to pretend he is his father's right hand. He campaigns openly to be King. He says it is time for his father to step down and cede the throne to him. He has some support for this. Clearly, the King is not what he once was, and there are those who think it best that he abdicate."

"Phaedon has no right to ask this," Arling interrupted.

Ellich smiled grimly. "Since when did decency ever stop that boy? The King hangs on mostly because he still hopes his son will change. He thinks that time will season him and he'll somehow become the King he should be. It is an impossibility, but my brother will not see this."

"So what are you saying, Uncle?" Aphen pressed.

The smile died away. "You are always so quick to intuit things. I am saying that any promises he makes to you today might be broken tomorrow. Tell him what you will, but remember that he needs to know that whatever has happened is not insurmountable. His heart is weak and his strength limited. If you can reassure him there are solutions to problems, if you can give him hope, if you can take on some of the burden, it will go a long way toward helping him deal with any demands being placed on his shoulders."

He paused. "Am I asking too much? From the look on your face, I think maybe I am."

"You will decide for yourself when you hear what I have to say." She put her hands on his broad shoulders. "I love you both, and I would do nothing to hurt either of you. But what I have to say can't wait and can't be softened. It is harsh and terrible, and it must be dealt with. I need Grandfather to be strong for this."

Her uncle nodded slowly. "Then we must do our best to help him be strong. Come."

They followed the path to the little side door she had entered not so long ago but which now seemed as if it must have happened in another lifetime. She had spoken to her grandfather about her order's plan to embark on a quest, but she had never told him exactly what the Druids were seeking. She had asked for the use of the seeking-Stones at that meeting, and now she must ask for them again. But this time there was a clear precedent for her request, one deeply rooted in Elven history, and she intended to rely on it.

A member of the Home Guard stepped out of the foliage to greet them, nodded approval for them to pass, and vanished as quickly and silently as he had appeared.

Ellich rapped on the door, and after a moment it opened and her grandfather was standing before her, smiling. "Aphen," he said, and took her in his arms.

She was shocked at how haggard he had grown, his age never more evident than it was now. His arms, encircling her, felt weak and brittle, and his weight had dropped noticeably. The strength that had once been evident was completely gone. It was as if he were hanging on by his fingernails.

She hugged him back. She could feel the tears in her eyes. "Grandfather. I've missed you so much."

"Well, then. We are well matched." He looked past her. "And you, as well, Arling." He released Aphen to hug her sister, patting Arling gently on the back. "I don't see enough of either of you anymore. Come in, come in."

Ellich followed them into the room and closed and locked the door behind them. They moved over to a pair of couches and sat, the sisters facing the King and his brother. There were pitchers of ale and tea on the low table between them, and Ellich motioned for Aphen and Arling to help themselves.

Aphenglow poured tea for all of them, and then she began to relate her tale of the events surrounding the fate of the doomed expedition and the discovery of the failing Ellcrys. She told them everything save what exactly the Druids had been searching for and how finding Aleia Omarosian's diary had provided the impetus for the expedition. She focused instead on the impending collapse of the Forbidding and the need to act at once to prevent it from happening.

She took a long time to cover everything, but she thought it important to leave nothing out. She could see early on the effect it was having on her grandfather and wished she could have softened the sharp edges of her news, but there was little softening to be done. Ellich was calmer, listening intently, nodding now and then, his strong face expressionless, his hands clasped loosely together as he leaned forward, resting his elbows on his knees.

Arling said almost nothing, only now and then adding a detail regarding the condition of the Ellcrys or the nature of the demands that had been placed on her as the Chosen the tree would send in search of the mysterious Bloodfire.

When Aphen had finished, there was a long silence. Then her grandfather surprised her by saying, "You are showing great courage, both of you. In the face of enormous responsibility and much danger, you are as calm as if this were no more demanding than a walk in the woods. I am proud of you."

Spontaneously, they rose and went to him, hugging him where he sat on the couch, bent over and frail, hands shaking as he hugged them back. "There, now," he said, his voice stronger than before. "It's all right. It will be all right."

Seated again, Aphenglow said to him, "Now that you know, I have a request to make. To find the Bloodfire, we must have the use of the Elfstones. You did not see fit to give them to me before, but this time I think you must. Without them, I will have only the directions recorded in the Druid Histories. That isn't enough. The High Council must be made to see this. Arling has been asked to carry the Ellcrys seed so that it can be immersed in the Bloodfire, and I will go with her to see that this happens. I have no clear idea of what this will require of us, but we cannot afford to fail. The Elfstones are the best way to protect us against the unforeseeable. Had the Druids been given the Stones when they went into the Forbidding, they might not have suffered so greatly. I do not think we can afford to let something of that magnitude befall us. We have to be protected."

"But the Elfstones would be our most valuable weapon against the things breaking free of the Forbidding," her grandfather pointed out. "How can I give them up in the face of so great a threat?"

She was ready for this question. Precedent must prevail. He must be made to see that.

"When the search for the Bloodfire was conducted last, in the time of Eventine Elessedil, the girl and the boy who carried the Ellcrys seed were given the Elfstones by the Druid Allanon." She paused. "Without them, the effort would have failed. The Histories are quite clear on this."

Her grandfather shook his head. "The High Council will not agree."

"Nor will Phaedon," Ellich added, drawing his brother's attention. "Emperowen, you must give her the Elfstones yourself. This matter should not be brought before the High Council. If it is, there will be endless debate and constant delay. You will be forced to stand up to them all and to your son, as well. You know this to be true."

It was a bold statement, one tinged by confrontation and demand. The King stared at his brother, and for a moment Aphenglow caught a glimpse of fury in the aged eyes.

But when her grandfather spoke, his voice was calm. "You wish me to simply give the Elfstones to Aphen? To ignore the Elven High Council and Phaedon entirely?"

"No, my King, I *wish* nothing of the sort." Ellich held his brother's gaze. "But I think it is necessary."

There was a long pause as they eyed each other, and then the old King nodded slowly. "I suppose I do, too."

Ellich turned to Aphenglow. "How will you go about this? Whom will you and Arling take with you?"

"Cymrian," her sister declared at once. She gave Aphen a stern look. "Don't you agree?"

Aphen nodded. "We will use *Wend-A-Way* as transport. She will serve our purpose well enough. She's small and quick and easily handled. The less notice we draw, the better."

"Which is a valid point," her uncle said. "We can't assume that whoever was trying to kill you earlier has given up. We have to assume there are those who might try to interfere with what you are attempting to do, possibly without even realizing what they are risking."

Aphenglow saw the wisdom in his warning. She couldn't be sure that whoever sought to stop their search for the missing Elfstones wouldn't try to stop this search, as well. Not because they sought to prevent a renewal of the Ellcrys—which they likely knew nothing about—but perhaps solely because it would go a long way toward putting an end to the Druid order. If Drust Chazhul was behind this, certainly he would support such an effort.

"I think we must assume that the Federation and Drust Chazhul will offer us little help," she said. "He has demonstrated his intentions where the Druids are concerned by attacking Paranor. There is no reason to think he will behave any differently toward the Elves. He hates and fears magic, and he would see it destroyed."

"I don't know about the Federation, but the Prime Minister is no longer a concern. He was killed in the attack on Paranor. A new Prime Minister has been selected, and Edinja Orle is an avid believer in magic's uses. We are watching her closely to see what she does."

Aphen was surprised. "I hadn't heard that. Maybe this changes things."

"When will you leave?" her grandfather asked.

"As soon as the Ellcrys gives Arling her seed."

"And you, Arling? Are you determined to go with her? Can you do what the tree is asking of you?"

Arling glanced momentarily at Aphen and then nodded. "I will see this through. But I will not lie to you, Grandfather. I do not accept that I am the one she needs. I am not settled on that. But I will go with Aphen and find the Bloodfire and see that the Ellcrys seed is immersed and brought back again. Then we will see."

There was a long silence, and for a moment Aphen thought her grandfather might rescind his decision to release the Elfstones without a stronger commitment from Arling.

But the old King only nodded. "I will wait until after you are gone to advise the Elven people of what is happening. They will have to be told, but not right away."

"The High Council and Phaedon, as well," Ellich added.

The King nodded reluctantly. "Agreed."

"Grandfather," Aphen said. "One thing more. I know how the Elven people feel about the Druids. But you might have need of us, and we might be able to offer help. Even as few of us as are left. Let me speak with Seersha. She is skilled in the use of magic, and I will ask her to do what she can to help protect the Elves and Arborlon. A few of the others who came back with me may choose to help, as well. Embrace their efforts. It would be a grave mistake not to make use of their experience."

Emperowen Elessedil smiled. "You sound so serious in giving me this admonition, Aphen. So I will take it as seriously as you clearly wish me to. I will see to it that the Elves make the best use possible of your friends if they are willing to offer their help."

"And I will see to it that you have the weapons and supplies you need for your voyage," Ellich added quickly.

Aphen rose. "Then we should say good-bye now. We have a lot to do before we can leave."

Her grandfather held up one hand to stop her. "One minute. You must have the Elfstones to aid you in your efforts. I will entrust them to your care and ask only that you keep them safe until your return."

He left the room, and when he returned moments later he placed a small pouch in Aphen's palm and closed her fingers about it, patting them gently as he did. "There. It's done."

"Thank you, Grandfather," she said. "Thank you for your trust in me."

He nodded without speaking and turned to Arling. "I am sorry so much is being asked of you, child. I wish I could do something to change that."

Arling went to him, bent close, and kissed his forehead. "I must find my own way, Grandfather."

The King put a hand on her arm. "As must we all."

They kissed and hugged their grandfather one last time before slipping back out the garden door and heading through the trees to the edge of the palace grounds.

"He doesn't look well," Arling said as they stepped out onto the roadway and started walking for home.

"No, he doesn't," Aphen agreed.

"I wish we could do something to help him. Something to reassure him things will be all right. Something to make him feel better."

Aphenglow was speechless. Arling, whose own situation was so unimaginably overwhelming that her grandfather's struggles paled in comparison, was more worried for the old man than for herself.

"Let's go tell the others how things stand," she said at last.

Hiding the tears that filled her eyes, she picked up the pace.

15

THE SISTERS RETURNED TO THE COTTAGE AND TOLD SEERSHA
and Mirai Leah what had been said at their meeting with the King,
emphasizing the deterioration of his health and the feeling of both
his brother and himself that the support of Phaedon and the Elven
High Council would be questionable. Other than the four of them
gathered now, only Emperowen and Ellich knew of the plan to go in
search of the Bloodfire.

"This is not good," Seersha said at once. "To keep what's happening secret from everyone? How can they expect to do that?"

"Only until we are safely away. Then they will inform both the
High Council and the Elven people," Aphen said.

"What will your grandfather say to them?" Mirai asked.

The sisters exchanged glances. "He didn't tell us that," Arling answered.

"So at some point he will be forced to reveal that the Forbidding
is on the verge of collapse, that the seed that will quicken it anew is
en route and in danger, and that both of you are gone from the city
bearing the only real weapon of magic the Elves can rely on if they
have to defend themselves?" Seersha was appalled. "I can't imagine
that this particular piece of news will be well received."

Aphenglow was chagrined. "I told my grandfather that even
though I would be gone and the Elfstones with me, perhaps he could

rely on you to help keep the Elves safe until I return. I told him you were skilled in the use of magic and would be invaluable to them."

Seersha glared at her. "You had no right to do that, Aphen."

"But I thought you would be anxious to help. It would mean traveling with an army to the Breakline in order to prevent any demon-led breakout. It would give you a chance to discover if there is a way back into the Forbidding, a chance to reach the Ard Rhys and bring both her and Redden Ohmsford out safely."

"Not if I have to spend my time looking after a thousand men and women who have no magic at all to protect them against the kinds of creatures our failed expedition ran up against in the Fangs. You weren't there, Aphen! You didn't see what it was like!"

Aphen flinched in the face of her fury and shook her head in dismay. "I didn't mean to put you . . ."

"What were you thinking?" Seersha interrupted, so angry by now she was no longer interested in hearing anything her friend had to say. "You were the one responsible for sending us on this hunt. Remember? We went because you found that stupid diary! And now you intend to go off with your sister while you send me—"

"Stop it!" Aphen snapped. "Don't say another word, Seersha!"

The Dwarf rose and stood looking at her. "You're right. I've said enough. Too much. I'm sorry. You do what you have to. But I intend to do the same, so please don't think that any pledge you might have made on my behalf will be honored."

She wheeled away and stalked out, slamming the door behind her.

For a moment, no one said anything. Then Aphen sighed audibly. "I went too far. I should have asked her before I said anything to Grandfather."

"You were trying to reassure him that the Druids would help," Arling said quietly.

"There are no more Druids," Aphen declared, her voice hard and bitter. "The Druids are finished."

Mirai gave her a quick glance. "Seersha's angry, but she'll get past it. You didn't do anything wrong. She's worried about the Ard Rhys, and she thinks it might already be too late to bring her back."

"She might be right. She's certainly right about what happened being my fault. If not for me, there would have been no expedition, and everyone who went on it and died would still be alive."

"You didn't decide there would be an expedition." Arling was suddenly hugging her. "You only suggested it might be worth doing. Everyone else agreed and the Ard Rhys made the decision. Seersha is wrong to blame you."

Mirai was on her feet. "Arling is right. I'm going after her and ask what she intends to do. If she's going back into the Forbidding to look for Redden, Railing and I will both be going with her."

She left quickly, leaving the sisters clasped in a tight embrace of shared sorrow in the sudden silence of their home.

Railing Ohmsford was up early that same morning, too troubled to sleep and still bitter and angry that he had been forced to leave his brother behind. He understood there had been no real choice in the matter, that if what was left of their little group hadn't boarded *Wend-A-Way* and sailed off with Aphenglow and Cymrian, they would have been overrun by the Goblins and killed. He understood, as well, that there was no way back into the Forbidding, and no real chance of rescuing his brother even if there had been. He knew all this, but knowing it and accepting it were two entirely different things.

So he had let the others convince him—Seersha, in particular, because she wanted to save Khyber Elessedil every bit as much as he wanted to save Redden—that the only reasonable chance they had was to return to Arborlon, regroup, and come back again better prepared. But the sense of betrayal he felt was acute and deep, and none of the arguments he was able to muster could tamp it down.

Now, awake again before dawn and at loose ends, all he could think about was hopping aboard an airship and flying back into the Fangs.

In the hope of distracting himself, he hobbled out to the pathway fronting the residence he was sharing with Crace Coram, Skint, and Woostra. The effort it required to get there was laborious and painful and served mostly to demonstrate how far he still had to go before he would be fit enough to help anyone. Seersha had set the bones and then splinted the leg during the return trip, repairing the damage well enough that it would heal perfectly in six weeks or so. But making the short journey to the end of the walkway only served to remind him that six weeks could be a long time.

Growing quickly frustrated, he settled himself on one of a pair of benches placed at the edge of the grounds so he could rest and think.

Going back to Patch Run and his mother was out of the question. He would rather face the Goblins on one leg than have to tell her what had happened to Redden. He could return to Bakrabru and Farshaun Req and see if the old Rover couldn't arrange transportation back to the Breakline or perhaps find someone who knew the wilderness well enough to do the job the Speakman had been recruited to do. But Farshaun would want him healed first, and it seemed unlikely anyone there could do more to hasten that process than the Elves, unless he chose to travel east to the Gnome Healers at Storlock.

He sat for a time in the shade of a chestnut tree, stewing about his situation, waiting for the steady aching in his leg to lessen, trying very hard not to think about what might be happening to his brother inside the Forbidding while he was sitting around inactive and useless.

Skint appeared and said a few words to him, and a little later Crace Coram. The latter told him not to despair, that Seersha would already be making plans to go back and that both he and the boy would accompany her when she did. His reassurance helped ease Railing's distress, and finally he went back inside and washed himself and dressed in fresh clothes, having realized he was still wearing his clothing from the day before.

The morning passed while all four of them sat around waiting for something to happen. Eventually Aphenglow would appear with news of the Elven response to her report. What was to be done about the Goblins breaking free of their prison, though, was not something she had chosen to discuss with them, although Railing was pretty sure she would have talked it over with Seersha. Whatever the case, action would have to be taken, and it would have to be taken soon.

The boy was also anxious to see Mirai, who was as concerned

about Redden as he was, and to whom he could best open up about his desperate need to do something to help his brother. But midday came and went, and Mirai did not appear, either.

He was back on his bench in the early afternoon when Seersha trudged up the pathway looking less than happy. She came over and plopped down beside him. "Sleep well?"

"Poorly," he snapped. "Is there news?"

She shrugged. "Aphenglow and Arling went to their grandfather to advise him of things and to talk about what could be done for the Ellcrys. I think they made a plan for it."

"You don't look too happy about that."

She stretched out her arms and dropped them listlessly at her sides, frowning. "Aphen and I had an argument. I lost my temper. I don't usually do that, and I wish I hadn't this time. Aphen is my friend. But this whole business has gotten completely out of hand, and no one really knows what to do about it."

"I know what to do," he said darkly.

She nodded. "Go back into the Fangs and save your brother. But it won't be that easy. It might not even be possible."

"Don't say that."

"I have to say it. I have to convince myself. You and I want the same thing—to go into the Forbidding, find the Ard Rhys and your brother, and bring them out again. Simple enough. But there are larger concerns. If the Ellcrys fails and the creatures imprisoned there break free, they will overrun the Four Lands. It isn't just the Goblins; it's other things, much worse things. We lack the magic and the numbers to hold them back. And without the Ellcrys, we have no way to lock them up again."

"I'll worry about that later, after I've gotten Redden back," he insisted stubbornly.

"Except there won't be a 'later' if we don't address the collapse of the Forbidding first. I don't like it any better than you do, but I accept the fact of it and that's why I am not very happy just now."

They were silent for a moment, mulling this over. "What are you going to do?" the boy asked her finally.

"I don't know. That's what the argument was about. Do I go back into the Fangs and find the Ard Rhys, or do I stick around here and help the Elves fight off the demonkind that are breaking free? Aphen will go off with her sister to find something called the Bloodfire so the Ellcrys can be saved. She wants me to stay here and do what I can for her people. It's a difficult choice. I'm still thinking about it."

She looked at him, her fierce face tight and hard. "I can tell you one thing, Railing Ohmsford. You are not going anywhere until that leg heals. And that will take weeks unless you do what I tell you."

He stared at her, not at all sure where this was going. "What do you mean?"

"Mirai has a level head on her shoulders. She will likely exercise better judgment than you when it comes to helping your brother. So I want you to promise me you will listen to her and do what she says when it's time to go after him. Do that, and I'll see to it that you're healed. Today."

He straightened up at once. "You can do that?"

"I can and I will. Do I have your promise?"

He nodded quickly. "You do."

"Don't give it lightly and don't think you can go back on your word and not pay a price for doing so. Mirai is loyal and will stick with you on this, but if you betray either her or myself, you will live to regret it. By giving me your word now, you are promising that no matter what happens, you will do what she tells you."

"I'll keep my word," he said. He couldn't imagine going up against Mirai, in any case.

She held his gaze for a long moment. "Good enough. Come with me."

They retraced Seersha's footsteps, moving at a pace that allowed Railing to keep up. They had gone only a short distance when they encountered Mirai coming toward them. Railing tried hard to hide what he was feeling just at the prospect of having her close again.

"Where are you off to?" she asked, coming up to them. Her eyes shifted from one to the other. "Is everything all right?"

"I doubt it," Seersha replied. "But I've told Railing we might at least do something about his leg. Is Aphen still at the cottage?"

Mirai nodded. "Is your argument with her over?"

"Over and done. She's my friend. I reacted badly. But that's in the past. Want to come along?"

The three of them continued walking, Mirai linking her arm in Railing's to give him added support as they went. "I'm glad you're here," he said.

She gave him a smirk. "So I can nurse you back to health, no doubt. What does Seersha have in mind for your leg?"

"I don't know. She hasn't said."

"Are you rational today?"

"What does that mean?"

"It means that during the entire trip back here, you did nothing but rant and rave about how you were going back for Redden and no one could stop you and anyone who tried would regret it. That, and a lot of other wild nonsense. I was tempted to agree when Austrum threatened to bind and gag you."

At the mention of the big Rover's name, Railing felt his mood sour quickly. He remembered Austrum kissing Mirai. He remembered how she had failed to do anything about it afterward, not even warn him against trying it again.

"He would have regretted it," he muttered.

She gave him a quick nudge. "Why don't you stop trying to be so fierce? I like you better when you're gentle."

"I don't feel like being gentle."

"Which is something you should work on. Like Redden has."

He didn't know where that came from, but he didn't feel like pursuing it and let the matter drop.

When they reached the Elessedil sisters' cottage, they found Arling gone and Aphen packing clothes and making up a list of supplies for the journey. She told them she had already visited with Cymrian, who had appeared not long after Seersha left and was already off collecting an airship crew for their flight. She greeted Seersha effusively, and they apologized to each other. Railing stood by awkwardly until the conversation turned to him.

"Railing needs his leg repaired if he's to be of any use either to himself or to the rest of us," Seersha announced. "We can't afford to wait around for it to heal normally, so I think a little magic is in order. You are the best at this sort of thing. Will you give it a try?"

Aphenglow looked at him, and Railing at once felt the difference in their ages and maturity. She wasn't that much older, but her confidence and poise so far surpassed his own that it made him feel like a child.

"Is that what you want?" she asked him. "For me to use magic on your leg?"

He nodded. "If you can heal it, yes."

She glanced at Seersha and then at him again. "Magic of this sort works best on others. I can heal you more easily than I could heal myself when I was injured at Paranor. Unfortunately, it won't hurt any less."

They placed him on Mirai's bed in the spare room, loosening his clothes and making him comfortable. Aphenglow cut away his pant leg all the way up above the knee of his bad leg and took off the splints and bindings. When his leg was completely revealed, she gave him something to drink and then a bitter-tasting root to chew that immediately made his mouth go numb and eventually his body and limbs as well.

"Just be still while I do this," she told him. "No sudden movements. There will be some pain. To help you stay still, I'll have both Mirai and Seersha hold you. Don't panic. It won't take long. When it's over, you will sleep."

He nodded, waiting impatiently, the first twinges of doubt starting to erode his confidence. "Just do what you have to. I'll be fine."

She placed a cloth over his eyes and stroked his face. Then she placed both hands on his broken leg and began to move them lightly over the surface. She worked at this for a long time, and he could hear her murmuring softly. Once in a while her fingers probed.

Then a slow, steady ache began to build deep inside the bones of his damaged leg, rippling through him from thigh to ankle. The medication Aphen had given him dulled it, but did not prevent it. He could feel Seersha's and Mirai's hands tighten on his wrists and ankles. He held himself as still as he could manage, the pain building on itself in slow waves until eventually it was all he could do to keep from screaming. He clenched his teeth and focused on an image of Mirai—the image strong and alive in his mind. The murmuring and touching continued and the pain raged on, but he forced it all away and went down inside where his heartbeat gave him a lifeline to grasp and Mirai's voice whispered over and over, *I like you better when you're gentle.*

Then, finally, he lost consciousness and slept.

For Arling Elessedil, it was a traumatic day on several fronts. Her visit to her grandfather and Uncle Ellich, followed by her sister's argument with Seersha, had been troubling enough, but later she was forced to call a meeting of the Chosen to discuss the deterioration of the Ellcrys. It was becoming apparent that there were problems with the tree. The first signs of wilt and decay had begun to appear, and while the Chosen worked diligently to heal the damage, all of them suspected the same thing. The tree was failing and needed to be renewed.

They knew, as well, that for a renewal to happen, one of them must be given the Ellcrys seed and sent in search of the Bloodfire.

Once, such knowledge had been carefully hidden from virtually everyone, the myth of immortality part of the old legends of the creation of the Forbidding and the locking away of the demonkind. But that had changed during the reign of Eventine Elessedil, when the last Ellcrys had failed and the truth about her regeneration become common knowledge.

Now there were enough who knew the truth of things that pretending the tree could never die or need replacing was pointless.

Arling and Aphen had discussed earlier in the day how the meeting should be handled, and they had agreed that Arling should keep the fact that she had been selected to go in search of the Bloodfire to herself. Doing so would provide another of the order the opportunity to step forward and volunteer to do what she could not.

She was still not ready to accept that she was the right choice to become the tree's successor. She had talked with the Ellcrys nightly after Aphenglow's departure for the Breakline, trying to convince the tree that choosing her was a mistake. But the Ellcrys had deflected her efforts, continuing quietly to insist that she was the only one who would do. Nothing Arling had said during their discussions seemed to make any difference at all.

But now, perhaps, confronting the other Chosen with the enormity of the need facing them all might cause one among them to step forward and indicate a willingness to act as bearer of the seed.

This turned out to be wishful thinking. The other members of her order listened patiently, but none of them offered to be the one who bore the seed to the Bloodfire. If anything, they were reluctant to believe that the need was immediate. Surely there was more time than Arling believed. Shouldn't they examine the tree more thoroughly? Weren't there healing skills and medicines that could be employed? Objections were raised and questions asked, and the dismay that settled over those assembled seemed to inhibit any of them from doing more than listening.

By the time they had disbanded to go home for the night, not a single Chosen had seemed ready to accept what she had told them.

They were not so different, she realized afterward, from herself. She had been no more willing to believe when the tree had revealed its condition. She had been no better prepared for it, no more anxious to act on the tree's behalf, no more eager to wish for selection. Oddly, she was not surprised. If anything, it only deepened her growing sense of fatalism.

At midnight, when the rest of those staying in her little cottage were asleep, she slipped out the door and went through the nighttime darkness to the Carolan and down into the Gardens of Life. She crept through the flowering shrubs and bedding plants, through the trellis vines and ornamentals to where the Ellcrys stood alone, shining crimson and silver in the moonlight. She knelt beneath her canopy.

"I am here, Mistress," she whispered.

A slender branch lowered and came to rest on her shoulder.

–You are still afraid, child. You are feeling so alone. No one wishes to take from you the burden I have given you to carry–

"I told them what is happening. They could not bring themselves to believe it. I wanted one of them to say they hoped they would be the one you selected. I wanted just one to show a little of the courage I lack. It did not happen."

–At the time of your choosing, when I laid my branches on each of your shoulders, I sensed there was something that set you apart. Even then, I knew–

Arling did not believe she could be the only one; she had never believed it, although the tree had said so repeatedly during their nighttime discussions. In her efforts to reassure Arling, the Ellcrys had said this was always so. The choosing was the time in which she was best able to determine who should serve as her successor should she become too ill to continue. It was no different for her as a sentient tree than for Elves or Humans: The elders of a species always measure the fitness of the young to take their place.

"I did not tell them the whole truth," Arling said after a moment. "Only that you were failing—something they could already see for themselves—and that a renewal must take place. I did not tell them you had already selected me."

–You still hope one of them will ask to be the bearer–

"Yes."

On her shoulder, the Ellcrys's branch shifted slowly to stroke the back of her neck.

–I cannot wait for that to happen, child. There is no time for it. I am infected with my illness, worn down by my age, and fated to pass into history. I have served for so long. It has been my privilege to do so, but my service is ending. My seed must be carried to the Bloodfire and quickened–

"We are not yet ready for that," Arling said at once, a surge of fear penetrating all the way to her heart. "There are still preparations to be made." She swallowed hard. "I can't do it."

The silence that followed was as cold and hard as ancient stone. Arling bowed her head and closed her eyes. *Don't ask this of me! Don't tell me I must!*

–Would you leave me bereft of hope? Would you abandon your people and the Races of your world to their fate? I do not see that in you–

"I cannot do this!"

She screamed the words, their sound so piercing that she flinched in shame and dismay. But the branch on her shoulder did not lift away or cease its steady stroking of Arling's neck, a soft and soothing touch, a calming presence.

–You can do this and much more, child. You are strong–

Arling shook her head, tears filling her eyes. "I am a coward!"

–You are what I was all those years ago. You struggle as I did. You require courage and peace of mind in order to believe–

Inwardly, Arling collapsed. She could barely bring herself under control, the weight of what was happening crushing her. She fought back against her tears, against the wall of fear moving inexorably toward her, against her base and shameful instincts. She did not want to be like this. She did not want to appear desperate and weak. But she could not seem to help herself.

–There is no other to help me but you. You have the courage and the resilience that is required. There is no other to do what is needed if you refuse. Child, you are all there is, and I am only seeking that which I saw in you when you entered into my service–

Arling shook her head, wiping at her tears. "What you saw wasn't really there. You were mistaken about me. I am not what you hoped I would be. I am just a girl, and I want to live out my life!"

She shuddered and clutched at herself, shoulders heaving as she cried. The tree did not respond, but seemed to wait on her. "I want to be brave for you," she whispered. "I want to be strong enough and willing enough to be the bearer of your seed. I want to save the Elves. I want it, but I cannot make it be true. I cannot!"

The Ellcrys moved the end of one branch until it was touching her cheek.

–We never know what we can be or do until the need is there and we are tested by it. I thought as you did. I was afraid, and I fled with my fear to where I thought I would be safe. But necessity will always find us, and our sense of right and wrong will always find a way to make what is seemingly impossible the reality of our lives–

"No. Not here. Not with this."

–Yes, Arlingfant Elessedil, with this and even more, should the need be there and the call sounded to embrace it. Yes, best of my Chosen, strongest and bravest of my children. Hold out your hands to me–

Arling could not speak. She shrank back inside herself. She shook her head no.

–Hold out your hands–

The command was spoken again, and this time the words touched something inside Arling that she found she could not turn away from or ignore. Still riddled with pain and fear, she did as she was asked, whispering to herself as she did so, *No, no, no.*

She felt the tree stirring, sensed a gathering of its limbs. She had closed her eyes, and she kept them closed against what she knew was coming. She held her hands cupped before her, trying to hold them steady, trying to keep herself strong. It was surreal and terrifying, a contradiction of what she knew she must not allow and what she also knew she must accept.

She felt a weight settle into her hands—smooth and round and warm. She knew without looking what it was, and a moment later, when she opened her eyes, she found a small, silvery egg-shaped sphere resting in her hands.

The tree's branches drew back, and the Ellcrys went motionless and silent in the darkness and did not speak or move again.

16

---◆---

In that same darkness, in Arishaig, the assassin Stoon slipped down mostly empty streets and alleyways, avoiding the drunks and homeless who huddled in the shadows, staying clear of the voices that whispered now and then from doorways and alcoves where men like himself carried on their business. He was wrapped in his cloak and hooded against the possibility of being recognized, and his tall, lean frame gave him a sinister appearance to the one or two who caught sight of him on his way to his meeting with Edinja, causing them to move quickly away.

Why she had decided on a meeting at this time of night was troubling. Why she had asked that it be conducted at her home rather than in the quarters of the Prime Minister was equally so. She had invited him there only once before, when Drust Chazhul was newly dead and she was still in hiding. But since then, all of their meetings had taken place in the bedchamber of her official living quarters, and he had come and gone through the secret passageways he had used when in service to the unfortunate Drust.

A less confident man, a less skilled professional, might have thought twice about the change in meeting places, might have read into it that it signaled a shift in the direction of the wind, one that might sweep him away. But Stoon was not such a man, and to refuse to meet with her as she asked or to seek a change of venue would only demonstrate weakness. So here he was, creeping along through the city well after midnight to the spectral, forbidding tower whose black stone façade and gargoyles were recognizable—and religiously avoided—by everyone who resided in Arishaig.

The grounds lacked walls and gardens to distance the tower from the streets that bordered it on two sides, leaving it close up against the corner crossing, casting its black shadow. There were stories about Edinja's residence: of screams and shrieks emanating from within, of foul smells and strange rumblings, of moving shadows glimpsed behind the curtained windows—things that were clearly not entirely human.

He had seen none of this in his single visit. Nor heard the sounds or smelled the scents. Stories whispered by superstitious people, he had decided after he had departed. Rumors that perhaps she herself had created to warn off the curious.

He skirted the tower's rough edges when it came into view, avoiding the front entry, moving instead to a tiny door just off the street that was sheltered by shrubbery. He moved quickly and without hesitation, resisting the urge to stop or give further thought to what he was doing. There was no point. If her intentions were bad, he would not be able to tell from out here.

Once through the door and inside, he climbed a spiraling stairway that took him to the rooms at the apex of the tower where she made her bedchamber. As he neared the end of his climb, he saw the soft glow of candlelight emanating from her open door and felt a small measure of relief. If she had meant him harm, she would not have bothered providing him light with which to see. Not when she saw so much more clearly than he in the dark, and had the services of Cinla to help dispatch those she suddenly found too troublesome to bear.

His footsteps were soundless on the stone steps, his passage less evident than a breeze, yet before he reached the doorway she was calling to him.

"Come, Stoon. Don't keep me waiting. Isn't this just like old times?"

The corners of his mouth twitched in response—the closest he ever came to a smile. He went through the door and found her reclined on her lounger, the big moor cat that served as her protector and familiar sprawled in front of her. Given its position, he decided he was not being invited to go directly to her, so instead he moved to a chair that had obviously been prepared for him. A comfortable throw was draped across its arm and a glass of wine set next to it on a small table. A candle sat beside the wineglass, its flame a bright flicker of light in the near darkness. A second candle burned on the table next to her.

"Mistress," he greeted, giving her a small bow.

As always, he was dumbstruck by her beauty. Dusky skin, silver hair, slender limbs, and angular features gave her an exotic look. She was distinctive and stunningly lovely. But as with those snakes whose bite was instantly fatal, it would be a mistake to venture too close without exercising caution.

"Try the wine," she said to him, sipping at her own. "It is quite wonderful, and we are celebrating this night."

He picked up the glass and drank. He didn't hesitate. Life was a risk when you consorted with venomous creatures. The wine slid down his throat easily and warmed him deep in his belly. "Extraordinary," he said, keeping his eyes on her.

"Aren't you going to ask me what we are celebrating?"

He shook his head. "You will tell me when you are ready. I would not presume to rush you."

"Oh, you are so very cautious!" she exclaimed. She put down her glass and straightened, clapping her hands in approval. "I rather like you that way. I am celebrating us. Today it is exactly one year since we began our relationship and entered into our agreement to be lovers and co-conspirators. Do you remember now?"

He did not, precisely, but smiled and raised his glass to her. "A fine agreement it was, too."

"Wasn't it?" She clasped her hands in front of her and leaned forward. "I thought it fitting we meet here to commemorate our union. Now tell me your news."

He nodded. The reason for this meeting in the first place. "Our creature in Arborlon has sent word that the Druid expedition has failed and that the order was all but destroyed in the process. Only two of their number survive; the rest were lost. Those two have re-turned to Arborlon with a handful of others. Apparently, the Druids are no longer any kind of threat at all."

She smiled. "If a single Druid lives, they are a threat. Make no mistake about that, Stoon. Still, the destruction of the order and the fact that the Druids have abandoned Paranor—now, *that* is some-thing to build on. But their search did not succeed, you say?"

"Apparently not, although we still don't know what it was they were looking for. Whatever it was, it apparently ate them up and spit them out. Even the Ard Rhys did not return."

Edinja considered, a frown creasing her smooth brow. "What should we make of that, I wonder?"

"Indeed." He took another drink of the wine. "There is more. An-other expedition has been mounted by the Elven girl, Aphenglow Elessedil, one of the two Druids who survived. A much smaller expe-dition, formed in secret and with little notice."

"And its purpose?"

Stoon shook his head. "Unknown, as yet. Nor do we have infor-mation regarding its destination. We will know everything eventu-ally, of course. Our creature will find out. But, for now, we know only that it departs Arborlon soon, probably today. This has all come about very quickly. I sense a need for haste and a certain amount of desperation."

He paused. "One thing we do know: Aphenglow was given the blue Elfstones, the so-called seeking-Stones, by the Elven King. It was done secretly, without the knowledge or permission of the Elven High Council. It appears she is looking for something."

Edinja's frown deepened. "What could be so important that the old King would allow this?"

She was silent a moment, thinking. Stoon finished off his wine and considered the advisability of leaving his seat long enough to pour himself more from the decanter he could see sitting on the side-board. But in the end he decided to remain where he was.

"She flies an airship on this latest expedition?" Edinja asked sud-denly.

Stoon shrugged. "I would presume so. Our creature seemed to suggest as much."

"*My* creature," she corrected him instantly. "Be careful not to lay claim to any part of what isn't yours."

He bowed deferentially at the coldness of her voice. "Of course. I apologize. *Your* creature. I would never suggest otherwise, Mistress."

Her smile was quick and hard. "I didn't think so."

She rose and walked over to him, took hold of his hands, and brought him to his feet. She wrapped her arms loosely about his waist and brought him against her so that their faces were close.

"I want you to go after her," she whispered.

There were few tasks in this life that Stoon was reluctant to undertake, but this was one of them. The memory of his near-death experience at Paranor was still fresh in his mind. Bad enough that he had been foolish enough to attempt to overpower Aphenglow Elessedil once. But to risk his life doing so a second time smacked of madness.

"Mistress, I would do anything for you that I believed would advance your cause. But I have encountered this girl once, and once was more than enough. I do not expect that if I were to come up against her again, I would survive it. She is extremely dangerous and more than a match for me."

Edinja reached up to touch his lips with her finger, running the tip back and forth slowly. "Since when do you accept failure so willingly?"

"I do not like admitting this, especially to you, but I must accept realities I cannot change. My instincts warn me to avoid her. They foretell my death at the hands of this girl." He paused, sensing her displeasure, realizing he had crossed a line. "Nevertheless, I am yours. I will go after her if you command it. Tell me what you would have me do. Do you still wish it of me, knowing how I feel? Because if you do, then I will go."

She wrapped her arms around him and pulled him tightly against her. "My big, brave assassin. Afraid of a mere child."

"Call it what you will. I believe in instincts and hunches and foretellings. They have kept me safe more times than I care to remember. They warn me now about Aphenglow Elessedil. She is no mere child, Mistress. She is too much for me."

Edinja Orle laughed, and her laughter was filled with sly cunning and tinged with a clear hint of disparagement.

"What if I were to give you help in this matter?"

He hesitated. "What sort of help?"

"The sort that will tilt the scales in your favor."

He shook his head. "What exactly am I expected to do about her? Am I tracking her to discover what she seeks? Am I to take the Elf-stones away from her and bring them to you? Am I to dispose of her or make her my prisoner? What is it you are asking?"

She stood on tiptoes, and her hands wrapped around his neck as she kissed him on the mouth. He never felt the small sliver of glass she embedded deep under his skin. "Whichever you deem appropriate. It's your choice." She released him and stepped back. "I seek answers. I need information. If what she is doing is dangerous to us, you make one choice. If she can be persuaded to ally herself with us, you make another. If she lacks any discernible use, you make a third. You are a free agent in this matter."

"I am to make my own decision regarding the Elven girl?" He could hear the disbelief in his voice. "That is bold. What if I choose wrongly? What if you disapprove?"

She shrugged. "You face the consequences. Are you not prepared for that? Does that not enter into your thinking whenever you under-take a task for me? You chose the time and place to dispose of Drust Chazhul. You knew what you were risking then, yet it did not stop you from doing what you saw was needed. What good are you to me if I cannot depend on you to act on your own and act wisely? What is the point if I must always be there beside you?"

He considered, saying nothing for a moment, his sharp eyes locked on hers. She was taunting him by asking these questions; he could feel it.

"I thought you had decided not to attack the Druids as Drust did. I thought you wanted to keep the order intact and to subvert it to your own purposes."

"That was before the order was broken. All the Druids but two are gone." She shrugged. "It might be better to finish them off and start over. I could make myself Ard Rhys. I could choose my own follow-ers and establish my own order."

He found this arrogant and dangerous, but he kept his thoughts to himself. It would be a mistake to underestimate Edinja Orle. She was determined and ruthless in spite of all her smiles and sweet words, and if you were an obstacle in her path you were likely to find yourself crushed.

"Tell me something of this help you would give me," he said finally. "How would you give me an edge if there were to be another encounter with Aphenglow Elessedil?"

She walked back to her lounger, picked up a heavy robe, and threw it over her shoulders. "I will do better than tell you. I will show you. Wait here with Cinla until I return. Drink as much of the wine as you like. Dream sweet, wicked dreams of me."

She crossed to the back of the room and touched something in the wall; a jagged section of stone swung open with a grinding sound. She passed through, and the section of wall closed behind her, leaving Stoon alone with a watchful Cinla.

She was gone for almost two hours. During that time, he finished off the decanter of wine, wandered her bedchamber and perused her possessions, stood looking out the window at the city, sat looking at Cinla—who never moved—and took long moments to consider if perhaps he had gotten in over his head. Edinja Orle's seduction of him had been welcome enough, the lure of her promises and her ability to deliver on those promises a far better risk than the one he'd been taking by remaining with Drust Chazhul. But she was a viper and fully capable of turning on him without warning, and he did not think himself the least bit safe from her venom.

By the same token she was irresistible, and the attendant risk in staying with her was intoxicating. He was balanced on a wire, and whichever way he tumbled he would likely be killed. The only reasonable choice was to stay on the wire.

When she returned, she materialized in a rustle of clothing and a shimmer of silver hair. She brought him awake from where he dozed in his chair. Then she led him to the hidden door in the wall and from there to a stairway that descended through the tower and deep underground. Together they passed down countless steps, and the air grew stale and the stone damp. She said nothing as they went, her eyes on the way forward, her hand clutching his. He followed duti-fully, thinking as he did so that this is how it would be until the end, that he would always allow her to lead him, even to what one day would prove to be his death.

When they reached the bottom of the stairs, a passageway bur-rowed ahead through a scattering of smokeless torches and shadows. They traversed it in silence, and he began to hear whispers of voices and the rustling of movements from ahead, muffled and unrecogniz-able. He could not identify their source or their purpose, but they sent chills down his spine and unpleasant images through his head. They grew louder the farther in he went, and the effect on him grew more pronounced.

At the end of the passage was a huge iron door. Edinja touched it lightly twice, so quickly he could not remember afterward which bolts in which sections she had fingered, then the door swung open in a creaking of iron against iron.

Stoon had seen many strange and terrifying things in his life, and there wasn't much that could give him pause. But he was not pre-pared for what waited behind that heavy door.

"Cat's blood!" he hissed softly.

Men shambled about a cavernous chamber of stone blocks, iron racks dripping with chains and shackles, and, in the dim recesses of the far back wall, cages. But these were not men in the accepted sense of the word; these were something else entirely. Resembling men, they stood mostly upright and were possessed of two legs and two arms, but they were otherwise misshapen in unnatural ways, their faces so severely blunted and warped that their features had virtually disappeared. They muttered and huffed like cattle as they trudged about the chamber, but they did not converse. They seemed to know what they were supposed to do, but they paid no attention to one another or to anything that was going on about them.

"What are they?" Stoon asked.

Edinja was smiling. "They are my creatures. Assembled and shaped in ways that I alone determined. Answerable only to me. They do what I wish without argument. They carry out my orders without question." She looked at him. "Are they not the sort of servants every-one wishes they could have?"

He nodded, thinking as he did so that no one wanted creatures like these prowling around their homes. No one but Edinja. These were aberrations—humans mutated into monsters, men made into beasts. Where had they come from? They might have been men once, even if they were clearly something much less now. What had she done to them? They looked to have had their brains reconstructed, their ability to think and react scrubbed down and selectively erased.

"Come," she said, taking his hand and pulling him forward. "Meet your new companions for your voyage."

She took him to the cages at the back of the room, passing them by until she came to the final three. In each was a prisoner of reasonably normal appearance—big, heavily muscled men who had seen hard work and lived hard lives. Ragged and dirty, they screamed curses at Edinja as she stood safely out of reach. They grasped the bars and shook them violently, throwing themselves against the cage doors so hard Stoon wondered that the chains securing them did not give way.

"Not very well behaved, are they?" she said to him, stepping away so that a handful of her creatures could lumber forward and begin their work. They opened the cage doors and hauled out the prisoners one by one, dragging them like wild animals across the chamber floor to be securely shackled and chained to heavy wooden tables set side by side. Stoon could not help but notice the stains in the wooden planks; many of them had been made by blood.

Though enormously strong, Edinja's captives were no match for her creatures. Though they struggled mightily, they were held down and secured, their heads and bodies immobilized. Flexible metal funnels with clamps and short tubes were forced into their mouths and down their throats. The prisoners wailed and roared in fury and terror, thrashing wildly but unable to break free.

Then Edinja said to him, "Do you have your knife?"

He nodded, pulled it free from beneath his clothing, and showed it to her.

"Cut yourself. Across your palm."

He hesitated a moment, then did so. She took his bleeding hand, held it over a beaker, and let the blood drip into the muddy fluid contained inside. After a moment, she moved his hand away, swirled the liquid around in the beaker, and nodded. "Watch."

She stepped over to the men on the tables, going to each in turn, prodding their throats while whispering until—even though their mouths continued to gape and their bodies to strain—they could no longer make any sounds. Once they were quiet, she began pouring doses of the liquid from the beaker into the funnels and down their throats. The liquid steamed as it disappeared into the funnels and the bodies of the prisoners convulsed. Edinja poured and whispered, moving from the first to the second to the third, three times each until the beaker was emptied and her captives had grown silent and unmoving.

She removed the funnels from their mouths. Then she turned to Stoon and beckoned him closer. He came reluctantly, not wanting any part of this, already wishing he had said nothing to her about his fear of Aphenglow Elessedil. When he was beside her, she gripped his arm in both delicate hands and held him close.

"Watch."

The prisoners were beginning to change. Whatever magic she had employed, it was remaking the men in front of his eyes. One after another, they took on a different look, their features tightening and stretching, their bodies growing larger and filling out even more with muscle, and their eyes snapping open and growing feral and dark with animal hunger. Hair sprouted in knots from their faces, from their arms and legs, from their hands and feet, all of it thick and dark.

When the change was finished, they had taken on a different look entirely. Now they more closely resembled animals than men, creatures built to hunt and kill, their bodies powerfully built, their faces wolfish and equipped with muzzles and sharp teeth. Their eyes snapped open and they looked about with a predator's cunning, clearly taking the measure of things, growling and snapping at the air they breathed, flexing and straining against their bonds.

Edinja stepped forward to where they could see her clearly. At once they went quiet, watching her intently. She spoke to them in small hisses, her voice too indistinct for Stoon to hear any words, though the response of her new creations was clear enough. They were listening and they were doing so because she was now their master.

"Come, stand beside me," she ordered. "Let them smell you."

Again, he stepped forward obediently, aware of the hungry gazes now shifting to find him, of the looks that said he would be nothing more to them than prey should they be set free.

When he was next to her, she began making fresh sounds—animal noises, small grunts and growls—and he could see her newly created creatures were listening. He watched the once-men shift their gazes from her to him, fixing on him, watching intently.

"There," she said finally. "It is done. They are yours to command. They will do what you tell them, and they will act as your protectors against anything that threatens you. They will hunt all day and all night, if you ask it. They will fight until they win or are destroyed. They are enormously strong and impervious to pain and weariness. They feel nothing and require no care. You can set them a task, and they will pursue it until it is completed."

She paused, giving him a wicked smile. "Even a Druid will have difficulty standing against all three of them. Even one as troublesome as you find Aphenglow Elessedil to be."

"But they will not kill her if I do not ask it, will they?" He remained unsure of these creatures. "I need to know, Edinja. Will they do exactly what I tell them with Aphenglow Elessedil?"

She gave him a sharp look. "Why are you suddenly so concerned for her? What are you saying?"

He had unwittingly crossed a line, but he was quick to recover. "This has nothing to do with being concerned for her. I need to know what I can expect of your creatures. If it becomes clear that the best course of action is to kill the girl and seize the Elfstones, then these creatures should be perfect. But what if there is good reason to keep her alive so that she can be brought to you? What if she has information that only you can extract? Will these things let her live or will their animal instincts govern them in spite of what I ask?"

"They will not go against your wishes. They will do as you ask." She paused. "But that's not what's bothering you, is it? You are afraid they might turn on you."

He shrugged. "I would be a fool not to consider the possibility. They don't look as if it would trouble them much." He hesitated. "I want to test them here and now. I want to see if they'll do as I say."

Without answering him, she walked back to the tables on which her creatures lay and released their chains. They sat up at once, cat-quick and eager. But they did not try to attack her. Instead they crouched atop the tables as if waiting for direction.

She looked over her shoulder at him. "Tell them what to do. Tell them to get back into their cages. Give them a command."

He did as she asked. Without hesitating, the three bounded off the tables and loped back across the room to their cages, pulling the doors closed behind them after they were inside. Edinja walked over, snapped shut the locks on the chains that secured the doors, and turned back to him.

"I need the truth behind the failed Druid expedition so that I can understand what is happening. I want you to find the girl and her companions and track them. I want you to discover what it is they seek. If it involves magic in any way, I want to know. I want both of the Elessedil sisters brought here to me. With the Elfstones."

"Is that all?" he deadpanned.

She smiled. "You are my right hand, my steady guide, my dependable and loyal consort. I rely on you to do what is needed."

He shrugged. "I will do my best."

She came over to him, once again took hold of his hands and looked deep into his eyes. "I hope so. Because I will know if you don't."

Then she reached up and kissed him ever so gently on the mouth.

17

APHENGLOW ELESSEDIL SPENT THE FOLLOWING DAY PREPAR-
ing for their departure with Cymrian and Arling. She had thought at
first to send her sister off to the Gardens of Life to be with the other
Chosen, giving the appearance that everything was normal, but she
quickly abandoned that idea. She hadn't forgotten that someone had
been stalking her ever since the day she had uncovered Aleia Omarosian's diary. There was no reason to believe that the danger she had
faced was past or that whoever was behind it had given up. Nor was
there reason to think that the danger to her hadn't spilled over onto
Arling. Whoever was behind it knew about the diary and the Elfstones; why wouldn't they know about the Ellcrys seed, as well?

So she kept Arling close to Cymrian and herself, while preparing
Wend-A-Way for the upcoming flight.

It was not a difficult undertaking. It involved little more than
gathering up materials and weapons, supervising the loading of both
onto the airship, and interviewing the crewmembers Cymrian had
chosen to accompany them. At first she had resisted the idea of taking anyone else. Better to keep this among the three of them. But
Cymrian was quick to point out that he and Aphen alone could not
safely fly the airship. Arling lacked the proper training, and at least
several others would be needed to take shifts at the helm if they were
to get any sleep or if either of them became sick or injured. He was

right, of course, so Aphen backed down, irritated that she had not seen this before he did.

She was also forced to reconsider using the Elfstones before they departed to get a sense of where they were going. Any use of magic would alert other magic users, and those alerted might be the very ones hunting her. She could not be sure this would happen, but there was no point in taking chances. She already knew that what they were hunting was hidden somewhere in the Wilderun. So all they needed to do was to fly there and then use the Elfstones to pinpoint their destination. By then, they would be far enough away that they wouldn't be as likely to be identified.

An air of suspense and expectation infused her efforts during the assembling and loading of supplies and equipment. Time and fate seemed to press down on her in equal measure, urging her to move faster, to perform more quickly, to finish and be off. She worked steadily throughout the day, and more than once caught Cymrian staring at her, a mixture of surprise and disbelief reflected on his lean features.

Once he said to her in passing, "This isn't a race, you know."

To which she had replied, "You're wrong. That's exactly what it is."

Late in the afternoon, the ship almost ready, she told the other two that she intended to say good-bye to Ellich and Jera. She had thought at first she might forgo the visit; it might be better not to speak to anyone before leaving. But she needed to believe that someone cared enough to see her before she left.

Cymrian immediately announced that he was coming with her, but she told him that it would be better if he stayed with Arling and kept watch over her. She didn't say so—she didn't need to—but she was better able to protect herself, and leaving Arling alone with the Ellcrys seed was not a good idea. She promised she would be careful and, after a short visit, would come right back.

She made her way from the airfield and took the roadways that led to her aunt and uncle's home, skirting her own cottage, where Cymrian and Arling had promised to wait for her, and her mother's, where only disdain and disappointment could be found. She turned down smaller roads and finally pathways, and in short order she was standing at the front door, knocking hopefully.

Ellich and Jera provided the succor she needed. Warm and welcoming, they sat her down in their kitchen, fed her hot tea and muffins, and said they would miss her terribly and she must do everything she could to stay safe and well until her return. No mention was made of her sister, and Aphen could not be certain if her uncle had told his wife that Arling was going, too. So Aphen said nothing about her sister's plans, including the fact that Arling now carried the Ellcrys seed and was entrusted with the future not only of the Elven nation but also of the other Races. It was a secret charged with dangerous possibilities, and it made Aphenglow want to bury it so deeply that it could never even be glimpsed.

Throughout their conversation, Aphen was reminded of her own carefully kept secret. The Elfstones were buried deep in a pocket of her cloak, and she found her hand straying to them frequently—an involuntary reflex generated by the need to reassure herself that they were still safely tucked away.

But her visit went well, her self-indulgence in gaining their farewell was satisfied, and she departed with a feeling of contentment.

Twilight was falling by then, and she was reminded of another visit she had made to her aunt and uncle not so very long ago. She had been attacked on her way home on that occasion and forced to kill a man. Almost without thinking about it, she began looking around, peering into the deeper shadows, angling as she walked to parts of the pathway that were still light. Her hand strayed again to the pocket where she had hidden the Elfstones. Foolish of her to obsess like this, she told herself as soon as she realized what she was doing. But she took the Elfstones out of her cloak pocket and put them inside her tunic, where she could feel them pressed close against her body.

She mulled over the details of the departure they had planned for the following day. Their journey would take them out through the Valley of Rhenn and then south past Drey Wood and the swamps below to the Rock Spur and from there to the Wilderun and the peak known as Spire's Reach. The time required would be less than three days by airship. She had not been down into that part of the world, but she knew Cymrian had. She was relying on his experience to see them there safely.

She found herself thinking again about Arling and the enormous struggle she was undergoing. Her sister would be carrying the Ellcrys seed, but with no clear intent of what she would do with it once it was immersed and quickened. If she did not intend to use it herself—and it seemed clear at this point that she did not—she would have to find another Chosen willing to take her place.

A failure by Arling or any of the others to make the sacrifice required to renew the Ellcrys would doom the Elven people and likely the whole of the Four Lands to a fresh war with the demonkind—a war that might never find a resolution. It would betray the heritage of the Elves as protectors of the talisman that had kept the dark creatures of Faerie locked away for all these centuries and return the world to the chaos that had existed before.

Would Arling permit that to happen?

She didn't think so.

But she didn't think her sister would sacrifice her life, either. She didn't think she was capable of it.

She sensed another presence then, her instincts warning her this time, and was quick to respond. Her wards came up at once, and she turned toward the source of the danger. But nothing happened. She listened and stared into the darkness, searching.

Nothing.

Yet she was not mistaken. Something was out there.

She started toward home again, suddenly furious. She was sick of being stalked and attacked and made to feel that she wasn't safe anywhere. She was tired of not knowing who was behind it, always suspicious that it was someone she knew, someone from Arborlon. A secret enemy, a creature with plans about which she knew nothing specific. It wanted the diary and the Elfstones and probably the Ellcrys seedling. It wanted to hurt her and already had. Maybe it wanted her dead. But why was it doing all this? What did it hope to gain?

Then her thoughts flashed again to Arlingfant, waiting in the cottage for her return, and she broke into a frightened run.

She had never run so hard and at the same time taken so long to reach a destination. She imagined a hundred terrible results, a hundred horrific scenes, and she was all but exhausted by the time she tore up the front walkway and burst through the door into their tiny common room with its reading chairs and its small table for eating.

Arling, stepping out from the kitchen, stopped in surprise. "Aphen? What's wrong?"

Aphenglow stopped where she was and scanned the room quickly to reassure herself. "Nothing. Are you all right?"

Her sister stared at her. "Of course I'm all right. You can see that for yourself. But you don't look so good."

Cymrian appeared behind her and took one look at Aphenglow. "What's happened?"

"Something was tracking me—just now—after I left Ellich and Jera. I couldn't see it, but I could feel it." She took a deep breath and exhaled. "It was there, and then it was gone. I was afraid it was coming here."

Cymrian stalked to the windows and peered out, his face grim. "This is the second time you've had something like this happen right after visiting your uncle. That's a big coincidence."

"Wait a minute," Aphen objected. She could see where this was going. "Ellich wouldn't be a part of something like this. I've known him all my life. He's been my friend and supporter and champion the entire time. Even when my mother refused to have anything to do with me, he was always there for me."

"Aphen's right," Arling spoke up. "Uncle Ellich is our best friend—even closer to us than Grandfather."

Cymrian started to say something more, then just nodded. "Whatever the case, we can't stay here any longer. We have to leave. Right now."

"But I'm not ready!" Arling objected at once. "We agreed to wait until tomorrow! We haven't even gotten any sleep!"

"We can sleep on the ship." Cymrian was already moving into the other room where they had packed and stored their personal belongings earlier in the day. "We have everything we need. There's nothing keeping us here. Besides, the weather is changing and not for the better. We should just go." He was rummaging about, moving things. "Finish what you have to do and make ready."

Arling looked at Aphen in despair. "I haven't been to see Mother," she whispered. "I can't go without telling her. Without even saying good-bye? What if . . . ?"

She couldn't finish. Aphen came to bend close and put her arms around her sister's shoulders. "You can't tell Mother what you are doing, anyway. You can't say anything to her. We agreed. None of us can say one word about this to anyone. It has to be kept secret. Mother would understand."

"Mother would understand?" Arling's laugh was quick and shrill. "Are we talking about the same person? Why would you say that? You, of all people!"

"I know. It sounds ridiculous." She could feel the flush come to her cheeks. "But that just reinforces what I'm saying. There's no point in going to see her."

"Not for you, maybe, because she won't talk to you anyway! But she still talks to me. She still relies on me to tell her what's happening. She doesn't have anyone else but Ellich, and he barely speaks to her! I don't intend to tell her anything specific. I just have to tell her I'm leaving so she won't worry when she finds out I'm gone."

"But you can't go to her now, not at this time of night! She'll be asleep. You'll just worry her if you show up in the middle of the night and say you're going away!"

"Which is why I can't go *now*!" Arling snapped, flinging herself away from her sister. "Don't you see?"

Cymrian reappeared. "Quiet down, both of you. You'll wake everyone up and down the lane if you keep this up."

"You stay out of this!" Aphen snapped at him.

He hesitated, then turned around without a word and left the room.

"I have to tell her!" Arling's voice was low and hard, and she stood glaring at Aphen with fists clenched against her sides. She took a deep, calming breath. "What if I don't make it back, Aphen? What if she never sees me again, and I didn't even say good-bye to her?"

Aphen nodded slowly, resigned. "Then I'm going with you. She doesn't need to talk to me. She doesn't even need to know I'm there. But I won't let you go alone."

Arling came to her at once and hugged her. "Thank you for doing this. I'm sorry I yelled. I love you."

"I love you, too," Aphen replied.

They set out at once, hurrying along the pathways that led to their mother's cottage. It was not far away, close enough that Aphen felt reassured they would be all right—especially since Cymrian had insisted on going, too, and was somewhere back in the shadows. She led the way as she usually did, the province of the oldest, and Arling trailed along silently, lost in thought. Aphen had helped her sister pack the Ellcrys seed in a leather pouch that was hidden under her cloak, fastened over one shoulder with a strap. She already regretted getting angry, was embarrassed that she had been so insistent on her not doing this. She knew Arling was still close to their mother, that she felt a special obligation toward her now that Aphen was no longer living in Arborlon. She should have just agreed in the first place and let her sister do what she felt she had to and avoided all the acrimony.

She felt a weariness seep through her. Maybe it was the stalking that was wearing her down. Maybe it was the expectation and worry over what they were about to do. Maybe it was the enormity of what she was undertaking.

And maybe she should just stop trying to make excuses.

She forced herself to pick up the pace.

It was dark and close inside her mother's home, the windows closed, the curtains drawn, the air stale and dry, and the silence deafening. Arling's mother was huddled on a couch set well back in the shadows, her presence apparent by little more than the rough sounds of her breathing and the dark outline of her body.

In Afrengill Elessedil's world, inside the home she almost never left, time had stopped advancing long ago.

Arling fidgeted, searching for a place to begin. She had left Aphenglow and Cymrian waiting outside, her sister's insistence on letting her go in alone unshakable. She knew it was meant to be a gift, a way of removing herself from the meeting so that she would not prove a distraction. If Aphen were to try to come inside with Arling, she would be refused as always, and immediately her mother would become mired in one of her darker moods. Aphen wanted Arling to be able to speak to her mother without that happening, to make this visit be something as close to pleasant as was possible.

But just at the moment it didn't seem in the least possible. Her mother had greeted her with a sullen grunt, clearly less than happy to have her here at this hour. She had motioned Arling to her usual chair, settled herself on the couch, and waited in silence. She had not said one word to her daughter.

Arling now believed that Aphen had been right and that coming here, no matter the depth of her need to see her mother, had been a mistake.

Nevertheless, she resolved to make the best of things.

"Mother, I have to go away for a while," she said finally. "Perhaps for as long as several weeks."

Her mother did not respond, but simply sat there staring at her. Her eyes glittered in the gloom like tiny flecks of starlight.

"I'm sorry to have to come so late at night and with so little notice, but I just learned of my leaving. I didn't want to go without saying good-bye. I didn't want you to worry about me."

She watched her mother's eyes shift slightly, a flicker of movement, and then her mother said, "Is this your sister's doing?"

It caught Arling by surprise, but she was quick to recover. "It has nothing to do with Aphen," she lied. "This is work for the Chosen, a pilgrimage the order requires I undertake."

"Your sister is a bad influence, Arling. She is not to be trusted. I wish it weren't so, but it is. You should stay away from her."

Arling shook her head in denial. "Aphen is a good person, Mother. She doesn't try to influence me or ask things of me." She felt tears fill her eyes. "And she loves you."

"She loves herself and her Druid friends. She loves the power that being a Druid bestows on her. False beliefs and foolish endeavors are what she embraces. She betrayed us all when she chose such things over us."

"Mother, please . . ."

"Stay away from her, Arling. Open your eyes to what she is, and shun her as she has shunned us."

Arling took a deep breath. "Can we speak of something other than Aphen? I came to say good-bye. I just want to tell you . . ."

She trailed off. What did she want to tell her mother? What could she tell her?

Her mother gave a dismissive snort. "Well, go then. Leave me like your sister left me. Abandon me to my sorry, empty life."

"Mother, please! I am not abandoning you."

"By leaving me, you abandon me. Who else will come to see me? Who else will bother to look after me?"

"Uncle Ellich will come. Aunt Jera, too. They'll keep watch over you until I return. If you will let them."

Her mother seemed to draw farther into herself, pulling up her legs and tucking in her arms, becoming a dark, shapeless ball on the couch. "I will miss you, child," she said softly.

The depth of feeling in her words caught Arling by surprise. They emerged sudden and unexpected from amid the anger and sadness, bright and welcome.

"I will miss you, too," she replied quickly. "I will think of you every day until I return."

She got to her feet and went to her mother, enfolding her in her arms in a gentle hug. But her mother was rigid and unresponsive, and Arling held her only for a moment before releasing her again and stepping away.

"I have to go now," she said, desperately wishing she could avoid the need for doing so. It was more than her reluctance to be the bearer of the Ellcrys seed, more even than her fear of what might be required of her once the seed was quickened. Her mother was so alone and needed her so badly; what would she do if Arling failed to return? What would become of her?

"What is it you go to do?" her mother asked suddenly, still huddled on the couch. "What is so important that you would leave me like this?"

Arling almost told her. Why shouldn't she know? Why shouldn't she be made aware of what her daughter faced? Why shouldn't she think well of her for making a sacrifice that would possibly save them all?

"I can't tell you that, Mother," she said finally, backing away from her impulse to say more. "I am sworn to secrecy by the order."

"Yes," her mother said after a long silence. "Like your sister."

Arling felt stung. "This isn't—"

"Go!" Afrengill Elessedil shouted, springing up suddenly from the couch and advancing on her. "Get out of my house! Lies! You tell me lies! Go join your sister and become what she is! That's what you're doing, isn't it? Isn't it?"

Arling shrank from her mother's fury, tried to say something to defend herself and failed. She couldn't find the words, couldn't make herself respond. Instead she turned and fled from the home and her mother, back through the door and into the night. She ran blindly down the pathway until Aphen stepped out of the shadows and caught her up, wrapped her arms around her and held her close.

"Shhh, shhh," her sister whispered. "It's all right. I have you."

Arling nodded, tears streaming down her face. "I know."

But it wasn't all right and might never be again. Even her sister's comforting presence couldn't change that.

On the other side of the darkened house, tucked up under the eaves and close by the window through which it had been listening to Arlingfant and her mother converse, the creature that served Edinja Orle watched as the sisters moved down the walkway and out of sight. Then it dropped to the ground. Long and lean and feral, it flexed its limbs, relieved to be back in its natural state. Or at least the state to which it had been rendered during one of Edinja's ongoing experiments. It had been an Elf once but had fallen under the power of the Federation witch and now served as her eyes and ears within the Elven home city, believed by all to be the one whose identity it had assumed.

But it wasn't that person, of course. That person was long since dead and buried with no one the wiser.

The creature would have preferred to return to its nest. It would have liked to lie down and sleep, but it had a chore to complete first. So it crawled into the trees that crowded up against the back of the house, slinking through the long grasses and between the mossy trunks, safely hidden from prying eyes and chance discovery, until it had reached the cottage where the sisters lived.

Fully reverted to its natural physical state by now, the creature nevertheless retained the memories and intelligence of the Elf it pretended at being. It knew how to act the part. It understood it must remain safe when it was not necessary to go out. It knew to protect itself when its identity was threatened, but to otherwise stay hidden. It knew to report whatever it heard from or about members of the Elessedil family, particularly the old King and the young Druid, back to its mistress. It was instinctive by now; it was an effort that required almost nothing of it.

So it crouched in the darkness and waited, and after a while the sisters emerged carrying packs and weapons, cloaked and hooded and moving cautiously so as not to attract attention.

Too late for that, the creature thought with a sense of satisfaction. Way too late for that.

It began tracking them through the city.

Aphenglow walked with her arm about her sister's shoulders, consoling and reassuring her following their mother's verbal assault. Arling had stopped crying, but seemed beaten down and was leaning against her, head lowered. Sometimes Aphen forgot how young she was. Still so vulnerable. In the distance, storm clouds were mounting an assault, dark thunderheads filling the skies north and west in huge banks. Cymrian had been right about a change in the weather.

Preoccupied with her sister and not really believing that anything would happen when they were this close to the airfield, Aphen failed to sense the creature's presence until right before it attacked.

They were passing through a grove of elm and oak when a black shape hurtled out of the darkness ahead of them and slammed into the sisters. Because Cymrian was trailing, he couldn't respond quickly enough, and the creature was on top of its victims before he could stop it.

All three—the sisters and the creature—went down in a tangled heap. The darkness within the trees was so complete that it was impossible to tell one from the other. Aphen's magic exploded out of her in a flash of brightness that catapulted both the creature and Arling away. The creature had hold of Arling's cloak and tore it from her as it tumbled away. But it was up again almost instantly, coming at the girl once more, trying to get at her a second time. Aphen howled in despair and threw her Druid magic at the creature, knocking it off stride, staggering it. Arling was trying to crawl away, to reach her sister, but she was clearly stunned and seemed unable to make her limbs move.

Then Cymrian flew into the attacker, knives flashing, hammering it backward and away from Arling. The combatants thrashed and twisted as they fought each other, and Aphen saw Cymrian bury one of his knives in the creature's back.

But then the two broke apart, and the creature regained its feet, took a quick look over at Aphen, and raced away into the woods.

Cymrian started to give chase, but Aphen shouted to him. "No! It wants to get you alone!"

The Elven Hunter halted, turning back. "Then let's get to the airship. Now!"

Aphen helped Arling back to her feet. She might have lost her cloak, but her sister had a death grip on the leather pouch that contained the seed. She gave Aphen a determined smile. Other than scratches and bruises to her face and arms, she seemed to be all right.

The three raced ahead through the woods and out into the open road that led to the airfield. Though they watched for the creature, anticipating a further attack, it did not return.

At the edge of the airfield, the creature watched as the sisters and their protector raced over to the Druid airship. A crew of Elves was already aboard, raising light sheaths and fastening radian draws. A flurry of activity ensued as the newcomers boarded and the last of the baggage and supplies were loaded. The anchors were released seconds later, and the airship began her slow, steady ascent into the night sky.

Within minutes, she had turned east toward the Valley of Rhenn.

Which was what the creature had been looking to discover all along, and what its attack had been designed to reveal. It had counted on the attack to disrupt the concentration of the three and cause them to react rather than think.

That way they wouldn't bother trying to hide their choice of escape routes.

The creature bounded away, moving swiftly into the deep woods. Less than a mile away, a distance it covered in less than ten minutes, it reached a small, windowless blockhouse. The building was constructed of heavy stones, its walls sealed up save for a single iron door that was chained and barred. The roof consisted of heavy metal grates that could be removed if you knew where the locking devices could be found and if you could avoid the poison darts that would be triggered if you stepped wrong. Inside, a clutch of arrow shrikes—the messenger birds favored by magic wielders since the days of the Warlock Lord—huddled together, waiting to be dispatched.

The creature leapt onto the roof, lifted off one of the grates, and chose a bird from the second pen. There were two pens; the birds in the first were meant for the mistress and those in the second for her man. How the bird managed to find either, the creature neither knew nor cared. Holding the bird gently, the way it had been taught, the creature told the bird without speaking but with images formed in its mind what it wanted the bird to tell the man.

Then it released the bird, waited until the winged messenger was out of sight, and silently bounded away, back toward the city.

18

It was just after midnight when *Wend-A-Way* lifted off, a sleek and silent shadow silhouetted against a sky rapidly filling with dark clouds that already blocked the quarter moon and stars. Cymrian was at the helm, and the crew of three worked the lines and sails, channeling the power from the diapson crystals nestled in their parse tubes port and starboard, drawing down stored power in the absence of direct light. They rode a southeasterly wind that blew chill and brisk from out of the deeper darkness of an approaching storm that promised heavy weather within the next several hours. Cymrian ordered the light sheaths rolled back and the radian draws made fast as the wind quickened and the yaw of the vessel increased from slight to heavy.

"This won't be pleasant!" he shouted over the wind's whistle to where Arlingfant and Aphenglow huddled together forward of the pilot box.

Neither had to be told. Both knew enough of airships and storms to recognize what was coming, but Aphenglow, as the more experienced flier, was especially concerned. The size of the front and the strength of the wind told her this would be very bad, and they might even have to put down somewhere until it passed. If that proved necessary, it would remove any advantage they might have gained by leaving Arborlon in secret and under the cover of darkness.

But there was no help for it. The weather wasn't something anyone could control—not yet, at any rate, although there were rumors of efforts aimed in that direction by the newly emboldened scientists of the Federation, who claimed to be on the brink of developing a way to use diapson crystals to manipulate natural forces. Aphenglow hoped that wasn't true. If it were, it would open the door to the possibility of a power struggle that would eclipse anything the Four Lands had seen since the time of the Great Wars.

She took a moment to consider the possibility, a dark forewarning of something she had thought about before. The Druids had feared for some time now that diapson weapons even more destructive and dangerous than those already employed by the Federation were on the horizon. How could it not happen, with the Races and governments of the Four Lands constantly at war, each seeking a way to gain the upper hand? A confrontation between those who cultivated and employed magic, mostly Elves, and those who embraced science, mostly Men, was inevitable. She did not know what form that confrontation between past and present would take, and did not think she would be there to see it, but it would come.

Overhead, the mainsail billowed under the thrust of the wind, and the radian draws sang like discordant harp strings.

"Some wind," Arling said, leaning close. Her dark eyes were big, and the concern on her oval face gave her the look of a child.

"Are you all right?" Aphenglow asked, looking deep in her sister's eyes. "About what you are setting out to do, I mean?"

Arling shook her head. "I don't know. I guess so. I've come to terms with things. I know what is needed if the Ellcrys is to live, and I want her to. I know what it means to all of us. Not just to the Elves, but to everyone in the Four Lands. She has to be renewed if the Forbidding is to hold, and it must hold. What else is there to say?"

"That you don't want it to be your responsibility. That you don't want this to happen."

"Too late for that. It's happened already. I have been given the seed. So now it's mine. I am settled on that, Aphen. I am."

"But you don't want this. You've said so repeatedly."

Her sister reached out and put an arm around her, pulling her close. "I don't think any of us wanted most of what's been given to us these past few weeks. We didn't want any of it to happen. But it has. I think I understand what that means. It means we must exercise grace in the face of fear and doubt and loss of belief. It means we must understand that this is how life works—that it challenges us; it tests us. It gives us burdens to bear, and the measure of who we are is how we manage those burdens. I don't wish to have mine. Of course I don't. But what sort of person would I be if I refused them? Or cast them away?"

Aphen said nothing, letting the matter drop there, not sure if her sister had convinced herself that she could transfer the seed to a different successor. Something else was at work here, but it seemed clear that Arling didn't want to talk about it.

She leaned into her sister. "That was well said," she said. "I admire you for it."

Arling bent her head into her arms. Her shoulders shook. She might have been laughing or crying, Aphen couldn't tell which. "*You* admire *me*? Don't you have that backward?"

"No. You have courage and determination and great heart." She gripped her sister's arm and squeezed hard. "Do me a favor. Lend me some of each. All three have been drained away from me."

Arling snorted. "I doubt that!" Then, without looking at her, her sister punched her hard on her arm. "There. Now you have them. All three. Use them wisely."

"Aphen!" Cymrian shouted down at her from the pilot box. "Get up here!"

She left Arling and groped her way around the walls of the box and climbed inside. Rain as well as wind was lashing *Wend-A-Way* by this time, the storm's fury building steadily. Cymrian gestured behind him, and she turned to see an enormous black cloud bearing down on them rapidly—a massive giant that would engulf them within minutes.

"Where are we?" she shouted.

He pointed. She could just make out the pillars that framed the pass at the far end of the Valley of Rhenn. "If we can make that and get safely through, we will have some shelter on the lee side of the hills when we swing south. But we'll have to hurry!"

Wend-A-Way lurched ahead, running at the front of the storm, her crew scrambling like madmen to keep her aloft and steady. The force of the wind increased, howling with fresh fury, the rain pummeling the decks of the airship and her passengers with droplets that stung like needles. Aphen crouched next to Cymrian, who had to stand in order to maneuver the controls and keep the vessel from smashing into the valley walls. She peered through the shroud of gloom and rain, watching the pillars appear and then vanish as if everything were a mirage and nothing was real.

Time slowed, and for a few desperate minutes their flight toward the pillars seemed endless. Aphen was certain they were going down, and she shouted to Arling to get off the deck and inside the pilot box with her. But her sister didn't seem to hear, hunkered forward of the wall, her head lowered and her shoulders hunched, wrapped within her cloak.

Abruptly, they were abreast of the cliffs, the stone monoliths stark and jagged to either side. The ship yawed heavily and then, with breathtaking suddenness, catapulted through the opening as if shooting rapids on a raging river.

Wend-A-Way rode the tide of wind and rain and, once clear of the pass, Cymrian swung the bow sharply starboard and down along the forested heights beyond. *Wend-A-Way* shuddered, then lurched ahead into a patch of diminished turbulence where she found her footing and steadied once more.

Impulsively, Aphenglow leapt to her feet and threw her arms around Cymrian, laughing like a child.

A short distance farther south, concealed within a defile that opened deep into the cliffs bordering the pass and with a clear view of it, Stoon stood on the foredeck of a Federation warship and watched the first gusts of windblown rain sweep past the opening of his hiding place. With him waited the warship's captain and crew, a rough bunch whom he had accepted without question, all of them chosen by Edinja Orle and presumably loyal to her. They seemed competent enough as sailors, and they handled the airship with experienced hands. So as long as they obeyed his orders, he was content to let them go about their business.

The mutants were another matter. Tucked away down in the hold, they were out of sight if not out of mind. If Stoon had his way, they would stay that way until the end of time. They might have started out as men, but now they were beasts of a sort that made him shiver when he was near them. So far they had followed his directives on the few occasions he had given orders—but he was not convinced he could depend on them to do so when it mattered. They reminded him of hunting dogs—reliable when they were in their kennels, but unpredictable when they sensed prey.

In spite of Edinja's reassurances, he had reason to worry that at some point they might turn on him.

The captain of the warship came up to him. "This storm is much worse than I thought it would be. It might be wise to stay here until it passes."

Advice Stoon did not think the man should be giving him, but he only nodded and said, "If the ship we track passes us, storm or no, we will go after her. That is a direct order, Captain."

The other man nodded, tight-lipped and sullen, and stalked away. He knew who was in charge here. That much was certain. Stoon was confident Edinja would not undercut his authority deliberately. Not when she wanted so badly to discover what was happening with the Druids and their mysterious search. The shrike's message had made it clear that the Elven airship was coming their way. She would have to pass through the Valley of Rhenn before setting any further course. Odds were good that she was heading east or south. From their position in this defile, he would be able to tell which.

He lifted the spyglass to his eye and scanned the mouth of the pass, his tall, lean form bending forward out of habit as he did so. No sign of her yet. Sometime soon she would appear, unless the storm grew so bad it obscured everything. That was a risk, of course, but there was nothing he could do about the storm. Not that Edinja would see it that way if he lost his quarry now. But positioning themselves directly in front of the pass made no sense at all. It was dangerous enough to get this close. He still didn't like it that he was tracking the Elessedil girl. Even the idea of it was unsettling. But he could not go against Edinja, no matter how he felt. So he had resolved to make the best of it.

He lowered the spyglass and rocked back on his heels. He wondered again about the spy Edinja had placed in the Elven camp. He understood better now where her spy might have come from after having watched her change those three men into mutants. Perhaps it, too, was a form of mutant answerable only to her. But who could get close enough to the Elessedils and their friends to gain access to the information she was now privy to and still not draw suspicion? How had she managed that?

There was no way of knowing, of course. Not unless she chose to tell him, and she was unlikely to do that. Perhaps at some point he might meet this mysterious person. But for now, the spy was little more than the sum of the messages sent by the shrikes.

In the distance, something moved against the deep blackness of the storm. He brought up the spyglass quickly and studied the murky roil at the mouth of the pass.

An airship.

Smaller than his own and sleeker, a vessel built for speed and maneuverability.

He turned at once. "Ready the ship, Captain. We're going out."

Aboard the *Wend-A-Way*, Aphenglow had relieved Cymrian at the helm and was steering the airship on a steady course south along the Westland forests bordering the Streleheim. The storm had swept through the pass behind them, rolling across the whole of the upper Westland in the process, all blackness and fury as it gave chase. Aphen could tell already that they were not going to be able to outrun it; the best they could do was ride it out. Failing that, they would have to set down somewhere along the way and wait until it passed.

But the plains offered little in the way of shelter, and trying to set down in the forest during a blow of this magnitude was dangerous. She had already resolved that unless they were in danger of crashing, they would do neither.

"Arling, get up here!" she shouted at her sister.

This time Arling responded, climbing to her feet and making her way around the pilot box to the opening that allowed her to climb inside. Cymrian was gone by now, out working the lines with the crewmen. Fearless, that one. Aphen smiled at the memory of the look on his face when she had hugged him. Shock and pleasure both—she liked that. He hadn't known what to make of her impulsive gesture, but he had clearly welcomed it. She thought about how far they had come in their once-strained relationship, how much more comfortable they had grown with each other. They were friends now, and their friendship transcended the mistrust and suspicion that had kept them at odds before.

She could almost imagine having him around on a regular basis. Almost.

But she was wary of getting close to people just now, even as friends. She was still hurting from the loss of Bombax. She was still devastated by the destruction of the Druid order and the decimation of its Troll guard. She had been close to all of them, and the pain of their deaths discouraged her from seeking new friendships of any sort. Now there was Arling to worry about, as well. It was difficult for her to let herself become close to others, and she thought it would be a long time before she could do so again.

Not that she didn't appreciate having Cymrian there. Not that she would have wanted it to be any other way.

She watched him move among the other Elves, swift and sure-footed, his white-blond hair plastered against his head in the rain, his clothing already soaked. He seemed tireless to her, impervious to exhaustion and weakness. She marveled that he could always seem so fit and ready when she felt so worn.

As the wind blew with fierce purpose and the rain sheeted in torrents across the decking, she stood at the helm in the darkness and wished again that things could be different.

Arling nudged her arm. "We should put down, Aphen. We're going to rip apart!"

But Aphenglow shook her head. "She can take it. *Wend-A-Way* is built to withstand this."

She said it, but she wasn't entirely sure it was so. The storm was on top of them now, a monstrous force of nature, and it felt as if every wire and plank and nail were rattling. It was taking everything Aphen had to hold the ship even marginally steady as she jerked and yawed sideways and underwent sudden, breathtaking drops. She found herself wondering how much power was left in the diapson crystals; a storm like this one would drain their power quickly. If they had to try to change out the crystals in this sort of weather, it would be an unbelievably treacherous job.

Arling was clinging to her arm, holding on as if doing so were the only way she could stay safe. Aphen let her, finding fresh strength in her sister's touch, in the clear sense of dependency. It made her want to wrap Arling in her cloak and shelter her from the world. It made her want to find a way to keep her safe forever from the dark things that were coming to steal her away.

"Aphen!"

Cymrian was beside her suddenly, pressing close to be heard. His face was slicked with rain and drawn with tension. "There's an airship tracking us. There."

He pointed beyond the stern of *Wend-A-Way* into the blackness. Aphen peered into the gloom.

"I don't see it."

"Wait for the lightning!"

A second later a jagged streak lit up the sky, and she saw it. A warship, she thought, big and black within the roiling center of the storm. "What do we do about it?"

He gave her a puzzled look. "What do you think? We lose it."

Stoon realized too late that the Federation warship was overtaking the smaller craft. Sensing the danger, he screamed at the captain to slow her down, and when the captain failed to respond quickly enough, he raced back from the bow to confront the man. But by then the damage was done. The Elves had seen them, and their airship had put on a burst of speed and was flying west toward the cover of the forest.

Raging at the captain for his stupidity, Stoon ordered the warship to give pursuit. They had lost the advantage of surprise, their identity and likely their intent revealed. The best he could hope for now, even after all his care and planning, was to force the other vessel down and make prisoners of her passengers. What the chances were of that, he had no idea. At least, it would give him a chance to see firsthand how effective his hunters were, how obedient to his orders. He almost hoped it would end with all of them dead, Elves and mutants alike. He would risk what that would mean when he returned to Edinja, just to have this business behind him.

But maybe it would all go another way. Maybe the mutants would prove more than a match for the Elven girl. Maybe they would be stronger than her magic. Maybe they would dispatch the crew and overpower her, she could become his prisoner, and he would cart her off to face Edinja in the privacy of her dungeons.

Staying close now to the captain, afraid to leave his side for fear that he would do something else stupid, Stoon searched the blackness ahead, peering through sheets of rain and shifting phantasms of gloom and mist. The edges of the forest loomed, vast and sprawling, just visible as the warship drew close.

Then lightning flashed anew, and the assassin saw everything ahead of them clearly revealed.

The Elven airship was gone.

19

---◆---

APHENGLOW WAS SHAKEN AWAKE FROM A DEEP SLEEP, LOST IN a dream that she immediately forgot. She was so disoriented that for a moment she could not remember where she was.

"Aphen, wake up."

Cymrian. She could not see him. She struggled against the blanket wrapped about her, aware that she was lying on hard planking. The smells of damp wood and caulking overlaid with pungent aromas of old-growth forest invaded her senses, and she remembered.

She sat up too quickly, struck her forehead against a low crossbeam, and was immediately dizzy. She slumped back, trying to find her balance. Hands caught her and held her. Cymrian again. "Steady."

"Where are we?"

"Hiding. But it's time to move along. It will be daylight soon, and that warship will be searching for us."

She nodded, her head against his chest. She could smell the damp in his clothing. "The storm?"

"Passed about an hour ago. It went on for hours. Worst I've seen in quite a while."

"But they didn't find us?"

"They didn't find us."

She remembered the rest then. They had sprinted ahead recklessly to outdistance the larger ship, catching her off balance while she was still at half speed, and had reached a jumble of rolling terrain where they were able to slip down into a heavily shadowed gap in the forest. They could not have been easily seen from the air even in good weather. In the wildness of the storm, they were virtually invisible. Resting less than ten feet above the ground and surrounded by trees much taller than the ship's mainmast, they had hovered in silence and watched the larger ship pass overhead without slowing.

Not wanting to risk discovery by moving again too soon and less than eager to put themselves back in the air in the teeth of that storm, they had decided to lay low for several hours. Cymrian had persuaded the sisters to bed down belowdecks, and Aphen had gone straight to sleep.

She lifted her head away from his chest, swallowing against the dryness in her mouth. "Arling?"

"Topside already. She was awake before you."

She started to get to her feet, her dizziness fading. Cymrian's hands still held her, even though she had not asked him to, guiding her from a prone to a standing position. *Wend-A-Way* was steady, no sway or rock to her, and even though she must still be hovering, it felt to Aphen as if they were settled on the ground.

"Did she come back again after missing us on the first pass?"

"The warship? No. We've been alone since then. I don't think they could have retraced their route even if they had tried. Not in that storm." One of his hands moved to her arm. "Come. Walk with me. Give your eyes a chance to adjust."

She allowed him to guide her to the wooden ladder that led from belowdecks. She climbed obediently, catching a hint of light through the open hatch. But when she arrived on deck, she found the world a place of heavy mist and layered clouds that closed away the sky and shut out the moon and stars. Ambient light that lacked an identifiable source reflected off particles of rain and mist, a wraith's glow that lit the whole of the hazy shroud in which they were wrapped.

Arling was standing by the port railing watching the Elven crewmen, who were changing out the diapson crystals. She turned at the sound of her sister's approach and smiled. "You were so sound asleep, I didn't want to wake you."

Aphen laughed. "Do you see anything out there?"

"Only mist and more mist. Cymrian says we need to lift off and find our course again before it clears."

One of the Elven crewmen glanced over. "The sooner, the better. That was a Federation vessel chasing us."

Aphen turned. "Federation? You're sure of that?"

The man nodded. "I'd know one of those black devils anywhere."

"You have to wonder what they thought they were doing," said another. "We're too quick for anything that big. Too easy for us to hide, too, in these mountains."

"Still," said the first. "Better if we don't take chances."

"Let's eat something before we leave," Aphen suggested, turning away.

So bread, salted meat, and fruit were brought out from the food storage locker and consumed with glasses of ale. The crew joined the sisters and Cymrian, but no one had much of anything to say, content to remain in silence. Aphen's dizziness had finally passed. When it was time to set out, she told Cymrian that she would man the helm. To his credit, he didn't offer any objection and instead moved to the bow to take up the forward watch.

Arling moved into the pilot box beside her sister and stood without speaking as the anchors were raised and the airship began to lift off. The plan was to move back to the edge of the Westland forests in which they were hidden, continue south past Drey Wood and the Pykon, and make their way into the Wilderun. The heavy mist should hide them from discovery, and with any luck at all it would last for a few hours past sunrise. The chances of encountering the Federation warship again would be lessened considerably if they flew low against the backdrop of forests and mountains and kept careful watch for what lay ahead of them. They would fly swiftly and without stopping until they were at the Wilderun, manning *Wend-A-Way* in shifts and outdistancing their pursuit using a combination of speed and endurance.

It was a solid enough plan, but like all plans it could go wrong quickly if chance and bad luck combined to thwart it. So no one was taking anything for granted, and everyone was prepared for the unexpected.

The sisters and Cymrian discussed using the Elfstones to track the progress and position of the Federation warship in order to gain an edge in the pursuit, but in the end chose not to. The problem was the same as before—using the Elfstones could give them away to any magic users looking for them, and they had no way of knowing if there was one such aboard the warship. Aphen was pretty sure there was magic at work somewhere in this business, given the nature of the attacks on her in Arborlon and the seeming ability of whoever was carrying them out to know each time exactly when to strike. It wasn't a risk worth taking, especially since a single use of the Elfstones would not be enough to guarantee escape and more than one use would be tempting fate.

They decided to hold off on employing the Elfstones until either the need was so obvious they could not pretend otherwise or they were close enough to the Bloodfire that it became necessary to pinpoint its source. Caution and sharp eyes and ears would better serve them at this point.

It was a view that was borne out as time passed and the mist remained thick and impenetrable. Aphen eased *Wend-A-Way* ahead at a slow, steady pace, keeping the airship just above the treetops, doing her best to make the airship disappear into the haze.

She found herself wondering if this had anything to do with Edinja Orle. It had to be someone in the Coalition Council hierarchy if they could command a warship like the one hunting her. But what was the point? If they knew of the failing of the Ellcrys, why would they want to prevent its recovery? The danger to them was as great as it was to the Elves. Could they be hunting her for the Elfstones, for the magic they commanded? Edinja was a magic user. Perhaps the temptation of gaining possession of the Elfstones was too strong for her to ignore.

Her gaze was directed forward into the screen of mist and damp, and it settled now on Cymrian, a fixture against the forward railing just to the starboard side of the bowsprit. She found herself staring at him, fascinated by the fact that he had been standing motionless in that same spot for the entire time since they had set out.

"How does he do that?" she whispered to Arling.

"Do what?"

"Stand like that for so long without moving."

Arling glanced at her first, then out at Cymrian. "I don't know." She paused. "He's a patient man. You, of all people, should realize that."

"I suppose that's so. I've watched him."

"Watched him?" Arling gave a soft snort.

"I don't mean just here. At other times, too. Lots of times. He knows how to wait on things."

Arling shook her head. "You are so hopeless."

Aphen looked at her. "What does that mean?"

"It means that sometimes you don't see anywhere near as much as people give you credit for." She gave her sister a look. "I thought you would have figured it out by now, Aphen."

"Figured what out? What are you talking about?"

"Cymrian. I'm talking about Cymrian!" Arling gave an exasperated groan. "You still don't understand what he's doing here? Why he came in the first place? Why he's put himself in such danger for the both of us when he just as well could have stayed safe and sound back in Arborlon?"

Aphenglow hesitated. "Well, he . . ." She brushed back her hair where it had fallen over her eyes, damp strands knotting. "What are you saying?"

"I'm saying he's in love with you!"

Aphen frowned. "No, he's not."

"He is. He has been for years. You wouldn't know because you've been all caught up in your Druid life and haven't paid any attention at all to what's going on back here, but he's been in love with you since you were in training together, years ago. I think everyone knew it—even if they didn't tell you."

"But that's just ridiculous! He barely knows me. Or I him. I didn't even remember who he was, at first!"

Arling gave her a look. "Yes, you're right. How could anyone you don't remember still be in love with you years later?"

They stopped talking for a while, staring out at the mist in silence, concentrating on the movement of the airship through the haze. At the bow, Cymrian brought up his hand sharply and signaled for

Aphenglow to swing to the starboard as they altered course. Aphen watched the terrain below them change as the trees began to thin and grasslands to appear. They were back out on the lower Streleheim, clear of the forests and heading south.

"You're serious about this, aren't you?" Aphen said finally.

Arling nodded, keeping silent.

"But he's never said . . ." She trailed off.

"He wouldn't. He's not like that."

Aphen shook her head in disbelief. The idea of Cymrian being in love with her was so unexpected, she could not bring herself to accept that it was possible. But he must have had a reason for agreeing to be her protector back at the beginning. She had been so dismissive of the idea—and of him—that she might have missed the truth. Then afterward, she had been mourning Bombax, and there had been so many changes and upheavals in all their lives that she hadn't questioned his motives or his presence but simply accepted both as a given.

"Listen to me, Aphen," her sister said suddenly. "I'm telling you this because I think it's time you knew. Way past time, in fact. But I know how you are. You see what you think you need to see and miss other things in the process. This is one of them. Cymrian's put his life on the line for us. Repeatedly. He's doing so again now. I think you need to understand why he's doing it. On the other hand, I don't want you telling him that you know. Or worse, that you think it's a mistake. You're already thinking of telling him that, aren't you?"

Aphen shrugged. "He shouldn't be doing this because he thinks he loves me!" She sounded indignant, even to herself, as if this whole effort on Cymrian's part were some sort of personal affront. She shook her head in dismay and held up her hand in a warding gesture. "I didn't mean that. That was wrong."

"Yes, but you said it to me and you probably would have said it to him." Arling was scolding her now, something she almost never did. "Don't. Keep this to yourself. If you don't want to love him back, fine. But don't diminish his sacrifice for us by telling him he shouldn't have made it. You don't know what he's been through, and you shouldn't assume that what he's done is a mistake."

Aphen stared at her and then smiled. "You are such a fierce little bird, Arling Elessedil."

But Arling didn't smile back. "Maybe it's because I'm being forced to grow up all at once, and I can't afford to be timid."

Aphen let the smile drop. "All right. I'll do what you ask. It bothers me, but I won't let what I know get in the way of things. I promise."

Her sister nodded and put a grateful hand on her shoulder. Aphen turned back to the task of steering the airship and searching the shifting haze, mulling over what she had been told, trying it on for size the way she would a new set of boots.

What she found was that she wasn't at all sure about the fit.

Stoon stood watch on the forward deck of the Federation warship, growing increasingly worried as he stared out at the mist breaking up beyond their cliffside hiding place.

Once it had become clear they had lost the Elven ship in the storm, he had ordered the captain to turn their own vessel south and make for calmer air and better weather. He had considered for perhaps ten seconds turning back and searching for their quarry, but then quickly abandoned the idea as foolish. They would never find anyone in the morass of wind-driven rain and fog assailing them. Better to give it up until the weather improved.

So he had taken a calculated risk. The Elven ship had left Arborlon by way of the Valley of Rhenn and turned south. It was a better-than-even bet that their destination lay in that direction, probably much farther away than closer. Given the supplies they had stocked aboard and the size of the airship, he could assume they were anticipating at least several days' travel there and several more back. He could also assume they would resume their previous course on their way down, and if he didn't get too far south himself, they would cross paths again.

By morning, his ship had escaped the storm and gotten down into the stretch of Westland forest known as Drey Wood. Here, still north of the Matted Brakes and the Pykon, they had found another hiding place for their ship, this time edging far enough back into the trees that there was almost no chance they could be seen. Once in place, Stoon had dispatched a pair of flits with orders to place themselves at strategic points where they would have a clear view of the plains and any airships passing south. With the storm dissipated and the mist breaking up, they should have no trouble finding the one they were searching for. Once they did, they were to slip away and return to the warship quickly enough for her crew to mobilize and intercept their quarry.

This was twice now he had tried this approach, and at the start of things he'd had reason to think that this time he might be more successful. But now it was well past midafternoon and there was still no sign of the Elven vessel. More than once he had thought to abandon his hiding place and go out in search of it himself. But he had managed to tamp down the urge, knowing that a mistake at this point would likely put an end to any chance he had of managing to intercept it.

Still, he had to admit to himself that he was no longer particularly interested in tracking the Elves. It was conceivable he still might be able to follow the Elven girl, as Edinja wanted. But realistically he thought this was now impossible. The warship had been seen, so the Elven girl and her companions not only knew they were being pursued but that it was a Federation vessel pursuing them. Better, he thought, just to bring the Elven ship down and put a quick end to her passengers and crew, as he had decided to do earlier. This chase needed to be over and done with.

He scuffed his boot on the decking, conflicted. Increasingly, Edinja was using him in ways that were troublesome. He was an assassin, and he preferred to work alone when he hunted. Instead, he was saddled with those animals down in the hold and with a captain and crew who were reluctant and in need of watching. For the first time since he had terminated his partnership with Drust Chazhul, he found himself missing the man. Even though he had overreached his grasp at the end, Drust had always known how Stoon could best serve him. Edinja seemed to think there were no limits, possibly because she saw no limits in herself. Drust had lacked Edinja's power and prestige in the Federation hierarchy and he had never possessed her cunning, but he had been predictable. Stoon had always known what to expect from him.

He exhaled sharply, frustrated. Shouldn't the Elven vessel have reached them by now if it was coming this way? He wondered again at its purpose. All these Druid expeditions—what were they attempting to accomplish? Edinja was convinced that it was important for her to know, but what did she care why the Druids had mounted their expedition into the Westland? How reliable was the intelligence they had been given by the spy she had placed in the Elven camp? The information had been sketchy at best. That was true of this latest expedition, as well. No reason had been given for why the Elven girl was leading it or why she had taken her sister with her. No suggestion had been offered as to what it had to do with the still unresolved expedition taken by the remainder of the Druid order.

Too many unknowns.

Gaining possession of the Elfstones was the only thing that mattered, and Edinja didn't need the Elessedil sisters alive to accomplish that. Taking them prisoner felt like a waste of time. Edinja was a magic user; surely she could find a way to unlock the Stones' fabled power.

His brow furrowed and a dark look settled over his face. He didn't like how things were going. He didn't like it that he was being dragged this way and that by the reports the spy was giving and as a consequence was much less the master of his own destiny.

Maybe it was time to change all that.

As if in response to that thought, a flit appeared, winging toward the warship.

"The mist is breaking up," Arling murmured, still standing next to Aphen in the pilot box.

"No more cover while we're in the air," Aphen agreed.

As planned, they had eased their way south along the border of the Westland, hiding in the brume as they found their way to the beginning of Drey Wood. Now they were midway down its eastern edge, heading for the Matted Brakes, and there had been no sign of the Federation warship.

Cymrian was already making his way back to them in his easy, loping stride, his hair whipped by a fresh breeze that had started up out of the south.

"You should give him a chance," Arling said.

Aphen did not reply, letting the comment hang unanswered. She kept trying to picture him as someone in love with her, but couldn't quite manage it. All she could see was the wry, taciturn protector who had first come to her in Arborlon to apply for the job all those weeks ago.

"Let me take the wheel for a while," he said, climbing into the box. "Fresh eyes are needed. Mine are worn out."

Without a word, she stepped away and went down onto the main deck, heading for the bow. Around her, the three Elven crewmembers worked the rigging, attaching and detaching radian draws, bringing up fresh sails, reconfiguring light sheaths to catch more of the sun's rays as the mist dissipated in the growing brightness.

I don't want him to be in love with me, Aphen thought.

She caught a flash of something dark off the starboard bow as a shadow emerged from Drey Wood in ominous silence, sliding out of the trees. A warship, her light sheaths unfurled and billowing out, her railguns and fire launchers pulled forward and ready for use, and her ramming bow extended and locked, was coming directly toward them.

"Cymrian!" she screamed in warning.

She was an instant too late. A single burst from the forward starboard railgun tore away a portion of the mainmast rigging, splintering spars and shredding portions of the light sheaths. One of the crewmen was caught directly in the blast and disappeared over the side.

Cymrian reacted swiftly, drawing back on the thrusters and taking *Wend-A-Way* skyward at such a steep angle that Aphen lost her footing and slid all the way to the stern railing before she caught herself. The remaining Elven crewmen hung on as the masts and rigging swayed and shook with the force and suddenness of the lift. Aphen heard other railguns release and felt the impact as dozens of metal projectiles slammed into *Wend-A-Way*'s hull in staccato bursts, splintering timbers and planks, embedding themselves in the wood.

But Cymrian had made the right choice by lifting away rather than diving and so prevented further damage to the sails and rigging. The warship angled upward in response to his maneuver, sweeping hard to port to bring the rest of her railguns and the bulk of her fire launchers into play. Cymrian had anticipated this, however, and executed a controlled fall that took *Wend-A-Way* down and out of range in a quick sweep to the south, increasing speed as she went, leaving the warship with weapons trained on empty blue sky.

Even so, *Wend-A-Way* had suffered sufficient damage to her primary light sheaths that gathering fresh power would require changing them out, and that was time the Elves could not afford to take. So they flattened out parallel to the grasslands and drew as much power as the diapson crystals could expend in an effort to outdistance their pursuer. Aphen regained her feet and stumbled back to the pilot box to rejoin Cymrian and Arling, and the crewmen positioned themselves where they could manipulate the rigging and sails.

Aphen glanced over her shoulder and saw that the warship was already coming after them, huge against the backdrop of the northern horizon.

"We don't have weapons enough to stop her," Cymrian shouted when he saw where she was looking. "Can you use the Elfstones or your magic to help?"

She made a quick measurement of the distance. "I can try."

She leapt out of the pilot box and rushed to the stern railing, having already decided what she would do. She didn't want to risk using the Elfstones in this situation. Her footing and balance on the airship were too uncertain, and if she dropped even one of the Stones, the search for the Bloodfire was effectively over. She would use her Druid magic instead. She lacked the strength of a practitioner such as Bombax or even Seersha; her practical usage was of a more nuanced variety. She would deter rather than try to disable their pursuer. Cutting radian draws and shredding light sheaths might help, but a Federation warship of that size carried too much sail and rigging to be effectively stalled out unless Aphen let her get right on top of them before striking—and then Aphen would probably only get one chance. At best, it would be extraordinarily risky to try. Better to keep their enemy at arm's length and not limit herself to a single chance.

Steady.

She dropped to one knee against the heavy railing and braced herself. With her arms stretched out toward the warship, she began to use words of power and accompanying gestures, feeling the magic surge through her as she created wind out of still air to either slow or turn aside their pursuit. She felt the force of her magic release and could actually see the turbulence it caused. The Federation airship's sails collapsed on themselves and the vessel bucked against the force of her attack. But then the airship came on again. However many diapson crystals she was using to power her engines, it was more than sufficient to overcome Aphen's magic.

Aphen watched the warship draw closer.

Don't panic.

Then she dispatched a swarm of hornets into the faces of the men aboard the airship, and for a moment everything turned to chaos. Everyone aboard ran screaming and shouting, swinging their arms to fend off the stinging insects, all of them abandoning their posts to find shelter. But she could not sustain the attack, and not enough damage was done to cause the pursuit to fall off.

Think!

Efforts at setting fire to the vessel's sails and decking fell apart as the crew quickly extinguished the flames. An attempt to damage the controls failed, as well. Too much shielding warded them, and the distance was too great for her to make a precision strike.

By now the airship was much closer, her black hull looming over the smaller ship, her ramming bow pointed directly toward Aphen.

"Aphen!" Cymrian shouted, desperation surfacing in his voice.

On the mainmast, the *Wend-A-Way*'s crew was engaged in changing out the light sheaths, working frantically to set their rigging and attach radian draws that would siphon off fresh power for the diapson crystals. But it was all going to be too late. The warship would be on them before the effort could be completed.

"Aphen, get out of there!" Cymrian screamed.

But she held her ground stubbornly. If she were to be given only one chance, she would take it, no matter the risk. She watched the warship draw close enough that she could make out the individual planking nails, the knots on the cleats, the openings in the parse tubes, and, most terrifying of all, the muzzles of the fire launchers swinging down to take aim.

Swiftly she summoned and gathered together the magic she needed, staying calm as she watched the warship draw even with them.

Then, at what she believed to be the last moment, she released all of it in a thunderbolt of power. It exploded out of her in a fiery burst that struck the Federation warship's mainmast and broke it in two. Down came the top three-quarters, dragging with it all of the light sheaths and rigging, whereupon everything burst into flames.

But an instant later the fire launchers aboard the Federation ship fired a broadside barrage that raked *Wend-A-Way*'s decks from bow to stern. Planking and railing splintered and burst apart. The charge that struck closest to Aphen razored off a section of railing and balustrades that slammed into her head, flinging her backward. Explosions rocked the Elven vessel, and fires broke out all across the decking.

Aphenglow remained conscious just long enough to realize that the entire length of the Elven ship had been swept clean, everyone had disappeared in a mix of fire and smoke and ash, and the ship was going into a steep, precipitous dive. Then everything went black.

20

◆

REDDEN OHMSFORD WOKE FROM A RESTLESS SLEEP AND immediately wondered whether this was the day he would finally be killed. He lay on his bed of straw in his darkened cell, the stone block walls damp with moisture and the air chill and stale. There were no windows and only a single heavy door. A tiny horizontal slit cut into the door's thick wood admitted a glimmer of light from pitch-coated torches burning in the hallway and a hint of fresh air that wafted down into the depths into which he had been cast.

Here, any semblance of normal life had been extinguished. No sounds, no movements, no anything. Hallways like the one without, doors similar to his, and a pervasive suffocating silence that shrouded everything. He knew this much only because of what he had seen while being brought here by his jailers. How long ago had it been now? Days? Weeks? He had no way of telling. This deep underground, time stopped entirely. He ate and drank his prisoner's meals, he slept on the straw in his squalid accommodations, he sat in the darkness and fought to keep his fears and doubts in check, and he waited for the inevitable.

At some point in time, they were going to kill him. They were going to come for him and they were going to drag him out. And no matter how hard he pleaded with them, they were going to kill him.

They would kill the Ard Rhys, as well, if they hadn't already done so. He had no way of knowing at this point if she were alive or dead. He hadn't seen her since the two of them had been brought to this fortress, to this massive sprawling complex of walls and towers and battlements built of black stone rimmed in iron and situated on a bluff that rose a thousand feet above the lands beneath it. Here inside the Forbidding, this keep was the home of the Straken Lord and the seat of the supreme power that dominated this monstrous world.

The journey to reach their imprisonment had been nightmarish. They had been hauled in wagons fitted with cages. Khyber Elessedil was sprawled on the wooden floor across from him, both of them bound and gagged and chained to the bars so they could not reach each other or even speak, Pleysia's head spiked on a pole just outside, where they could watch it bounce and sway as the wagon rolled across miles of desolate country. Huge beasts that vaguely resembled oxen hauled the wagons, while whip-wielding drivers that looked like huge toads sat stone-still atop wooden seats, their eyes directed straight ahead. Wolves prowled the perimeter—huge shaggy beasts, eyes burning with hunger. They growled and snarled and snapped at one another and everything around them. Now and again, they lunged at the cages as if intending to tear them open and devour the prisoners inside.

And the creatures that served the Straken Lord as soldiers and handlers and minions stalked without. They were Goblins for the most part, but other things, too—things that had no recognizable names or origin or even purpose, hunching and shuffling and slogging to keep pace with the wagons.

Dust and grit clogged the air, stirred up from a dry, dead earth in which almost nothing grew. A deep haze hung over everything, mingling with grayness that never changed in this world reduced to perpetual twilight. The sky was masked by clouds that hung low against the earth from horizon to horizon; the landscape was bleak and colorless, the smell of it fetid and the taste rank and bitter.

Miles of this desolation passed, and time slowed to a crawl as Redden stared across the cage at Khyber Elessedil and she stared back at him.

Until they came in sight of the horror that was their destination, a fortress that was black and massive and terrifying, and the boy knew instinctively that this was a place from which no one ever returned. Up the winding road they went to the summit of the bluff, and then huge iron gates and craggy walls swallowed them up. They were hauled from their cages while their captors and their animals howled and huffed and snorted and growled and breathed on them from so close at hand, they could feel their heat and smell their odors.

Dragged into the bowels of the formidable keep, away from the last real light and air he or the Ard Rhys would probably ever see again, they were brought into a windowless room and chained to a wall, side by side, their arms and legs spread, their torsos pinned in place, fastened so that they could barely move and still could not speak. Redden remembered the hard cold feel of the stone pressing up against his back as he sagged against it, exhausted and deeply ashamed of what had become of him. He remembered his fear as he waited to discover his fate, far away from his home and his brother, deep in a savage land he barely understood. He remembered the companions and friends who had stumbled unwittingly into the Forbidding with him, all either dead or lost now. Gone.

He remembered exchanging a single look with the Ard Rhys, a look that said more than any words could hope to express.

The Straken Lord had entered the room then, his minions bowing or dropping to their knees instantly, acknowledging his power and position without hesitation or restraint. Tael Riverine was big and powerfully built, standing close to seven feet, his body studded with spikes and rippling with muscle. He wore leather garments that barely covered him, all of them draped with colorful feathers and ribbons, and there were blades strapped everywhere. His nearly feature-less face was expressionless, and his blue eyes hard and bright with purpose.

He gave Redden a brief glance and then turned to gaze for a longer time on Khyber. "You are not her," he said finally.

She stared at him, not comprehending.

"You are not the Straken Queen!" he roared with such fury that everyone cringed away from him. "Tarwick!"

A lean feral creature that looked as if a strong wind might blow it away bounded from the crowd of onlookers and dropped to the floor in front of his lord. "Master?"

"Fit them with the collars."

The creature scrambled up, produced a pair of metal collars, and locked them in place about the prisoners' necks. Then it released Redden and Khyber from the wall, unshackling them from their chains, freeing their arms and legs, and letting them drop to their knees.

"You wear conjure collars," the Straken Lord told them. "While you wear them, you must obey me. They will teach you to do so. Disobedience or disrespect will result in punishment." Khyber Elessedil started to rise. "No, stay where you are. On your knees. Bow to me."

What followed was the lesson he had intended to teach them all along—a lesson that was to establish his dominance and their servitude. When Khyber continued to rise, the Lord of the Jarka Ruus gestured casually and she jerked upright with a scream, consumed by a terrible pain. As she collapsed and Redden tried to catch her, he was treated to a similar demonstration. The pain was excruciating, radiating out from the collar all through his body, and he dropped to the floor and lay writhing in shock for long seconds.

"This is how it will be if you fail to do as I wish," Tael Riverine advised. "If you fail to call me Master. If you speak out of turn and without being asked. If you attempt to remove the collar for any reason. If you try to use your magic."

He saw the stunned looks on their faces. "Yes, I know of the magic you wield. You have been watched and your powers noted. You are no mystery to me. You are only slaves. You are mine to do with as I choose. Do you understand? Answer me."

Both had murmured, "Yes, Master," and their servitude had begun in earnest.

It was the beginning of their imprisonment. Since that day they had been confined to separate cells, always kept apart and solitary. They lived within their tiny dark spaces and awaited their Lord's pleasure. Their magic, which should have served them well, was useless. Redden had tested his early, and the resultant pain had persuaded him not to try again. He had fiddled once with loosening the conjure collar and suffered a similar fate. He assumed it was the same for Khyber. He had examined his cell from wall to wall and floor to ceiling, searching for a way to escape. There was none. He had considered trying to overpower his jailers, but they almost never appeared when he was awake and then only in force.

He wondered anew what had become of Khyber. In that first meeting, Tael Riverine had demanded to know what had become of the Straken Queen, how Khyber dared to call herself Ard Rhys, how she had found her way into the Forbidding, who else knew there was an entry, and so on. Dozens of similar questions were thrown at her, one after the other. When she had failed to answer him fully enough, fast enough, or respectfully enough, he had used the lash of the conjure collar on her until finally she collapsed unconscious at his feet.

He had not bothered with Redden. In truth, the boy was not even sure why he was still alive.

By now, he had come to believe it didn't matter. His life was over in any event. No one was coming for him. No one knew how to reach him. Not even Railing and Mirai—though he believed they would try—could save him from this.

He looked down at himself. He had not washed since he had been brought here. He had not shaved or cut his hair. He wore the same clothes in which he had been captured. He smelled and he itched from things he did not want to think about. He was miserable all the time, and what small hope he had harbored at the beginning of his misery had long since faded away.

Now and then, he found himself thinking about the reason he had come here in the first place—to search for the missing Elfstones. How far away that seemed. How unimportant. He thought of it as a monumental miscalculation, an effort that never should have been attempted, a foolish and reckless undertaking that had killed more than half their company and left them with nothing to show for their loss.

If he had to do it over again . . .

But he didn't, so there was no point in dwelling on it. Each time the subject surfaced he quickly let it slip away.

He did, however, wonder frequently about Tesla Dart. What role had she played in the fate of the expedition? Had she arranged their capture or had she tried to warn them away from it? He was uncertain even now. Tesla had appeared and vanished again too often for him to know what to think. It might have been her intention to help them, but she might just as easily have been leading them into a trap.

He had no way of knowing this, just as he had no way of knowing much of anything else, and trying to come to terms with his uncertainty was the worst part of his suffering.

Then, all of a sudden and for no discernible reason, his jailers came for him, accompanied by the creature called Tarwick, and brought him to a room where a tub of hot water waited and allowed him to bathe. Afterward, they cut his hair and gave him clean clothes and hot food. They took him to a different room—still a cell, but with a barred window that allowed in light and fresh air and let him look out over a ragged, rolling landscape as riven and desolate as everything else.

The only favor they did not do for him was to remove the conjure collar, but he had no illusions about that happening. They might be treating him better—relieving a fair amount of his discomfort—but they had no intention of giving him a chance to escape. To emphasize the point, they continued to lock the door to his cell day and night.

This new, improved treatment continued for the better part of a week, and he felt his strength and self-confidence returning. He wondered if similar consideration had been extended to Khyber Elessedil, but he never saw her and no one spoke about her. Once, right at the beginning of his change of circumstances, he tried asking Tarwick what had become of her. But the Straken Lord's servant quickly put a finger to his lips and lightly touched the collar about Redden's neck.

There was no mistaking his meaning.

Then one day Redden was taken from his cell and marched up into one of the towers of Kraal Reach, a climb of hundreds of steps around a winding staircase that bypassed floor after floor of closed doors and ended at the tower's pinnacle. Once there, he was brought into a tiny room off the entryway and left alone to wait.

Long minutes later the door opened, and in walked Khyber Elessedil, flanked by another pair of jailers.

He started to get to his feet, but she made a small hand movement that told him to stay where he was. They remained facing each other until the door closed behind them, then she came over to him and hugged him warmly.

"We don't want them to know more than necessary about us," she whispered. "Are you all right?"

Looking at her, he wondered if he was. If he looked anything like she did, she was right to be concerned. Her face was haggard and drawn, her graying hair hanging loose, and her body thin enough that the clothes she wore hung on her as if she were a scarecrow. She was washed and freshly clothed, and he assumed she had been given the same treatment he had. But there was a dullness to her eyes that reminded him at once of his own sense of hopelessness.

"I'm all right," he whispered back.

"This hasn't been pleasant. I'm so sorry I brought you into it."

"Don't worry about me. Have they hurt you any more?"

She shook her head. "And you?"

"The same."

"I saw this keep in Aphenglow's memories of the Elfstones' vision. It's called Kraal Reach. Grianne Ohmsford was imprisoned here . . ." She trailed off, exhaling sharply. "We're going to get out of this, Redden."

"I don't see how."

"There is always a way."

"There wasn't for some of us. All the others are dead, aren't they? All the ones who came in with us? And maybe even the ones who didn't. Maybe even Railing?"

She reached up and gripped his shoulders hard. "Listen to me. I've been in a lot of hopeless situations through the years. In the time of the Druid rebellion against Grianne Ohmsford, things were so bleak there were times when I wanted to give up and just let go. But I didn't, and I survived. I will do so here, too. And so will you. Will you believe me?"

She was so fierce that he found himself nodding his agreement. "I will."

"Have you tried using your magic?"

"It didn't work. It just triggered the collar, and the pain dropped me like a stone. We have to find another way."

She turned abruptly and moved away as the lock snicked and the door began to open. *Patience,* she mouthed silently as she placed herself against the wall several feet away from him.

Tarwick stepped inside the room, looked them over, his gimlet eyes bright, and beckoned them to follow. Without a word or a look to each other, they did so.

A handful of Goblins surrounded them once they were outside, providing an escort. Right away, Redden started to worry. For a week now, guards had seemed a formality. Now, all at once, there was a reason for them. An urge to bolt swept over him, irrational and impossible, and he had to fight not to break away and run.

They followed a corridor that circled left around the tower until they reached a pair of huge iron doors that stood open.

Inside, the Straken Lord sat slouched on a bench atop a dais, robed in black and drinking from a metal cup that steamed and spit as if its contents were boiling. Tarwick led them forward until they were less than six feet away and then dropped to his knees and bowed until his forehead was touching the floor. Unbidden, Redden and Khyber Elessedil did the same.

"Address me properly," said the Straken Lord.

"Yes, Master," Khyber said at once.

"Master," Redden echoed quickly.

"Rise," he said, and they did. His impassive face turned away from them, and his gaze shifted to an open window. He was quiet for a long time. "What should I do about you?" he asked finally.

That he spoke their language was a puzzle Redden had not been able to solve, but he assumed it had something to do with the collars, even though he could provide no good reason for thinking this and it was at best an educated guess. In any case, hearing this creature speak words he could understand was not as jarring to him now as it had been during their first encounter, when everything had revolved around domination and pain.

The Lord of the Jarka Ruus looked back at them, straightening on the bench and leaning forward slowly. "Where is the Straken Queen?

Where is Grianne Ohmsford? Wait!" He held up his hand abruptly. "This will be the second time we have had this discussion. There will be no third time. Think carefully before you answer. Be truthful. I will know if you are lying. Tell me where she is."

He pointed at Khyber. "You."

Khyber nodded, looking weary and defeated. "She is in the Four Lands, outside the Forbidding, Master. But she is no longer Ard Rhys. She left years ago and lives alone now in the mountains."

Tael Riverine studied her. "You have succeeded her as Ard Rhys?"

"I have, Master."

"I wish her back. I wish her to be my Queen. How can I make this happen?"

Redden felt his heart stop. Grianne Ohmsford had been gone for over a century, and even if she were still alive she would be very old. But this was not what the Straken Lord wanted to hear. It was not what they could tell him.

"She will not come back to you, Master," Khyber answered. "She ran from you. She was afraid of you."

"She is meant to be my Queen and bear my offspring, and I will have it so." He talked as if he hadn't heard her, as if nothing she said mattered. "Will she return if it means your lives?"

Khyber shook her head. "No, Master. She will not come back for us. She will let us die first."

Tael Riverine seemed to think this over for a moment, his strange flat features revealing nothing. Then casually he gestured, and Khyber Elessedil jerked as excruciating pain exploded through her body, causing her to scream and drop to the floor of the tower, twisting and writhing in shock. He left her that way for long seconds, watching her suffer with studied indifference. Then he motioned toward her again, and she collapsed sobbing.

"I told you not to lie to me," he said softly.

Khyber hauled herself to her knees, gasping and choking. "I didn't lie. I told you the truth!"

"I did not sense that. You lied."

"No, she didn't!" Redden cut in abruptly. He cringed as the Straken

Lord wheeled on him. "Master," he added quickly. "She speaks the truth!"

He waited for the inevitable gesture, but Tael Riverine only stared at him for what seemed an endless amount of time before leaning back again on the bench and looking away.

"You lie as well. But I expect nothing less." He looked back at his prisoners. "The walls of our prison are collapsing. Soon we will return to our old world, the one from which we were driven. I will lead the Jarka Ruus back through the shattered walls and reclaim what is ours. There is nothing anyone can do to stop this."

He paused. "Anyone except Grianne Ohmsford. She can prevent this from happening. If she returns to me and if she mates with me and bears my children, the Jarka Ruus will remain within their own lands and forsake yours. You have my word on this."

He would abandon his plans for invasion of the Four Lands if Grianne became his? Redden almost laughed out loud. Now who was lying? Granted, Tael Riverine was clearly obsessed with the former Ard Rhys and would apparently do anything to get her back, but giving up the chance to seize control of the Four Lands and its people when there was no reason to do so felt patently false.

Khyber remained on her knees, still shaking from the attack. "You cannot promise this for all of the Jarka Ruus! The Drachas, for instance, are not yours to command. And there are others equally rebellious. Some will break through and do as they choose."

Tael Riverine nodded. "Some is still better than all. Those beholden to me will not transgress against me. You will keep your world and your lives. But Grianne Ohmsford must accept my offer."

That would never happen, Redden thought. Besides, even if it could, he had already realized there was no reason to think the Straken Lord's word was worth anything.

But Khyber Elessedil was struggling to her feet, saying to Tael Riverine, "We would have to find her first. We would have to explain your offer. We would have to persuade her to accept it and then bring her here. That won't be easy. But we can do it."

His eyes fixed on her. "Address me properly, woman."

"Master," she said at once, and bowed deeply.

He shifted his gaze to Redden. "What do you say to this?"

"She is family to him, Master," Khyber said quickly, clearly afraid for Redden's safety if this creature thought him useless. "He is an Ohmsford, too. He will be effective in persuading her."

The strange blue eyes flickered with something dark and unexpected, and Redden was suddenly certain that Khyber had made a mistake in telling him this.

"You are blood kin?" the Straken Lord demanded of the boy.

There was nothing he could do about it now, so Redden nodded.

"Would that matter to her?"

"I don't know, Master. She's never seen me. She doesn't know me."

Tael Riverine looked back at Khyber. "But she knows you. You are her chosen successor. She named you so. Did you not say this?"

Khyber stared, unable to answer. Finally, she nodded. Redden felt the floor drop away, and he was overcome by a sinking feeling that they had signed away their lives.

The Straken Lord rose suddenly, towering over them. "I have decided your fate. Your usefulness is limited. You are weak and unreliable, you are not to be trusted, but you may still serve a purpose. Bow to me. Address me properly."

Redden and the Ard Rhys both went down on their knees and bowed low to the floor to Tael Riverine. "Master," they said to him.

"Now rise and stand before me."

Redden climbed back to his feet and with Khyber next to him stood in front of Tael Riverine, his head lowered deferentially, burning with rage and humiliation. If there had been a way to get at the Straken Lord in that moment, a way that would have provided him with a real chance of killing the demon, he would have taken it in spite of the likely consequences.

The Straken Lord looked at Khyber Elessedil. "You will face me in the arena tomorrow at midday. You will provide entertainment and an object lesson. If you kill me, you will be sent home unharmed along with this boy. If not, the boy's fate is mine to decide. Tarwick!"

At once they were surrounded by Goblins who fastened them anew with chains and fitted gags to their mouths. Neither made any attempt to resist. Redden was stunned and disbelieving, still trying to comprehend what he had just heard, as if perhaps it wasn't true and in a moment he would hear it all rescinded.

A moment later they were hauled from the room and back down the tower stairways and through its corridors. Just before they were separated, Redden got a quick final glimpse of Khyber Elessedil's face.

He had never seen such ferocious determination.

21

♦

Afterward, returned to his cell and his solitude, Redden Ohmsford sat alone in the silence and tried to keep from falling apart.

It took him a long time to recover himself sufficiently that he could consider rationally what had just happened. He felt overwhelmed by how unexpectedly the meeting with the Straken Lord had ended. Devastated, shocked, and adrift in the knowledge that he was helpless to do anything, he just sat on his bed with his hands clasped and his head bent, staring at the floor.

He did not for a moment believe that Tael Riverine would let Khyber Elessedil leave Kraal Reach alive. He didn't care what the Straken Lord had promised or the conditions he had set; the outcome of the battle was a foregone conclusion. No matter how hard Khyber fought for her life, no matter how clever or strong or brave she proved, she was doomed. The Straken Lord would not allow any other outcome. In sentencing her to trial by combat, he had sentenced her to death.

How he would accomplish this, Redden wasn't sure. But there was no other purpose in arranging this. A spectacle, perhaps, for the benefit of his minions—or perhaps simply for his own gratification. But it would be a spectacle nonetheless, not a true opportunity for the Ard Rhys.

Which would leave him as the final surviving member of the ex-

pedition that had come into the Forbidding, the last loose thread in a
tangled web of destruction and murder. He didn't think for a moment that Tael Riverine could resist pulling out or cutting off that
loose thread and putting an end to the entire business.

Redden hugged himself and rocked back and forth as anguish
threatened to engulf him. He would not cry, he told himself. He
would not give in to what he was feeling. He would be as fierce and
strong-willed as Khyber Elessedil had been when they parted. He
would be her equal in courage, though what faced him was so vast
and inexorable that there was no reasonable chance of finding a way
through it. Tears were spilling from his eyes, but he remained silent
and stoic even so.

Eventually, his despair passed and he regained control of himself,
and he was able to master his sense of hopelessness sufficiently to
consider what he might do to help himself.

Khyber Elessedil seemed to think there was hope. He had seen it
in her face. She was contemplating hand-to-hand combat with a
creature twice her size and infinitely stronger, and very likely more
experienced in battle. She had not been told the rules of the fight or
the choice of weapons she would be offered or anything substantive
of what was to take place. Yet still she was evincing confidence in her
chances.

He must do something to help her. He must search for a way to
throw off the conjure collar and summon his magic. The wishsong's
power was considerable, after all, evolved through generations of
Ohmsfords and tested personally by both Railing and himself. He
knew what it could do. If he were given even one chance to use it
against Tael Riverine, there would be no more Straken Lord.

But the day drifted away without any further idea about how to
make that happen. His jailers brought him food and a jug of water
and left him for the night. He slept poorly, plagued by dreams of con-
flict and darkness, of battles fought between good and evil, between
combatants who were faceless and nameless and yet somehow managed to make the struggle feel personal. The air cooled and the gray
mix of clouds and haze swallowed everything until he could see only
pinpricks of light cast by torches burning through the gloom.

When he woke, he was no more enlightened as to how to free

himself or aid the Ard Rhys than he had been when he went to sleep. The day was iron-hard and dry, and the cloud ceiling had lifted to allow a sharp, clear view of the bleak countryside from mountain ranges to hardpan flats and barren hills to fields of broken rocks. He stared through the bars of his tiny window at this grim tableau and felt the weight of his desperate circumstances return.

Breakfast was accompanied by something that resembled ale, but of which he was suspicious and so ignored. No one spoke to him. He ate in silence and alone and waited for something to happen.

Sometime toward midday, they came for him.

He was waiting when the door opened and his jailers appeared. He was escorted from his cell and down countless halls and stairways until he was brought outside into a vast courtyard. Creatures and animals of all shapes and sizes—horned and tusked, scaled and spiked, big and small—milled about. The terrible wolves that had prowled the perimeter of his rolling cage on his journey to Kraal Reach roamed freely.

He was taken to another of those wheeled cages and placed inside. The denizens of Kraal Reach and minions of the Straken Lord crowded close to examine him. Twisted, dark faces pressed in, and parted jaws revealed teeth made for tearing flesh. He was oddly calm in the face of this—perhaps because he kept telling himself that nothing was meant to happen to him on this day, at least. Even when he felt their fetid breath and smelled their rank bodies, he did not cringe away or show fear. Even when they growled and hissed and spat at him, he simply looked away.

I will not give in to this.

He spoke the words in the silence of his mind. But he knew they were a fragile shield, and in the end would not be enough to save him.

A roar from the crowd of creatures heralded the arrival of Khyber Elessedil. Surrounded by Goblins, she was marched through the crowd, her head held high in the face of their fury and hunger, her gaze directed straight ahead. She was wearing what appeared to be a form of flexible body armor, and she had weapons strapped everywhere—everything from long knives and daggers to short swords and throwing stars. She looked surprisingly fit and strong and ready for what was coming. She saw him as she approached and gave him a small nod and a slight smile. As if to reassure him that everything was all right, that she had matters under control.

They brought her to the cage, opened the door, and waited for her to climb inside. Without a glance at any of them, she did what was expected of her.

She sat down next to Redden, close enough that he could see she no longer looked either haggard or beaten. If anything, she looked better than he had ever seen her.

"I know. I don't look the same, do I?" She leaned close. "This morning they gave me something to drink that they said would make me stronger. I was weak from fear and lack of sleep and saw no reason to refuse it. How much worse could things be for me, even if I were being poisoned? But they were telling the truth; it was an elixir meant to strengthen my body and sharpen my instincts. I could feel it working on me right away. All of my despair and weariness disappeared. I felt better immediately."

Redden shook his head. "Why would they do that for you?"

"Because the Straken Lord wants this to be a fight, not an execution. His pride and his manhood demand it. This is supposed to be a battle, so he must have an opponent who will provide a sufficient challenge. Make no mistake about this. I am to be killed—but not too easily. I am to provide entertainment and a few thrills first."

"They've given you enough weapons for it."

She glanced down at her assortment of blades and smiled. "After giving me the elixir, they took me to an armory and let me choose what I wanted. I took this armor and the blades and throwing weapons. They will provide me with a lance or spear of some sort once we arrive at the arena."

She paused. "They said they will remove the conjure collar, as well."

He stared at her in disbelief. "They will?"

"So they say. A mistake, I think, if they do so. But this is part of the spectacle. If I can be rendered immobile with a gesture, there is no point in the fight. If I can be subdued at any point, there is no suspense or even purpose to the battle. What this is meant to be is a demonstration of the Straken Lord's power. He keeps his creatures in thrall by never allowing them to think for even a moment that he isn't the equal of them all. Fear binds them to him. But fear must be instilled anew on a regular basis. I am to be the next best example of what could happen should they transgress."

"But you believe your magic will give you the edge you need?"

"I think it might."

She looked so confident and ready in that moment that Redden's spirits were lifted. "Then we might escape this, after all."

"We might. He may have overreached himself by giving me this opportunity. He thinks women are weak—all but Grianne Ohmsford, whom he worships. I learned this from the creature Tarwick. Tael Riverine has never forgotten her, his Straken Witch—the only female sufficiently strong enough to bear his children and extend his line. He is fixated on having this happen. He plans to dispose of me and then send you back to tell everyone what happened and what to expect. He assembles his army to march into the Four Lands and will do so as soon as the last of the Forbidding falls."

A whip cracked and the rolling cage jolted forward, departing the courtyard. The crowd trailed after it, throngs of creatures and animals pressing close, pushing and shoving to gain a better position. Goblins, kobolds, Gormies, Harpies, and others Redden could not put names to. The demon-wolves roamed among them, growling and snapping at one another and anyone who got close. Every so often they would converge on an unfortunate creature that had caught their attention and drag it down, thrashing and screaming. None of the other creatures paid any heed to this. Those who were close just moved out of the way, avoiding the carnage and doing their best not to draw attention to themselves. The rest didn't bother doing that much.

Dust rose from the rutted road onto which the procession had turned after passing through the fortress. The air grew thick with it—heavy clouds that rose dozens of feet into the grayness and blanketed everything. Buried in the haze were the grunts and snorts of the beasts hauling the rolling cage, and the shouts and cries of the creatures keeping pace, all of it a surreal, frenzied mix.

"Listen to me, Redden," Khyber instructed, her voice suddenly urgent. She bent so close to him that their heads were almost touching. "I will try to find a way to defeat the Straken Lord, one that will give us a chance to escape. When that happens, I will come for you. Be ready. If we can persuade Tael Riverine to remove the conjure collar earlier or if you can manage to do so by yourself, that would help. But whatever happens, I will come for you."

He nodded. "I'll come to you first, if I can."

"Then we have our plan." She paused, and her expression changed. "But if our plan fails and I am killed, do not despair. Remember what I told you. He will release you anyway. He will send you back into the Four Lands as his messenger. That is his intent. I will try to disappoint him, but you will be freed if I fail."

"You won't fail," he said quickly. "You will be stronger than he is and you will succeed."

She sat back, nodding slowly. But she did not speak again.

They continued traveling through the scrub-covered landscape, through terrain blistered and raw and empty of visible life. Their journey took longer than Redden had expected—a long slow downward angling into a cluster of valleys—and it was only much later that the boy finally looked back to find Kraal Reach receding into a screen of dust and gloom, looking oddly tiny and insignificant.

The cage rolled on, its retinue of beasts and creatures trudging and slouching along in its wake, their collective gaze fastened on the prisoners. But at last the wagon crested a rise and started down toward a broad circular embankment thick with Jarka Ruus that must have arrived earlier. Tall gates opened into the embankment's interior, and the cage was pulled through. Within, the arena stretched away a hundred yards, its uneven, cracked surface littered with broken rock and bones that gleamed bare and white against the dark earth. Howls and screams of expectation rose from those gathered—a primal roar infused with rage and bloodlust.

Cringing inwardly, diminished by the fury of the sound, Redden kept his eyes averted from the source.

"Steady," he heard the Ard Rhys say.

The cage was brought to a halt before a set of risers constructed of iron bars and wooden planks. Creatures that were robed and hooded sat surrounded by Goblin bodyguards. At their center was the Straken Lord, draped in black, with Tarwick at his side. As the wagon pulled to a stop and those attending it dropped to their knees and bowed, he leaned over and whispered to his Catcher. Tarwick came to his feet and threaded his way through those occupying the risers until he stood before the cage door. Signaling to the guards, he had the door opened and Khyber Elessedil removed. But he motioned for Redden to stay where he was. When the boy tried to climb down anyway, the Catcher held up one hand, palm out, in an unmistakable gesture. Frustrated, Redden motioned toward his collar, signaling he wished it removed. Tarwick shook his head firmly.

Redden slumped back as the cage door was closed and locked anew. He watched as the Goblins led the Ard Rhys away from the viewing stands and the Straken Lord.

She did not look back at him.

They took Khyber to the center of the arena and brought her to a halt. Tarwick took a moment to check her body armor and weapons; he reached up and carefully removed the conjure collar from around her neck. He hesitated a moment afterward, perhaps waiting to see if she intended to do anything. Then, satisfied that she did not, he stepped away and allowed one of the Goblin guards to offer her a short spear, one perfectly suited to her size and weight. She took it without a word and watched as they turned and walked back toward the risers.

She could have killed them all, could have decimated them without effort, but what would it have gained her? The only one that mattered was Tael Riverine. She needed to save her strength for him.

She stood waiting, her gaze shifting between the risers and the cage that still held Redden Ohmsford captive. She had hoped he might be taken out and given some small measure of freedom, but the Straken Lord must have foreseen the possibilities for escape, however remote, and had chosen to shut them off completely. She knew the boy was disappointed and afraid. She didn't have to look at him to know what he was feeling. But there was nothing she could do about it.

She gazed around at the grayness of the land and sky and thought that this was a miserable place for anyone to die.

Atop the risers, the Straken Lord rose to his feet and started down. When he reached ground level, he threw off his black robes and revealed that he was dressed as she was, in lightweight black body armor. He bore similar weapons. He accepted a short spear from one of the Goblins, hefted it in one hand to test its feel, and nodded in satisfaction. Then he turned to those gathered on the viewing embankment and thrust both arms skyward. A deafening roar of approval greeted the gesture, his minions chanting and screaming, leaping up to mimic him, arms raised, fists pumping the air overhead.

The Straken Lord turned from the crowd and began to stalk toward Khyber.

She stood where she was, holding her ground. She had already begun to summon her magic, and she found it strong and ready as it gathered at her fingertips. The shouts and roars of the faithful had resumed; they cheered for Tael Riverine, urging him on. Let them howl, she thought. She would try to give them something to really howl about. She would kill him quickly. She would catch him off guard and overconfident, and she would end his life before he could end hers.

But, instead, he was the one who caught her off guard. Still moving toward her, he went into a sudden crouch and flung his spear directly at her with a strength and accuracy she would not have believed possible. She flung herself aside just in time, barely avoiding being skewered as the deadly missile whizzed past. She rolled and came back to her feet to see him racing toward her, blades in both hands.

She had only seconds to respond, but that was enough. She gathered up the threads of her momentarily scattered magic, hardened them into a solid mass, and sent it hurtling toward Tael Riverine. But he deftly sidestepped the dangerous attack, barely slowing. Even so, he could not escape her second strike, which followed close on the heels of the first. It caught him squarely in the chest and threw him backward like a straw man.

Fresh screams rose from the assembled masses, but Khyber was paying no heed now, consumed with her struggle to stay alive. She drew on her magic again, moving toward the Straken Lord as she did so, closing the distance between them. He was sprawled on the earth, smoke rising from his damaged armor, but he was quick to rise. Aside from the scrapes and cracks in his armor, he appeared whole. Knives flashed from his hands as he sped toward her, and she barely managed to use her magic to knock them down. Others followed, and she found herself on the defensive as he closed in on her.

She took a few steps backward. She did not want him to get close enough to grapple with her. If that happened, she was finished.

Moving sideways now as she gathered fresh magic, she barely eluded another pair of knives and then she attacked. She caught him with another strike, this one to his head, flinging him away, tumbling him head-over-heels across the rocky earth, spines tearing at the ground as he rolled. Yet almost immediately he was up again, shrugging off whatever pain and injury she had inflicted.

Then he charged.

She could not recover fast enough to bring another strike to bear, so she snatched up the spear she had left lying on the ground and used it to sweep his legs from under him as he reached her. She leapt aside as he tumbled past, then backed away quickly and braced for his recovery. He spun around and came for her, but she clenched her hands and drove him backward with a fresh explosion of magic. Then she struck at him once more, another surge that caught him midsection and thrust him away. He was on fire now, all of his spines red-hot and steaming, his armor half melted, and his dark body singed and peeling in a dozen places. Most of his weapons were gone, either expended in his earlier attacks or lost during the course of their battle. He dropped to his hands and knees, shaking himself like a dog, gasping for air.

Finish him!

She summoned fresh magic, intent on doing exactly that. This was her chance, and she could not afford to let it pass.

But something was wrong. She felt the magic respond, then immediately dwindle. Confused, she summoned it again, willing it to life—to her fingertips and her service. Again it sparked, and again it quickly failed.

In the same instant, she felt her strength begin to fade. A sudden weakness overcame her, as if all of her energy had been drained away. She tried to collect herself, to harden her resolve against what was happening, to recover the power she had possessed just moments earlier.

But it was gone. It was all gone.

She experienced a sinking feeling as she realized what had happened. The elixir she had been given had a finite life. It was never intended to sustain her for long; it was always meant to fail. The Straken Lord had wanted her to give a good account of herself, and so he had given her a measured amount to allow for that. But, in the end, she would be left helpless.

With a sudden sense of desperation, she threw herself atop Tael Riverine, the long knife in her right hand flashing downward. But he had either seen or sensed what was happening to her, and he knocked the blow aside and rolled out from under her.

Slowly, deliberately, he rose to his feet, kicking her down again when she tried to get up with him. Moving close, he pinned her to the ground with his foot. She struggled to break free, but could not manage it, betrayed by the elixir on which she had depended, deserted by her magic and her strength, bereft of everything.

She looked up at the Straken Lord as he towered over her, his spines rigid, like tiny spears extending from his powerful body, his dark face expressionless. His strange blue eyes fixed on her, willing her to meet his gaze, looking to see the fear he expected she would display. She stared up at him, but there was no fear and no despair. There was only grim resignation.

He studied her for a moment longer, then drew the short sword from his belt, the last weapon he possessed, and drove it through her heart.

22

SEERSHA STOOD AT THE FRONT OF THE ROOM, ARMS CROSSED, watching with her one good eye as Mirai Leah took a seat next to Railing. She was the last of them to arrive. The Druid had called them all together—those returned from the ill-fated expedition—in the house the men and the boy shared as communal lodging.

Railing, assessing the situation, believed from the urgency of her summons and now the serious expression on her bluff face that she had something important to tell them.

He glanced from Crace Coram seated right across from him, to Skint sitting next to the Dwarf Chieftain, to Woostra tucked back in a corner by himself, and finally to Mirai beside him. He couldn't be sure from their faces, but he guessed they probably thought the same as he did.

"I've finished an audience with the King, Aphenglow's grandfather, and with his brother, both of whom are aware of what is happening to the Forbidding. I have asked to return there, and the King has agreed to it."

"Finally!" Railing exclaimed, unable to contain himself.

"Better hear me out," Seersha said, cutting him short. She took a moment to be sure he was listening. "The King will provide a company of Elven Hunters to go with me. Or perhaps it's me going with them, depending on how you read things. Sian Aresh, who is Captain of the Home Guard, will lead these men. We will travel back into the deep Westland until we reach the Breakline. The Elves are under strict orders to stay outside the walls of the Forbidding, even if an entry presents itself. They are to keep watch for an attempted break-out by those trapped within. Reports are to be sent back to Arborlon, but the Elves are to hold their position until a more significant force can be assembled, equipped, and flown west in warships to join them. At that point, any attempt to invade the Westland is to be met with force and thrown back."

Railing felt his heart sink. There was no mention of a rescue at-tempt, no suggestion of anyone going in after either his brother or the Ard Rhys.

"A significant force," Crace Coram repeated carefully.

Seersha made a face. "We all know the history. The war between the creatures of Faerie ended with the creation of the Forbidding. Until then, the two sides had been evenly matched. But the Forbid-ding gave the edge to the Elves and their allies. If the Forbidding col-lapses, as it appears it is in danger of doing, it will probably take all of the Races working together to keep from being overrun by the dark creatures imprisoned within. We've already had a taste of what that would require—all but Woostra, and I am sure you will agree he is much the better for having avoided it. So, no, the Elves alone—even a 'significant force,' whatever that means—won't be enough."

"So we're buying time for something else to happen?" Skint guessed.

Seersha nodded. "We are, in part at least, and that is what we are here to discuss."

"I want my brother back," Railing declared.

Seersha nodded impatiently. "We all know how you feel. But get-ting your brother back is no more important to you than getting back Khyber Elessedil is to me. We are both looking for the same resolu-tion. The question is, how do we get it?"

"But if you have to stay outside the Forbidding and hold your ground, like you say . . ."

Seersha held up one hand quickly. "The *Elven Hunters* have to hold their ground and stay outside. Not me."

"So you will go in after them?"

"Just as soon as I am able to do so. Will you let me finish, please?"

"I'm going with you."

"Let me finish, Railing."

He went still again, biting back the rest of what he wanted to say, tamping down the frustration and impatience that ruled his every waking minute, reining in his fears and doubts regarding his brother's safety. What he wanted to do was to commandeer a sprint, fly into the Forbidding, find his brother, and spirit him out. Now.

But he knew it wouldn't be that easy. And he knew that Seersha had already decided what they were going to do.

"Let's get this out of the way, Railing," she said to him suddenly. "I am going back into the Forbidding, but you are not."

He started to leap up and object, but she put him back in his seat with a look and a quick gesture. Again, he tried to speak, but he was pinned in place and now he found he couldn't speak, either.

"There are reasons for this," she continued, ignoring his thrashings. "Good ones." She paused. "You are going to hear them whether you want to or not. Do you understand me?" She waited until he quieted and gave her a brief nod. "Then pay attention. You are not fit enough to make this journey. Aphen's magic is healing your broken leg, but it still has a way to go. The time required for the healing to become complete is uncertain. I can't put others at risk by gambling that it will hold up if we are attacked. Yes, you have the magic of the wishsong to aid you, and it is a powerful weapon. But be that as it may, you still need time to finish mending, and I intend that you should have it. As well, you are the wrong person for this effort. You are brave and committed, but you are not experienced enough. So I am giving you something else to do, something every bit as important and perhaps more so."

Everyone was listening closely now, intrigued by this unexpected possibility. Railing, rendered silent and immobile, seethed at his predicament, but listened anyway.

"The Ulk Bog who found Crace Coram and Oriantha was very insistent that the Straken Lord seeks a way to bring Grianne Ohmsford back into the Forbidding so he can breed with her. He has retained this fixation for more than a hundred years, and it appears to remain undiminished. This is not a rational expectation, but the Straken Lord does not appear to me to be a rational creature. So what if we could find a way to make it happen? What if we could produce Grianne?"

"Wouldn't she be dead and buried by now?" Skint asked doubtfully.

"Not if she used the Druid Sleep. Not if she retains her magic and her Druid skills. She could still be mentally and physically strong enough to be every bit as effective as she was when she escaped him before. If so, she becomes a very potent weapon we could use against him. We have two considerations here. First, saving our friends, and second, putting an end to the threat of an invasion by the Jarka Ruus into the Four Lands. What if Grianne Ohmsford could provide both?"

She looked around the room, ending with Railing. "I want you to find out if this might be possible. Go with Woostra and search the records at Paranor to see if we can find out what happened to her. Take Mirai and Skint with you. If you find anything that tells you where she can be found, go to her and tell her what is happening. If half of what I've read about her in the Histories is true, she will want to help us. You are her descendant—you and Redden. You are all Ohmsfords. Talk to her. Persuade her. Bring her back and let us face him together."

There was a long silence.

"This seems something of a stretch," Skint said finally.

Seersha nodded. "Everything we try at this point will be something of a stretch. Even finding a way back into the Forbidding and into the Straken Lord's fortress to free the Ard Rhys and Redden Ohmsford seems unlikely. But it's too late for what's possible and what's not to suddenly become a concern."

"But hasn't Woostra already studied the Druid Histories at length?" Mirai asked. "Is there anything new to find?"

Seersha gestured at the little scribe. "Woostra and I have already discussed this."

Woostra shrugged. "The Druid Histories say nothing about what became of Grianne Ohmsford after she left Paranor. But there are writings from both Grianne and Khyber Elessedil in the archives from that time period. I have not researched all of these. There might be something there."

Skint was not persuaded. "But no one's heard anything about her—anything—for more than a hundred years. Is this even a possibility?"

"I'll admit it feels like the beginnings of the search for the missing Elfstones all over again," Seersha replied. "A hunt through old journals, diaries, writings of people dead and gone, lost to us for too many years. But maybe this time we can make something good come of it. The Elfstones are still lost to us, but maybe Grianne isn't. She was a powerful witch and a fierce Ard Rhys during her life. Perhaps she's still something of both."

She moved to an empty chair and plopped down. "What else do we have to do but find out? Go back to the Forbidding and try to get inside again? Go back into that madness that has already killed most of us and hope it does not take the rest?" She gestured at Railing. "What do you want to do, Railing?"

The boy discovered he was free of his restraints. He could move again, and he could talk. Still, he hesitated. "What I want to do is whatever it takes to save Redden. Do you really think this might be the way?"

"I think if it isn't, there's still time to try another. The Straken Lord made prisoners of the Ard Rhys and your brother for a reason. Whatever we do, we have to hope that means he wants to keep them alive and well long enough for us to save them. We have to hope there's a way. While you search for Grianne Ohmsford, Crace Coram and I will search for a way back inside the Forbidding. We will attempt to bring your brother and Khyber out. We won't just be sitting around with the Elves."

"Remember that Oriantha is still in there, as well," the Dwarf Chieftain added. "I saw what she could do when that dragon carried us off. She is someone to be reckoned with, and she is looking for your brother, too. I think Seersha is right. Nothing you could do at this point by way of searching for him would add to our chances. Stay here and look for the Ilse Witch."

Seersha looked at him sharply. "Don't use that name. The Druids don't call her that anymore."

Crace Coram nodded. "Doesn't matter what the Druids call her. That's who she was, like it or not. That's who she still is—if she's still alive—somewhere deep down inside. Maybe that's who you want to find if you expect her to stand up to the Straken Lord."

Railing was thinking it through. He had listened to the Dwarf Chieftain relate the story of his experiences inside the Forbidding several times. He had heard him speak of Tesla Dart and of what she had insisted was true about the Straken Lord and his obsession with Grianne Ohmsford. It seemed clear enough that he would do anything in his power to bring Grianne back, and that almost everything else was secondary. It was a fresh form of madness, and it might make him vulnerable. They needed to find a way to breach his defenses and undermine his control over the Jarka Ruus, and perhaps by doing so disrupt things enough to allow them to reach Redden and Khyber Elessedil. All that was true.

But it was also true that every day he was kept away from his brother left him riddled with guilt. Every day seemed to increase the chances they would never be together again. The Speakman's prediction still haunted him. Only one would return. Only one. What if that one was Crace Coram, and those still left inside the Forbidding—his brother included—would not be coming back?

The others were talking again, Skint questioning Woostra further on the chances of finding anything new about Grianne Ohmsford and Seersha adding something about Aphenglow's experience with the Elven writings. But Railing wasn't listening.

"If you go," Mirai said quietly, leaning close to him, "I will go with you."

He nodded without looking at her. He knew she would. He would have been surprised if she'd said anything else.

But this felt like such an impossibility that he couldn't make himself believe there was any real chance of it coming to pass. Could he abandon his plans, however ill formed, for rescuing his brother immediately? Could he put off what needed doing yesterday and gamble on finding someone missing and long presumed dead, hoping she could alter the course of events if she appeared, but not knowing if she would even consider doing so? Did this make any sense at all?

"What do you say, Railing?" Seersha repeated.

But nothing was clear to him anymore. Everything that had made sense in his life had been left behind at Bakrabru when he had flown west into the Breakline with the ill-fated Druid expedition.

"I'll go," he said, just like that.

"And I," Mirai said at once.

Skint gave a curt nod of agreement, and Woostra said, "I've already said I would go. How soon do we leave?"

"An airship will be arranged for you," Seersha said, getting to her feet. "You can leave as soon as you want."

When she left, Seersha took Crace Coram with her for a meeting with Sian Aresh to discuss preparations for their departure for the Breakline. The two old friends walked side by side in silence toward the city proper and the compound that housed the Home Guard. Elves passing by gave them covert glances, these two Dwarf warriors, scarred and worn from hardship and years. "You don't believe anything you told that boy," the Dwarf Chieftain said finally.

"A little of it," she answered. "Enough of it that I could speak the words without feeling they were a lie."

"Do you really think that Grianne Ohmsford is still alive? What chance is there of that?"

"What chance is there that his brother is still alive? Or Khyber? It's all the same."

"But you gave him hope."

"Hope is all we have." She stopped and faced him. "I told Khyber— I promised her, when she left with the rest of you to go through that waterfall that wasn't a waterfall at all—that I would not let anything happen to Railing Ohmsford. He already had a broken leg and she was taking his brother with her. She knew it would be dangerous and she might not come back, and that Redden Ohmsford might not come back, either. She did not want both brothers to die. She had told their mother she would bring them back, and if she could not bring them both back, she would at least bring one. She was insistent about this. She would make certain at least one of them returned home."

"So you're sending him on this hunt for ghosts and shadows to keep him safe? To keep him from going into the Forbidding?"

She reached over and tapped him lightly on the forehead. "And to think they say you're slow-witted."

They started walking again, moving off the smaller pathway they had been following onto the main road. "He won't appreciate it once he finds out what you've done."

"He'll appreciate it if we bring his brother out of the Forbidding," she said. "And if we don't, likely we won't be around to hear about it, will we?"

They walked the rest of the way in silence.

Still sitting in the common room with his companions after the Dwarves had departed, Railing watched dust motes floating in the sunshine that streamed through the window. "You think trying to find Grianne Ohmsford is a waste of time, don't you?"

Skint grunted. "If we thought this was a waste of time, we wouldn't be going with you."

"Seersha was adamant that I do this," he said.

"She does seem to have made up her mind that you're not going into the Forbidding with her," Mirai agreed.

"She thinks I would be underfoot. She worries I would do something foolish because I want to help Redden so badly. She thinks I'm young and impulsive and don't have enough experience." Railing shook his head. "I can see her point, even though she's wrong."

"I've always wondered about the Ard Rhys Grianne," Woostra said quietly. "What happened to her?" He was still sitting at the back of the room, separated from the others by more than the distance between them, an outsider suddenly pressed into service with them. "She vanished completely after Shadea a'Ru and the rebel Druids were dispatched."

"She must have said something about her intentions to someone," Mirai said.

"Not a word. She gave over the leadership of the order to Khyber and a couple of others, then boarded an airship and left. It's all in the Druid Histories. But there's nothing written about what happened to her after that. Not that I've been able to find, and I've read it all at one point or another."

"So this is a waste of time, after all."

Woostra got up and came forward to join them, taking the seat vacated by Crace Coram. "I don't think so. She kept a journal; Khyber once told me so. Grianne gave it to her for safekeeping when she left the order. But Khyber put it away, and no one ever saw it afterward. I asked her about it once, and she said it was where it belonged. It's worth taking time to look for it." He shrugged. "And there might be other writings. Khyber kept a journal, as well, tucked in a drawer in her sleeping chamber. I've never read it—never thought I had the right or the need to do so. But I'm willing to take a look at it now."

"But even if you find something, even if Grianne Ohmsford is still alive out there somewhere, what sort of shape is she in?" Skint pressed. "I heard what Seersha said about the Druid Sleep and the magic and all that, but even so Grianne would be more than a hundred years old. I don't care what you do to help yourself, what sort of magic you command, you aren't going to be as fit and strong as you were a hundred years earlier. What help is she going to be able to give us?"

"I considered that," Railing said quickly. "But then I thought, maybe she knows something about the Straken Lord that would help us get Redden back. Maybe she knows a weakness that even now, a hundred years later, she could use to destroy him. Or maybe she knows a way to outwit him. Or confuse him enough to give us a chance."

He threw up his hands. "What I know for sure is that I can't sit around here doing nothing! If I can't go into the Forbidding with Seersha, I'll do this."

"I just think we need to be realistic about our chances," the Gnome Tracker muttered.

"Maybe we should talk about who else is going," Mirai said, clearly anxious to turn the conversation in another direction. "We should take a crew to man the airship and maybe a few Elven Hunters for protection."

"No," Railing said at once. "I don't want anyone to go with us. It should just be the four of us."

Skint made a rude noise. "That's just nonsense, boy. Woostra and I don't know anything about airships, and if something happens to you, Mirai would be left to manage alone. You're supposed to be heal-ing, remember? We need a crew to keep things running smoothly. And a little protection wouldn't hurt."

"He's right," Mirai cut in before Railing could object further. "We don't want to try this without help. We don't know where our search will take us. Let's be smart about this."

"How do we know who to trust?" Railing replied. "Look what happened to Aphenglow."

"That was about something else—probably to do with the search for the missing Elfstones and that journal she found. We're on a dif-ferent mission entirely."

"We can be careful about who we take with us," Skint said. "We can find people we can trust. That Rover fellow. Farshaun Req. Why don't we send word and ask him to come with us? He's someone you trust. He can bring his own crew of Rovers, too. Skilled fliers, those fellows. Then we can spend our time worrying about what it is we're trying to do and let them fly the ship and watch our backs."

Railing immediately thought of Austrum and Mirai, and he al-most dismissed the idea out of hand because of what he feared might happen if the two were brought back together. But that was foolish thinking; if Mirai wanted to be with the big Rover, it would happen one way or another. She would make it happen.

"Getting him here will take time," he said instead.

Skint made a dismissive gesture. "A day, maybe two, at the most, if we send word now."

Railing looked from face to face, seeking and finding approval. Still, he hesitated. This search was what he had agreed to, yet he re-mained uncertain. There were reasons to reject it, even now, even after he had verbally committed to the idea and made it his own. Lay-ers of doubt clouded his confidence, making him wonder if he

shouldn't take this last chance to abandon the plan and try something else.

But what else was there to try? What other road was there left for
him to travel?

"Send word to Farshaun," he said finally. He was speaking to
Mirai. "Tell him to bring *Quickening.* Tell him we'll be waiting."

23

---◆---

They flew out of Arborlon two days later with Far-shaun Req at the helm and a crew of four men he had brought with him from Bakrabru working the lines. It was early morning, and the skies were bright and clear. The Rovers had arrived in Arborlon at twilight of the previous night, much faster than Railing had expected, and they had already stocked *Quickening* with supplies, weapons, and spare parts so that she was ready to depart at once. Railing was tempted to do so, to leave under cover of darkness to avoid the chances of being seen by unfriendly eyes. But common sense won out, and after consulting with Farshaun and Mirai it was agreed that allowing the Rovers a meal and a good night's sleep was the better choice.

Standing in the pilot box with Farshaun as the buildings of Arborlon dwindled and disappeared behind them, he leaned close and said, "I didn't know if you would come."

"Why wouldn't we come?" the old man asked in surprise. "Redden is one of us, as much a part of our family as he is of yours. We want him back safe, too."

"But after what happened in the Fangs? You lost all your men, friends and family both—all but Austrum—when the *Walker Boh* went down."

A shrug. "We're fliers, Railing. We're used to losing men to the skies. We don't measure our loyalty or our sense of responsibility by things like that. We know the risks, and the risks never change."

Railing watched the Rovers scurry about forward of them, tightening the radian draws on the mainsail. The sailcloth billowed in the favorable following wind, and the lines sang with the strain.

"You know what? Austrum never said a word about the *Walker Boh* when I asked him," Farshaun continued. "Just said he would find three more men and be ready in two hours. Good as his word, too. That boy has grown up a considerable amount since saving our skins in the Fangs."

Railing nodded wordlessly. He didn't like to be reminded of the virtues of the big Rover, but he wasn't the sort to diminish another's accomplishments or disparage his contributions. Austrum had saved them, and he did seem somewhat less bombastic this time around. What was even more unexpected was how distant he and Mirai acted toward each other. They had greeted each other coolly, and since then when they spoke it was without any particular heat or special sign of interest. Railing had watched for something more, but it hadn't been there.

So now they were on their way, and the enormity of what they were undertaking was blocking out other concerns. Its weight pressed down anew every time he considered the odds against finding Grianne Ohmsford. Since he was already riddled with guilt for not going after his brother directly, the weight seemed even heavier.

At one point, he left Farshaun and went back to talk with Woostra, who was huddled in a niche between crates of light sheaths lined up along the stern railing. The gawky, angular scribe looked very out of place. Railing walked over to him and sat down.

"What happens when we get to Paranor?" he asked.

Woostra cocked his head and stared off into space as though he had not considered the matter and needed a moment to think it through. Then he shrugged. "We go inside."

"But then what?"

"We look around."

"But isn't there magic that protects the Druid's Keep?"

Woostra gave him a look. "Don't overthink this. When we get

there, you and I will go into the Keep and study the readings. No one else—just the two of us. Only Druids are allowed within, and I can't have a bunch of Rovers and such tramping through the halls. I'm only taking you because you're an Ohmsford and you might see or recognize the importance of something that I would miss. You'll bring fresh eyes to the effort, and you share a family history with Grianne. Don't worry about the Keep's magic; it's no longer warding against entry. Aphen took care of that." He paused. "At least, I hope she did. I guess we'll find out. In any case, you and I will go in alone."

Railing wasn't reassured in the least by any of this, but he wasn't in a position to argue. Woostra was the only one of them who could access Paranor, and he would just have to hope the scribe was right about the Keep's magic being back under lock and key.

Toward midday, after spending the morning alternating between conversations with Farshaun and taking his turn at the helm, he found a moment to be alone with Mirai in the pilot box. They had almost completed their crossing of the Streleheim Plains by then, and the peaks of the Dragon's Teeth had come into view—a jagged, broken line that stretched across the eastern horizon.

He stood beside her as she worked the steering and for a moment didn't say anything. She reached over and put a hand on his shoulder. "It will be all right, Railing. We'll get him back."

"I can't stop thinking that this might all be a waste of time," he confessed. "I'm flying away from Redden, not toward him, and it might all be for nothing. I know rationally what we're doing. I understand the reasons for it. I even believe it has value. But it just feels so . . ."

He trailed off, unable to find the words.

She squeezed his shoulder reassuringly, and that alone was worth anything she might have said to try to comfort him. They stood in silence for a while longer before she spoke again.

"If we don't find anything at Paranor, if you don't feel right about what we're doing at that point, we can go back and find Seersha. We can travel all the way to the Breakline, if you want. I'll go with you. I'm not giving up, either."

"I know that. I never thought you would."

She smiled at him. She was so pretty, he thought. He wanted to tell her so. He wanted to lean over and kiss her. But they were standing out on the open deck with people all around them, and he couldn't make himself do it. He loved her, but he wasn't sure enough of himself to risk finding out that she didn't love him in return. At least, not in that way.

He stared off into the distance. If he were Austrum, he wouldn't have hesitated. He would have just done it.

But instead he made up an excuse about needing to talk to Woostra and left her there alone. Conflicting thoughts jumbled together in his head. *How can I even be thinking about Mirai like that when Redden's life is at stake? How can I be so selfish? Why didn't I go ahead and kiss her? She wouldn't have minded. She didn't mind Austrum doing it. But it doesn't matter about Austrum. What matters is Redden, and I can't let myself think about anything else.*

He raved on for a few moments more and then angrily swept everything aside and went down into the hold to sleep.

He was awake again when they reached the Dragon's Teeth, and then all the way through the peaks and across the Forbidden Forest to the spires of Paranor. By then the day was easing toward sunset, and the sky to the east was darkening. Woostra had them set down in the same clearing where he had landed with the Elessedil sisters and Cymrian weeks ago when returning to discover information about the Bloodfire.

Then, leaving the others to keep watch, the boy and the Druid scribe departed with Railing for the tunnels that led into the Keep.

It took them little time to find the hidden entrance and make the underground journey into the fortress. Torches helped them navigate their way through the darkness, and no obstacles appeared to hinder their progress. Although Woostra proceeded with no apparent concern for what might be lying in wait, Railing couldn't help listening for noises and searching for movement. He couldn't seem to help himself, even though he knew that if anything were hiding in these tunnels, it would be on them before he could do anything about it.

But nothing happened, and once inside the walls of the Keep and aboveground, Woostra started directly for the tower where the Druid Histories and accompanying papers were concealed and where Khyber had her sleeping chamber. Evidence of the Federation's attack on the Keep had not been removed. Debris from broken walls and parapets still littered the courtyards through which they passed, and damage from fire launchers and rail slings still scarred the buildings surrounding them. Bodies lay everywhere, now picked apart by birds of prey and other scavengers. The Keep itself was silent and devoid of life, and it was clear that the Federation had made no further attempt to occupy it.

"Guess the scavengers decided they could feast on the dead after all," Woostra muttered. He glanced over. "Stay close to me. Don't wander off."

Fat chance of that, the boy thought. The heaped bodies and the extent of the carnage inflicted by whatever magic warded the Keep unnerved him. In the best of times, Paranor would be an intimidating place—cold and cavernous and filled with strange sounds. But turned into a charnel house, it was terrifying. The hairs on the back of his neck prickled, and as they passed down the lifeless corridors he could feel cold spots that froze his blood.

"Why isn't the Federation army anywhere about if the magic's gone back to wherever it came from?" he whispered.

Woostra glanced over. "They don't know that Aphen has locked the magic away again. And they have no way of knowing what's here without coming back inside the walls. They're not about to do that after what happened to their fellows." He paused. "Besides, Drust Chazhul is dead. Without his insistence on pursuing the attack, they've retreated to Arishaig. Edinja Orle will have a different take on things."

Railing listened to the silence, unbroken save for the sound of their footsteps as they climbed flights of stairs and traveled down empty, echoing passageways crisscrossing the building. Rooms came and went, all of them deserted. Paranor felt as if it had been abandoned for centuries and not weeks. He tried to imagine what it would be like to live here, to be a Druid in residence, and he could not do so. It felt too closed away, too claustrophobic. He was a creature of open air and sunlight, and walls felt unnatural and unfriendly. He thought of his great-aunt living here, of her days as Ard Rhys, but any image he could form was incomplete and tinged with what he knew of her dark life, and it felt forced and unreal.

"Here," Woostra said, many floors and passageways later, standing at a set of heavy doors that were closed and locked. "We begin our search in these rooms."

He manipulated the locks, and the doors opened to admit them. Together they entered the first of what Railing could see was a series of rooms with wall-to-wall bookshelves and cabinets and floor space crammed with worktables and desks. He looked around in dismay. How in the world would they ever find anything in this jumbled mess?

"We'll begin here," Woostra announced. "We won't need to look through the Histories themselves; I'm familiar with what they contain, especially regarding recent times. There's nothing in them that will help." He saw the look on the boy's face. "Don't worry. I know where to search for what we need."

So search they did, through notebooks and journals, through stacks of letters, files thick with official Druid documents and piles of odd notes and scraps of paper with cryptic comments. They did not find Grianne Ohmsford's private diary as they had hoped to. They found, in fact, exactly nothing that would help explain what had become of Grianne after she left Paranor.

It took them all night to discover this, and at the end Woostra simply shrugged. "Unfortunate. We'll try the sleeping chamber of the Ard Rhys."

They left the document chambers and went up another flight to Khyber Elessedil's private rooms. Woostra took the boy inside, and together they resumed their search. There was a desk and a writing table, but neither yielded anything of value. Because this was primarily a sleeping chamber, the search went quickly and finished when Railing, looking through a nightstand, found a series of journals belonging to Khyber Elessedil beneath a false bottom in a drawer containing a collection of loose documents.

He thought at first he had found what they were looking for and was flushed with anticipation as he handed the journals to Woostra.

But the Druid scribe, after carefully paging through each, shook his head. "These were written by Khyber Elessedil. And they aren't what we want. They don't go back far enough. There is at least one missing, the oldest. That's the one we need to find."

So they went back to looking, working their way from the obvious places to the least obvious, trying to work out where the Ard Rhys could have hidden another journal. They looked for the better part of an hour but in the end came up empty-handed.

"I don't understand it," Woostra admitted. "Why would she hide one journal and not the others?"

"Maybe there aren't any besides the ones we've found," Railing said. "Maybe that's all there are."

Woostra shook his head. "I don't believe that. She would have started keeping a journal right from the start of her term of service if she was going to keep them at all. She's always been very thorough. She's hidden that one deliberately. We have to look some more."

Railing glanced around at the already ravaged room. "Where? Should we start tearing out the walls?" He paused. "Wait a minute. Could she have used magic to hide it? Redden and I used to do that with all sorts of stuff. If the journal's so important . . ."

Woostra was on his feet. "That's exactly what she's done. She's done it before with important documents." He looked around expectantly. "Can you use your magic to look for it? Can you try uncovering it that way?"

Railing stood up quickly. "I think so."

He glanced again at the journals they had already read through. All of them looked the same. So he pictured another like them and began to hum, calling up the wishsong. He felt the magic respond, felt the familiar warmth and the tingling at his fingertips. Holding the wishsong steady as he hummed, he began a slow scan of the room. He felt the magic spread away from his hands, lighting here and there, revealing patches of color, bits of detritus from earlier magic. The room was filled with it, and he realized he was sweeping over years of magic use, all of which probably related to the journals in one way or another and none of which gave him a clue as to the whereabouts of the one missing. The leavings were especially thick around the writing desk, which confirmed his thinking.

He stopped his search and told Woostra what was happening. "We have to find another way. Something that will set the hiding place of the journal apart from all this other stuff."

They considered the problem in silence for a long time, and then Woostra said, "If she hid it, she must have left a way to find it. A way that a Druid would understand. But we don't have a Druid with us to ask."

"What if she put something in one of the other journals?" Railing asked. "A key to the one that's missing."

"She would have done that right at the beginning, assuming she wanted it hidden right after Grianne left the order." Woostra took out the earliest journal and paged through it quickly. "Nothing written in here stands out."

"It wouldn't be something written." Railing took the journal from him and studied it. "Let me try another approach."

He called up the wishsong a second time, humming first and then shifting into words that just came to him as he envisioned a link between this book and the one missing. He sang of a need for rejoining, for assembling all of the journals as a unit, for a reunion and an end to separation.

At first, nothing happened. But then he felt a tugging and the sudden launch of the blue light, flaring out and sweeping through the room. Almost immediately it settled on the stone blocks of the south wall about midway up, flaring once as it revealed a series of red lines, then consuming the lines and turning dark again.

Woostra crossed quickly to the place in the wall upon which the magic had settled and began fingering the surfaces of the stone blocks and the crevices between. It took him only moments to discover what he was looking for, and abruptly one of the stone blocks popped loose, extending out far enough for Railing to pull it free and set it aside.

There, in the space behind the stone, was the missing journal.

Together they sat down and began to scan the contents.

Railing brushed strands of his unkempt hair out of his eyes. "I can't read any of this. What language is this?"

"Old Elfish," Woostra answered, giving him a look. "Interesting that she changed languages after filling up this first journal. She made a choice at that point to make the others more readable, so that they would be more accessible to anyone who found them. Why not this one?"

He scanned a few pages, searching.

"Read me something," Railing pressed. "How does it start?"

Woostra sighed, a hint of irritation flashing across his seamed face. "All right. First page, first entry. She uses a dating system I don't recognize. But here's what she's written."

I am Ard Rhys now, the legacy of the Druid order passed on to me by decree of my predecessor and by circumstance, as well. Though more newly come to the Druid order than others, I am asked to serve in this capacity. Trefen Morys and Bellizen have been with the order longer, but neither hesitated to defer to me. The others are too new and too unsure of themselves to take on such responsibility. So I am left with the choice of accepting what is asked of me, knowing it will likely consume my remaining years, or of rejecting it knowing it will instill within me an irrefutable certainty that I have failed Grianne Ohmsford.

So I have made my choice and taken on the role. I have given myself over to the demands of being Ard Rhys of the Fourth Druid Order. I wonder how I can make myself do this, knowing what I am giving up, knowing what I am embracing. I wonder how Grianne stood it for so long, even to the end of her days when she was betrayed and her life thrown into such upheaval.

I wonder if she has found peace where she has gone.

I wonder if I will one day find peace, as well.

"This is what we've been looking for!" Railing exclaimed excitedly. "Isn't it?"

"It appears so." Woostra seemed less enthused. "But let me look ahead and see if the answer we seek is actually here in these pages. Be patient a moment."

He began scanning the journal's pages, reading carefully, taking his time. He turned the worn sheets one by one, and with each Railing waited to hear that the answer they sought had been found. But Woostra just kept reading, shaking his head, muttering to himself, pausing now and then to decipher something that was unfamiliar to him.

"Some of this language is obscure, even to me," he said finally, looking up. "Most of it I can translate. She talks about how she will reform the order. She sets out the parameters and goals she intends to adopt. She mentions Grianne frequently, drawing strength from her example, repeating how she will . . ."

He was still scanning as he was talking, and suddenly he stopped doing both. He held up one hand to silence Railing and read the page he was on carefully. Then he went back and read it again.

He looked up, distraught. "Listen."

After much consideration, after weeks of delay, I have decided to keep my promise to Grianne. She asked it of me when she departed with Penderrin Ohmsford and confided that she would not be returning. She gave her journal into my keeping and told me that if I wished to read it, I could do so. Only yesterday, I did. It explained in detail what she intended to do. It revealed the immensity of her heart and courage. It revealed, as well, the depth of the suffering she has endured and what it has brought her to.

I am to give the journal to Penderrin and his descendants to keep safe. I am to tell him that he must read it and remember her story and pass it on to those Ohmsfords who come after so that they will understand the nature and importance of their history. I wonder if they would not understand that anyway, but perhaps she is afraid it will all be seen a different way if her writings are lost. Why she chooses that it be kept within her family rather than by the Druids, I don't pretend to understand.

At first I did not intend to honor my promise. I thought instead to keep the journal here, safe at Paranor, safe in the hands of the Druid order. Better that I fail her than allow the journal to be lost. It belongs with the others, here in the place where she was most at home.

But I have changed my mind. I will honor her wishes and give

*the journal over to Penderrin on my next visit to his home in
Patch Run.*

*I thought it odd, before reading the journal's last entries, that
she wished it given to her nephew rather than to his father, her
brother. But I know now she shares something with her nephew
that is different from what she shares with Bek. Something that
transcends all other considerations. Something that dictates her
decision regarding the fate of the journal.*

Something that requires I do my part for her.

"So the journal isn't even here?" Railing asked in disbelief.

"I would guess that it is somewhere in your home," Woostra answered. "If it hasn't been destroyed."

Railing thought a moment. "We have a trunk in which writings made by Ohmsfords since the time of my great-grandfather have been kept. Everything before that was lost during a period when it seemed all of the Ohmsfords had died out. The trunk came to us and my father took it into the attic of our home and left it there, bound and locked. We have been careful to preserve everything in it ever since."

"But you must have looked in it?"

"I don't think anyone has. Not since my grandfather died." Then he paused suddenly, and a startled look crossed his face. "Except for . . ."

Realization flooded his eyes. "My mother."

24

---◆---

HE EXPLAINED HIS MOTHER'S INVOLVEMENT TO WOOSTRA after they had returned Khyber Elessedil's journal to its hiding place in the bedchamber wall and sealed it up again.

"I saw her looking through the trunk once, not long after my grandfather died and it was delivered to us by my grandmother. I was by myself; I don't remember what Redden was doing. I do remember I was still pretty young and didn't know the history. I only knew that it had come from Grandfather, and that Father considered it very valuable."

"You never looked inside it yourself?" Woostra was leading him back through the empty corridors of the Keep and out into the courtyard past the desiccated bodies and piles of debris. "Or maybe your brother?"

"If Redden had looked, he would have told me. We tell each other everything." He did not mention Mirai. "I didn't look because I just didn't have any real interest. After a while, I sort of forgot about it."

"But you saw your mother?"

"She was kneeling by the trunk, and the lid was raised. She was holding papers and had others stacked beside her. Maybe there was a book or two, as well. Maybe even the missing journal. I can't remember. I almost said something, but the look on her face—I remember it so well. She was very upset. I didn't know why but I knew enough not to disturb her. I watched for a minute more and then left. I told

Redden, and later on when Mother wasn't around we went into the attic where the trunk was stored for a look. But it was locked again, and we didn't know where the key was. We thought about breaking the lock, but if we did Mother would know what we'd been up to and we decided it wasn't worth it. Just a bunch of old papers and books, we told ourselves."

He shook his head. "We never went back. Mostly, we didn't think it was important enough."

They crossed the courtyard and retraced their steps down into the tunnels. They might have found a way through the gates or over the walls, but Woostra never seemed to consider going another way. He was silent for a time after Railing finished his story, and it was only as they reached the far end of the tunnel and the hidden entry they had passed through coming in that he turned once more to the boy.

"Your mother is no friend to the Druids. Especially not to the Ard Rhys. She still blames the order for your father's death. You know all this, so you know we can't just go to her and ask to look in the trunk."

"We can't go to her at all," Railing declared. "She thinks Redden is safe. She can't be allowed to find out he isn't. If she sees me without him, she'll know something is wrong."

Back outside in the open air, the entrance to the tunnels sealed anew, Woostra turned to him again. The woods were dark save for where shards of moonlight sprinkled the forest floor in strange patterns.

"We have to go to Patch Run if we want to know what happened to the journal," he said quietly. His scarecrow form was hunched over as he bent close to Railing. "It may be that your mother has destroyed it. We can't discount that possibility. She was angry and distraught after your father died, and she might have done it out of spite. Whatever the case, we can't discover the truth unless we get a look in that trunk. Do you know where she keeps the key?"

Railing shook his head. "I've never seen it. It could be anywhere, I guess. Probably it's in her bedroom somewhere. What's the difference? I can't ask her to tell me. I can't let her even see me. I can't go back without Redden."

Woostra rocked back on his haunches. "I don't see that you have

a choice. If you want to find out what's become of Grianne Ohmsford, we have to look in that trunk. It's up to you. Better make up your
mind here and now, before you have to face the others."

Railing stared at him a moment and then looked away. The scribe
was right. They didn't have any other option. They didn't have time to
find another option even if there was one. He wondered if his mother
had destroyed the journal. If she had, none of this mattered. Even if
she hadn't, there was nothing to say it contained anything they
needed to know. But this had always been a long shot, right from the
first. He had known that. There had never been anything better than
a small chance that they could find Grianne Ohmsford and return
her to the Forbidding.

"You already know my answer," he said. "I don't want to give up.
But we have to find a way to do this that won't let Mother know that
anything has happened to Redden."

Woostra grunted. "It won't be the first miracle we've performed
since all this started."

Back on the *Quickening*, it was Mirai who came up with a solution to
their problem of how to gain access to the contents of the trunk without exposing Railing's presence.

"Sarys doesn't need to know you're there at all, Railing," she told
him. "Not if I'm the one who goes to see her."

They were discussing the matter on the foredeck—the Highland
girl, the boy, Woostra, Skint, and Farshaun. Austrum was in the pilot
box, and the other Rovers were lounging about nearby, but all were
out of hearing. Woostra had just finished relating what he and Railing had discovered at Paranor, concluding with the boy's recollection
of the trunk being delivered to the twins' home in Patch Run.

"I could go up to the house," Mirai continued, keeping her voice
low enough that the others had to lean close to hear, "and tell Sarys
that her sons are still safe and sound in Bakrabru, but busy with the
Ard Rhys. The Ard Rhys never said anything about how long they
would be gone, so Sarys has no reason to question me. I could say
that I've come home on an errand for my father and decided to visit
long enough to let her know everything is fine. Deliberate lies, but

necessary ones. If we do it in daylight, I can entice her out of the house. While we're visiting, Railing can slip in through the back door, find the key, open the trunk, and have a look."

There was a long silence. "But you don't know where the key is," Skint pointed out to Railing. "You'll have to hunt for it."

"You don't know if the missing journal is in the trunk," Farshaun added.

"You don't know if you can read the journal even if it is in the trunk," Skint continued. "It might be in whatever language Khyber was using in the other one. Old Elfish or whatever. This whole plan sounds like a disaster in the making. Isn't there a better way?"

"We're listening, if you know of one," Woostra snapped back irritably.

Mirai shook her head. "Stop arguing and listen for a minute. There isn't a better plan. There isn't even *another* plan. The facts are simple. Only Railing or I could even approach Sarys without drawing suspicion. The rest of you wouldn't get through the front door. Since Railing can't do this, it has to be me. And I wouldn't be offering at all, believe me, if I didn't think it was possible. I just have to distract Sarys long enough to give Railing a chance. If he can't find the journal, then at least we've tried." She looked directly at Railing. "Isn't this what you want to do?"

He nodded quickly. "I made the decision coming back to the ship. I can risk being disappointed if this doesn't work out, but not living with myself if I don't even try."

"Well, it will take a lot of trying and a lot more luck than skill." Skint was conceding nothing. "I don't know how you can manage it."

"Would it help you if I told you that I know where the key to the trunk is?" Mirai said, cocking one eyebrow.

Skint stared at her for a long moment. "On the other hand, this boy does seem to have more luck than most." He gave an elaborate shrug. "I suppose we had better give him his chance."

They lifted off and flew on through the remainder of the night, passing out of the Dragon's Teeth, across the Mermidon, down the length of the Runne Mountains, and out over the broad sweep of the Rainbow Lake. The skies remained clear and they passed only a handful of other airships as they traveled down the flight corridor that ran from Tyrsis and Varfleet south, easing their way toward their destination.

Railing slept again for a time, at Mirai's behest, aware that the few hours he had managed so far were not nearly enough to give him the rest he needed. The stress he was feeling by anticipating what lay ahead only added to that he was already experiencing from worrying about his brother. Mirai told him again as she accompanied him be-lowdecks that they would get Redden back. They would not abandon him; they would not give up on finding him. It didn't matter what they found in the trunk or what they had to do to find Redden him-self. They would get him back safe.

Then she lay next to Railing and snuggled up against him, and both were asleep in seconds.

It was dawn when Skint came down to shake them awake. "We're there," he said.

Farshaun was in the pilot box when they came back on deck. He gave them a quick once-over and nodded enigmatically, as if satisfied with what he saw. "We're just west of Patch Run." His gaze shifted to Railing. "Your house is farther down the shore, but not far. We'll land *Quickening* in one of these coves and lie at anchor while you take a flit the rest of the way."

The boy and the girl nodded. "I'll drop Railing off just before the house is in sight. He can walk in and slip around back while I draw Sarys outside."

"You'll have to be quick," Farshaun said. "You won't have all that much time. Sarys is sharp enough to sniff out a deception if you daw-dle."

Both Railing and Mirai knew this well enough not to have to be told, but they nodded anyway. Timing and stealth would mean every-thing if Railing was to avoid discovery, and they were aware of what would happen if he were found sneaking into his own house.

Farshaun swung *Quickening* into a cove only a short distance from the Ohmsford home while still safely out of sight. Once the air-ship was settled and moored, Austrum rigged one of the flits and with help from the other Rovers released it from its mooring cradle by removing the blocks and ropes that held it fast.

"Remember," Woostra told the boy as he started after Mirai for the flit. "If you find the journal, bring it with you whether you can read its contents or not. We may have need of it for reference purposes. We don't want to have to rely on memory if there's a question later."

Railing nodded and climbed into the flit, cramming himself into the narrow cockpit behind Mirai. The girl unhooded the parse tube that contained the single diapson crystal powering the tiny craft, and they slowly lifted off into the early-morning light.

They eased their way down the coastline, staying just above the water and below the tips of the trees bordering the shore. Both knew where they were and how far they could go before risking discovery, and so they said nothing as they flew east toward Patch Run.

When Mirai maneuvered the flit into a landing site, Railing was not surprised to find that it was one he had used hundreds of times before, one he would have chosen himself if he had been at the controls. Mirai released the restraining straps that buckled them both in place, and Railing extricated himself from the cockpit and climbed free.

"It's maybe fifteen, twenty minutes' walk from here," he said to her. "Give me a chance to get close to the house before you fly in. When I see you come out with Mother, I'll go in the back way. Give me as much time as you can." He paused. "I forgot to ask. Where does Mother keep the key to the trunk? And how do you know this?"

Mirai couldn't contain her grin. "It's in the bottom drawer of her nightstand. I gave her a necklace last year that I brought back from one of my trips. A gift. After admiring it, she put it in the nightstand. I was there when she did it. I caught a glimpse of a large iron key at the back of the drawer—perfect for opening a trunk. I'm guessing there's only one locked trunk in your house?"

He returned the grin. "You are full of surprises."

She nodded without answering, giving him a wink, and with a parting wave he started off.

He went quickly through the trees, staying back from the shoreline now, wanting to come in from behind his home. The day was warming and sunlight streamed out of the bright, clear sky. He wrinkled his brow in response to the glare. There would be no help from clouds or mist on this day. If he made even the smallest mistake, he would be revealed.

When his home finally came in sight, he was still well back of it. He worked his way around to where he could see not only the house but also the pathway leading down to the docks where Mirai would rope off the flit once she flew in. Crouched down amid trees and brush so that he was safely hidden, he waited. Memories surfaced unbidden of Redden and himself— of adventures shared, challenges met and overcome, and lessons learned. The longing to go back was so acute that tears filled his eyes. He wanted things to be the way they had been. He wanted his brother back, and he wanted to come home.

He had just taken a deep, steadying breath and cleared his eyes when he saw Mirai appear on the pathway. She never looked in his direction, her eyes turned toward the house, and a moment later his mother appeared, coming out through the door in a rush to embrace Mirai warmly and usher her onto the porch. He could hear snatches of their conversation, but not enough to determine what they were saying. Then they disappeared from view, and for endless minutes he could neither see nor hear them at all.

Long minutes later, they reappeared carrying a pot of tea and cups and a plate of muffins that they took to the table and benches set out on the lawn, seating themselves where they could look out across the broad sweep of Rainbow Lake.

Railing got to his feet at once and moved back through the trees until the house blocked his view of the women; then he hurried for the back door. It was unlocked, and he was inside quickly and moving toward his mother's bedroom. Her sleeping room was on the first floor because she had ceded the rooms on the second floor to her sons, so he got to it quickly. Kneeling in front of the nightstand, he reached down to open the lowest drawer. It wouldn't budge. He tried again, thinking it might be stuck. Still nothing. But there wasn't a keyhole. If there was a lock, where was the keyhole?

He was still in the process of trying to find a way to open the drawer when he heard someone come in from outside.

He had only seconds to hide. He heard the footsteps cross the common room and start down the hall. Dropping flat, he squirmed under the wood-frame bed, remembering as he did how he had done so as a child when playing hide-and-seek with his brother. It was a much tighter fit now, but he managed to squeeze himself in and inch his way toward the far side.

He watched his mother's legs appear through the doorway. To his surprise, she moved toward the nightstand and knelt before it. He shrank deeper into the shadows of his concealment and stopped breathing, praying she wouldn't stoop any lower. If she did and glanced beneath the bed, he would be caught.

But instead Sarys did something else, something he couldn't see. Seconds later he heard a distinct click, the release of a catch, and the lower drawer sprang open several inches. His mother opened it all the way, reached inside, took something out, and closed it again.

He waited until she had left the room and gone back outside, her footsteps indicating she was descending the porch steps, and he was back out of his hiding place and searching the surfaces of the nightstand for the lock release. He found it after only a few experimental pressings—a peg knob located near the back panel, the third in a line of four. It gave at his touch, and the drawer sprang open a second time.

He looked inside. Jewelry, some letters bound in a ribbon, some coins, a few artifacts . . .

And a trunk key.

He snatched it up, closed the drawer carefully, and headed for the steps leading to the second floor and the attic above. He paused as he neared the stairs, aware that if his mother was looking into the house she might see him going up. But Sarys had her back turned, engaged in deep conversation with Mirai. He thought the latter might have glanced his way, but quickly dismissed the idea. Mirai wasn't stupid.

He went up the stairs, his passage swift and silent. At the top, he rounded the banister and went down the hallway. A second set of steps, enclosed by a wall and shut away behind a door, led up to the attic. He eased the door open, peered upward into the dark, and began to climb.

The attic was deeply shadowed and thick with gloom. A single window set at the front of the house let in what light there was. Dust motes danced on the air where the sun streamed through the glass, and shadows layered furniture and boxes draped in cloth coverings. It had been a long time since Railing had been up here, and he took a moment to orient himself. More memories of childhood flooded his mind—images of Redden and himself as young boys playing games in this storage space—but he set them aside and began to search for the trunk.

He found it quickly enough. It was tucked back behind some boxes, covered with a sheet and wrapped with cord. He studied the cord for a moment to memorize how it was wrapped before loosening the knots and pulling off the sheet. He knelt in front of the trunk and tried the key in the lock. It turned easily, and the lock fell away.

Carefully, he raised the lid and looked inside. The trunk was stuffed with books and papers of all sorts, some labeled, some not. There were logbooks, journals, maps, charcoal and painted portraits, and other recordings both written and drawn. He glanced at the whole of it momentarily and then began to go through it systematically, again being careful of the order of things so that he could put it all back the way he had found it.

He discovered what he was looking for after only a few minutes. The journal was tucked down by itself against the front wall of the trunk, apart from the rest of the stacks, clearly taken out at some point in the past and then put back again so that it could be easily found. Railing knew at once that his mother had read it, and whatever she had found had caused her to place the journal aside from the rest of the contents.

He opened it to be sure of what he had and found Grianne Ohmsford's name written on the inside of the cover. He skipped quickly to the back of the diary, to the last few paragraphs written, and began reading.

This will be my final entry as Ard Rhys of the Third Druid Order. It will be my final entry of any kind, as I will leave tomorrow with Penderrin Ohmsford for Stridegate, there to keep the promise I made to myself weeks ago when the boy came for me inside the Forbidding and brought me out again. That he should have come for me, that he should have saved me when all other efforts would surely have failed, that he should have risked so much for someone he knew so little about, cannot go unrewarded.

He has sacrificed much for me; now I must sacrifice for him. I will fly to Stridegate and set free the girl he loves, who was taken from him by the tanequil in exchange for the staff that would provide me my freedom from the Forbidding. I will repay my debt, and by doing so I will step down from my position as Ard Rhys and leave forever my life as a Druid.

There was much more that followed, but no time now to read it all. Railing closed the book, tucked it into his tunic, and began replacing the contents of the trunk in the order in which he had removed them. When he was finished, he closed the lid, draped the sheet back in place, and retied the cords so that everything looked exactly as he had found it. He didn't think his mother would notice any changes, but there was no point in taking chances. His mind was racing as he worked, excited that he had discovered what he was looking for, already anticipating where it might lead. He could barely concentrate on what he was doing, so anxious was he to get to a place where he could read the entry uninterrupted.

Finished, he departed the attic, returned the key to his mother's nightstand, and slipped out the back door.

Neither his mother nor Mirai saw him go.

He returned through the woods to where Mirai had left him earlier, having agreed that they would meet back here when both were finished. Mirai would take a while longer with his mother to be certain that he had enough time to find what he was looking for—if it was there to be found. Sitting back against a tree trunk in the shade, where he could escape the heat of the day, he retrieved the journal from his tunic, opened it anew, and began reading through it in detail.

He was reading it for the second time when he heard the flit approaching and watched Mirai settle it down smoothly in the clearing. Railing rose and went over to her immediately.

"I found it!" The words just burst out, his excitement too strong to contain them.

"I'm glad," she said, but didn't sound very glad.

"What's wrong?"

"Nothing much. I just spent two hours lying through my teeth to someone I happen to like a lot and who trusts me to tell her the truth. She's your mother, and I deceived her badly, and I didn't much like doing it. That's all."

"Mirai, I know you . . ."

"She asked how you and Redden were, Railing. She told me she was worried about you, and I said you were both doing fine."

He stared at her in stunned silence.

"I just had to get that out. Just so you know. We don't have to talk about it again." She beckoned. "Climb on. Let's go."

They flew back to the *Quickening* in silence.

25

RETURNED TO THE *Quickening*, RAILING SAT HUDDLED WITH
Mirai, Skint, Woostra, and Farshaun Req at the bow of the airship
while he first related the history of his family in the time of Grianne
Ohmsford—including the revolt of the rebel Druids at Paranor—and
then read the final entry in Grianne Ohmsford's journal aloud. No
one interrupted while he did this, and for a few long moments afterward the silence continued. The day was winding down, the sun
drifting west toward the horizon and the light beginning to wane. It
had taken longer than he had expected to travel to Patch Run, retrieve the journal, and return to the vessel. Railing could feel time
slipping away, its passage swift and unstoppable, running through his
fingers like grains of sand.

"Let me get this straight," Skint said finally. "Your great-aunt, once
the Ilse Witch, then Ard Rhys, simply walked away from the Druids
in order to exchange places with this girl, this Cinnaminson? She
gave up everything to become a slave to an ancient magical creature
that took the form of a giant tree and made young girls into spirits,
invisible creatures that live in the air?"

"She felt she owed it to her brother's son, because the tree took
Cinnaminson as part of its payment for giving Penderrin Ohmsford
its branch as a talisman that would allow him to pass through the
Forbidding and back again." Railing felt a surge of irritation at the

way the Gnome was putting things, but he managed to stay calm as he spoke. "The girl he loved had been taken from him, and Grianne Ohmsford believed she should be returned. To do that, she had to change places with her."

"But don't you see?" Mirai added quickly. "It's more than that. She was unhappy, and she knew she would never be happy as long as she was connected to the Druids. She could not continue as Ard Rhys. She was hated and distrusted in too many quarters. People would not forgive her. Haven't you heard the stories of her time as the Ilse Witch? Too many knew them and could not forget or forgive. And once you've become as marked as she was, no matter how much good you do or how many people you help later on, you never entirely escape what you were. We are the sum of our lives and not simply pieces of them. We are the whole of our time in this world. Grianne Ohmsford couldn't live with what that meant. She was looking for a way out."

"So she found it as an aeriad in service to the tanequil," Woostra said slowly. He gave Skint a look. "She wasn't a slave, Skint. Not from the sound of her words in that final entry. Not from the little we have written down in our histories of the tanequil and the aeriads that are bound to it. The symbiosis might not be entirely clear to us, but there was never a suggestion that the voices speaking to Penderrin were troubled or miserable, or that slavery was involved."

"If you say so." The Gnome Tracker was clearly not convinced. "But look at what we are left with, even if your interpretation of things is true. We have to undertake a journey to this place called Stridegate—which I, for one, have never been to—to find this tree and persuade it to release Grianne Ohmsford from her service so that she can come back with us into the Forbidding and confront the Straken Lord. Think about that. Why would the tree agree to do this? Before, it wanted an exchange of bodies—Grianne Ohmsford for the girl. Whom do we exchange? Or how do we persuade it that no exchange is possible, so it has to release Grianne and never mind that other little detail? Then there's the matter of Grianne being well over a hundred years old. Sort of ancient to be going into combat against demons and such, don't you think? And that's if she even agrees to come back with us in the first place! Would you do something like that? If it were me, I would tell you to push off."

"I won't dispute any of those arguments." Railing gave a shrug. He even managed a smile. "Why would I bother to try? You're right about every one. But it doesn't matter. I'm going anyway. I have to. If there is even one chance in a thousand that we might get what we want, that we might be able to bring my great-aunt back with us and free Redden, then I have to take that chance."

He looked around at the faces of his companions. "I'm not asking anyone to go with me if they don't think they can do so willingly. Mirai and I have made our decision. The rest of you have to do the same. I only read the journal entry so that you could hear it for yourselves and make your own judgment."

"You might remember that only a couple of days ago we weren't in the least convinced that the writings we uncovered even existed," Mirai pointed out. "We had no real reason to think they contained anything at all about what became of Grianne Ohmsford. We thought she was dead and gone and her disappearance would be a mystery forever. Now we have reason to think otherwise. We know she's out there and very likely still alive. We know that at least once before someone in service to the tanequil was released to come back. And Railing's grandmother came back whole and unchanged!"

She took a deep breath. "Here's what I think. This search is all about faith. Faith that what's clearly impossible might somehow turn out not to be. Faith that we can do what we never would have thought we could. Faith to keep going when everything tells us we should turn back."

She exchanged a quick glance with Railing. He gave her a small nod and a smile and waited. The silence deepened.

Then Farshaun cleared his throat and shifted positions on the decking. "My bones don't tolerate hard surfaces like they once did. Too many years of riding airships and sleeping on hard ground. But I don't fancy making any changes in my life. I don't have enough time left to try experiments." His eyes locked on Railing's. "I'm all in on this. I like the sound of it. Maybe Mirai is right. Maybe this is a good chance to find out something important about the limits of possibility."

"You just want to keep an eye on us," Mirai deadpanned.

"I'll go, too," Woostra said. "You might need someone who can explain how an Ard Rhys thinks, how her mind works. Whatever she is now, however we find her, Grianne Ohmsford will still think like an Ard Rhys."

They all looked at Skint. "I didn't say I wasn't going," the Gnome said defensively. "In point of fact, I am. At least I know how to find my way around in that country. None of the rest of you could find your behind with both hands. I just wanted to be sure you understood how this was likely to turn out. You have to go into something like this with your eyes wide open."

"That's exactly what we need you for." Farshaun gave him a look. "To help us keep our eyes wide open."

Skint grimaced. "Glad you understand. Now, when do we leave?"

It was decided they would depart at first light, flying north toward their destination. Skint believed they could find their way as far as Taupo Rough without much trouble, but it might be a problem after that. They would have to find someone who knew where Stridegate could be found. Likely it was in the Charnal Mountains, and they were wide and deep. This was a journey that could take them weeks, and it didn't seem to him they had weeks to spend.

That prompted Railing to suggest they leave at once. Since time was precious, they couldn't afford to waste it. But Farshaun suggested they would be better off waiting until daylight because they were traveling into strange country and would likely encounter dangerous situations on their way, even apart from Gnome raiders and sky pirates.

A compromise was reached. They would travel now to the far shores of Rainbow Lake, where they would find shelter and anchor east of the city of Varfleet. After a good night's sleep, perhaps the last they would get for some time to come, they would wake at sunrise and continue north to their destination.

This wasn't entirely satisfactory to Railing, given his desire to reach their destination in as little time as possible, but he understood the need for caution, too. So they crossed Rainbow Lake as the sun slipped west and by nightfall were moored in a secluded cove ten miles east of Varfleet and safely out of view. Farshaun had insisted earlier that Austrum and the other Rovers be informed of what they intended to do, and while the company ate its dinner the old man explained to his younger companions the general nature of their journey without getting too specific. He stayed away from what he knew about the Forbidding and the demons and stuck to the reason for their search—to discover the fate of Grianne Ohmsford. Mirai pitched in, picking up loose threads and adding information where she saw it would help. Austrum asked the most questions, but Mirai was there to provide the answers each time. Railing watched how attentive he was to her, how he listened without argument and was deferential and polite. A far cry from his brashness of earlier, the boy thought, vaguely irritated all over again.

In the end, the Rovers agreed to sign on, young and bold enough to accept the risks for the promise of an extraordinary adventure, sure enough of their strength and resilience to reject the possibility of dying. Their elders had a darker view of the risks involved, but the young Rovers were all enthusiasm and confidence. Railing remembered feeling like that when he and Redden had set out with the Ard Rhys and her company for the Breakline. But all of that had been knocked out of him in the struggle to survive the horrors that had attacked them in the Fangs. All of that belonged to someone he had been and not who he was now.

He went to sleep shortly afterward, more tired than he had realized. Mirai was still awake when he rolled into his blanket, talking with Austrum. They spoke in whispered voices, their heads inclined close. Railing wanted to interrupt them, to put a stop to it. He didn't like what he was seeing, but he knew enough about Mirai to accept that she would do what she wanted no matter what he thought about it.

He closed his eyes instead and slept.

It was still dark when he woke again, the sky clear and bright with stars, the world a silent and wondrous nightscape. He lifted himself on one elbow and looked around. Someone had called his name, but everyone around him seemed to be sleeping. Dreading what he would find, he looked over to where he had last seen Mirai, but Austrum had gone and she was sleeping alone. He watched her for a moment, then threw off the blanket and got to his feet. He looked around the starlit darkness at the sleeping men and finally found the big Rover well off to one side near the pilot box. Then he heard his name again, and he scanned the decks of *Quickening* from bow to stern, in search of the source. Everyone was asleep—even the sentry sitting near the stern where it faced back toward the shoreline. They were anchored several hundred yards offshore, and when he walked from the port to the starboard railing he could find no trace of another vessel from which the voice might have come.

Perplexed, he stood waiting for his name to be called again, listening intently to the silence, trying to convince himself he had not been mistaken.

But instead of hearing his name, he saw a light appear on the shoreline—a tiny flash that came and went in a steady blinking. He watched as the light began to grow brighter, and finally he realized that it was moving toward him. He backed up a step and almost called out for Mirai. But by then the light was right on top of him, and he found his voice had disappeared in his sense of wonder and surprise.

When the light abruptly disappeared, a young girl was standing before him. She was no more than ten or twelve years old, her hair white-blond and her eyes a stunning depthless blue. She smiled and stretched out her hand to him, and he surrendered his own.

The light returned, enfolding them both, closing them away. Everything around them disappeared, and there were only the two of them standing face-to-face, joined by the meeting of their eyes and hands. Railing tried to ask who she was and what she was doing, but his voice had deserted him completely. She seemed to know that he was trying to speak, however, and even though she remained silent, she gave him a reassuring smile and a squeeze of her hand.

Then the light flared once, bright enough that even the girl disappeared within it, her hand releasing his as she faded away, and when the light was gone and his vision had cleared sufficiently that he could see in the darkness again, he found himself alone.

But he was no longer aboard *Quickening*. He was standing on the shore where he had first seen the light. He looked down at his feet to make certain of where he was and then out into the cove to where the

airship was lying at anchor. His first thought was that he was dreaming, even though he knew deep down inside where truths are always
revealed that he wasn't, that this was actually happening in his waking life and it was real.

"As real as the search you undertake for the Ilse Witch, Railing
Ohmsford," a voice whispered to him.

He turned and found an old man standing behind him, a
white-bearded ancient cloaked in robes that were worn and ragged,
his tall, lean body stooped with age and perhaps the weight of something much greater, something that was reflected in his eyes as he
studied the boy with an intense but not unfriendly gaze.

"How do you know about Grianne Ohmsford?" Railing asked,
finding that his voice was now returned to him.

The old man made a dismissive gesture. "Oh, I know quite a lot
about most things. It is my business to know."

Railing shook his head. "I have the strangest feeling I should know
you."

"Or at least know of me."

"You have use of magic, don't you? Are you a Faerie creature?"

"I am. I was well known to others in your family. I have helped
them now and then over the years by offering respite from weariness
and stress and advice about how to continue. Sometimes they took
both and sometimes they took only one and sometimes they did not
take either. Once or twice, I gave them talismans. Like this one."

He held out his hand, his fingers closed about whatever lay within.
Railing hesitated. "Take it," the old man said. "Would you reject a gift
from the King of the Silver River?"

Railing stared in surprise, then quickly extended his hand. The
old man dropped a ring into it. The ring had a very odd look to it. The
band was formed of a series of gold strands that had been interwoven
in an intricate, delicate design. There were perhaps a dozen threads
in all. At the apex a single gemstone, milky white and opaque, had
been fastened in place. Railing had never seen anything like it. He
tested the strength of the woven strands to see how much give there
was to the metal and found to his surprise that there was scarcely any.
The metal felt hard and fixed.

"Slip it on your finger," the King of the Silver River suggested. "Go on, it will not harm you."

Railing did as he was told. The ring fit perfectly, the metal suddenly soft and malleable, molding itself to his finger as if it were a living thing. The boy studied it a moment, admiring its look, and then tried pulling on it. It came off without difficulty and turned rigid and unyielding again.

The old man nodded. "It belongs to you now until you choose to give it to another. Should another try it on while it is yours, it will not respond."

"What does it do?" Railing asked. He was still trying to get used to the idea that this was the legendary Faerie creature who had appeared to members of the Ohmsford family at various times over the centuries, always with a willingness to help when their lives seemed darkest and their need greatest.

"It does what you need it to do when you cannot find your way." The King of the Silver River smiled. "That's what I have come to talk to you about. Finding your way."

"Can you help me find Grianne Ohmsford?" the boy asked excitedly. "Can you tell me where she is?"

The old man shook his head. "I am not here for that. The ring can show you the way once you know what you are looking for. I am here to talk to you about what you *should* be looking for. I know the quest you undertake, and I know the reasons for it. I have listened to your conversations on both sides of the Rainbow Lake and seen the writings you have uncovered. I know your heart. I can feel your passion. But you travel down a road that may lead to your ruin."

Railing started to ask for an explanation, but the old man had already turned away. "Come sit with me while we talk. My bones are weary from tracking your efforts. I need to rest them."

They sat together on the trunk of a fallen tree, looking back across the water at *Quickening* and the star-filled skies that silhouetted her. For a long moment, the King of the Silver River did not speak.

"This is going to be difficult for you to hear, Railing Ohmsford—and even more difficult for you to believe. Perhaps you won't heed me. Perhaps you will dismiss me out of hand. But at least I will have spoken the words and you will have had a chance to assess their worth. And perhaps, if you allow yourself to do so, you will take them to heart and weigh them carefully. If not now, then at another time in the not-too-distant future, before it is too late."

"What is it?" the boy asked him. "What would you tell me?"

"You search for Grianne Ohmsford, Ard Rhys of the Third Druid Order. You believe that by finding her, you will find, as well, a way in which to bring your brother back to you. But you should understand that what you seek is not necessarily what you will find."

The old man folded his hands in his lap. "The Grianne Ohmsford you seek is lost to you. She has been gone for a hundred years, since she gave herself to the tanequil in exchange for the girl who became your grandmother. What's been gone for so long cannot be brought back. Not as it once was. Not whole and complete again, perhaps not even alive. Understand, Railing. She is transformed. She became another creature entirely by choosing to live as an aeriad. She cannot take that back, and you cannot expect to find a way to make her."

"I can try," Railing interrupted, upset by now with how the conversation was going. "Grianne switched places with Cinnaminson. Why can't it happen that someone switches places with her?"

The King of the Silver River nodded. "It would seem that such a thing would be possible. But the switch between Grianne and your grandmother happened only weeks after your grandmother gave herself to the tanequil. Only weeks, Railing. Not more than a hundred years. You can expect things to stay pretty much the same in weeks, but not after a century has passed."

"What are you saying, then? That I should just give up and go home and forget my brother? That there is nothing I can do for him?" Railing was so incensed by the idea that he was shouting. He caught himself, glancing out at the dark shape of *Quickening*, but there was no sign that anyone aboard had heard. He looked back at the old man. "I won't do it. I won't abandon Redden."

"Nor am I asking you to. Nor would I expect it of you." The aged eyes seemed to look right into him. "But finding Grianne Ohmsford may not be the answer. It may end badly for everyone involved. It may not yield the result you hope to achieve."

"You can't know that. You can't know how it will end!"

"I am a Faerie creature, and I have the use of magic and the gift of premonition. While I cannot know the answers to all things, I can sense if they will be good or bad for those involved. It is so here. My sense of it is very strong."

Railing took a deep breath to steady himself, not wanting to blurt out what he was thinking. "What are you telling me to do?"

"Only this. Make your choice wisely. Do not become wedded to the idea that there is only one way."

"I already know that."

The King of the Silver River shook his head. "You only think you know. In the end you may discover you are a child playing with matches and in danger of burning everything around you to the ground. Think carefully. Do you really wish to continue on after what I have just said, or will you turn back and go into the Forbidding alone?"

There was a long silence as the boy and the old man faced each other. In the distance, something splashed in the waters of the cove, and the dark shape of a bird of prey winged skyward with food for her young.

"I cannot give this up," Railing said.

"You can give anything up just as you can take anything up. But once the choice is made, there are consequences. And you cannot change those consequences. You can only live with them."

The insistence in the old man's words was daunting. Clearly, he believed what he was saying. Railing hesitated. Neither of them knew exactly what would happen if Railing persisted in his search for Grianne Ohmsford, but the King of the Silver River seemed certain that it would not be anything good. Yet even creatures of magic could be mistaken. Even they could be wrong. The history of the Ohmsford family had demonstrated that often enough.

Railing was no fool; he knew he should consider carefully what he was being told. He had until at least sunrise to do so. And he had all the days of his journey after that, as well, didn't he? He would not dismiss the old man's warning out of hand. He would think on it for as long as there was reason to do so.

"Will the ring guide me to wherever I choose to go?" he asked the other.

The King of the Silver River shrugged. "Or out of wherever you've been, should that become necessary. But know this. Unlike some magic, it has a finite life. It will show the way each time you ask for it, but each time one strand of its woven threads will disappear until all are gone. Save the stone for when the threads are gone and your life is at such risk there is no other magic you can call upon. That time may come sooner than you think."

Railing took a deep breath. "I thank you for the ring and the advice. I will consider carefully everything you have told me."

"Will you?"

The boy nodded uneasily. The old man seemed to see right through him. "How do I get back to the ship from here?"

The King of the Silver River smiled. "Who is to say you ever left?"

Then he disappeared, and the shoreline and the trees and any view of the airship anchored in the cove disappeared, as well, and Railing woke from what might have been only a dream still wrapped in his blanket and lying on wooden planking, and he was aboard *Quickening* once more, and all that remained was the silence and his memory of the Faerie creature's words.

It might have been a dream if not for the ring that nestled deep inside his pants pocket.

Railing was awake for much of the rest of the night, mulling over what the King of the Silver River had told him. He was conflicted in every conceivable way, even as to whether what had happened was real.

He wanted it to have been a dream—in spite of the ring's presence—mostly because he didn't want to believe that what he had been told had any value. Even accepting that there was a possibility things wouldn't work out as he wished, that Grianne Ohmsford was indeed beyond their reach and would never return, he did not want to abandon his search. Because if he did, if he gave up on trying to find Grianne, he would be forced to do what the old man had told him he ultimately must. He would be forced to go after Redden himself, into the Forbidding, a place much, much worse than the one he had barely escaped before, and with no idea of how to go about finding, let alone rescuing, his brother.

Just thinking of it terrified him. Once he had been so sure of himself, so certain that he could just hop a flit, charge back into the Forbidding, and save his brother. No more. He was ashamed of his fear, but he could not dispel it. He might be brave enough flying a Sprint into the wilderness of the Shredder, but that was child's play compared with what he would face inside the Forbidding. He'd had time to think about it, to understand better what it meant, and his fear was so overwhelming that he could not come to terms with it.

As a result, he could not give up the idea of finding Grianne and persuading her to stand with him against the creatures of the Forbidding.

It could happen. It must.

He agonized until sunrise and then rose with the others, moving about the *Quickening* as if half dead, consumed by fears and doubts and confusion. He knew he should tell someone about what had happened to him during the night. He knew he should reveal what he had been told. But if he did so, the search was over. Skint, for certain, would turn back and try to persuade the others to do the same. Austrum and the other Rovers would give up, as well. Maybe even Mirai would abandon him, in spite of having said she wouldn't.

"Ready to set out?" Farshaun Req asked him as they sat around on the foredeck eating breakfast.

All eyes turned toward him. He fingered the woven strands of the ring that he had kept concealed in his pocket.

He was surprised at how quickly he responded. "Ready," he said, and felt the world drop away inside.

26

Amid a pungent haze of smoke and ash and mist, cloaked in gloom and wrapped in pain, Aphenglow Elessedil opened her eyes. Somehow she was still in one piece. The last thing she remembered was clinging to the stern railing of the *Wend-A-Way* as the airship, shattered and burning, plunged earthward, completely out of control and seemingly doomed. She had been thrown backward off the railing with the last explosive attack of the fire launchers mounted on the Federation warship and stayed conscious for only a moment or two afterward—just long enough to feel *Wend-A-Way* begin to fall. Then everything had gone dark.

What she knew for certain was that she shouldn't be alive. She should be dead.

She looked around, still sufficiently dazed that she couldn't seem to get her bearings. Where was she? She wasn't aboard the airship any longer. She was lying on the ground; she could feel the cool dampness of the earth and grasses beneath her. She shifted her position slightly and caught the red glow of dying embers through the haze. The remains of the airship, she thought.

Then she remembered Arlingfant and Cymrian and the Elven Hunters who had been aboard the airship with her, and she forced herself into a sitting position. A wave of dizziness swept through her, and she seemed to hurt everywhere at once. But when she tested her arms and legs, one by one, she could tell that nothing was broken. Her ribs were another matter. At least several were cracked and perhaps worse. She took a moment to use her magic to layer her midsection with a healing wrap that gave her some relief from the pain.

Then, ignoring what pain still lingered, she forced herself to her feet and took a few steps toward the glow of the embers. She could tell the airship had come down in a forest; the trees closest to her were scarred and ripped by the force of the crash. Pieces of the vessel lay everywhere, scattered about like the bones of a dead thing. She found one of the Elven Hunters only a few feet away, what was left of him barely recognizable. Shivering at the implications of what this might mean about her sister and Cymrian, she stumbled ahead more quickly, looking everywhere at once.

She found the larger part of *Wend-A-Way* some distance farther on, her hull holed in a dozen places by enemy fire and her decking collapsed. The glow she had seen earlier was emanating from sections of wood planking that were still smoldering. The masts were shattered, and lengths of them lay all around the wreck. One was even caught up in the branches of one of the trees. The parse tubes and light sheaths had been thrown all across the space where the airship had come down. Yards of radian draws hung from the trees like spiderwebs.

She found parts of another of the crewmen nearby, able to tell that it wasn't Cymrian from the markings on the one remaining forearm. She pushed on through the haze, coughing as the acrid smoke and ash entered her lungs, peering about for signs of her sister and their protector. But she couldn't find either. She was widening her search to the areas outside the immediate crash site when she remembered the Elfstones. She had chosen not to use them when they had been attacked, relying instead on her Druid magic. But where had she put them? She began searching through her pockets without success. If they had fallen out somewhere during the crash, she would never find them. They had to be on her somewhere.

And they were, tucked in an outside pocket of her pants, down along her thigh. She felt their distinctive shape through the fabric and breathed a sigh of relief.

"Aphen."

She turned to find Cymrian coming toward her from out of the haze, his clothes soaked, wild and streaked with mud. Blood from a deep cut on his forehead ran down his face. She felt a sudden rush of emotion that surprised her—a sense of relief coupled with something much stronger.

"I can't find Arling," she told him at once. "Have you seen her?"

He shook his head. "I just now found my way to you. I was thrown off the ship when she came down. Right into a bog. Arling? I don't know. She might be anywhere."

"Let me see that cut," she said, moving over to examine his head.

She cleaned the wound as best she could with the sleeve of her tunic and then used a small bit of magic to close the gash and initiate the healing. He stood quietly while she did so, his lean features intense, his eyes turned away. "Are you all right?"

"Better than you, I think. Mostly I'm just sore. We have to find her, Cymrian."

He nodded as she finished and stepped away. "We will. Can you walk?"

"As far as you need me to."

"Then let's conduct a sweep of the area. Spread out from here. We'll find her quickly enough."

They began a slow outward circling from the ruins of *Wend-A-Way*, searching the brush and trees as they went, careful not to neglect the possibility that Arling was caught up in the branches of one of the trees. Around them, mist and smoke swirled through the night, thick and pungent. They were barely able to find their way, but they pushed steadily onward until at last they were far enough from the airship's remains that the haze had dissipated and they could see clearly again.

"This is close to where I landed," he said at last, stopping. "Maybe we're guessing wrong. Maybe she didn't even get off the ship. She could still be inside, trapped belowdecks. It looked as if the ship collapsed in on herself, so . . ."

He trailed off. "We'd better go back and have a look."

Aphenglow didn't need to be told what he was thinking. If Arling was in the airship wreckage, she had probably been crushed to death on impact.

They took a direct line back to *Wend-A-Way*. Cymrian left Aphen outside to wait as he began searching through the inside of the hull. He was gone a long time before reappearing. "Nothing," he said.

They stood together once more, looking everywhere but at each other. "I'll have to use the Elfstones," Aphenglow said finally. "It's risky, but I can't afford to worry about that. Arling could be dying out there."

To his credit, Cymrian didn't argue. He simply nodded.

She pulled out the Stones and dumped them from the pouch into her hand. Closing her fingers about them, she stretched out her arm and formed a picture of her sister's face, holding it firmly in her mind as she summoned the magic.

The blue light blazed to life and then spun away to their left. She wheeled quickly to square herself up to its beam, fixing the direction as it traveled only a short distance to a jumble of branches that had been torn away in the crash. Beyond was a tangle of grasses in which a body lay prone, nearly invisible against the muddied earth. The light held fast for a moment to mark the spot, then flared and was gone.

Cymrian was already moving. She hurried after him, jamming the Elfstones back in her pocket. It took them only minutes to make their way back through the trees and the brush. Arling lay just a short distance from where they had turned back from their earlier search. Aphen gritted her teeth in fury. They had been only steps away.

She rushed over to her sister and knelt. Arling was covered in mud and bleeding from her nose and mouth. She was breathing, but just barely, and her pulse was weak and unsteady. Quickly, Aphen checked for other injuries without finding any. But since Arling was unconscious it was difficult to be certain.

"She's in a bad way," she told Cymrian. "I'm afraid to move her."

"Can you tell if anything is broken?"

"Doesn't seem to be." She felt up and down her sister's arms and legs without finding any sign of broken bones. She explored Arling's body, as well. Nothing. "Can you lift her? By her shoulders, but don't let her head move when you do."

Cymrian did as she asked, and she felt underneath her sister's back. She had almost finished her exam when her fingers found metal splinters. Her breath caught in her throat. That last barrage from the Federation fire launchers must have done this. There were at least two, and perhaps more, of those splinters embedded in Arling's back. It was impossible to tell how deeply they had penetrated, but it seemed likely they were the source of the problem. The splinters, and the impact of Arling's fall from the ship, would explain a lot.

She took off her cloak and spread it on the ground beside her sister. "Can you roll her over on her stomach?" she asked Cymrian, indicating the cloak.

The Elven Hunter did so—carefully, tenderly, keeping everything as protected as he could manage. Aphen helped by turning Arling at her hips and legs as Cymrian turned her at her shoulders. It took only a moment to lay the injured girl on her stomach. Now both her sister and their protector could see the splinters and the blood that seeped from the wounds they had made. The splinters protruded from halfway up her back, close to where her heart was.

"I'll have to take them out," she said, looking at him. "But I don't know what that will do to her."

"If you don't take them out, you know for certain what it will do," he answered.

She called up her magic and layered her sister with a deadening spell that would numb her body against the pain and help to seal off the wounds as soon as the splinters were removed. She cut away Arling's tunic to expose her back and was horrified to find that in addition to the larger, more obvious wounds, there were dozens of smaller ones, as well. Arling must have been caught in a hailstorm of metal shards in that last attack. A wave of fear swept through her. If she made a mistake now or if she failed to do enough, she was going to lose her sister.

Before any further thoughts of that sort could take hold, she began the process of extracting the splinters. One by one, she removed them with steady, practiced movements, ripping off the sleeves of her tunic to wipe away blood and debris, pouring small amounts of liquid from her aleskin onto the wounds to help with the cleaning. She worked as quickly as she could, refusing to be distracted by her fears. Cymrian knelt beside her, watching silently. It seemed to her that it took an inordinate amount of time. The larger splinters came out easily enough; they were deeply embedded, but didn't appear to have penetrated or damaged any bones or the spinal column. The smaller shards were a different matter. Some of them were long and thin and not easily located. She reached inside her sister's body with her magic, extracting the splinters one by one.

When she had the last of them she cleaned the wounds and sat back, staring down at her sister's still body. Her breathing hadn't changed. Her pulse was still irregular. Something wasn't right. Taking out the splinters hadn't been enough to solve the problem.

She shook her head, knowing she had to do more, that she had missed something.

Across from her, Cymrian suddenly turned and looked off into the trees. "Someone's coming."

She hadn't heard anything. But she had learned by now that his ears were sharper than hers, in spite of her instincts and her magic. He would not be mistaken about something like this. She stared at him in confusion, saw the look on his face, and quickly said, "Don't go."

"You'll be fine," he said, already on his feet.

"It's not me I'm worried about. If you go, you'll be all alone."

"It doesn't matter. I can't let whatever's coming reach you and Arling. I have to stop it."

"Wait a few more minutes. I'll come with you."

He shook his head. "We don't have those minutes." He moved over and knelt beside her. "Take as long as you need with her. Whatever's out there, I will find a way to stop it."

She glanced down at her sister, knowing she was losing her, knowing at the same time that she was about to lose him, as well. "Cymrian, no."

He gave her a momentary smile. "It's my job to protect you, Aphen."

She made a small sound in her throat and reached for him, pulling him to her and kissing him hard on the mouth. She held the kiss for a long time, desperate to keep him close, realizing for the first time how terrible it would be to lose him. How many times had he saved her? How many times had he been there for all of them? She hadn't realized it before—hadn't let herself accept it, perhaps—not in the way she understood as she kissed him now. But there it was, full-blown and alive in her heart.

She cared for him every bit as much as he cared for her, in spite of all her efforts at distancing herself from his long-held affection for her.

When she released him, he said, "Be strong. I will be back for you."

Her eyes held him fixed in place for a second more. Then he turned away and was gone.

Stoon was not happy. The Federation warship had come out on top in the encounter with the Elven vessel, but as a consequence of the damage inflicted, the latter had gone into a steep dive and disappeared into the depths of Drey Wood, lost beneath a tangle of tree limbs and clouds of mist that obscured the entire forest. To make matters worse, the Federation ship had lost her steering capabilities and so much sail that it had barely managed to land for repairs. Spars, radian draws, and parse tubes alike were smashed and severed and exploded in such numbers that it would take hours, if not days, to put things right.

Realizing that by then they would lose track of the survivors of the crash—if there were any—he made up his mind to go after them on foot. Unfortunately, that meant he would have to release the mutants in the hold, because he certainly wasn't about to go mucking around in the forest alone. He lacked the necessary skills for that sort of work, and he imagined the Elf who served as Aphenglow's protector was much better trained in it than he was. Plus, he was not about to wager that any of them were dead, the crash notwithstanding, and he didn't want to find out the hard way that they were alive and well and enraged enough at what had been done to them to want to make an example of him.

So he would have to use the creatures Edinja had provided. As much as he hated the monsters, he might as well make use of them in the way in which Edinja had intended. He would make up a story later about what had happened—how he had tried to capture the girl and her companions alive but been unable to do so; how the mutants had overreacted to the threat; how he had been lucky to escape with his life. Edinja would have her doubts, but there would be nothing she could do about it at that point.

"Captain," he announced, once repairs were under way, "I am taking those things in the hold out for a walk. We'll hunt for the Elves on foot. Stay with the ship. Wait for me. I'll find you when it's over."

He could see the relief in the other's face and smiled to himself as he started down the ladder into the hold. No pretense of courage in that one. No danger that he would step outside the lines. The captain would be here when he returned.

Belowdecks, submerged in gloom and the dank smells of old wood and stale air, the assassin moved over to the cage. The animals inside were already stirring, hulking forms just visible as they rose from their crouching positions to face him. Their features were blunted and empty of expression, but their eyes watched him carefully. Huge, muscular creatures, any one of them could snap him in two with barely an effort. A part of him was terrified of them, even given his unmatched proficiency at killing. But Edinja had assured him they would do whatever he asked, and she wouldn't have sent him all this way just to have him killed. So he pushed back his fear, closed off his doubts, and kept his face as blank and fixed as theirs.

He came up to them and stopped. "I'm letting you out. You are to hunt for three Elves—a man and two women. They are out in the surrounding forest somewhere. I will point you in what I think is the right direction. Then you will search. When you find them, I want you to kill them. No hesitation, no stopping to think about it, no mistakes. Kill them. Do you understand me?"

They grunted, one after the other, an indication that they did. Good enough.

He unlocked the cage door, opened it, and stepped back. They lumbered through the opening, stretching their huge arms and hunching their shoulders. They looked about warily, and then faced him, waiting.

"Come outside," he ordered them, satisfied.

They climbed the ladder and emerged onto the warship deck.

Gloom and brume surrounded them, and they could barely see beyond the ship's railings to the closest of the trees. The captain and crew had moved well away to the stern. Several of the men held blades at the ready. Two of the crew were even manning one of the fire launchers. Stoon shook his head in disgust. What fools. They would be dead before they could bring any of those to bear, should the creatures with him wish it.

He gave the captain a farewell wave and walked to the rope ladder that had been thrown over the side, with the beasts trailing after him. Down the ladder they went, and when they were on the ground, Stoon chose his direction as best he could recall it from when he had seen the Elven airship spiral downward. By then, the Federation ship had herself been sideslipping, so he couldn't be sure. He hoped his hunters were equipped with good instincts and sharp senses; he hoped they were the hunters Edinja had promised.

But there was only one way to find out.

"Hunt them," he ordered, pointing west into the mist and trees.

The creatures stood where they were for a moment, sniffing the air, casting about like dogs before a hunt. They did not look at one another. They did not look at him.

Then one caught a scent that intrigued it and began to move away, the others following.

Stoon, fingering the blades strapped to his waist and legs and body to reassure himself he was ready for whatever would happen next, went after them.

With Cymrian gone, Aphenglow went back to work on her sister's wounds. She used a fresh infusion of magic to try to wake Arling, but the other's body resisted such intrusion and refused to respond to the effort—a clear indication that whatever was still wrong was serious. She backed away from her efforts, once again doing a slow, careful examination of her sister's back and sides where all the damage from the metal shards appeared to be the worst. But everywhere she looked she found the same thing—all of the splinters had been extracted, and blood from the wounds was barely seeping into the bandages.

Aphen sat back. It must have been the impact of her fall. She must have suffered broken ribs or worse. Perhaps a head injury. But without obvious bruising or evidence of broken bones, she needed sharper eyes than her own to see inside her sister's body.

Different eyes.

She took a deep breath to steady herself. Time was slipping away. For Arling. For Cymrian. For all of them.

Then she made the call for help, a deep-throated cry that reverberated through the forest silence. She made it three times and sat back to wait, eyes on the misty dark.

The owl, when it came, was small and nondescript, its colors unremarkable, its presence nonthreatening as it landed on her shoulder and perched there, perfectly still. A bore owl, not well known outside the Westland, and even there seldom seen. She did not look at it, did not acknowledge its presence. Instead she called up the magic she needed to bond with it, to make it her familiar, and when she was done the owl's eyes were her own, her vision so sharply enhanced that she could see as it did.

Like the owl's, her eyes stayed open and steady as she began a new search for her sister's injuries. But now she was seeing so much better than before. Every scratch, every pore, every tiny hair was visible—the ridges on the surface of Arling's skin, the tiny scars, the shadow of her bones, the minuscule places where wounds had split the skin but had already closed over. And inside her sister's body the pulsing of veins and capillaries, the slow rise and fall of her lungs, the soft beating of her heart—Aphenglow could see it all.

She searched with owl eyes and Elf fingers, an excruciatingly slow process given the urgency she felt. Where was the damage? Where was the thing that was stealing away her sister's life?

She found it when she was working her way up her sister's left side. There, beneath her arm, barely visible even to Aphen's owl eyes, was a pinprick from which nothing protruded and no blood flowed. Dirt and sweat had obscured it so thoroughly that it was virtually indistinguishable from the skin surrounding it. But when Aphen pulled back the skin from either side of the wound, she saw the sharp glint of metal. She held her finger to its tip without moving it in any direction and sent her magic down its long, slender length to discover that it was nestled against her sister's ribs and breastbone and buried inside her heart.

She had missed finding it before, thinking it only a part of Arling's bones. She had rushed herself; she had worked too fast. And it had nearly cost Arling her life.

Aphen sat back, terrified. Six inches of jagged metal, driven into her sister's heart. She had to extract it at once, but she could do nothing that would cause it to go deeper or cut further. It had penetrated far enough and done such damage already that it was close to ending Arling's life. It would take only a single mistake to finish the job it had started.

From somewhere not all that far away, she heard the sounds of a struggle and then a howl of anguish.

Faster! She had to work faster!

But that was exactly the wrong thing to do, of course. That was the mistake she had made before. She had to do exactly the opposite. She had to take her time.

Her owl eyes fixed and steady, her fingers splayed to either side of the wound so as to pull back the skin, Aphenglow Elessedil reached downward into the wound with her magic, wrapped its strands around the length of the metal shard, softened the edges and the razor-sharp spurs, and began to pull it out. She had only heard of the procedure; she had never done it herself and never seen it done. The Ard Rhys, it was rumored, had twice performed this form of extraction—but only once successfully. It was immensely difficult. Her invisible grip on the sliver of metal slipped repeatedly—more times than she cared to remember later.

Her face felt hot and damp, and the effort of keeping her eyes open and fixed caused her to experience an ache that threatened to flatten her. But she held firm, stayed steady, and continued her task.

She heard Arling groan. She felt her start to move. *No!* She stopped what she was doing, waited without breathing, without doing anything but willing her sister to sleep.

After a few mind-numbing seconds, Arling did. Aphen went back to work at once. She was close, so close.

In the distance, another howl. This one was much worse, chilling and raw.

Then the sliver came free, and as it did so she heard Arling give a long, soft sigh. She let the metal shard drop and used her magic to close the wound so that healing could begin. She bent to her sister, feeling for her pulse, listening for her breath.

Both were smooth and even again. She was resting quietly, asleep but no longer threatened.

Aphen removed her tattered cloak and laid it across her sister's body. Then she was on her feet, racing into the trees.

27

---◆---

STOON LOPED THROUGH THE FOREST, WORKING HARD TO KEEP pace with the animals ahead of him. The mutants were moving swiftly now, the scent they were following clearly growing stronger as their prey grew nearer. For such large creatures, they were surprisingly agile and silent, bounding ahead like great cats at the hunt. Even as disgusted as he was by what they were, and as contemptuous as he felt of their reduced state, Stoon could admire their athletic skills and feral instincts.

Maybe they would be as good as Edinja had promised. Maybe they would put an end to the Elves and to this foolish and pointless pursuit.

The mist was thickening, swirling close to the ground, wrapping about the tree trunks and filtering through the gloom in tendrils. The way was sufficiently obscured that Stoon had to work hard to keep up. If he fell here, he would lose the mutants completely by the time he regained his footing. So while haste was important, caution was equally so.

Fortunately, the beasts ahead seemed to sense this and reduced their speed just enough to allow him to keep up. The thought of it irritated him—that such creatures would condescend to him—but he managed to soothe his discomfort by assuring himself that the end result would make up for it. A few minutes more and it would all be over, and he would—

A cry of rage and dismay reverberated through the silence and brought him up short, his nerve endings instantly jagged and raw. What had happened? Had his creatures brought the Elves to bay? He dropped into a crouch, searching the surrounding haze. One thing he knew: Someone or something was dead. He waited for a further indication of the source, but no other sounds reached him. He had lost sight of all three creatures, and he couldn't hear them now, either. The gloom muffled and enfolded everything more than a few feet away, a swirling soup creating phantasms and wraiths that appeared and vanished in the blink of an eye. Stoon wasn't used to such conditions and didn't like to hunt when the weather was a factor.

He rose and started ahead once more. He wouldn't find out anything by staying put. He kept his pace deliberately slow. Since he could no longer see the mutants, there was no point in stumbling ahead blindly and finding himself unexpectedly in the middle of a dangerous situation. After only a few yards, he found evidence of his creatures' passing—crushed grasses and heavy footprints in the damp earth. The mutants had thrown aside caution and were charging ahead wildly. Something had happened to change the nature of their hunt, and Stoon didn't like what that meant.

He kept listening, waiting for a sound that would give him a direction in which to go. But everything remained silent, expectant.

He found the first mutant a hundred yards farther on, its body sprawled amid a cluster of hardwoods, decapitated. Its head lay twenty feet from its body, cleanly severed at the neck. From the placement of head and body and the look of the wound, the mutant had never even seen its attacker, and the force of the blow that had killed it must have been very great indeed. A quick survey of the area gave Stoon no clue as to who or what might have done this, or why the mutant had failed to realize the danger until it was too late.

Stoon hesitated once more. If he were up against a hunter this proficient, he might want to wait until he saw how the other two mutants fared. But then he risked losing contact with the hunt.

So he set off anew, following a trail of matted grasses and vague footprints, doing his best to stay alert for any indication of the danger he was up against. He moved more cautiously than before, stopping often to listen, calling on his vast experience to avoid detection, staying hidden within the mist. He had his favorite knife out—a long slender blade forged of carbon-infused steel rendered hard enough by fire and hammer to penetrate armor. It was the killing weapon he used most frequently, the blade he knew he could depend upon to stop anything.

Whatever he was up against, he assured himself, it wouldn't be the equal of this blade and his skill at using it.

Even so, he remained uneasy. He still didn't know what was out there, and he wasn't used to that. As an assassin, he always made it a point to know his victims before he hunted them, to familiarize himself with their personal habits and to learn what to expect from them. None of that was possible here. Even the terrain in which he found himself was unfamiliar. Everything was working against him. He was seldom required to defend himself, but he thought it entirely probable that he would have to do so here.

Cymrian was crouched in the deep shadows of fog and trees when the mutants shouldered into view, big and menacing and dangerous beyond anything the Elven Hunter had ever encountered. He didn't know what they were, but he knew at once he was no match for them in a straight-up fight. These were not creatures he could subdue or trick as he might other foes. They would have to be killed and killed quickly. His only hope was to isolate and eliminate them one by one.

He waited as they passed him, moving ahead into the trees, each separated from the others by perhaps ten or twelve feet as they hunted. They had his scent, but they didn't yet know where he was; he could tell by the way they were hunting. When they were out of sight again, he left his hiding place and went after them. He followed at a safe distance, letting them stay well ahead. They were aggressive hunters, but they did not have the look of forest creatures, and this was his country, not theirs.

When one of them fell slightly behind the others, he moved up on it swiftly. He had his short sword out, and he was on top of it before it knew he was there. With both hands locked around the handle, he

swung the blade in a quick, hard arc. The creature's head flew off and
the rest of it collapsed in a heap. Cymrian was already moving, darting back into the gloom. But one of the others caught a glimpse of
him and howled with rage.

The Elven Hunter fled, leaping and bounding through the scrub
and deadwood, and still only barely managed to escape. His hunters
were much quicker than they looked, and soon enough he could hear
the sound of their ragged breathing. But he darted between the
trunks of trees that were grown so close together that his much larger
pursuers had to go around to get through. By then Cymrian was lost
again in the concealment of the gloom.

He did not slow. The mutants were hunting him and would track
him until they caught him.

He angled away from where he had left Aphen and Arling, working his way through the trees while seeking a place to set an ambush.
He had to find something quickly, because he suspected his hunters
were much stronger and their endurance greater. He did not think
for a moment that anything would turn them aside or draw their attention away from him. They would keep coming until he was dead.

He wondered about the origin of the things. He didn't give a second thought to the possibility that they were creatures native to the
region; the Elves would have encountered something this big and
dangerous before now. Most likely they had come from the Federation warship, which suggested strongly they must have been brought
along for the express purpose of hunting Aphen and Arling and had
only focused on him when he attacked them. But who would want to
do this? Who would be desperate enough to go to this much trouble
to hunt down a pair of young women? The same people who were
behind the earlier attacks in Arborlon. Were they seeking to steal the
blue Elfstones, or was there something more involved?

Without slowing, he vaulted into a tree whose branches hung sufficiently low that he could swing himself quickly into the cover of the
foliage. He climbed from there—a rapid ascent that took him well
into the forest canopy—and then he leapt to a second tree and from
there to a third, their branches all closely linked. When he reached
the third tree, he settled back to wait.

The mutants charged past moments later, still following his scent.

But in their efforts to overtake him quickly, they were past his hiding place before they realized they had lost him. By then, he was back on the ground, a pair of long knives drawn. He heard them thrashing about just ahead, then suddenly they went silent.

Instantly he froze in place. There was no sound from ahead—or from any other direction.

They were waiting on him, he thought. They had realized what he was about and set an ambush. He hesitated, undecided. Going forward risked becoming trapped between them. Waiting risked losing any advantage he had gained.

He was still debating when he heard fresh sounds at his back—a slow, creeping approach by someone coming up from behind.

No longer certain what was happening, he eased backward into the heavy brush, squirmed into a shallow depression amid the grasses, and settled down to wait.

Stoon was almost into the clearing before he sensed the other's presence. It wasn't smell or sound or movement that alerted him; it was instinct. He could *feel* the other—a kind of tingling of his nerve ends, warning him that someone was lying in wait. He stopped where he was and dropped into a crouch, making himself as small as he could manage and going completely still, wondering if it was too late, if he had been seen, if he was already a dead man. In this cat-and-mouse game, had he become the mouse?

But moments passed and nothing happened. So he began the process of discovering where his adversary was hiding. There was no question as to who it was. It was one of those his creatures were hunting—probably the women's protector, the one with all the hunting and tracking skills. He tried to imagine what sort of cover the other would choose, how he would go about concealing himself, and what he was attempting to accomplish. He wondered, as well, where the remaining two mutants had gone. Surely they weren't dead. If they were, he should turn around and get out of there as swiftly and silently as he could manage.

He put his senses to work, trying to gain some scrap of information, some clue as to what was happening.

Nothing.

He stayed where he was. Moving ahead now was suicide. If his adversary didn't already know he was there—something he highly doubted—he would certainly know the moment Stoon moved even a few paces toward the break in the trees. This hunt had become a waiting game, and no one was better at waiting than Stoon. The advantage would go his way so long as he kept still and didn't panic. If the Elf tried to move at this juncture, Stoon would hear him and know where he was. And that would be the end of this standoff.

But everything remained quiet. Suddenly there was a change in the light just off to his left—a slight drift of darkness in the dim haze that appeared and faded in less than a second. It might have been the mist, but Stoon didn't think so. He tightened his grip on his knife, which he held down by his side, ready for use. He shifted his eyes ever so slightly toward the change, holding the rest of his body perfectly still as he did so. There it was again, that small darkening. Its source came from somewhere back in the trees—a slight shading that, once again, might have been nothing more than the movement of the mist.

Stoon tensed for the expected attack, knife ready to slash upward and then cut down, eviscerating whatever came at him. He would have to be quick. He would have to be . . .

A second movement caught his eye, this one coming from the other side. It wasn't a change in the light this time, but a movement of the brush that was windless and otherwise still. Something *else* was back there, and he was caught between them.

He stayed frozen in place a moment longer, trying to judge whether it was best to ease farther backward or bolt forward toward freedom and fresh cover. He chose the former, pressing himself even closer to the ground as he scooted slowly, silently back into the trees, eyes shifting left and right, trying to see everywhere at once.

But again, nothing revealed itself, and no sounds broke the stillness. He felt the heat of his anger rising in response to his frustration. He was going to put an end to this nonsense. He was finished with all of them—mutants and Elves alike—and they would all be dead and buried before he was done with this business and on his way back to Arishaig and his old life.

He was almost to the thickest of the shadows that clustered behind him when a sudden hush, a stilling of the air, made him pause.

Something was about to happen.

Cymrian was flattened against the earth, ready to spring up and attack, when everything abruptly went quiet. His hunters had sensed his presence. He waited several minutes to make certain they had quit advancing, and when there were still no further noises or hints of movement, he decided not to wait any longer. Staying low to the ground, he began to inch his way backward into the trees, having already chosen a position that would be difficult for a pursuer to reach without becoming exposed. He assumed this would not be something his hunters would want to risk, so he kept retreating until he was completely layered in shadow, the mist so thick that it hung directly over him in an impenetrable blanket. He could see nothing of what was out there but was content to rely on his other senses as he waited to see what would happen.

Then something moved off to his other side—a second presence, very likely one of the creatures he had been tracking earlier. The momentary sound of its approach was so faint, he almost missed hearing it—the barest scrape of a passage through dry leaves. He froze, but the sound was lost in the heavy brume, its exact location impossible to pinpoint. The most he could determine was that it was off to his right, while the earlier sound had come from his left. He was caught between two stalkers, and he could not be certain how close either was.

Give her whatever time you can, he told himself, thinking of Aphenglow. *At least enough time to save Arling.*

He knew he was in trouble. There were at least three of them, two of them mutants, the other an unknown. Good odds if the latter was a normal man, even one possessing skill and experience. Bad odds if he was subhuman or worse. He had to assume the latter, having seen close-up the mutant he had killed. He had been lucky with that one. He had caught it unawares and dispatched it quickly, but he could not expect such luck a second time. With creatures of this sort, all it took was a single mistake and they would have you.

He took a deep breath and exhaled slowly. He would have to choose which of the two closing in on him he would try to disable first.

He chose the mutant.

Turning in that direction, he began to creep forward, pausing every few seconds to listen, waiting for some small movement or sound that would give away his adversary's position. He had the short sword gripped in his right hand, ready to use. His mind was calm and his heart quiet. He was wary, but not afraid. He believed himself ready to do what was needed, and he did not for a moment believe he was going to die.

He never believed that.

Steady.

Listen.

He heard the sound of breathing almost right in front of him— a rough exhalation as the creature paused in its hunt. He waited only a moment, then launched himself through the haze in a blind attack. Sword lifted, gripped in both hands, he rushed his invisible enemy and went right past him. He caught sight of the creature as he flew by, but it was too late. It had shifted its position just enough so that he was left swinging at empty air. He whipped back around, but by then the mutant was ready for him, armored forearms raised, its huge ax ready to cut him in half.

Cymrian feinted left, drew the swing of the ax toward his head, and rolled right, tumbling past, but leaving the short sword buried in the creature's exposed side. The beast roared in fury, kicking out at him, then wheeled to follow, the ax still swinging. Cymrian came back to his feet, fresh blades in both hands. He sidestepped the ax and left a second blade buried in the other side of the creature's thick body.

He was swinging back around for a fresh attack when the second mutant materialized out of the misted tangle of trees, a juggernaut bearing down on him. He threw himself aside as the creature's arms sought to entangle him, slipping clear just as a flash of steel flew by his head, out of nowhere.

The mutant roared and twisted violently, a blade buried deep in its neck, sending it to its knees as if it were a puppet whose strings had been severed.

A second later Cymrian, still confused about what was happening, felt a blow to his back, about shoulder-high, followed by excruciating pain, and he pitched forward.

Stoon had come out of hiding the moment he heard the struggle begin, charging into the fog without hesitating, seeing a chance to put an end to the hunt. He could hear the sounds of weapons clashing, of grunts and gasps, of bodies thrashing in the woods. It would be the Elf and one or both of the mutants, tearing at each other.

If he moved quickly enough, he realized, he would have an opportunity to see them all dispatched.

The mist had grown thicker and was shifting in a slow clockwise motion, giving the impression that the whole world was fluid and unsteady, but the assassin never slowed, homing in on the struggle. He came on it quickly enough, finding the Elf facing off against one of the mutants, blades in both hands, sidestepping the other's ax with a combination of speed and agility that spoke of skill and experience Stoon didn't care to test.

Instead he unsheathed a throwing knife. Weaken the Elf and the mutant would finish him quickly enough. Then he could decide what to do about the mutant. He waited only a moment, searching for an opening, the throwing knife balanced between his fingers. Then the second mutant appeared, rushing in to join the fray. The Elf spun clear as it reached for him—a clear opening for Stoon—and without hesitation the assassin hurled his blade.

But the combatants shifted unexpectedly at the last moment, and his knife struck the mutant instead.

He did not pause. A mistake was a mistake. There was no fixing it now. A second knife was in his hand instantly. This time he was more successful. The blade buried itself in the Elf's back, causing him to stagger and drop to his knees. When he tried to rise, Stoon sent a second blade to join the first, and the Elf collapsed in a heap.

Stoon moved forward, wanting to get close enough to finish the job. But the mutant he had mistakenly struck with his first blade was back on its feet and lumbering toward him, its huge body jerking and twisting as it sought to regain control of muscles that no longer worked properly. Its eyes were bright with hatred as they fastened on Stoon, and there was no mistaking what it intended. Whatever control he had enjoyed over this monster before, whatever loyalty Edinja had instilled in it, was gone.

He glanced quickly at the Elf. He was back on his knees, he saw, and the second mutant was closing. It was over.

He shifted his attention to the mutant coming for him, drew out a heavy hunting knife, and held his ground. When the mutant was close enough, Stoon feinted and darted inside the creature's arms and thrust the hunting knife up through the beast's jaw and into its skull. The mutant collapsed, dead before it struck the ground.

But by taking time to dispatch the creature, he had been forced to shift his attention away from the Elf, who had somehow risen to his feet. He was every bit as proficient as Stoon with a knife, and his arm was a blur of motion as he flung his blade at the assassin and caught him in the chest. The force of the blow knocked Stoon backward, and he tumbled to the ground.

He had just enough time to realize that the final mutant had shifted its attention back to him—either because of what it had seen him do to its companion or because the blood pouring from its wounds had disoriented it—before it was on him.

Cymrian watched as the man tumbled backward, the blade buried in his chest, his eyes wide with shock and pain. The Elven Hunter was on his feet again, fighting to remain conscious, to stave off the effects of his own injuries, knowing he needed to ignore the pain and the ebbing of his strength if he was to have any chance at all. He saw the remaining mutant close on the man, take him by the neck, and shake him. He had a fresh blade out by then, aware that he was down to his last few, and he flung the knife at the mutant with as much force as he could muster. His aim was true, and the blade caught the beast in the neck, severing vital arteries and cords. The beast hunched over and released its grip on the man, who flopped backward like a rag doll.

Cymrian was already attacking, short sword in hand, swinging for the creature's head. But he was unsteady on his feet, and the mutant blocked his effort and backhanded the Elf with such force that it knocked him all the way across the little clearing and left him lying dazed and helpless. He watched as the creature tried to rise and then fell back, jerked once, and lay still.

Everything had gone quiet. No one was moving. The clearing was stained with blood and littered with bodies. In the trees, the heavy mists continued to swirl and the shadows to glide.

Then Cymrian saw the man across the clearing roll onto his side, his eyes finding the Elf and fixing on him. A knife appeared in one hand, drawn out from beneath his dark clothing. Cymrian tried to move, but his body would no longer obey him. Whatever damage he had sustained, it had left him helpless.

He watched with grim acceptance as the man began to drag his broken body across the clearing to reach him, the knife gleaming.

28

APHENGLOW RACED THROUGH THE FOREST TOWARD THE sounds of the battle, knowing that she would never forgive herself if Cymrian's efforts on her behalf cost him his life. She shouldn't have let him go. She should have made him wait until she was finished working on Arling. There would have been time enough then. Their enemies wouldn't have reached them that quickly.

But he had felt otherwise, and his judgment in such matters was final. His experience was deeper, and the decision had not been hers to make.

She ran faster, the sounds ahead all gasps and grunts and cries of pain and rage. She was doing nothing to hide her coming, unwilling to slow down to mask her approach, certain that time was not something she could afford to waste—not even a second of it. Mist and shadows swirled about her, creating a confusing miasma that threatened to lead her astray. But the sounds were close now, and she could track her destination by that alone.

Abruptly she burst into a clearing in which bodies lay everywhere and blood soaked the greenery in bright patches.

Movement caught her eye, and that was when she saw the man who had tried to kill her during the battle for Paranor, the assassin who had thought to catch her unawares and strike her down from behind. She would never forget his face, and on seeing it now she bared her teeth and rushed at him. He was dragging himself toward Cymrian, a knife gripped in his hand. Even now, as she raced to stop him, he tried to use it, stretching out his arm toward her protector, slashing and stabbing wildly in an effort to finish the job.

But Cymrian was just out of reach, and Aphen was on top of the assassin before he could crawl closer. She stripped him of his weapon and pinned his arms against the earth so that he could not reach for another. She could feel him struggling beneath her, could hear the harsh labor of his breathing.

"You're . . . crushing me!" he gasped.

She stayed where she was. "Who are you?"

"No . . . one."

He could barely speak now, his strength ebbing. His wounds were terrible, and she could tell at a glance he would not survive them. "Why are you trying to kill us? You don't even know us!"

He laughed, a terrible rattling in his throat. "I . . . don't have to . . . know you . . . to kill you."

She took a chance. "Is it the Elfstones? Is that what you are after?"

He nodded once. "She . . . wants to . . ."

He couldn't finish, blood spilling from his mouth.

"Wants to what? Tell me."

"Wants . . . to know."

She was getting nowhere, and she needed to go to Cymrian. She glanced over. He was lying on his side, watching her through pain-fogged eyes, listening to what was being said. She could see the blood on his body and the blade buried in his back. But she needed to continue with what she was doing.

She bent close to the dying man. "You said 'she' wants to know. Who? Give me a name!"

The assassin laughed.

"Don't die and leave her safe! Tell me who she is!"

His eyes found hers, and she could see death clouding them. "Why . . . not? She's . . . killed me. Maybe she will . . . kill you . . . as well."

He was racked by a sudden fit of coughing, and for a moment Aphen was certain she had lost him and would never know the name of the one who had sent him.

But then he gathered himself and whispered, "Edinja . . . Orle. Now, you . . ."

But then his voice faded, and his eyes fixed in a vacant stare. The life went out of him with a soft sigh, and he was gone.

She stared down at him a moment longer, then got up and went over to Cymrian, kneeling beside him, her hand on his cheek.

He smiled up at her. "You got here . . . just in time."

"Don't talk." She bent close to him, searching for his wounds. She found the worst of them quickly enough. The knife that had caused the first was still buried in his back. A deep penetration to his chest marked the second, although the blade was no longer there. Both were bleeding freely, the rents ragged and gaping. She reached for his hands, gripping them in her own. "Close your eyes. Keep them closed."

She sent a wave of numbing magic all through his body to ease the pain, and then followed it with an infusion of sleep magic that put him under completely. When that was done, she began work. She stanched the flow of blood to the chest wound, searching for internal injuries to his vital organs. Finding none, she pinched the edges of the torn skin and muscle together and sealed it with a fusing of tissue. It took a long time and deep concentration, and she worried all through it that she was sacrificing the back wound in the effort. But she knew this injury was the more serious, and that the loss of blood from the other wound was not as severe.

While she worked, Cymrian made small noises, but was otherwise still. She stroked his brow once and kissed it afterward, anguished by what had been done to him. He had defended Arling and herself against all of these creatures, mutants and assassin alike. He had sacrificed himself for them, and she would never doubt again what her sister had told her about his reason for taking on the job of protector.

That he loved her.

That he had always loved her.

She hadn't believed it before. She couldn't conceive of it being true. So many years had passed since she had even seen him. So much had happened since they were children, and yet none of it seemed to have mattered. None of it had diminished his feelings for her. She wondered at his obstinacy, at his dogged determination to have her—how else could she think of it? But she knew even as she thought it that this wasn't it at all. It was more akin to the taking of a vow. It was making a commitment to something he believed in so utterly that he would wait as long and do as much as was necessary to see it fulfilled.

Even though the effort cost him his life.

As might happen here, if she failed to heal him.

She finished with the chest wound and moved on to the damage to his back. She laid him out facedown and extracted the knife, reaching along the razor-sharp edge of the blade to its tip with her magic to make certain he was shielded as she worked on him. His lungs and heart were unscathed, the injuries he had incurred confined to muscle and tissue and a complex network of blood vessels. The blade removed, she began the effort of mending arteries and veins so that the ends joined perfectly, tying together sinew and ligament, repairing torn muscles, and cleansing the whole of possible infection.

By the time she was done, she was exhausted. She took time to bind up both wounds with strips of cloth she tore from the clothes worn by the dead assassin. Then she closed her eyes for what she expected to be a moment's rest and promptly fell asleep.

Arlingfant Elessedil is dreaming.

She rides in an airship, high above the ground, lost in clouds that seem to buoy the vessel in the manner of an ocean's waters. Through holes in these clouds, Arling can spy the earth far below—a distant patchwork of green woods, blue lakes, silver rivers, and brown mountains, all of it perfectly formed and reassuring. She is pleased to be able to observe it, but to remain above it, too. She can see it without touching it, can witness its presence without having to descend.

She is afraid it might not be real.

Aphenglow rides next to her. Her sister wears white robes that billow and flow like gauzy streamers. She smiles when Arling glances at her, further reassurance that all is well. Arling speaks to her, although she is uncertain of the words she uses. But Aphenglow doesn't answer; she only smiles again and then points.

Ahead, looping through the clouds, is a flock of giant birds, their wings as wide as the airship is long, great predators in search of food. But they do not seem to notice the airship and continue their flight without paying it the slightest attention.

When Arling looks to her sister for an explanation, Aphen is gone.

Seconds later she sees her sister in the pilot box, standing at the controls. There are others aboard the airship, too. She cannot see who they are, but she knows instinctively they are Elves. They scurry along the decks and climb the rigging of the masts and work the radian draws and trim the light sheaths. They do sailors' work, and nothing inter-rupts or distracts them from their efforts, even her calls of encourage-ment.

Suddenly the airship lurches and drops before steadying again. Ar-ling seizes the railing against which she has been leaning, catching herself so that she does not fall. She feels her heart in her throat, and she is suddenly afraid. The airship jolts and drops a second time, and now she looks to the pilot box for Aphen. But her sister has vanished, disappeared into the ether. Nor are the other Elves still aboard. All are gone, as if they never were.

She is alone.

Terrified, she struggles across the deck as the airship begins to spi-ral downward, dropping swiftly earthward. She is intent on reaching the controls so that she can slow the vessel's descent. But even though she fights her way across the heaving deck, she can never seem to get any closer to the pilot box. She is moving steadily, but the deck stretches out and grows longer. The airship drops through layers of clouds, sink-ing into them one moment and then abruptly falling back out again. Because she is no longer standing at the railing, she cannot tell how far she has fallen or how close the ground is beneath her. She senses that the time left before impact is very short, but she cannot find a way to measure it.

Then the airship catches fire. She screams for Aphenglow, but her sister does not respond. She is truly gone, and Arling cannot depend on her for help. She must save herself. She continues to crawl toward the pilot box, but the flames are everywhere and the heat is too intense. She begins to slide backward toward the railing and then the railing disap-pears and she falls over the side and . . .

She is in her mother's arms. Her mother holds her, cradles her, protects her, and she is safe again. The airship has disappeared and the falling has ended. She lies on soft grasses amid flowers and green plants. Trees form a canopy overhead, their leafy boughs swaying in a wash of gentle breezes. She stretches out with her head and shoulders in her mother's lap. She feels comforted and loved, and all of the fear she felt only moments ago has dissipated, replaced with a sense of well-being.

"Child," her mother whispers in her ear and rocks her gently.

"Mother," she replies, realizing suddenly that something very good has happened and her mother is herself again, no longer the harsh, embittered woman she became when Aphen went away.

"I have you now," her mother says. "I have you and will hold you forever. You are mine, and I will never let you go."

Arlingfant loves hearing these words; she revels in their sweetness. She lies there and does not move, does not think, does not seek more than to be in the moment in which she finds herself.

"Dark skies," her mother whispers. "Stormy weather. Hold tight."

The air above them is blackening, the light dying, everything turning gloomy and unfriendly. The trees and grasses and plants disappear. The colors fade. Arling knows they should rise and go inside where it is safe, but she cannot make herself move, cannot make her body respond to her commands, and when she looks up at her mother, her mother is no longer there.

Again, she has been abandoned.

"Mother," she whispers.

But there is only the darkness and the feel of the earth pressing up against her body, as she lies helpless and alone.

The dream faded, replaced by darkness and silence. She smelled woods and damp, but she could not make her eyes open or her muscles respond. She was wrapped in what felt like yards of cotton wadding and heavy blankets of softest down. A deep, abiding lethargy infused her. She listened and was surprised to hear very close to where she lay . . .

Voices.

"She cannot be more than a young girl."

"She wears knives strapped to her waist; she's no stranger to combat. Look, there is blood on her clothing."

"But she only sleeps. She's not dead, is she?"

Hands probe. Fingers explore.

"She is injured. Perhaps she dies."

"We should help her, Sora."

"We help ourselves, not strangers. You know that. You speak like a child. What have I told you?"

The voices faded. Arling waited, but weariness overcame her and she slept anew. This time there were no dreams. When she woke again, the darkness and the lethargy were still there.

And the voices were back.

"She should not be left alone."

"Others have been here with her. Not that long ago. They will return for her soon enough. We should be gone when they do."

"We cannot know if they will return, can we? Those who were with her may have abandoned her. They may think her dead. Or even wish her so."

"There is nothing to suggest any of that is true."

"Why was she left alone, then? Why does she lie here untended? If they are family or friends, why would they go off and leave her even for a moment's time?"

"This isn't our business!"

"Helping others is everyone's business. You sound so cruel when you say such things! Where is your compassion?"

"I have enough trouble looking after you and me! Stop arguing about this. You know we can't become involved!"

A long silence. This time she did manage to open her eyes, if only a little, seeing loose pants tucked into work boots on one, ragged skirt hanging over worn, scuffed half boots on the other.

Her eyes closed again.

"Well, I won't let you leave her like this. We found her, and now she is our responsibility. She should be taken to where she will be looked after. This crash was not her fault. Her injuries were not her doing."

Arling tried to speak then, but the words would not come. Instead, she could only manage a low groan, one that sounded frightened and painful even to her.

"There, you see? She needs us! She is begging for our help!"

"She said nothing; she made a sound, and it could signify anything."

Help me, Arling thought, suddenly afraid that she would be left alone again— that even as her sister and her mother had left her, so, too, would these unknowns who hovered over her. She did not want that to happen. She did not think she could stand to be left alone again.

Hands touched her once more, this time resting gently across her forehead for long moments before moving away.

"She has a fever. She needs medicine and rest. Leave her here and you are killing her. Deliberately."

"Her companions will look after her."

"What companions? Do you see any? Besides, if they were any sort of companions at all, they would be looking after her now."

"And if you are wrong about them, and if they come looking for her and find her missing? Then what? They will come looking for us! That might not be so welcome as you seem to think."

"You always expect the worst. Try looking at it a different way. What if we save her life?"

"You ignore reality when you talk that way. You act as if you lack knowledge of the world."

"I would rather it be my way than yours."

A pause. "It doesn't matter what you say. We should not involve ourselves. What would you have us do, anyway? I won't stay here and risk being caught."

"No, I don't suppose so. Something else, then."

"There is nothing else!"

"Don't just dismiss me like that. Think of something!"

Arling drifted away again, riding the crest of her lethargy and weariness, returning to darkness and silence. Nothing disturbed her journey. She was buoyed by a deep sense of peacefulness, wrapped in a promise of safety and well-being. She could not determine its source, could not decide from whence it came. But it bore her on through time and held her with the firm gentleness of her mother's arms and she gave herself over to it.

When Aphenglow Elessedil woke, not knowing how long she had slept, her first thought was of Arling. She had left her to come to Cymrian, but she had not intended to leave her sister this long. She had not intended to fall asleep. Anything could have happened to Arling in the interim, and it would all be her fault for abandoning her.

Cymrian was looking at her. "I think I might live," he said, with a shaky grin.

She blinked and yawned. "I think you might. How badly do you hurt?"

"Hardly at all. Whatever you did, it took away the pain." His quirky smile surfaced. "You saved me."

She blushed in spite of herself, shaking her head. "Not yet, I haven't. I can still do a little more. I can make you stronger so you can travel." She sat up. "Here. Give me your hands."

He did so, and, conjuring the magic that was needed, she sent an infusion of strength washing through his body, careful not to overdo it, to keep it moderate and controlled so that it would not disrupt the healing that was already under way. When she finished, she looked at him for approval, one eyebrow lifting quizzically.

"Better," he agreed. "Much better. I can feel the difference. Amazing. I should be bedridden for weeks, but I think I can even walk."

"You'll have to. I can't carry you."

"No, I wouldn't expect that."

She stood up. "I'm sorry, but there's no more time. We have to hurry."

"Arling?"

"Sleeping when I came to find you. I found the problem and fixed it. But she's very weak."

He sat up gingerly and flexed his shoulders. "We'll do whatever we have to for Arling. At least we won't have to worry about being hunted. Not right away, anyhow." He nodded toward the bodies surrounding them. "There's one more farther back—another mutant. Ugly things. Men, once, but something much less now."

"Who made these creatures?" she said. "Edinja Orle?"

"It's possible." He climbed to his feet, testing his weight, looking down at himself as if to make certain he was all in one piece. "I know her. A witch. A member of a powerful Federation family, most of them practitioners of magic. She was one of the candidates for the position of Prime Minister of the Federation Coalition Council when Drust Chazhul got selected as a compromise choice."

She gave him a look. "How do you know this?"

"I keep up on what's happening in the camps of our enemies. I'm surprised you don't."

She shook her head. "I've had no time for keeping up. I've spent almost a year shut away in a cellar looking at ancient documents. I've lost touch with a lot of things." She paused. "Things I should have been paying better attention to."

She placed her hands on either side of his face and kissed him on the mouth. When she drew back, she kept her eyes fixed on his. "But I might want to think about changing all that."

Without waiting for his reply, she started away. He fell into step beside her, his movements still tentative. "Let me know if I can do anything to help," he said after a moment, and the smile was back once more.

They returned the way they had come, finding the path easily enough. Aphen was anxious to make certain Arling was all right. Her sister had been sleeping soundly enough when she left, and the danger from the shards that had penetrated her body seemed under control, but you could never be certain with wounds of that sort. In other circumstances, she would never have left her, but abandoning Cymrian to his fate when he was risking so much for them was unthinkable. Hard choices both, and she hoped she had made the right one.

The woods thickened, and the mist grew steadily heavier. Shadows floated all around them, cast by tree trunks, limbs, and things unseen and unknown. The woods were still, and there was an odd sense of emptiness about them that was troubling. Aphen picked up the pace, suddenly worried.

She had reason to be. When they reached the clearing where she had left her sister, Arling was gone.

29

---◆---

THE PITTED STONE BULK OF KRAAL REACH ROSE AGAINST THE gray smudge of the horizon, easily the most formidable keep that Oriantha had ever seen. Hidden in a thick cluster of boulders to the west, she studied the fortress in silence.

Next to her, Tesla Dart shifted restlessly. "We should not be here."

Oriantha nodded. "But here we are, anyway. Is there a way in?"

The Ulk Bog stared at her in horror. "We do not go in there! You did not see what they do? Somehow you are made blind?"

Tesla was speaking of Khyber Elessedil's head, spiked atop the east gates, ravaged by the elements and picked over by scavenger birds. Oriantha had crept close enough with dawn's approach to make certain of what she was seeing. Such a terrible thing to witness, but it was not the first and would not be the last. Not while they remained inside the Forbidding.

The shape-shifter and the Ulk Bog had come looking for Khyber Elessedil and Redden Ohmsford almost a week ago—immediately after leaving Crace Coram to make his way back through the break in the Forbidding's wall. If the boy and the Ard Rhys were still alive, Kraal Reach was where they would be found. Tesla Dart was certain of it. All of Tael Riverine's prisoners were taken to his fortress as a matter of course, and that's what would have been done with them.

Not that Tesla Dart believed for one minute that being here was a good idea. From the moment that Oriantha had told her what they were going to do, she had bemoaned their impending fate, railing against the foolishness of such a decision. But Oriantha was determined. She had made up her mind that even though her mother and most of those who had come with her were dead, she was at least going to bring back the two who remained alive. She was not going to leave them behind; she was not going to save herself without first doing what she could to try to save them.

And she had made it clear that the Ulk Bog would help her whether she wanted to or not.

Mostly, it was because of the boy, she thought. Redden Ohmsford. There was a quality about him that reminded her of herself. It spoke to her, intrigued her, drew her. Maybe it was the magic, a vast store of power and possibilities that were a birthright like her own—inherited, not learned, an inseparable part of who they both were and which defined them in ways that none of the others would ever entirely understand.

So after coming down out of the Dragon Line Mountains, they had journeyed on through the Pashanon, avoiding Furies and Harpies and several dozen other dangerous species, the Ulk Bog guiding them and Oriantha keeping a careful watch on her while she did. Pleysia's shape-shifter daughter had learned the hard way to be cautious. She didn't trust Tesla Dart. Her part in the demise of the Druid company was still suspect. Whatever had happened to Oriantha's companions was not going to happen to her. Because of her shape-shifter heritage, she was much closer to being one of the things that were confined to the Forbidding than had been any of those who had come with her. If Tesla Dart did anything to arouse her suspicions, she would sense it and be able to act on it.

She had pointed this out to the Ulk Bog early on, warning that any suggestion of betrayal would result in swift retribution.

Tesla Dart, for her part, denied that she had played any role in bringing harm to Khyber and her followers. Quite the opposite. She had done everything she could to save them—everything they would let her do, at any rate. But in the end, they had brought about their own doom by ignoring her warnings and going off without her. It was because they hadn't trusted her, she pointed out, and it would be tragic if Oriantha were to make the same mistake. She was not the shape-shifter's enemy; she was her friend. Hadn't she agreed to come on this impossible mission? Hadn't she promised to show her the way and kept her safe? Wasn't she risking her own life by placing herself in harm's way, all for the sake of two people who were probably already dead?

Yet the shape-shifter remained unconvinced, and the tension between the two remained. To Oriantha, Tesla Dart's motives were a mystery. The Ulk Bog talked of her uncle Weka and how much he had done to help the Straken Queen Grianne, and how this obligation had been passed down to her. She talked of obligation and loyalty and blood heritage. But none of it really explained what had brought her to them in the first place. She claimed she had been waiting for Grianne Ohmsford's return, had been looking for this miracle as if she truly believed it was possible. But her intimate knowledge of Tael Riverine and his creatures—and of Kraal Reach and its secrets— was troubling. While she claimed she knew these things through her odd relationship with the Chzyks, Oriantha wasn't convinced. Tesla was hiding something, and that made the shape-shifter nervous.

Their uneasy relationship did not prevent them from completing their trek to Kraal Reach, however—although they watched each other guardedly for the five days it took. They walked the entire way, traveling by day, hiding by night, kept safe from the ever-present dangers that threatened them by Tesla Dart's knowledge and experience and by Oriantha's instincts and caution.

When they arrived, almost the first thing they saw was what remained of the Ard Rhys's head spiked atop the gates, and the shape-shifter's first thought was that they were too late to save Redden, as well. Tesla Dart insisted this was so. If one prisoner was dead, so was the other. Especially if the one who was dead was Khyber Elessedil. Tael Riverine did not keep his enemies alive unnecessarily, and the Ard Rhys had been the one who mattered. The boy meant nothing to him.

Now, crouched close to the fortress walls, the argument resumed.

"I'm not asking you to go inside with me," Oriantha pointed out. "I'm asking you how I can get in. Do you know a way?"

"You walk in, you will be carried out. In pieces!" The Ulk Bog was having none of it. "Forget this!"

"Do you know a way?" Oriantha repeated.

"Over the wall. Climb it, you get in!"

"No secret passageways, no hidden doors? Did Weka Dart teach you nothing?"

"Not talk that way of him!" The Ulk Bog was beside herself. "He dies for Straken Queen! Is that not enough? Doesn't owe you, her or me!"

Oriantha looked away, studying the fortress some more. Apparently she was going to have to make it the rest of the way on her own. *Climbing might work,* she thought, *but how do I find my way once I am inside? How do I find Redden?*

"Don't do this," Tesla Dart said suddenly, grasping her arm. Her voice had dropped to a whisper, as if in speaking louder she might be heard by others. "He is dead. Let him go."

Inwardly, Oriantha was afraid this was so. But she was determined to make sure, nevertheless. She was resolved not to leave him if he was alive.

"We will wait here until it's dark, and then I will scale the walls and search for him. In my shape-shifter form, I will not be so easy to spy or to catch. If I don't find him by morning, I will come back out again and we will leave."

Tesla Dart sagged back with a moan of despair, shaking her head so hard the clusters of hair sprouting from it quivered. "You will not come back," she said. "You will not."

High within the imprisoning towers of Kraal Reach, Redden Ohmsford sat alone in the cell to which he was confined, staring at the patterns of the stonework on the floor. The seams between the slabs ran this way and that, forming endless rivers of grout that crisscrossed and angled and curved from wall to wall. There were bits of dust and debris, the carcasses of dead bugs and stains that interrupted the otherwise intriguing flow, and he kept coming back to them as his eyes wandered listlessly through the maze. He should remove them. He should clear them out so that nothing blocked the way. He thought to do so over and over, but he couldn't seem to muster the strength.

In point of fact, he couldn't muster the strength to walk to the window and look out over the countryside. Bleak as it was, empty and pitiless, it nevertheless would have offered him a change of view. Wouldn't that be better than just sitting where he was, studying the slabs and grout of the flooring? But if he did that, he would end up glancing down at the east gates—because curiosity would demand it of him—thinking that this time her head would be gone from where it had been fixed on the spike atop the ramparts. In the beginning, he was sure they would leave it in place only a few days, a reminder and warning. But days later, it was still there, the scavengers picking at it, reducing it to something unrecognizable—to a horrific caricature of what she had looked like in life. Finally, he had quit looking out the window at all, quit exposing himself to the feelings that tore at him, quit letting hope interfere with reality.

Let the dead rest in peace. Give the Ard Rhys that much. Or as much as could be expected, given the nature of her demise and her subsequent treatment.

Khyber Elessedil.

Gone with the rest of them.

And now he was the last. The very last.

He couldn't know this for sure. He had seen most of them die right in front of him, had seen the bodies or pieces of the bodies afterward, so of those he had no doubt. Oriantha and Crace Coram were unaccounted for, but he was certain they were dead, too. He could sense it in the same way he could sense what it would do to him to look out the window. They had been carried off by a dragon and had died in a faraway place, but they had died all the same. There was no point in pretending otherwise.

Just as there was no point in pretending any longer that he might find a way out of this nightmare.

He would have cried, thinking of it, but he was all cried out. He had shed all the tears he had left to shed. He was frightened and desperate and burdened with an unshakable sense of hopelessness. His chances of ever going home again, of ever returning to his old life, were gone. All prospects of such a miracle had dimmed to darkness. He was passing his time now awaiting the arrival of his own death. It was coming to claim him; he could feel it. It was just a question of when.

His days had grown endless. He had lost all track of time. When he had been brought back to the fortress following the battle between Khyber and Tael Riverine, he had been taken immediately to this cell and left there. No one had spoken to him during the return trip. The only words uttered were those of the rabble that tracked his cage as it rolled through the countryside, an indecipherable barrage of taunts and jeers. He could still recall the sound, a cacophony rising up from the mob's dark mass. His champion had died defending herself, and his turn was coming. What weapons did he have to call upon? What magic did he have that could defeat the power of their Straken Lord?

None, he knew.

He had no weapons and no magic that would ever make a difference. Not while he wore the conjure collar.

He felt the weight of the collar around his neck, a constant reminder of his reduced state. Even thinking of it caused him to wince involuntarily. He had tried over and over again to remove it or at least loosen it to relieve its pressure. But each time the pain it had generated was so intense that it doubled him over and left him writhing on the stone floor. Each time the extent of his helplessness had been reinforced.

Until at last he had stopped trying.

Until finally he had accepted that it was never coming off.

There was nothing left for him after that. He sat in his cell, his prison, his jail, and waited for his inevitable execution. He had no meaningful expectations left. What expectations could there be? That a miracle would happen and someone would come for him? That he could still find a way out of this madness? Impossible! Who even knew where he was? Even those who had remained behind, stranded on that ledge with the Goblins coming at them from every direction, were probably dead by now.

Even Railing.

But he didn't believe it. Oddly, it was the one hope he clung to. Railing was still alive, still out there somewhere searching. His brother would never give up. It might be hopeless for him, but it wouldn't be for Railing. Not now, not ever. Railing was his twin, his other half, his shadow self, and he was alive and well and hunting for Redden. Railing would never be satisfied with leaving things as they were. Even if it killed him, he would find a way to reach his brother.

Of course, he was aware of the impossibility of this happening. And the thought of Railing dying, too, brought down by his efforts to reach him, was more than he could bear.

They brought him food and water, and sometimes he ate and drank. But mostly not. Sometimes they pulled back the metal plate set in the cell door that served as a peephole and looked in on him to see what he was doing. He never bothered to look up, never cared if they were looking at him or not. He ignored them. He tried to pretend they didn't exist.

For a while, he tried disappearing into memories, but that hurt too much. Memories were reminders of what he had lost, and what he could never have back.

So he ended up studying the floor and tried not to think of anything. He just sat there, staring at the lines of grout that connected the stone slabs of the cell flooring, fascinated by the intricacy of the workmanship.

That worked much better.

Except that without realizing it he was slowly disappearing from the real world. He was slowly treading his way down an endless spiral stairway that descended into darkness and finally insanity.

And then, unexpectedly, they came for him.

Oriantha was stretched out in the shade of an overhang among the boulders, taking a short nap while she waited for the cover of darkness, when she heard an earsplitting creaking of iron fastenings followed by two massive booms. She was up instantly, catching sight of Tesla Dart charging back into the rocks from the perimeter where she had been keeping watch.

"He's coming out!" Fear was etched deep in her wizened features.

At first Oriantha thought the Ulk Bog was speaking of Redden Ohmsford, which made no sense at all. But then she realized Tesla meant Tael Riverine. Moving swiftly through the rocks, she reached their perimeter just as the first ranks of the Straken Lord's army appeared through the west gates and moved out into the open in a semi-organized procession of creatures that marched, plodded, shuffled, trudged, rolled, and crawled in what soon seemed to be an endless line. There were members of all of the species imprisoned within the Forbidding save for dragons, which she assumed even Tael Riverine could not find a way to control. Even the terrifying Furies appeared at one point, a ragged cluster of them, cat faces contorted, hissing and screeching, prowling this way and that. A phalanx of Goblins, split into two ranks, bracketed them in a way that kept them from straying too far out of line. How the Goblins managed to keep them in check defied Oriantha's understanding, though she made a mental note to ask Tesla Dart later.

The Straken Lord's army was so huge that it was still winding its way clear of the gates of Kraal Reach an hour later. Amid the ranks of creatures were wagons of various sizes and shapes, although there was nothing to indicate what was in them. There were no siege machines or catapults or other mechanized weapons, and she presumed this was because an army comprising creatures such as this hardly needed such cumbersome tools. Even without experience of what it could do, she was sufficiently informed of the possibilities based on what she had endured while coming through the Fangs and finding herself trapped in this monstrous world. The denizens of the Forbidding, she had discovered, wasted little time on subterfuge. These were creatures that hunted and fought and killed by getting close enough to look you in the eye. These were creatures that attacked in a barely controlled frenzy and did not stop until the last semblance of life had gone out of you or them.

"What's Tael Riverine doing?" she asked Tesla Dart.

The Ulk Bog gave her a look. "What I said. What I warned. He takes his army into your world to destroy it."

"Now? But how can he do that? The Forbidding isn't down yet!"

Tesla Dart looked confused. "The wall crumbles. A place to cross will be found. No reason to wait longer. He will begin his search."

"Search? Search for what?"

"Are you stupid? Her! His Queen! I told you. He wants the witch Grianne. He demands her return. Give her to me, he will say. If she comes with him, he will turn around. If not, he will use his army to grind all those who stand in his way to dust and take her anyway."

Oriantha searched the ranks of the army as it wound its way across the countryside, but there was no sign of the Straken Lord.

"Where is Tael Riverine?" she demanded of Tesla Dart, but the Ulk Bog only shrugged and shook her head.

Then, unexpectedly, a wheeled cage rolled through the gates, surrounded by wolves and Goblins, with a lean, feral creature riding in the driver's seat. As a pair of massive bull-like creatures strained against the traces, the driver snapped his long whip and shouted at the beasts, urging them on. Alongside the cage, the wolves snarled and snapped their jaws at both the vehicle and its lone inhabitant.

Oriantha caught her breath.

Redden Ohmsford, chained and imprisoned, hunkered down in a pile of straw at the cage's center.

"He lives!" Tesla Dart hissed in disbelief.

"Lives and breathes and waits for us to save him. And save him we will, Tesla."

The Ulk Bog turned to look at her and then began laughing madly. "Should be easy! Only thousands stand in the way. Should not stop big strong shape-shifter you!"

She continued to chuckle, but Oriantha was already thinking of ways she could manage to even the odds, disrupt the flow, get through the sentry lines, do whatever was needed to reach the boy and free him.

The last of the procession, the final ranks of the army, cleared the gates, which immediately began to swing shut behind them. A shrieking of metal hinges, a crashing of ironbound portals slamming into place, and Kraal Reach was sealed once more.

Overhead, scores of Harpies appeared, crooked black carrion creatures flooding the skies, trailing after the army. The shape-shifter and the Ulk Bog held their places within the rocks as the half birds, half women passed, patient and watchful. When the Harpies had gone, Oriantha waited awhile longer. There was no urgency. It would be easy to keep pace with an army the size of this one.

She let it get almost a mile ahead before saying to her companion, "Now we track them."

Tesla Dart groaned in dismay but got to her feet anyway. Together they set out, following the clouds of dust raised by the army's passing.

"Wait!" Tesla said suddenly, hunching forward and casting about. "Can use Chzyks to track! Chzyks be anywhere, and no one sees them. Come back to tell us everything they learn. Better than us getting too close."

"You can summon them?"

"Always."

"Then do so tonight and let's have them take a close look at that cage and the guards watching over it. Can you get them to do that?"

"Always, with Lada. I call, he is here. Very smart. Do whatever I ask of him." She glared at Oriantha. "Why? Do you think me stupid, Halfling? I say so, it be so!"

"All right. Calm down. I was just asking. It would help us to know how closely they watch Redden."

Tesla snorted. "Close so that if you can see him, they can see you. That close. This is a foolish chance. All yours to take. But not me."

Oriantha believed she could live with that. She had never expected Tesla Dart to do more than provide information and guidance. But if she used her Chzyks, she would be able to offer firsthand information regarding the location of the cage and guard arrangements. That would be enough.

So bold, she thought. *I am so bold, and I have no reason to be so. Mother would hate it.*

But her mother was gone, and with her most of what Oriantha had thought would become her new life.

"Halfling!" the Ulk Bog snapped, grabbing her arm and pulling her to the ground, then falling on top of her to keep her pinned.

"What are you—" she began.

"Don't move!" the other hissed, and motioned skyward. "Look!"

A dragon was rising out of Kraal Reach—a huge burnt-red monster that was at least as big as, if not bigger than, the one Oriantha had ridden with Crace Coram in what now seemed another lifetime. The beast shrieked and swung north after the departing army, winging hard to catch up.

Astride the dragon's long neck rode a solitary black-cloaked figure.

The shape-shifter girl knew at a glance that it was Tael Riverine.

30

APHENGLOW STARED AT THE EMPTY CLEARING IN SHOCK AND
then started to rush forward. "Cymrian! Where is she?"

He caught her arm. "Wait. There will be signs to tell us. Let me
have a look."

He released her and moved slowly toward the place where they
had left Arlingfant, stepping carefully, crouching often to study the
ground, searching for indications of what had happened. He reached
the flattened grasses and bloodied earth where she had lain and
paused. Then he began to move slowly about the spot, one cautious
step at a time. Aphen waited impatiently, desperate to find her sister,
frantic for her safety. Arling could not have gone off by herself.
She wasn't strong enough for that. So someone—or something—had
taken her.

She had a momentary vision of those mutants, and a shiver went
up her back like a blade's razor edge. "Have you found anything?"

He held up his hand in a gesture that asked her to hold on and
continued his search. He was moving away from where Arling had
been lying, heading across the clearing, apparently having found
something. He was moving steadily now, still reading the signs but
not pausing as often as before to consider what he was seeing.

Finally, he straightened and beckoned her over. She rushed to his
side. "She was found and carried away by two people, a man and

perhaps a woman. Both wore boots that are old and worn. Their tracks show they are not young, but not physically impaired, either. They were strong enough to pick up Arling and carry her off. They came in from this way"—he pointed ahead of them—"and left pretty much the same way."

"Why would they do this? Why would they take her?"

"Hard to answer that without knowing who they are. Come on. We can track them."

They set out, Cymrian reading the signs as they went. Because the ground was thick with grasses and brush, footprints were indistinct and passage was hard to determine. Aphen could make out nothing at all, and if not for the Elven Hunter she would have been lost. But Cymrian seemed able to find what he was looking for, and so they made their way forward.

Nevertheless, Cymrian was badly weakened from his battle with the mutants and the assassin, and his strength was limited. He could not go quickly even if he wanted to, and Aphen had to fight down her impatience to go charging ahead. She could not stand the thought that something bad might have happened to Arling—that it might be happening even now. Speed was imperative.

But there was no help for it. They could only go as fast as Cymrian's constitution and his interpretation of the trail would allow.

It began to rain, a squall appearing out of nowhere, the gloom and mist of Drey Wood deepening. Water sheeted down and quickly layered everything, the whole of the forest taking on a shimmery, reflective look. The dampness increased and pools of water began to cover the ground. Soon, Aphen knew, any traces of footprints or similar signs would disappear into the murk and damp and they would lose the trail completely.

Finally, they broke through the screen of tree trunks and found a narrow trail that wound through the murk. The path was barely wide enough for two people walking shoulder-to-shoulder, and yet when they bent to study the rutted earth, they found the imprint of wagon wheels.

Aphen was flushed and angry. "What would anyone be doing with a wagon this far into the woods?"

Cymrian shook his head. "Hunters, foragers, tramps, Rovers,

travelers—take your choice. And a cart made these tracks, not a wagon. A mule pulled it. The signs are clear enough. But . . ."

He didn't finish, kneeling now, bending even closer to study the wheel marks and hoofprints. Aphen realized the problem. The trail did not end where they stood. It ran both east and west. The hoofprints and wheel marks did the same. Because of the rain and prior usage, it was difficult to tell in which direction the wagon had gone this time.

"What do we do?" she said.

He looked up. "We make an educated guess. They carried Arling to the cart and put her in the bed, and now they are taking her somewhere. Either deeper into the woods west, or back out onto the Streleheim east."

He stood up. "If they live in these woods, if they have a cabin or a hut, they might live deeper in. If they live elsewhere, they would have gone back out onto the plains. It's too far to the western edge of the woods for this trail to go all the way through. It dead-ends somewhere farther on, but we can't know for sure how far that might be." He glanced west. "There's not much to sustain anyone living in these woods. I think they went back out to the east."

They set off at once, Aphen unwilling to waste even one more second debating. She thought repeatedly about using the Elfstones, but worried that the magic would give them away. Better to wait until calling up the magic became the only alternative. She thought Cymrian was right about what had happened to Arling in any case, and he was the one best able to read the signs.

She considered leaving him behind and going on ahead, moving fast enough that she could catch the wagon and its occupants before they got out onto the plains and disappeared. But if they turned off the trail at any point, would she know? She couldn't read the signs the way Cymrian could, and if she lost her way without him she might lose him, as well. So as difficult as it was to restrain herself, she slowed her pace to stay with him and trust that their progress was sufficient.

Who would have taken her sister like this?

Someone who was trying to get to her.

She gritted her teeth, furious at herself for falling asleep after helping Cymrian when she should have stayed awake and gone back for her sister. She hadn't meant for that to happen, but that didn't make her feel any better. She had left Arling alone, and what was happening now was the consequence of her foolishness.

The rain was increasing, turning from a squall into a full-blown thunderstorm. Overhead, the skies were roiling and black. Lightning streaked the darkness in brilliant flashes and thunder boomed out in long, deep peals.

Resolutely, she pressed on.

Irritable, Sora tried to ignore Aquinel's constant complaining, but in the end found it impossible.

"Will you stop talking about it, woman? The matter's decided. Let it be!"

"I just don't feel right about it," she replied. "In my bones. Don't you sense it? We don't know anything about these people."

She was small and stocky, tough as nails and hard to move once she set her mind. Right now he wished she would stop harping on the girl and what he had decided to do with her. Why couldn't she see it was an opportunity for them and a chance at life for her?

"We aren't equipped to care for injuries of the sort she's suffered," he insisted. "Did you not see the damage to her body? You were there when I opened her clothing and took a look. You saw the puncture wounds and bruising. She was hurt badly enough in that crash that it's a miracle she's still breathing!"

Aquinel nodded and didn't look at him. "That's not the problem and you know it."

"No, you're the problem. That's clear enough. You keep looking to find what's wrong instead of focusing on what's right! Woman, I swear you will be the death of me."

"You'll be the death of yourself long before I have any impact on your stubborn nature." She stopped and turned to face him, bringing the mule and the cart they were leading to a halt. "I know what you're about. You're thinking of what this can mean for you, not about the girl."

"Am I? Is that how you see it?"

"I see it clear enough. You want a reward for returning her. Or at least for giving her over and washing your hands of her. You think these people will give you coin for this. But you don't know that. You don't even know who they are or what they're doing here."

He sighed. Looking down the trail to where it bent toward their destination, he took a moment to brush the unkempt black hair from his eyes. "I know that this is fate working her hand in our favor, and when she does that you don't stop to question the why of it. Didn't I see the ship when she came down? Didn't I remember it when we set out with the girl?"

He started off again, pulling on the mule's halter, forcing Aquinel to stick with him. She was a good woman and a sturdy helpmeet, but she spent too much time questioning his decisions. It wasn't as if she knew more than he did and was better able to reason things out. It wasn't her place to guide the family. That was a man's work.

"We have to think about ourselves," he added sullenly.

They traipsed on through the damp and the murk, winding down the lane through broad-leaf trees that canopied overhead, ignoring the steady rainfall and the attendant chill, lost in their separate thoughts. Sora found himself wondering what she would say if she knew about the other—about what he had done when she wasn't looking. He wondered how he would break it to her.

Probably, he thought, he wouldn't. He would keep it a secret. Best that way. He would find a buyer and make some coin, and they would have a few good things for themselves that he could explain away. It wasn't as if he hadn't done this sort of thing before. It wasn't as if this was the first time that he found a little something knocking around that she didn't need to know about.

"We should have waited longer," she said for what must have been the tenth time. "We should have been more patient."

He shook his head. "She was injured and alone. We had no way of knowing who was with her or when they were coming back. *If* they were coming back at all. We had no time to go searching for them. We did what we had to do. We are doing what we have to do right now. What you asked for, remember? Find a way, you said. So I did. Now stop talking about it!"

She set her jaw. "I'll stop talking about it, but I won't stop thinking about it. I can promise you that!"

"Fine. I'll settle for that much."

The trail had broadened, and the woods had opened a bit. Ahead, Sora could make out the hull of the airship through the gloom and mist. She was a big one, probably some sort of warship. He slowed automatically, Aquinel with him. For a few moments, he reconsidered what he was about to do. Maybe this wasn't such a good idea. Maybe he should just take the girl to the nearest village and leave her there. Forget any reward for his trouble. It wasn't like he hadn't already found a way to get paid for this mess.

But greed won out over reason, and he abruptly pushed forward, clucking at the mule, pulling it and the wagon and the girl who lay in the wagon bed forward.

Already men from the airship had appeared on the decks and were watching them approach. One waved in greeting and started down the ladder to meet them.

"Remember," he said to Aquinel, "we're simple foragers. We gather mushrooms and sell them to the surrounding villages. We come here all the time. Today, we were on our way to our grounds and we saw this girl lying in a clearing. She was injured and alone, apparently abandoned. We don't have the means or ability to look after her. But we are responsible people and we want to see her safe and well cared for. We saw their ship, and we thought perhaps they could help. Thought they might even be friends of hers."

"I still think this is a mistake," Aquinel said softly.

He glared at her. "Hush, woman!"

"Hush, yourself."

The rains were beginning to diminish and the woods ahead to thin out and open up. The trail was muddied and the tracks they had been following virtually erased, but that no longer mattered to either of them. Aphen and Cymrian were still running as fast as the latter could manage, ignoring personal discomfort and fighting off weariness. Cymrian had assured Aphen that they were close to catching up to the cart and its mule and drivers, the last of the visible signs indicating they were just a short distance off.

But they were shocked nevertheless when all three appeared abruptly from out of the mists ahead, not fleeing but approaching them—a big man and a short woman, both stocky and plainly dressed, a mule walking with its head down, hauling a cart in trudging acceptance of its lot, no sense of hurry or concern about any of them.

They slowed as the man and woman saw them and drew to an uncertain halt. If anything, the pair seemed frightened of them, and Aphen, sensing this, gave a friendly wave of reassurance. The woman returned it. The man stood motionless, watching.

"Easy, now," Cymrian told her.

Aphen nodded, at the same time sizing up the couple in front of them. Foragers or farmers, not Rovers or townspeople, she decided. They'd lived hard lives and had little to show for it, but their bluff faces did not suggest they were either bad-intentioned or dangerous.

"Have you seen a girl?" she asked at once. "Small, young. We left her lying on the ground in the woods more than a mile back. She was injured, and we—"

Before she could finish, the woman wheeled on the man and struck him as hard as she could. "I told you we should have waited! Look what you've done!"

The man seized her by the arms to keep her from hitting him again. "Aquinel, stop it! We don't know anything yet."

"You have the girl?" Aphen asked at once, unable to contain herself any longer. "She's my sister. Her name is Arling. Is she in your cart? Is she all right?"

The man and woman exchanged a quick look. She could tell immediately by the looks on their faces that something was wrong. "What is it? What's the matter?"

The woman shook her head. "We didn't know you were coming for her. We thought she had been abandoned. Her clothes and all the blood, you see. So we took her with us to keep her safe. But then we saw the airship, and we thought . . ."

"They said they were friends, that they could take her with them, make sure she got the help she needed," the man said, cutting her off.

"We didn't know!" Aquinel wailed, and began to cry.

Aphen stared. "Are you saying you gave my sister to some men flying an airship? What did the airship look like? What flag did she fly?"

"She was a warship, I guess," the man answered, not looking at her, trying to find a way to comfort the woman, who was having none of it. "She was a Federation ship, I think."

Aphen went pale. *Shades. The ones who were hunting us.*

She didn't need to speak the words. Cymrian would be thinking the same thing. Arling had been given over to their enemies, to the ones who had brought the assassin and the mutants.

"Have they lifted off yet?" Cymrian asked, moving a step closer. "Have they left?"

The man shrugged. "They were still on the ground when we started back. That was maybe ten, fifteen minutes ago."

The Elven Hunter took Aphen's arm and pulled her ahead. "Quickly, now. Maybe we can still reach her in time."

They charged past the man and the woman and went down the trail in a rush. They did not look back.

Sora and Aquinel started walking again, neither looking at the other. The rains had diminished to a few scattered drops, and the wind-blown mists had begun to re-form and thicken once more.

"Elves," Sora said after a time. "Dangerous look to them, too. Did you see their clothes? All torn up and bloodied. The man was hurt. You could tell by the way he was holding himself."

He waited for Aquinel to say something, but she wouldn't even look at him.

"I did what I thought was right," he said again.

But he knew that wasn't entirely so. He'd done what he *hoped* was right and what he *knew* would net him a profit. He'd been right about the men on the airship. They'd been quick to reward him for his efforts in retrieving the girl, and they hadn't looked anywhere near as questionable as the Elves. Of course, the injured girl was an Elf, too, and she looked the same as these two. But who was to say what the real relationship was between them? Maybe the two women were sisters, but maybe not. How could anyone tell? Those Elves all looked the same to him, anyway.

He tightened his jaw. Come right down to it, this wasn't his business. His or Aquinel's. None of it. They were well out of it. Let the others sort it out. He glanced at his wife, marching along at his side, stone-faced. She was angry now, but she would get over it.

Even after she did though, he didn't think he would say anything about the silvery white stone he had found in the girl's clothing. A beautiful thing, it was. He had never seen anything like it.

Now it was his. He would keep it, sell it later on the sly, and pocket the money.

After all, he deserved something for his trouble.

HERE ENDS BOOK TWO OF
THE DARK LEGACY OF SHANNARA

◆

RAILING OHMSFORD STOOD ALONE AT THE BOW OF THE *Quickening* and looked out at the starlit darkness. They were anchored for the night, the airship nestled in a copse of fir and hemlock, the sway of the ship in the soft breezes barely noticeable. It was well after midnight, and he should have been sleeping with the others. But sleep did not come easily these days, and when it did come it was haunted and left him racked with a deep sense of unease. Better to stay awake where he could try to do something to control his thoughts, as dark as they were. Better to face his demons standing up, prepared to fight them off and hold them at bay.

He could not banish them, of course. He could not send them back to the empty places where they sometimes went to hide, although increasingly less so these days.

Not that it mattered. He knew their faces. He knew their names.

Fear: that he might not be able to find Grianne Ohmsford and bring her back to face the Straken Lord because she was dead. Or because she was alive but could not be persuaded to leave the sanctuary in which she had placed herself, unwilling to risk a confrontation of the sort he was proposing. Or simply because she was Grianne and she had never been predictable.

Doubt: that he was doing the right thing in making this journey into the back of beyond because of a hope that had so little chance of succeeding. Because he should have been seeking his brother in the Forbidding, hunting for him there and bringing him out again in spite of the odds. Because time was running out with every passing hour, and his brother was alone and had no one to help him and no way of knowing if help would ever come. Because Redden depended on him, and it must seem to Redden as if Railing had abandoned him.

Shame: that he was deceiving his companions on this quest, that he was keeping information from them that might dissuade them from continuing. The King of the Silver River had warned him that nothing would happen as he thought and there would be results he had not foreseen. Because the Faerie creature had told him he should turn back and travel instead into the Forbidding—the one place he knew he could never go, so great was his terror at the prospect.

He felt himself to be a coward and a deceiver. He was consumed by his doubts and his shame, and it was growing increasingly harder not to reveal this to the others. He tried to keep it hidden, masked by his false words and acts, but it was eating at him. Destroying him.

He was crying again, silently, and all at once, tears leaked from his eyes and despair filled his heart.

He left the vessel's bow and walked back toward the stern, moving quietly, trying not to disturb the sleepers. Some were on deck, wrapped in blankets; some were below, rolled into hammocks. All slept save two of the Rover crew, who kept watch fore and aft. He saw the one at the stern and turned aside before he reached the man to take up a position near the starboard railing. Small creaks sounded as ropes and lines pulled taut and released again, and snores rose out of the shadows. He liked this quiet time, this confluence of shadows and sleep. Everything was at rest.

He wished he could be, as well.

It had been only two days now since they had set out from the Rainbow Lake, even though it felt more like twenty. They had debated among themselves that morning, on waking, as to the best route for their journey. The Charnals were unknown country to all but Skint. Even Farshawn and his Rovers had not come this way before. Railing and Mirai had traveled the Borderlands while conveying spare parts and salvage to customers but had not gone farther north.

Railing favored coming up from the Rainbow Lake, following the corridor that snaked between the Wolfsktaag and the Dragon's Teeth to the Upper Anar, and then continuing on through Jannisson Pass east of the Skull Kingdom and its dangers and straight along the western edge of the Charnals to the Northland city of Anatcherae—very much the same route his grandfather Penderrin had taken while searching for the tanequil all those years ago. From Anatcherae, once resupplied, they could continue on to their destination.

But Skint had thought differently.

What they needed most, he declared, was a guide—someone who was familiar with the Charnals and could help them find the ruins of Stridegate, where it was said the tanequil might be found. There were few who could do that, and he was not one. In point of fact, he knew of only one man who could help them with this, one whose loyalty and knowledge they could depend upon. And even he would need persuading.

His name was Challa Nand, and he made his home in the Eastland town of Rampling Steep. But finding him would require that the company fly *Quickening* east of the Charnals and through the Upper Anar. It would necessitate abandoning the western approach to Stridegate and finding one that came in from the east. Challa could show them, if they were able to persuade him to their cause.

Railing knew he could rely on the ring given him by the King of the Silver River to show them the way, but using it would mean either telling them about his meeting with the Faerie creature or lying about where he had gotten the ring. The ring could always act as a backup if the need arose; the better choice was to keep it a secret for now.

So he agreed to Skint's proposal, and the others went along, all of them keenly aware that they were in unfamiliar territory and needed to reduce the risks they would encounter in reaching their destination.

Now here they were, on their way to Rampling Steep, anchored at the northern edge of Darklin Reach not far from where the Rabb River branched east into the Upper Anar. If he listened closely, Railing could hear the murmur of the river's waters as they churned their way out of the mountains on their journey west to the plains and from there to the Mermidon. It was a distance of hundreds of miles, and it made him wonder if anyone had ever followed the river all the way from end to end. He supposed Gnome or Dwarf trappers and traders might have done so at some point, but he doubted that any had ever made a record of it.

"What are you doing?"

Mirai Leah was standing next to him. He hadn't heard her come up, hadn't realized she was there. He shrugged. "Can't sleep."

"Standing out here isn't going to help. You need to get some rest. Are you all right?"

He gave her a quick glance. Her blondish hair was rumpled and she was yawning. "You look like the one who ought to be sleeping."

"I would be if I weren't worried about you. What is it that's bothering you, Railing?"

He could have given her a whole raft of answers, starting with how he felt about her and what it would mean to him if he caused her harm. But all he said was, "Nothing. I just couldn't sleep."

She draped an arm over his shoulders, and her touch made him shiver. "How long have we known each other?"

"Seems like forever. Since we were pretty small, anyway. I still remember when your parents brought you for your first visit. They came to see Mother. I didn't like you then. You were kind of bossy."

"Not much has changed. I'm still kind of bossy. So when I ask you what's bothering you, it's because I know something is. So what's up?"

He brushed his red hair back and faced her. "Leaving Redden is eating at me. I can't stand it that I'm not going after him."

"Then why aren't you?"

"Because I think this is the better choice."

"Because you believe Grianne Ohmsford is alive and will come to Redden's aid?" She studied him a moment. "We've already discussed this. I don't think that's what's troubling you at all. I think there's something else, something you are keeping to yourself. Maybe you ought to try telling me."

Here was his opportunity. She had called him out on what she clearly recognized, and he could unburden himself by telling her about his meeting with the King of the Silver River. He could admit what he was doing, how he was manipulating them. But that was something he would never do. He didn't want her judging him. He wanted her to love him unconditionally and fully. He always had.

He fingered the ring, tucked deep in his pants pocket. "I need to go back to sleep. I'm sorry I woke you." He started to walk away, then he stopped and turned around. "I want you to know I am doing the best I can. If anything happens to Redden because of me, I don't think I could stand it. I need you to believe that. I need you to support me and to . . ."

He trailed off. He couldn't make himself speak the words: *Love me.* "Good night."

"I will always support you, Railing," she called after him.

Without looking back, he gave her a wave and disappeared back down the hatchway into the hold of the airship.

He had thought he might sleep then, weary and heartsick. But after a short, unsettling nap he was awake again, wide-eyed and restless. There was a tugging sensation that brought him out of his blanket and back up the ladder to the deck, where he stood peering out from the ship's railing and over the darkened countryside.

Something was out there. Something he must find.

He couldn't explain how he knew this, but the feeling was so compelling that he did not stop to question it. He needed to find out what it was. Ignoring it for even another moment was impossible.

He walked over to the sentry at the bow and told him he was going for a walk, but that he would be careful. The Rover clearly understood it would be a mistake to question the leader of their company, though he offered to accompany him. But Railing insisted he needed to go alone.

Once off the vessel and out in the night, Railing gave himself over to his strange compulsion, following his instincts. He felt oddly unthreatened. It might have been because of what he had survived in the Fangs—the days of attacks by the Goblins and the constant use of his wishsong magic to throw back the hordes in the debilitating struggle to stay alive. He had proved something to himself in those terrible days when others had died all around him. He had found, through his magic, a source of strength and resilience that he had not known he possessed. Before, the wishsong had never been more than a means of ramping up the excitement on each new adventure, or of pushing ever harder against the limits that common sense told him not to exceed. But what he took away with him from the Fangs was something different. It was a belief that his magic provided him a shield and sword he could use to protect both himself and those close to him. It was a belief that fostered confidence.

So he proceeded through the night's shadows without fear. He did not hesitate in his search for what was calling to him or consider turning back. His mind was made up. The voice reminded him of his summoning by the King of the Silver River two nights earlier, and he wanted to know why that was. While it was different—different enough that he was certain it was something else entirely—it shared a kinship that intrigued him.

Railing.

His name, spoken clearly. Spoken by a voice he could not mistake because he had known it all his life.

It was Redden who called to him.

He brushed aside his shock and pushed ahead at a quicker pace, listening for more. Everything was still again, the voice gone as quickly as it had come. Yet the pull on him persisted. He pushed through woods and soon no longer knew in which direction he was going—or even from which he had come. He was proceeding blindly, responding to the lure with a heedless disregard for his own safety, and he finally began to wonder if he was in danger and did not recognize it.

Railing.

Again, his brother's voice.

Now he slowed, no longer willing to rush ahead, worried that he had overstepped himself. He was lost at the very edge of Darklin Reach, which was not only strange but dangerous country. He was moving away from the Rabb; he knew this because he could not longer hear its rush. The silence was deep and pervasive, and only the cries of night birds broke its hush.

Ahead, just visible through the trees, a silvery glimmer caught his eye.

He wove his way through the woods and stepped out at the edge of a small lake. Fog lay eerily across the lake's rippling surface. The waters lapped the shoreline and chopped about its windswept center in small bursts of spray. Though he tried, the boy could not make out what lay on the other side. Moonlight notwithstanding, it was too obscured by the mist. The trees ringed the lake like a palisade, trunks dark and thick and seemingly impenetrable ten feet from where he stood. In the distance, through the gaps, he could spy the peaks of mountains.

Railing.

"I'm here, Redden," he shouted back, feeling foolish for speaking aloud to a voice that was only in his head.

Laughter greeted his response, filling the air in long raucous peals that shattered the silence and spun out around the lake in waves. Railing took a step back, unsure of what was happening, knowing only that it wasn't his brother he was hearing but something else entirely. The laughter was unsettling, inhuman. The boy would have bolted if not for the continuous tugging from inside his body, which held him rooted in place.

Then, from somewhere out in the middle of the lake, a dark shape began to form, sliding across the surface of the water as it came toward him.

Raaaiilingg.

His brother's voice again, but it had a whining, pleading quality that it had never possessed before. He shuddered at the sound, unnerved by the neediness of its tone. But he stayed where he was, waiting on the thing that crested the lake's surface and drew ever closer. He did not feel the fear that might otherwise have driven him into the woods. What he felt instead was a deep, inexplicable revulsion.

When the dark shape reached him, it was fully formed. It stood upon the waters and looked down on him.

"Brother." Redden Ohmsford addressed him in a hollow, empty voice.

Railing was dumbstruck and could not respond.

"Did you think that if you did not come for me, I could not in my turn find a way to come to you? Did you abandon me with the expectation that I would simply vanish from your life and leave you in peace? Did you believe that, even in death, I would not find a way to rejoin you?"

Railing fought back against a rising tide of despair. "You are not my brother. My brother isn't dead. I would know it if he were!" He swallowed hard. "What are you? A shade? A changeling?"

The creature before him shimmered and began to transform again. "Perhaps I am you."

Just like that, Railing was looking at his mirror image—every detail recognizable, every line and feature in place.

"Why did you call to me? What do you want?"

"Oh, it isn't what I want. It's what *you* want."

"That's not true. This is all coming from you. And you are not me!"

"Well, then, descendant of Valemen and Druids, who am I?"

Railing wracked his brain for an explanation, for a memory, for a hint of who or what this thing was. But he could not seem to think straight while looking at a duplicate of himself.

"I have known your kin, and your ancestors great and small. I have spoken to some over the years. I spoke to Brin Ohmsford when she went in search of the Ildatch. And to Walker Boh when he went after the Black Elfstone." The laughter returned, whispery and prodding. "Does that not tell you who I am?"

In fact, it did. Abruptly, Railing found the answer—both from his memories of his family's history, and from the stories told him by his father and repeated endlessly by his brother and himself.

"You are the Grimpond. You are a shade confined to this world, chained to this plane of existence."

"An immortal creature who knows secrets that no one else does. A creature who possesses the ability to see the future. A being that might be of assistance to someone like you."

Railing knew that the Grimpond was a spiteful prisoner of this world, trapped here for reasons that no one knew, hateful of all the Races, treacherous and inconstant. Whatever words it spoke—even though it did know things hidden—were not to be trusted.

"I thought you dwelt further back in Darklin Reach, somewhere north of Hearthstone." It was coming back to him now, the whole of what he knew of this shade. "How do you come to be here?"

The shade rippled and changed again, and now it was his mother who confronted him, her face stern and unforgiving. "You were told not to let anything happen to your brother, and yet you did. What sort of brother does that make you, Railing? What sort of son?"

Railing ignored the insults and folded his arms defensively. "I'm wasting my time here. If you have something to tell me, just say it. Otherwise, I am returning to my bed."

"And you think you will sleep well, knowing what you have done? How you have betrayed and manipulated those who depend on you? How you hide a gift from a Faerie creature because you are afraid to reveal your possession of it? How you have become a thing much worse than what you think me to be? Oh, I seriously doubt that you will sleep well at all."

Railing fought back against his rising anger, and he deliberately kept his hands at his side and out of his pockets. "Since you seem to know me so well, you must also know that there is nothing you can tell me that will make a difference in how I feel about myself or my brother or my friends!"

"Nothing?" A meaningful pause. "Really?"

Railing took a deep breath. "What, then?"

"You are such a disappointment to me, Railing! Such a waste of possibilities!" His mother's voice, cold and scolding. Then the shade rippled once more, and suddenly it was a faceless shade, cloaked and hooded. "It is I who shall go to bed and leave you to your fate."

"You can know nothing of fate!" Railing's hands were clenched into fists. "Only of secrets. You are a master of trickery and deceit. My fate is in my hands."

The Grimpond went silent then, hovering like the fog from which it had emerged, the substance of it beginning to fragment and vanish. "If you are so convinced of that, go on your way. I am done with you. I would give you help, but you spurn me. You mistrust me, yet you refuse to see that I might have knowledge you lack. Knowledge you desire, Railing Ohmsford. Knowledge that you crave."

Railing stepped back, shaking his head slowly. "No, you would trick me with your words and your pretenses. You seek to play games with me. You did this with others in my family. The histories tell us so. You were never less than deceitful, and I will not become your latest victim."

The Grimpond came back together again abruptly. "Why not hear my words and judge for yourself? Can my words do so much harm that even to listen would undo you? Are so you frightened of me?"

The night closed down around the boy as he pondered a response. What should he say? Should he admit his fears and be done with it? Should he deny being afraid and demand that the other give him what he was promising? Should he walk away? The silence lengthened and the Grimpond waited.

"I want you to do what you think you should," Railing said eventually. "If you have something to say, I will listen. If not, I will leave."

The Grimpond chuckled softly and shimmered once more. But this time it did not change form and did not give a quick retort. Instead, it seemed to consider.

"Hear me, then," it said finally. "I summoned you to see what you were made of, that much is true. Had you been weaker, I might have tried to teach you a lesson. But now I will simply tell you what it is I know that you do not. You have come in search of Grianne Ohmsford. You would know her fate, and if there is a chance that she might be brought back to face the Straken Lord."

He paused, and the boy waited patiently on him.

"She lives, Railing Ohmsford. She lives and she can be what you need. She can do what you expect. If you wish that of her, you should continue on with the knowledge that what you seek is possible. Yet you should be careful what you ask for—an old phrase, but a good one to remember. All is not as it seems. There are threads that might cause the whole to unravel, like the threads of the ring you carry in your pocket."

Railing felt a surge of excitement. His efforts would not be wasted going in search of Grianne. His chances of finding her and bringing her back to face the Straken Lord—and save his brother and possibly the Four Lands—were real. He understood what the Grimpond was telling him about things not working out as he hoped, but he had known that from the first. And a chance was the best he could hope for.

"Is this the truth?" he asked the shade. "Are you lying in any way?"

"Not a word of what you've heard is a lie, but your expectations may turn my words to falsehoods. This is not my doing. Remember that. Keep the memory of what I have told you clear in your mind."

"I will."

The Grimpond shimmered and began to recede. "Enough of this. I came to say those words and I have said them. What happens now is up to you. I will watch your progress and record your reactions to everything that happens. It will be most entertaining for me."

The boy watched the shade trail away like a shadow lost with the light's passing—there one moment, and gone the next. It was still visible as it reached the fog and passed through.

Then it melted away in a scattering of tiny particles and was gone.

ABOUT THE AUTHOR

TERRY BROOKS is the *New York Times* bestselling author of more than thirty books, including the Dark Legacy of Shannara adventure *Wards of Faerie;* the Legends of Shannara novels *Bearers of the Black Staff* and *The Measure of the Magic;* the Genesis of Shannara trilogy: *Armageddon's Children, The Elves of Cintra,* and *The Gypsy Morph; The Sword of Shannara;* the Voyage of the Jerle Shannara trilogy: *Ilse Witch, Antrax,* and *Morgawr;* the High Druid of Shannara trilogy: *Jarka Ruus, Tanequil,* and *Straken;* the nonfiction book *Sometimes the Magic Works: Lessons from a Writing Life;* and the novel based upon the screenplay and story by George Lucas, *Star Wars:*® Episode I *The Phantom Menace.*™ His novels *Running with the Demon* and *A Knight of the Word* were selected by the *Rocky Mountain News* as two of the best science fiction/fantasy novels of the twentieth century. The author was a practicing attorney for many years but now writes full-time. He lives with his wife, Judine, in the Pacific Northwest.

ABOUT THE TYPE

This book was set in Minion, a 1990 Adobe Originals typeface by Robert Slimbach. Minion is inspired by classical, old style typefaces of the late Renaissance, a period of elegant, beautiful, and highly readable type designs. Created primarily for text setting, Minion combines the aesthetic and functional qualities that make text type highly readable with the versatility of digital technology.